D0365521

Sappho

the TENTH MUSE

Sappho

the TENTH MUSE

NANCY FREEDMAN

ST. MARTIN'S PRESS

NEW YORK

Grateful acknowledgment is given for the permission to reprint selections of Sappho's poetry from the following authors, translators, and publishers:

Willis Barnstone: *Sappho and the Greek Lyric Poets*. Copyright ©1998, Schocken Books. Reprinted by permission of the publisher.

Mary Bernard: *Sappho*. Copyright ©1994, Shambhala Publications Inc. Reprinted by permission of the publisher.

Guy Davenport: *Archilochus Sappho Alkman*. Copyright ©1980, University of California Press. Reprinted by permission of the publisher.

Jeffrey M. Duban: *Ancient and Modern Images of Sappho*. Copyright ©1983, University Press of America. Reprinted by permission of the publisher.

Suzy Q. Groden: *The Poems of Sappho*. Copyright ©1966, The Bobbs-Merrill Company. Reprinted by permission of the publisher.

Jim Powell: *Sappho: A Garland*. Copyright ©1993, The Noonday Press. Reprinted by permission of the publisher.

Beram Saklatvala: *Sappho of Lesbos: Her Works Restored*. Copyright ©1968, Charles Skilton Ltd. Reprinted by permission of the publisher.

Jane McIntosh Snyder: *Lesbian Desire in the Lyrics of Sappho*. Copyright ©1997, Columbia University Press. Reprinted by permission of the publisher.

Arthur Weigall: *Sappho of Lesbos*. Copyright ©1932, Frederick A. Stokes Co. Reprinted by permission of the publisher.

SAPPHO: THE TENTH MUSE. Copyright © 1998 by Nancy Freedman. All rights reserved. Printed in the United States of America. No part of this book may be used or reproduced in any manner whatsoever without written permission except in the case of brief quotations embodied in critical articles or reviews. For information address St. Martin's Press, 175 Fifth Avenue, New York, N.Y. 10010.

Design by Michaelann Zimmerman

Library of Congress Cataloging-in-Publication Data

Freedman, Nancy Mars.
    Sappho : the tenth muse / Nancy Freedman.—1st ed.
        p.   cm.
    ISBN 0-312-18660-6
    1. Sappho—Fiction. 2. Greece—History—To 146 B.C.—Fiction.
3. Women poets, Greek—Fiction. 4. Lesbians—Greece—Fiction.
    I. Title.
    PS3511.R418S27 1998
    813'.54—DC21   98-4992
                                                          CIP

ISBN 0-312-18660-6

First Edition: July 1998

10 9 8 7 6 5 4 3 2 1

FOR MY THREE DAUGHTERS

Johanna, Deborah, & Leslie

ACKNOWLEDGMENTS

KEN ATCHITY, who fell in love with Sappho

MADELEINE FINDLEY, for her expert guidance

DANA ALBARELLA, who made it happen

DEANE SHAPIRO, for his historical insights

PETER DOYLE, for his critical advice

JEAN SANFORD, for her technical help

PAT CARROLL, for her advocacy of the Muses

REBECCA FREY, for her careful verification

and always BENEDICT, for everything

SAPPHO REDISCOVERED

*S*APPHO, THE GREAT LESBIAN POET, LIVED SIX HUNDRED years before Christ, and her work was celebrated throughout the civilized world. Not only was she the first woman to reach such eminence and know such renown, she was the first to seek sexual equality and liberation, and as a result was banished from her island home.

Her lifestyle was extravagant, as was her life. In her banishment she taught Syracuse society how to put on an orgy. But in spite of her many lovers, there was a quiet, virginal spot reserved for her art, and no one intruded there.

Because of the bisexual and homosexual nature of her poems, they were burned centuries later by the early church. A concerted effort was made to erase all memory of her. This effort might have succeeded had her name not come down to us from ancient Roman writers, poets, and playwrights.

Plato called her "the tenth muse." Socrates "rejoiced" to call her work "beautiful." Strabo refers to her as "a miracle of a woman." Plutarch says, "There is magic in the songs of Sappho to enchant and bewitch." Horace rhapsodizes, "Still lives the flame this Aeolian girl committed to her strings." To which Pinyto adds, "Her words are deathless."

But through the centuries her words were lost. Then, in the 1920s, Professors Grenfell and Hunt, excavating Graeco-Egyptian cemeteries at Oxyrhynchus in the Fayum, discovered papier-mâché coffins composed of scraps of writing, which proved to be fragments of Sappho's poems. Here I quote Arthur Weigall, Inspector-General of Antiquities for the Egyptian government: "Out of the dust of Egypt there came one beautiful fragment after another. . . . Sappho's poetry is to be ranked among mankind's greatest achievements, and it is by her poetry that she must be judged."

This is what I have attempted. Through her passionate verse Sappho reveals herself, and I ask the reader not to judge her, but to come to know the very human person she was.

Nancy Freedman

Some say there are nine Muses
but they are careless, for look!
—there is Sappho of Lesbos,
who is a tenth.

Plato

I WANT, I WANT, I WANT!" THESE WORDS WERE MOST often on her lips when she was a child. What it was she wanted she could not express. For Sappho saw more when her eyes were closed and wanted things she did not know of.

She was the daughter of the noble Skamandronymos. An ugly infant, dark, small, and female, she would have been exposed at birth had her father not descended from Orestes, son of Agamemnon. Although male children came along afterward, it was Sappho her father found time to spoil. He was excessively fond of his daughter and invented her nickname, Little Pebble, for it was his contention that some pebbles have gems hiding in them. And certainly Sappho was a bundle of opposing traits: delicate as she was, her gaze scorched and burned. Her father sometimes wondered if she was alone in that small body, or if there were two Sapphos forever at odds with each other.

Their villa lay sprawled among limestone cliffs that leaned against the sea. The white walls of the garden half hidden in cypress and sycamore were meant to be a boundary to stay within, but Sappho preferred the rocky headlands with moss-waving manes. She liked to search among the humped reefs to see a crab startle, or poke an anemone with a stick and watch it retreat. She counted the colors of starfish that came each season by the hundreds to spawn, and played on the sand shore as children always have, running at the sea because it ran at her.

Perhaps the endless prayers of her mother, Kleis, that her firstborn be a son influenced Sappho, for she was bold and daring as any boy. She scrambled over spray-wet rocks in tides that might easily have swept a man away. Excitement charged through her at the fury of the water monsters born of Ceto and Phorkys. Her nurse and the other servants were afraid of the sea. From them she learned the waters of Ocean were a river that wound around the world. The singers called it the wet waste or sometimes the wine-dark sea. She found endless fascination in spume that one moment lashed the reefs, and the next became tame and gentle. She loved all of Ocean's moods. Most of all she loved the bubbling milky froth curling around her ankles. Holding a conch shell to her ear, she listened to Triton's horn and at times caught glimpses of the Nereids who played in the distant deep— Amatheis of the lovely locks, soft-eyed Halia, Galatea, Doris, and others whose names she did not always remember, but of whom her nurse told her.

She was quick for her years, and at an early age memorized her genealogy and could do simple sums. She knew she lived in the city of sea-swept Eresos on the west coast of Lesbos, to which the waves of the Aegean once washed the head and lyre of Orpheus. She knew her father was an exporter of the famed honey-sweet wine of the region and that the far-stretching vineyards, beyond which she had never seen, belonged to her family, as did the boats riding at anchor in the small, protected harbor.

She understood that as the daughter of the house she commanded slaves and they must do her bidding—but only after they had done everyone else's bidding. She was strangely loved by all in the house, and her smile, slow to appear, always delighted. The slave who had been purchased for his proficiency as a toymaker brought her dolls with movable limbs who lived among miniature furniture, carved as in the great house, with tiny pots and pans on which to prepare meals. There were also small boats, replicas of those her father sailed, with seats for rowers, keels, masts, storage areas, and lastly, string, so they should not be immediately lost to the surf. She had hoops, balls, hobbyhorses, a swing, and her own little cart, pulled by a pair of nanny goats.

She learned to play castanets and flutes. When she made them sound, she drew herself up like a figure on a vase, her fingers creating rhythms which her feet followed. She trod out the geometric frieze of urns and tapestries so exactly that the servants gathered around and her mother watched from the window.

Every hour of the day All-Mother Earth had more to show her. That is why she played outside. The sun didn't shine in temple or house, the narcissus and tamarisk didn't bloom in stone halls. It was in the garden and sacred grove that yellow crocus and the crimson wild rose clambered on walls. There were violets to discover, lilies, wind-flowers, and cloverlike melilot to pick. Sometimes, if she was very still, she could hear the bird with the secret name.

In the seventh year of Sappho's life a council was called by her father. Nurse told her the terrible Erinyes had been summoned to attend. Those daughters of Night with serpents twined in their hair had started their long journey, beckoning as they passed to the Gray Women, those monstrous birds with human heads, who, with their human arms protruding from feathered wings, passed around their one eye. All the gods and goddesses and those creatures spawned by them in the sea and air, the Hydra, the Chimaera, and the Gorgons, traveled toward Eresos. The coming of these misshapen beings, Nurse said, meant a great war.

Sappho watched the preparation for the council feast with a heart that struck against her small chest. Sun passed early to his rest, removing light, and tallow tapers were set flaming, making long shadows and leaving the in-between places dark.

Nurse bathed her from a golden ewer with the head of the Minotaur, rubbed her with sweet oils and braided flowers into her long black hair. A purple robe was cast over her, gold sandals fastened to her tiny feet, and she was led to the innermost hall, where a fire roared on the great hearth. Standing there were members of the council, of which her father was chief. Close by was her mother, with the fat baby in her arms and the two older boys holding to her skirt. Sappho crept as close as she could, dragging Nurse with her. A slave brought in two black rams dedicated to Apollo and an ox pledged to Zeus.

Her mother brought out the key to the door that was never opened, although all in the household knew what was kept there. The handle of the key was ivory, and Skamandronymos, taking it, shot back the bolt. Sappho strained to see the objects she had been told of, the bronze-shod spears and those of pelican ash, bows made from the horns of wild ibex hanging from a peg. Her father selected a bronze battle-ax with a handle of olive wood that shone in the firelight.

The sacrifices waited, anointed in barley meal, dark wine, and honey. Skamandronymos swung the ax in a great arc through the air and through the throats of the rams. They knelt in their blood which overflowed the chalice, and their bodies rolled to the floor. The broad-headed ox bellowed in alarm and had to be stunned.

Skamandronymos set up a chant, calling the gods to his side. Sappho began to tremble as the cadence of her father's voice rose and fell. There was grandeur in the sound, like that of blind Homer singing his great and terrible songs on craggy Chios long ago. A word repeated in each stanza: *Athens . . . Athens.*

In Athens, her mother once told her, girl children had no freedom to run about as she did. In Athens only males were taught music, the poetry of Ionian Homer, and sums. While it was never said to her directly, she knew that in Athens an unlikely female child would have been exposed.

A sudden haunting intonation in her father's voice indicated that the Gray Women and Erinyes had arrived. They seemed to her to crouch in the shadows, and she clung to her nurse. Abruptly the chant ended, and members of the council stepped forward. The air was filled with angry, exhorting speeches: Athenian merchants had seized the trading post of Sigeum, which Lesbos had established at the Aegean end of the Hellespont near ruined Troy.

Sappho began to understand that the five cities of Lesbos had declared war against Athens. She sought her nurse's hand, but Nurse withdrew it, whispering she was the daughter of the house and must set an example. So the seven-year-old squeezed in beside her father at the head table.

The smell of roasting meat filled the room, and her father poured libation, calling in the same awesome voice, speaking directly to great Zeus: "O Cloud-Compeller, son of Kronos, hear me! For you, Ever-living, know our cause is just. Let the Athenian ships founder. Let Folly, eldest of your daughters, close their eyes to their destruction. Send Ares, the unconquerable, to lead us to Athens. Grant that we who are assembled here live to see our wives and children and offer you fine hekatombs."

The singer who traveled between the five cities assured them that the oracle at Delphi was favorable. The holy Pythia upon her tripod, in a vision sent by Ares, saw the owl sacred to gray-eyed Athene, guardian of Athens, seized in the claws of the Lesbian vulture. The owl struggled helplessly, but the daughter of Zeus and Metis, born in a snowstorm of gold, was powerless to rescue her bird. Without her owl, that great queen of battle fell to her knees. By this token Ares, god of war, acceded to her father's request and promised supremacy to Lesbos.

Although Sappho brooded on the tale of struggling birds, and war was known to her through the recitation of many wandering singers, she did not yet understand that war would end the life she had known. So she tasted, then gorged, burning her small eager fingers on the flesh heaped on her plate. She sucked her fingers and stared at the entrails flung upon the hearthstones that foretold victory.

Her mother, paying no heed to omens, said fearfully, "Eresos is only five hundred stadia from Sigeum by sea, and will surely be attacked."

Her father inclined his head. "No one will be found here. You are to take the children to my brother Eurygyos, whose house is safe in the hills of Mitylene."

Hearing this, her mother wailed in a frightening way, all on one note. The attendant ladies did the same, and her brothers added to the din. The room was solid with noise, there was no place even for the thoughts in Sappho's head. Her large dark eyes moved from face to face. She felt a terror against which it did no good to cry, for her father welcomed dead heroes and ancestor-gods to the feast. Unseen, the Ever-living arrayed themselves with silent dignity to taste the fine barley bread, the dainties in woven baskets, the haunches of flesh and the spilled wine.

Her mother, quiet now, took Skamandronymos's greaves from a slave and fastened them herself about her husband's legs. Helping him draw on the breastplate of leather and bronze, she placed a close-fitting cap of plaited leather on his head and lastly the metal casque with its rim of wild boar's teeth and flying plume. This solemn ritual was broken by the howling of the baby, Larichos. Her father held the infant above his head before returning him to his mother, then pressed the two boys to him. He turned to Sappho last. "Little Pebble," he murmured into her dark hair.

She never saw him again.

In the morning the inlet was deserted. For the first time since Sappho could remember, not one of her father's ships rode at anchor. All were gone. She ran to the stables. The champing horses had been taken, and the wraps to spread over them. Even the stores of barley and rye were no longer there. Only the mules remained, and it was they, harnessed to a cart heaped with household goods, with which the family of Skamandronymos began the long journey to Mitylene.

Sappho had imagined much, but never that she would leave the sand shore, the encrusted rocks, the swing in the garden, her little cart and goats, or the house of her parents that clustered with other houses near the water.

The way was uphill and the slaves groaned under their burdens, for nothing was left behind. Linens, bedding, wardrobes, chests of toiletries, jars of oil and wine, baskets of bread, her father's high-backed chair richly carved and inlaid with gems—all were carried on the backs of servants. But not all—not the broad vineyards, not the garden, not the sand shore.

Sheep bleated as shepherds piped the stragglers. And Sappho, wrenching her hand from her nurse, looked back. The rocky headland of Eresos rose straight as though lifted by waves. The small harbor without the graceful black boats seemed alien. Trees were heavy with apples, quinces, and pomegranates, but the fruit was unpicked. Even the grapes in the vineyard were unpicked.

"Sappho, Sappho, don't look back." Her mother's tears fell on the child's upturned face.

They left the familiar cypress and sycamore; elms and willows now lined the path, the tamarisk too was thinning. Beech replaced the shady lanes of mulberry and honeysuckle. They climbed higher, through olive groves sacred to Aphrodite. Small rivulets from the hillside tumbled into glades of maidenhair fern. She no longer knew the way and in panic turned once more for a sustaining glance at her home, but it had disappeared.

They stopped at midday and ate roasted chestnuts served with fruits and dried fish. By the time they reached pine country, Sappho was asleep. With Eresos, civilization vanished. The party kept close by day and at night huddled around fires for fear of lions and wild boar. Sappho, wrapped in shawls, half woke and listened in a far-off way to the

talk of the grown-ups. She was not afraid of lions or boar, but of Phor-
cys's terrible children, the earth-dwelling Gorgons, dragons with wings,
whose look turned little girls to stone. When long-shadowed Night
waved and groaned, she clutched her mother and whispered her fears.
But Kleis told her such creatures were no longer upon Earth. Once,
yes, certainly there had been monsters, but now they were gone.

"Your father's brother," her mother said, "Eurygyos, has also gone
to the war. But his wife, Tyro, is kind. Barren women have to be, and
it is to this home we travel." To cheer her a bit, she added, "Mitylene
is a city I have heard compared to Rhodes and Corinth. When I was
a bride I visited there. The western side is spanned by bridges of white
stone, and there are two harbors, one on each side of the peninsula.
You have seen nothing like it. The market is set on a spit of land. So
many things to buy, wares from distant places, perfumes, baskets, pottery, candles, and such confections, such delicacies. We will go there,
Little Pebble."

"Don't call me that," the child said sharply and drew away.

On the third day, they came to washing springs and stone troughs.
But everything was deserted. The path had become a wagon road lined
with weather-beaten fig trees whose humped roots ran under the wall
of the city. From the bastions, sentries hailed the bedraggled band, and
they were made to state their family name and business before ap-
proaching.

Three massive bolts protected the gates of Mitylene. These were
not opened in such unsettled times, and the party entered by a small
postern door. Although she had visited her husband's brother years
before, Kleis had to ask the way.

The old soldier who admitted them stared hard at her. "You are a
relative and you do not know?"

"Please, we have traveled in flight from Eresos; the children are
tired."

The elder nodded, his face falling into deep furrows. "Then you
have heard no word of the battle?"

"A battle? So soon?"

"Athenian ships lay hidden by the crags of Chios. Our fleet was
burned and scuttled. The house to which you ask the way is a house
of mourning. They say Eurygyos, like Hector, went to his death with
open eyes."

Kleis's voice was tight in her throat. "Is it known who else . . . ?"

She is asking about Father, Sappho thought. But the old man didn't know.

Kleis pressed a coin into his hand and urged the servants to pick up their bundles. The wide streets had no one in them, except for some boys rolling hoops. They had been sent outside for this purpose and played without laughter or joy.

"Mother, I want to go back to Eresos, I want to go home."

Her mother didn't answer. She looked like one of the Gray Women.

The threshold of the house they sought was of stone. They stood there listening to the keening from inside. Red-eyed servants admitted them, calling their mistress. Tyro, wife of Eurygyos, embraced Kleis and the baby distractedly, then knelt and put her arms around Sappho. "This night, child, you will water the bones of your father."

Kleis's breath sucked inward. "Dead?"

"All. With the death that lays men at their length."

Kleis smiled at such nonsense. "He was with me four days ago. He told me, 'Take the children.' He told me . . ." She looked around. "How can it be?" She was still smiling.

"The gods looked with favor on the hekatombs of the Athenians. The owl of Pallas Athene escaped and betrayed our battle plans. For it is certain someone betrayed the route. In a cove west of Eresos our men died. My Eurygyos urged the rowers to a fast turn. An ax cleaved the nape of his neck. Still, they say, he gasped out instructions to save the ship, holding his nearly severed head clamped in his hands."

Kleis sank to the floor whispering, "No more, no more."

Tyro ordered that salts be brought.

Sappho wandered away. Slaves were attempting to start a fire. "How did Skamandronymos of Eresos die?" she asked.

An obese eunuch looked at the small travel-worn figure with disapproval. "I heard he was struck in the buttocks." This raised a general laugh and, encouraged by his audience, he continued. "The shaft of a spear was driven upward through his bladder and you might say when it burst, he drowned."

Someone nudged him. "The girl is his."

"Oh, Skamandronymos of Eresos, you say?" he said, suddenly polite. One had to be circumspect where the upper class was concerned. "Now that's a different matter. He jumped on the Athenian boat as if for the sport of it. And hurled fire upon their decks before he was overpowered."

Sappho walked on, stopping beside a maidservant busy with the preparation of mint. "How did Skamandronymos of Eresos die?"

"It was dreadful, that. A spear entered his eye and was driven downward, crashing among his teeth, knocking them every which way, cutting out the root of his tongue. And the Athenians burned him in his armor."

Another slave joined in. "I have it from one who was there that he was hit on the forehead, just at the rise of the nose. The bone cracked, and they say his two eyes, dripping gore, fell at his feet, and he crawled around trying to find them. *Then* they burnt him in his armor."

"You don't know at all, do you?" The small dark girl glared at them malevolently. "May strange dogs lap your blood from gutters in the street."

"What! Who is this miserable dark dwarf?"

Sappho stared them down. "In death there is a happy place reserved for heroes. My mother told me."

"Hush," one slave told the other. "She is of a great house by the way she speaks."

"If not how she looks." The other giggled.

Sappho's nurse had come looking for her. She laid hold of the slaves and shook them as though they were dust cloths. "Knownothings! She is Sappho, beloved daughter of the Lord Skamandronymos, and a guest in this house."

The arrival of messengers with laurel in their hair brought everyone to the courtyard. The messengers were given wine and when they had breath to speak cried, "Honor to Father Zeus, first in power!" They told that the bodies of their slain comrades were in the hands of compatriots. A great funeral pyre had been raised on the sand, a hundred feet high and in all directions a hundred feet. The bodies were washed, anointed with sweet oils, and wound in fresh cloaks. Their friends covered them with locks of their hair before carrying them by ladders to the apex of the mound, now surrounded by flayed sheep and oxen. Against the bier, jars of honey and unguents were piled. Six proved horses were killed and placed at the bottom of the burial hill. For each cup of wine drunk by their friends, one was spilled to the dead. And at the last it was the aureate wine of Lesbos that quenched the flames.

When the cremation was complete, the heroes' bones were separated from those of the offerings and laid, each in a golden krater, between layers of fat. They were wrapped in linen, and earth heaped over them covered by close-set stones.

The women wept as their loss was brought freshly before them, and servants led the messengers to food and rest while singers began extolling the fallen so that all might hear.

The child Sappho was carried to a room where a bed had been set up for her. Dreams born of Night sucked her beneath five thicknesses of darkness to Tartarus, the deepest pit under Earth, as far beneath Earth as Heaven is high. She saw her father and held out her arms to him. But he was pale and the sinews that bind together flesh and blood were no more. He did not approach her but sorrowfully shook his head, murmuring, "Little Pebble. Little Pebble."

She ran after him, wanting him to scoop her up in the old playful embrace. But her outstretched arms penetrated through Skamandronymos.

She woke screaming. It was the hour when the morning star brings light. True dreams pass through gates of horn, false dreams through gates of ivory. "It was a lying dream!" she shrieked. But she knew that dreams which come at dawn have passed the gates of horn. Her father was dead.

The war that killed him was to last ten years, until she was seventeen.

PITTAKOS

I DESIRE, I DESIRE, I DESIRE!" THESE WORDS WERE MOST often in her mind. Although what it was she desired she could not express. Sappho felt the world press against her and desired it without knowing what it was. Her mind seethed as music and words came together. "I long and I yearn . . ."

She had always sung her private thoughts, with a plea first to the Muses that the sacred Nine guide her. She did not regard the poems as something invented, but as given her. Sometimes she asked the Everliving why she had been so favored. Their rejoinder was gentle mirth and laughter. So she would slip away to the sacred grove where nature itself taught her to weave simple melodies, simply phrased.

> *Though few*
> *they are roses*

She had, over the years, grown in wild, untrammeled ways. There was no one to whom she must give way. Her mother was lenient, and Sappho was the leader of her brothers, who formed a free band, plunging into icy streams, climbing for chestnuts, running down to the sea for warmer bathing. They explored the forests, danced and sang in its glades and on the shore.

Sappho had a tortoiseshell lyre of four strings with a crosspiece joining two rams' horns on which she learned her lessons: the great epics of Homer, Hesiod too, she was made to memorize. "He's an old

woman, a scold," she stormed, impatient of Hesiod's many admonitions.
But hidden in all the moralizing she found the wonderful tale of Pan-
dora's chest. Two hundred years before, the crusty old poet sang: "Hope
was the only spirit that stayed there."

Sappho's memory for songs was faultless, and she made every passing singer sit with her until she knew each word of his repertoire. In
this manner she discovered that an Ionian, Archilochos by name,
ripped out his soul for a girl named Neobule—first in love, then in
hate. From him, Sappho discovered that pure rage uses short phrases.

She learned the lyric work of Eumelos of Corinth, and of Olympos
of Phrygia, inventor of the chromatic scale. She retraced the lines of
Tyrtaeos the lame, who made stirring songs to war, and Kallinos, who
a century before sang martial songs to his Lydian flute. She brooded
over the melancholy poems of Mimnermos of Smyrna; an old man now,
he once sang lovingly to Nanno, who accompanied him on the lyre
but never loved him. He commenced many of his songs with "The Fig
Tree Rune," which in other days was sung when humans to be sacrificed were pulled along the streets and beaten. Sappho reflected a good
deal on this oddly savage prelude to his tender outpourings. Were love
and hate one passion then?

She did not know. Those curious emotions had never touched her
half-child's heart. She had grown up in a city without men. There were
only boys—and at the suspicion of a beard, they too joined the endless
war, leaving women to rule not only Mitylene but all of Lesbos.

Sappho grew to womanhood without much thought of men. She
was unfamiliar with the sight, sound, or even the smell of them. At
seventeen, the usual age for marriage, she was quite untroubled that
there was no one available. The emotions that pricked her she channeled playfully in verse:

> *They say that Leda once*
> *found hidden an egg of hyacinth color*

She sang in a lyric Lesbian-Aeolic dialect using a variety of meters.
Many she invented. Spoken or sung, there was a conversational quality
about them; but her passion was inwardly directed, for she was her own
closest friend and confidante.

Familiar as she was with everyday Mitylene, she did not extol the sound of spinning or the smell of bread baking or any of the daily chores that went on around her. Nature filled her eyes and her poems.

Once, in her rambles following the course of a stream, she stopped, enchanted at the sight of a child gathering jonquils as yellow as her fine-spun hair. She was delicate and dainty as the long-stemmed flowers she held.

Sappho asked, "What is your name, little girl?"

"Atthis," was the shy reply.

Sappho picked up a jonquil the girl had dropped and, smiling, handed it to her.

The picture of the child remained with her. That evening, with a swift prayer to Erato, the Muse who played on a golden lyre, she sang:

> *I saw one day gathering flowers*
> *a very dainty little girl*

Since she could remember, Sappho had loved things of grace and delicacy. Therefore it was odd she should be disturbed when the first poet of Lesbos let it be known that he too intended to leave for the war. Alkaios had neither grace nor delicacy, but was loud and boisterous. He, the children, and a few white-haired elders who guarded the gates were the only males left inside the city. Plucking his lute, Alkaios liked nothing better than to gather a crowd and relate his amorous adventures. Sappho thought him a braggart, and said so, for she spared no one her thoughts. Yet when he sang his lyrics she listened, recognizing their perfect cadences and rhythms. And, although she took care not to let him know, it delighted her that a poet of Lesbos was sung in Lydia and far Sicily.

Alkaios departed for war, laughing and blowing kisses to the children and young women who ran at his side pelting him with roses and invoking the blessing of the gods on him, for the poet was beautiful, tall and fair as Apollo. He spied Sappho in the crowd and, his merry blue eyes twinkling, called, "What, not a word from Sappho of hidden harmonies?"

She flushed. "Do not let yourself be killed" was all she would say.

"Would you care?" The blue eyes were now serious.

"I was thinking of the many who love you," she retorted evasively.

"Of which you are not one?"

"I am never with the many, Alkaios."

He came close to her and, bending, whispered, "I heard the footfall of the flower spring."

It was something she had sung quietly in her room. She could not imagine how he had heard it, and she flushed more deeply than before. He went on his way, doing a twirl or two in the air.

The report reached Mitylene that Alkaios marched into battle, his flute at his lips. Then hearing the bones of a man's skull smashed inside his helmet rattling around like grape pits, he made an about-face and danced his way out of the fray, tossing aside his richly ornamented shield, which the Athenians seized and hung in mockery in their main temple. He returned to Mitylene, still singing. It was a scandal. The same children that had called after him adoringly now cried, "Coward!"

Alkaios laughed. "Wise man, little friends, with my brains inside my skull and my guts inside my skin. For I am here, and the vultures feed on other flesh, not mine." He was soon making the rounds of the few remaining taverns, voicing paeans to the wine. It was hard to be angry with him, for in spite of having run away he was an asset to Lesbos, which had not many accomplished or famous sons. Besides which, he had added a small, pointed, well-trimmed beard that enhanced his already charming appearance. His ribald ways were more or less condoned by all but Sappho, who was very hard on him. When they met, he was always humble and, if not sober, affected sobriety. His endeavors to please her made an impression on her, and she went to her mother.

"Mother, I know that I am not blond or tall. My features are not in the classic mold. Tell me—you are my mother—am I ill-favored?"

". . . You have a very sweet smile," her mother said.

"Thank you."

"Sappho, Sappho," Kleis called after her, but she was gone.

Sappho consulted her polished bronze mirror, finding fault with all but her eyes, which were luminous in their darkness as though just roused from sleep.

Alkaios began singing of her, and to her. One of the things he sang was:

> Your appearance is unmatched,
> intriguing,
> always different

These poems he declaimed in the marketplace, in the main square, and in the public houses. Sometimes he sang them outside the door of her house.

As her father had long ago suspected, there were two Sapphos. One of them was annoyed, one pleased.

A development in the war took her mind from herself. The town of Sigeum, retaken by Lesbos and her allies, was once more in Athenian hands. However, the Lesbians blockaded successfully with their black ships, and at this stalemate the enemies turned to arbitration. The wise man Periander, tyrant of neutral Corinth, agreed to preside as arbiter, and Athens and Lesbos pledged to abide by his decision.

It was the year of the forty-sixth Olympic Games. Lesbos was ten years weary. The priestesses of Dionysos consulted the sacred snakes in their caves, and far-seeing Perse with tangled hair rushed into the main street of the city. Froth was on her lips, she tore her robe, and her eyes rolled from the central place in their sockets to float in a sea of white. People knelt where they were, for this was one divinely possessed; the hand of a god was on her.

Sappho, who had gone picking pomegranates, flattened herself against a wall and let the basket fall. The fruit burst and splattered at her feet. Perse darted at one terrified form and then another. "One must be named!" she cried. "The Fates, those stern spinning women have spun you all at your birth. The shades of those dead in this long war must drink blood."

"An oracle! An oracle!" the crowd murmured. "Vipers of the cave make utterance through her mouth."

"One must be seized," raved the priestess. "No ram, no bull, no oxen. The tribes of the dead make treaty with the gods." A child screamed and clutched its mother in a spasm of terror. "Not the gilded horns of a heifer . . ."

The crowd chanted, repeating her words back to her: "Not the gilded horns . . ."

"Quickly, to the mountain. All will be done!" The prophetess, wild and disheveled, climbed the steep street.

The people streamed after her along the myrtle-lined road toward Lesbian Olympus.

Sappho seemed to have no will of her own; she followed with dazed steps. Priestesses stood along the way under shade trees, offering drink from goatskins. To Sappho alone was handed a golden cup embossed with gems. She drank. A numb feeling spread in her. Further on she was stopped again, another splendid goblet thrust into her hand. "In death is life," the priestess sang.

"In death is life," Sappho repeated. A strange sensation of power flowed to the tips of her fingers. She found she held a flute and began to play, improvising harmonies. "O Dionysos, the only immortal to taste death—you are in all places and all hearts. Your death brings life, your black blood renews Earth."

When she stopped again to drink, nimble fingers braided her hair with flowers. The white stone acropolis towering above shrunk to the height of mushrooms, while those things small, the blue squill and yellow gagea, assumed grotesque proportions, so that she seemed to dance along their petals.

It became harder to climb and there was little breath in her for singing. The people advanced, intoning prayers. The sound floated upward. Wildfowl, startled from the ravine, screamed overhead.

At the top was a worn green-veined stone, the navel of Lesbos. The stone spoke with the voice of a woman, and all who heard fell to the ground. The voice said: "The water of ever-flowing Styx, tenth stream of Ocean, commands you. And the golden generation who were in Kronos's time tell you these words: Not from the throat of sheep, nor the black blood of boar or oxen. The tribes of the dead, the kthonian people demand fresh blood for blood given . . . and great Zeus, Lord of the Aegis, hungers for it. Pour forth, that the mind of Periander the Wise be inclined toward Lesbos."

A girl-child was ripped from her mother.

"None live long and the young are pleasing." With these words the priestess with blank eyes slashed the girl's throat. "The gods would drink."

The mother's body struck the earth before the child's. Sappho fastened her eyes on the beautiful container of blown glass that filled quickly with spurting fluid. It gushed with a gargling sound, then flowed, then trickled. Every drop was caught and the vessel slowly turned in all directions that the sun might flash from it.

Sappho's eyes no longer saw. Above there seemed to be no sky, and Earth itself was unsteady beneath her feet. But anger for the slaughtered child took command: "Sing woe! Sing woe!" she cried.

The priestesses stopped their chanting and looked at her. And the people looked at her with wondering eyes.

"Death is an evil," she went on recklessly, her voice elevated to song,

> *We have the gods'*
> *word for it; they too*
> *would die if death*
> *were a good thing*

She was pulled backward, her mouth covered to stop her protest. It was Alkaios, who appeared from nowhere, panting in her ear, "You are mad to contest the priestesses of Dionysos." With her weight against him, he fell backward into a gully. Gasping and clawing bushes to slow their plunge, sobbing and incoherent, she tried to tell him about Earth falling away, having no bottom.

"We'll have no bottoms at the end of this." Alkaios set his feet forward like a mule and braced himself against a giant root, swinging her like a limp doll beside him. They were on the gravelly shore of a dry streambed.

"First . . ." Alkaios stood, groaned, and rubbed his backside. Then he walked to where water, having cut a new path, was meandering. "First, we wash your face, and perhaps some of the snake venom and baneful herbs they grind into their wine will leave you and you will begin to make sense. What thymos caused you to drink their potions?" He was splashing icy water over her.

"Oh," she said, and again, "Oh!" She began to wash herself with dripping hands, and Alkaios saw that she was shaking.

"The water is too cold?"

"No," she said.

"Never drink the wine a priestess gives you. It is made to confound the mind and delude the senses."

"Like your poems."

He laughed. "Poetry is stronger than magic."

"Poetry is magic," she retorted. Then, "She killed a child, Alkaios. She took her from her mother and drove a dagger through her throat. It stuck out both ends and then was withdrawn so the blood could flow unimpeded."

"Yes, yes, I saw men do such things to one another on the battle-field, and worse. It is why I did not stay."

"But it was a child . . . a girl." She passed her hand across her fore-head. "I think it was a child. Or did I dream?"

"Let's say you dreamed. But when it was done you called out . . ."

"Sing woe. Sing woe!"

"Sappho, one cannot rebuke those ladies. But Zeus is with you, for a treaty has been signed."

"A treaty?"

"Yes. While that drugged mob scrambled up the mountain to see human blood spilled, news came to the harbor. Periander's judgment went against Lesbos. The priestesses invoked their magic a bit late. Had they succeeded, your life would not be worth the dirt at my feet."

She stared at him. "Periander found against Lesbos? After ten years and a pile of dead that reaches to the sky?"

"His ruling is that each side will remain in possession of that they already have."

She continued looking at him in disbelief. "Give up Sigeum, that my father died to win back and all those since him? Lesbos will not accept such a treaty!"

"Lesbos has accepted it."

She shook her head, denying.

"The war is over, Sappho. The army is weary; the squadrons will no longer obey their captains who whip them to their posts. They will not fight anymore."

"It is the fault of those up here on the mountain who resort to old ways. They brought this misfortune of an ill peace upon us."

"So it will be said. And so you are safe."

"Stop," she said viciously. "I hate comfortable words." She sank down, her small body folding inward.

"Come Sappho, men and ships will be sailing into the twin har-bors—tired, defeated men. Mitylene must make them feel like heroes. There will be feasts and acrobats, wine and flowers. The sound of the lute must be heard, your aunt Tyro's and the good Kleis's tables must be spread with welcome."

She lifted her head and looked at him. "I will keep anger from the words I sing."

This was more difficult than Sappho imagined. Her island world was changing. As Alkaios predicted, the harbors that had been so serene filled with navy pentekoneters, and ships that had patrolled far out crowded dockside. Into her city through its crooked streets swarmed a race of strangers. Giants with unmodulated voices, they trampled the wildflowers with large, coarse-sandled feet. They gathered at taverns, roared their jokes, laughed harshly and unmusically. Their shouts when they hailed one another were enough to reach dark Tartarus. It was an invasion of creatures from some other world. They were called men.

Were they perhaps Poseidon's changelings, created by Kronos in ancient days? Or the offspring of the sky king, Uranus, whom Zeus imprisoned below the abyss that broods in unspoken darkness?

The city went mad. It welcomed these dolts as though they had been victorious and brought home great prizes. But the only prizes they had to bestow were themselves. Everyone seemed to think that quite enough. Petal confetti rained down on swaggering figures naked to the waist, glistening from scented oils the bemused girls rubbed them with.

Sappho watched this new race, exuding the lusty maleness of bulls and stallions, assume leadership in all things. They returned as masters in every house, and this was seen as natural. The best wines were brought from dark cellars and chill wells. Every kitchen competed in the making of jellies and preserves. The fattest among the flocks were slaughtered, and the maidens of Mitylene appeared in fine cambric with flowers braided in their hair. Music was everywhere: bells were fastened to the manes of horses, tied to chariot reins and over doorposts, accompanied by the sound of lute, lyre, and castanets.

Pittakos was the only Lesbian leader to return a hero. As the balladmakers and storytellers recounted the tale, Pittakos of Lesbos challenged the Athenian commander, Phynon, to single combat, choosing the art of wrestling-boxing. This seemed to give Phynon the advantage, as it was an event he had won years before in the Olympics. But now, at fifty, he was too old to fight and too proud to refuse. The Athenian met the Lesbian on the field. Pittakos, not trusting to his opponent's years, hid a net behind his shield. When they clashed, Pittakos, with a mighty heave, entangled his enemy and broke his neck.

The Athenians cried foul. But the Lesbians needed some claim to success, and for his deed Pittakos was the pride of the entire Lesbian army.

Sappho watched from her window as the hero rode through the streets with the merchant prince Melanchros and the noble Pinytos. It was plain to her that Pittakos was a rude man, a man of the people. In spite of this he held a strange fascination for her. She tried laughing at him. He did not know how to wear his himation, and the sureness of breeding was lacking, placed as he was between his betters—especially Pinytos of ancient lineage. One could see that Pittakos was flattered to be riding with these lords.

From then on there was a subtle difference in Sappho. During the day she wanted to be home in her chamber, where, looping the leather thong over her door stick, she could think without interruption. About whom? Pittakos, the unkempt commoner from Thrace.

Some god, she thought, has seized my mind, as rising in the night she pressed her lyre to her and sang the beauty of his limbs, when she knew he went unwashed, that even his beard was neglected and uncombed. She wondered at herself. This did not prevent her from intoning, "He knows wild things like a lion."

It must be that her father had guessed rightly, and there were two Sapphos. Otherwise, how to explain that she could not keep this trickster from her thoughts? For with one part of her mind she derided him; at the same time he seemed to her virile and powerful.

To rid herself of these conflicting emotions, she called a slave, asking for a ritual bath. They retired to the bathing room, with its slatted marble floor, and ewers of warm water were poured over her as she chanted prayers. She began to feel purified, free of loathsome thoughts. "Rub me with oils of Lemnos," she ordered.

A bed was set up on which she stretched herself, and the slave girl kneaded her body. She rubbed the inside of Sappho's thighs, letting the back of her hand, as though in carelessness, touch more private parts.

Sappho bit her. She would not allow this now she was grown. In one of the quick movements typical of her she was on her feet. "From this minute you belong to my brother, Kharaxos. I give you to him!"

The girl set up a noisy weeping and clasped her mistress's feet, Sappho kicked her and the girl crawled away. Alone, Sappho paced the room unable to find gentle Sappho. Lawlessness and madness, two sisters born of Night, had hold of her. And the cause was Pittakos. Pittakos, on whom ordinarily she would not bestow a word. Pittakos, whom not even a ritual bath had banished from her mind. Pittakos, whom she loathed and detested. Her small fingers pressed the palms of her hands, making fists. She struck herself about the body to dislodge the god who inhabited her, for it was not she who admired coarseness and had wayward thoughts of a great hulking male body. She, a virgin, denied it.

She wanted to use herself as she had the slave. If only she could say "Out of my sight!"

Alkaios brought attention to Sappho's work by repeating her poems with his. So when he invited her to attend the games at which contenders for the Olympics would be chosen, she agreed.

Kleis worried about her daughter's conduct now that the men had returned. "Sappho, to appear in public with a man of Alkaios's reputation . . . He is known as a drunkard, and, and—"

"I know his reputation, Mother. But Alkaios has been generous to me."

"If you want my opinion, he is furthering his own reputation by increasing yours."

"We are friends, Mother."

"But my dear, for a woman—"

"Do not speak of women. Or of men. I am Sappho."

"The returned warriors already say that you are too clever to make a good wife."

Sappho laughed. "They may be right."

"But, Daughter . . ."

Sappho no longer laughed. A new confidence born of her new poems was strong in her. She looked sternly at her mother. "Small I am. But a name which fills all the world will be mine."

Her mother drew back from her. "Has some god told you this?"

"I have told myself this."

When she appeared beside Alkaios in the stands erected for the games, there was a general movement in the crowd. They strained for a look at the diminutive figure and pointed her out to one another, for though only a girl, her songs were sung.

The first event was the chariot race. Her favorite brother, Kharaxos, the one next to her in age, was driving. So was the war hero, Pittakos.

She had not foreseen this. She pulled her eyes from Pittakos and tried to concentrate on the scene before her. A black bull without spot was slain to the deathless gods, and garlanded horses, their manes shining with oil, champed in their traces. The felloes of the chariot wheels were of gold, the eight spokes bronze and the naves silver, but the strength was in the oaken axles.

"The skill here is in wheeling around the post," Alkaios explained to her. "The chariots must not go wide in circling either end of the course. The nave of the wheel must almost graze the stone of the goalpost. One miscalculation, and the chariot is dashed to pieces."

Sappho nodded; she understood the race and had no need of Alkaios's well-meant instruction. She found herself praying as the charioteers took their places, but she did not name the one she prayed for. It was her brother Khar, of course.

How brutish Pittakos appeared beside her slim brother—how brawny, how strong. Again she forced her eyes from him. For Sappho was double-seeing. She saw him for what he was, an opportunist rising fast in the influential circles of politics. This upstart, this outsider, she was certain, intended to rule Lesbos. She resented the male resumption of power. Women had done very well for the ten years that Lesbos had been left in their hands. Their decisions had been wise and equitable. Now that the men had returned, all that went before was forgotten. Only she did not forget.

The contestants mounted their flower-strewn vehicles. An umpire gave the signal. The chariots leapt at air. "Lean to your left! Your left!" She was dancing up and down, catching only a glimpse between the shoulders and heads in front of her.

"Can you see?" Alkaios asked.

Sappho hated any reference to her size. "Of course," she said. "Khar should urge his right-hand horse, give him a looser rein."

Alkaios looked puzzled. Had he guessed that while she said Khar, she had described Pittakos, who was holding back, planning a last-minute spurt?

A horse fell, breaking its leg against the painted white stone; the chariot shuddered and overturned, pinning its driver. The scene was enveloped in dust. "Who is it?" Sappho screamed.

"Not Khar. He is well in front. He and Pittakos, they are both holding."

Sand and grit sprayed the drivers. Sweat from the animals fell in streams on the ground, and the wounded horse writhed under the chariot, while the man was still.

With bodies leaning toward the goal, the drivers made the final pass. Khar was wide of the post and Pittakos won. Sappho's face flamed with shame. She took it as a personal disgrace that one of her house should lose to that great bumpkin. The prize was a woman skilled in the arts of love and valued at four oxen.

As they moved to the waterfront for the next event, Alkaios drew her attention to a pigeon tied by a foot to a ship's mast. To cut the string was to win, to miss or kill the bird was to lose.

Next came the javelin throwing, and the naked bodies of the young athletes were sweet to gaze upon. Sappho thought, as she had recently, that the male had much equipment for love.

Footraces followed. The contestants, their bodies taut and gleaming with oil, their muscles tense, bent at the ready. Sappho studied their lean haunches, bulging calves, slender ankles, and dangling parts of love with foreskins drawn down and fastened securely to protect their manhood. Was it because of these instruments for cleaving and entering the body of women that they deserved to be lords over everyone? What god had decreed this? For it seemed a peculiar claim. Why were the qualities "larger, stronger" preferred over "delicate, kinder"? Why was the world everywhere under the control of men who gave no place to women and yet decided their fate?

The trophy was a mixing bowl of silver finely wrought by Phoenicians from beyond the sea. Second place brought a large ox and a talent of gold; this was won by Sappho's brother Eurygyos, named for the uncle in whose house they lived.

Discus throwers now took their stance. Sappho thought of the story of Apollo. It was in such a game that he accidently struck his friend Hyacinth, who died in his arms. "Alas, alas!" Apollo wept. And where his friend fell a hyacinth flower sprang up with "Alas!" etched on every petal.

The final contest of the day was the wrestling match. Sappho's attention was riveted once more on Pittakos, who, rested from his exertions of the morning, stepped forward to try his skill as he had with Phynon the Athenian. Sappho took in the raw power of his body, the naked, gleaming sinews of a lion. His breast heaved as he circled his adversary looking for an opening. They gripped tentatively, and moved apart. The opponent closed but Pittakos broke the hold. Again they were at each other like Zeus's lightning. The crowd thrilled to see them wind their bodies around each other in attitudes intimate as sex. Feeling the erotic arousal of the spectators, both men swelled like stallions. The crowd shrieked their pleasure at this proof of virility. The next instant, one of the stallions was on the ground, deflated, sweating from every pore and groaning. Pittakos had given him a tremendous knock behind the knees that sent him sprawling.

The audience yelled derisively as an old she-goat was led out. There were catcalls and laughter as the defeated wrestler got lumberingly to his feet and with chagrin led away his prize. The winner, Pittakos, was presented with a double goblet of handcrafted gold. He stood turning slowly for all to see—the cup, Sappho wondered, or his own magnificent torso?

Sappho was on her feet. Curving her hands about her lips she called, "Where's your net?" The mocking tone carried. There was a moment's silence while the joke penetrated. Heads wagged; sharp-tongued Sappho had hit the mark.

Laughter swelled against Pittakos, who seemed to shrink as he stood there, his role reversed from hero to butt. He turned and looked at the woman who had robbed him of his triumph. All who saw that look knew a struggle had commenced between the poet and the strongman.

Sappho smiled at him. She knew he knew lawless things and was without shame, and that he was her enemy. As her enemy she could withstand him, but if he turned his parts and passions toward her, she would be his slave. That she would not have.

The merchant prince Melanchros was declared Tyrant of Lesbos. He made a stern, inflexible ruler, and it became fashionable to quote Sappho:

You cannot bend a stiff mind

Melanchros made things worse by taking up the Spartan cry "No one belongs to himself, but all to the State." Would he segregate women then, Sappho wondered, and take their children from them? She saw that privileges taken for granted could easily vanish. But it was the tax laws, enforced with new rigidity, that had the common people openly muttering. Even the aristocracy were critical of Melan-chros's heavy-handed approach, and plots against him seethed. In the taverns men put their heads together; in many of the wealthy homes there were meetings that lasted late into the night.

Alkaios and his brother, Atreus, met often in the home of Sappho's aunt. Sappho sat with them and Kharaxos over spiced anchovies and nettles fried in oil, sipping wine, talking revolt.

There was a thought in her mind she had not expressed to the others. Her position was unique, she recognized this. Was she, the only woman, included because she was Khar's sister, Alkaios's good friend, because it was her aunt's home—or because she was Sappho? Until she could be more sure, she kept the question to herself.

Atreus struck the table with his fist. "Then we are agreed. The Tyrant Melanchros and his bribe-devouring council must go. And to-night one is coming who will help us accomplish this."

Who should walk through the door at that moment but Pittakos? Sappho could not believe what her eyes beheld. Trembling, she got to her feet. "You are here without invitation, sir."

"Sappho!" Kharaxos remonstrated, for the laws of hospitality were strong.

Her small face was white as a death mask. "I speak as I am minded."

"He is our guest," her brother said, "here by my invitation. I remind you, Sister, that all guests are from Zeus."

And when this formula failed to soften her, Atreus spoke: "Pittakos is our chance to rid ourselves of Melanchros."

Sappho did not relent. "Look at him. I have insulted him and he stands there to hear more."

Pittakos was a man turned to stone. He did not know how to battle in words. He did not know how to battle a woman, especially one who spat so fiercely. Atreus leapt to his defense. "Sappho, I, not Khar, asked Pittakos to come tonight. I tell you, the army is with him, and through him the Tyrant can be overthrown."

Sappho turned on him. "You are children! Would you trade the Tyrant Melanchros for the Tyrant Pittakos?"

Pittakos took a step toward her, he had found his tongue. "Sappho, songstress of Lesbos, your words are both true and untrue. It is true that I am a rude fellow unused to the company of such as you and your noble friends and brother. It is untrue that I would raise myself in rank, thereby placing in jeopardy all I have gained. As for becoming Tyrant . . . you could not have said it but in jest."

Sappho sank back in her place, her ever-ready words gone from her. She had never been so close to him. She watched as he took command of the little group. He was, after all, a commander of men. She felt the power in him, not only in his person but in the thoughts he set before them.

Pittakos spoke of democratic goals, a council in which all voices were heard.

"Even women's?" Sappho asked, bringing out the thought she had so long suppressed.

"Sappho." Khar was embarrassed. "What god puts such mad notions into your head?"

"Who do you think ran the city of Mitylene for ten long years?"

But it was Pittakos who, weighing his words, said, "It is good that a woman's voice be heard. For did not far-darting Athene spring from the head of great Father Zeus?"

The topic turned to various problems the city faced and how best to address them. Sappho did not follow this. She was thinking that Pittakos had spoken well, better than Khar, and the others had made no comment at all. A new young Tyrant with the juice of manhood in him might indeed be more generous toward women. She excused herself and went upstairs.

She sat statue-still in her room, waiting for the meeting below to break up. Then she reached for a cloak and slipped along the interstices of the house, using both interior and exterior staircases. Knowing the habits of the family and servants, she was able to avoid being seen.

She gained the courtyard unobserved, moving stealthily along its walls, lifted the latch, and, once in the street, ran. This she had done since she was a child, when she wanted to escape herself.

She felt her heavy hair fall rhythmically against her shoulders as she sped the night-darkened world. But tonight she could not outrun the many impressions that jumbled in her. Had she been mistaken? Had Pittakos magnanimously forgiven her public humiliation of him? How well he had spoken regarding far-darting Athene, to whose counsel great Zeus gives ear. Was it true he did not think of becoming Tyrant? Perhaps he should.

So absorbed was Sappho in introspection that she did not see the man until he stepped in front of her.

Where had he come from? He stood blocking her way in a narrow alley. She was not afraid, merely annoyed that he did not move aside. She was about to raise her voice to request this, for he was a common soldier, his single garment coarsely woven—when two rough arms took her and she was brought against a body like a boulder. One of the kolossos's arms was all that was needed to hold her; with it, he backed her against a building, bringing his face against hers. A rank man-smell combining sweat and wine and something more intangible made her frantic. But she was too shrewd to struggle.

"Well, well, what have we here?" The misbegotten creature smiled down at her, showing a space in his mouth through which wine dribbled. Protuberant lips fastened against hers and a callused hand felt its way inside her chiton. A thumb dug painfully into her buttocks, and she was tipped toward the blunt weapon of flesh rising under his tunic. It was a searching thing with a life of its own, groping for the center of the three folds which must not be violated.

"I am virgin." She hissed the words between their two mouths. "My family is powerful. You will die for this. Consider, is it worth it to have your parts hacked off, and your head afterward?"

Her body twisted to keep from being penetrated by that blind, thrusting organ. "My father is the prince Skamandronymos," she cried.

The soldier laughed. "He's dead."

"And Pittakos, that leader of men, was earlier at my house."

"And you would call on him? On Pittakos?" The man's laugh rumbled through his body. "He's the one who tells his friends to be on the lookout for a pretty morsel like you. Any girl who wanders alone at night is looking for trouble."

Sappho sank deadweight in his arms. He bent over her to hoist her up so he could finish his business. But she had positioned herself under him so she could knee him in the vulnerables, as vicious a blow as he'd ever been struck. He doubled over.

Sappho gave a shove and was under his arm, racing away. She didn't know which turnings she took. She ran wildly, her breath coming jerkily. A great rasping filled her lungs and the cavities of her head, and she thought she would strangle. She was not crying, but tears hung before her vision—*I am blinded like the Cyclops*—and she fell upon the stones of the street.

Lying in a heap, her skin prickling in anticipation of that rough hand falling upon her to finish what had been started, she slowly became aware that no one followed. And at the same instant the gods showed her herself, debased by fear, cowering in filth. Sappho, descendant of a noble house, humiliated by one of Pittakos's soldiers.

Her question had been answered. Pittakos had not forgotten, nor would he. He must know her habit of running about the streets at night. She had always done it, and thought nothing of it. But now the men had returned. Presenting themselves as protectors, they were violators lying in wait. And he encouraged them. Had he singled her out? Did he have her in mind when he let loose his dogs? Did he plan to ask for particulars, insist on details, deriving as much pleasure as though his rod committed the rape? And she had softened toward him, believed his glib, easy speech.

If only he had known. Had he himself come after her, she would have put up no resistance. And she cried for shame to be swept by unbearable desire.

What had become of the Sappho of old, who abhorred the rough and the vulgar? "O Artemis, Apollo's lovely twin, I will burn hekatombs! Pure virgin, help Sappho be as she was."

Zeus, capricious in all things, gave victory to the forces raised against Melanchros, and the Tyrant was exiled. Mysilos of Leanex became the new Tyrant. Atreus and Pittakos, as the chief architects of this political insurgency, were his closest counselors. Pittakos had the favor of the army and the mass of freemen, while the presence of Atreus soothed the aristocrats. Embers of Sappho's discontent continued to smolder, as the new Tyrant proved no less harsh than Melanchros. With this Alkaios agreed, but he shrugged. "In this world what is perfect?"

"It is clear to me," Sappho went on, "we must form ranks again and unseat Mysilos."

"Hold on, Sappho. We've had our revolution."

"I tell you," she said adamantly, "Mysilos must go, and Pittakos with him."

Alkaios gave her a long, shrewd look. "So it comes down to Pittakos."

In spite of Sappho's persistence, the conspirators would have disbanded had it not been for Atreus. He arranged for his brother to call a meeting but keep his coming secret. Alkaios simply said a comrade would join them. When Atreus appeared, the others were amazed and somewhat intimidated. For although not first in power, Atreus was one of the triumvirate. He approached the little group, hand on his heart.

"Speak then," Alkaios told his brother.

Atreus explained that he felt remorse at his part in bringing the new regime to power. Mysilos, with his profligate ways, was impoverishing the city, forever concocting schemes to defraud the people. It had come to the point, Atreus concluded, when a patriot could no longer stand by. If he could count on the support of their group, perhaps something could be done.

He saw their hesitation. But he had come prepared, and hastened to tell them he was in possession of information of such a shameful sort that it would topple Mysilos.

Khar shoved a goblet across the table at Atreus as a sign that he should tell what he knew. Into the expectant quiet, Atreus said, "Melanchros, our former Tyrant, is not in exile."

Sappho's face grew white. "Where then?"

"I can take you to the spot where his butchered body lies."

There was appalled silence.

"Oh, let me sing my anger," Sappho said softly.

And she did, asking in an anonymous poem where Melanchros was and suggesting that perhaps he was closer to home than any suspected. The verse was repeated the next day in the taverns, at the polished baths, and in the marketplace. By nightfall it was sung in every home.

The next morning the villa where Sappho lived was surrounded by soldiers. At the sight of them, her mother and aunt and the female servants set up a great wailing.

The captain saluted. "We have an arrest order for Sappho, daughter of Skamandronymos."

"In whose name is it issued?" Sappho demanded.

"It bears the seal of Commander Pittakos."

Sappho's lips smiled, but her eyes did not smile. She kissed her mother and aunt, assuring them, "It is nothing. He is not a lover of poetry, that is all." She walked lightly between her escorts, not looking at them but at the row of stately poplars they passed. If he wanted her silent, he would have to kill her. And as she plunged from time she would still sing his perfidy.

They passed a group of boys marching naked and in good order on their way to the school of the harpmaster. They looked curiously at her. She was taken to the portico of the town hall with its statues of gods and princes vividly painted and waxed.

Up the stairs they went to the great chamber. There, where a short time earlier Melanchros had presided, were her co-conspirators. Sappho's heart pulsed in her throat. All had been rounded up, not only Khar and Alkaios but such high-spirited dandies as Pelops and the firebrand Pinytos, as well as Kepalus. They greeted her in a subdued manner, Alkaios murmuring hurriedly, "Atreus has fled into Egypt."

"He was wise," Pinytos said. "The gods alone know what retribution will be taken. All sorts of allegations are spreading through the city." And he looked reproachfully at Sappho.

Pelops, the latest golden boy of Alkaios's passion, began to blubber. "If ever I burnt heifer, sheep, or these things . . ."

"Hush," Sappho said sharply.

Pittakos entered with his attendants. Seating himself, he looked with a mild gaze at the young troublemakers. When he spoke, it was courteously. "A harmful rumor flies around Mitylene from the white stone bridges that span the narrows to Mount Lesbos itself." He adopted the lecturing tone of a teacher with wayward children. At this condescension, Sappho held her head higher.

"Murder," Pittakos continued in the same patient tone, "is outside civilized law. Yet the rumor is that murder was done on Melanchros, whom we all know to be residing in Rhodes." He paused, giving them a chance to speak, wanting them perhaps to deny this. Seeing they would not, he continued. "I have word from my captains that Atreus has taken boat for Egypt. I do not know how deeply you youngsters were involved in his treasonous plotting. But I am inclined to think your only crime is that of being young, and of having a way with words that leads you to excesses." Here he smiled at Sappho.

To check her anger she dug her nails into the palms of her hands. "Apollo, god of Truth, looks over my shoulder when I sing."

"Yes, yes. But it is well to ascertain the facts before you sing."

She retorted haughtily, "The Muses themselves guide my mind. You perhaps do not know that Art was born in the temple and flowered in the sacred grove. If you use your power against me and my friends, let it be on grounds other than poetry. For if it be a lying song, it will die its own death. If it be true, then Melanchros's murder will be only the first."

"How you misunderstand me, young Sappho of a noble sire. Mysilos and I do not fear idle words, but neither do we want slander—it creates an atmosphere of unrest. Believe me, there has been no murder. Melanchros is as hale as I am. And a token will be dispatched by him from Rhodes, so that all Lesbos may know he prospers. And now . . ." His mood was almost fatherly. A crease of blood appeared on the inside of Sappho's hands. "I wish to persuade you that forgiveness is better than punishment. That is the lesson I want you to learn in this room." He smiled on them benignly. "Why linger," he said lightly, "when you are free to go?"

The miscreants looked at one another, unable to believe this clemency. There was a stir among them. Her brother went up to Pittakos and clasped his arm. Even Alkaios said to him, "You have spoken well."

Sappho said nothing, not to Pittakos or her companions. Alkaios, in high spirits at their reprieve, reached for her hand, which she tore from his.

"Do not meddle with the Pebble."

Sappho was bitter at being the recipient of Pittakos's leniency and angry with Alkaios for treating Pittakos as an equal. She was altogether out of sorts.

This was the moment her mother chose to speak to her of the young men who, with encouragement, might become suitors. "But," her mother continued in gentle reproof, "a girl who behaves so outspokenly will end up becoming what Aphrodite abhors most, an old virgin."

"I could always go to the priestesses of Dionysos and live in a cave with the sacred snakes," Sappho teased.

"Sappho, I am trying to have a serious talk with you." Nevertheless Kleis shuddered. She was afraid of those priestesses who communed with gods and knew the hour of each person's death. She sighed at her inability to oppose her small, imperious daughter.

A second person sought Sappho that day whom she treated no better.

"I have not forgotten my anger, Alkaios. Why are you here?"

"Sappho, stop playing the part of a spoiled child. Great happenings can be brought about."

She looked at him with curiosity.

"Would you still bring down the Tyrant Mysilos and his henchman Pittakos?"

Immediately she was on her feet. "Not here in the house. Come, walk with me by the columns of the loggia and tell me what is in your mind."

In the sunshine she felt free from prying ears and eyes. "You have some word of your brother?"

"You are shrewd, Sappho."

"But how? He has not had time to reach Egypt."

"He left a message that I just found."

"What is it?"

Alkaios hesitated. "The gods know, now that I am here I am afraid to tell you."

She laughed at him. "For what do you fear? Your heart or your head?"

"My heart you have danced on with heedless feet until it is squashed flat with no life in it at all. But I have given some thought to the creeping poison they say Mysilos uses."

She tossed her dark hair. "I do not fear him. And I don't believe there is a message."

He drew a folded sheet of papyrus from his breast and showed it to her.

She looked from it to him. "What is it? A map of the city?"

"First, is this my brother's genuine name-stamp and seal?"

She frowned over it. "Yes, of that I am quite certain. But these round dots?" Her frown deepened as she studied the sketch. "Could they be the stone markers pointing to the entrance of Mitylene?"

He nodded. "And the cross?"

She shook her head, puzzled.

"It has to be the spot that holds the body of Melanchros."

She grabbed his hand with all her strength, her eyes enormous in her face. "Alkaios, by the gods . . . Where was this hidden and why did you not find it sooner? Perhaps the papyrus was placed there by Pittakos?"

"You recognized Atreus's seal. The map was hidden under the sundial in my garden, a spot he and I used when we were boys."

"Why did you not look there at once?"

"It has been so many years. I told you, we were boys. But in thinking of it, it occurred to me that perhaps he had left a message, and I looked in the old place."

Sappho was double-listening—to him, and inside herself. "It could be a trap," she said. "Atreus could have been forced. It might be the price for a passage to Egypt."

Alkaios rejected this angrily. "My brother is of my house and lineage. He would not betray us."

Sappho threw her arms wide, abandoning herself to joy. "Then we have brought down Pittakos and his straw man!" Her voice dropped to a whisper, and she brought her face close to his. "Alkaios, what would you say to a decayed body wrapped in its poor winding sheet, left moldering in the very center of the market square for all Mitylene to see?"

Alkaios did not share her enthusiasm. "A moldering body? You mean . . . dig him up? Surely that is not a job for two poets."

"Why not? It is the highest duty of the poet to fight for freedom."

He shook his head. "I have no taste for this enterprise. If you want to know, the thought of what we may find turns my stomach. And you, Sappho, are"—he searched for an inoffensive word—"delicate."

She glared at him. "Small. That's what you mean, small. It doesn't matter—we will bring the others."

"There are too many to trust with the secret."

"Khar, then. Khar will help us."

Alkaios still wavered. "Suppose you are right and Atreus was forced? They will be watching the spot."

"We won't do it tomorrow, or the next day, or the day after that. Eventually they will grow tired and not watch."

"O Sappho of the violet hair. Why must we always be serious? If we are not engaged in plots, we are analyzing the work of Ionian Mimnermos, or Terpander of Antiss, or experimenting with lines based on different sounds and lengths. Why can't I take you in my arms like any other girl? Do you know I have never kissed you?"

A smile touched Sappho's lips, and she began to twist a coronet of thyme, interspersed with hyacinth. "You are my dear friend. We have too much to risk by such nonsense. Besides, you have your young lads. That was a sweet lay you wrote to the mole on the boy's throat."

"Yes. Well, all I know is, I am going to get drunk. Why wait for lamplighting time? The day has but a finger's length to go."

Sappho determined to be prudent, cautious and above all patient, traits for which she had not hitherto been known. She avoided Alkaios. She even avoided being alone with Khar. She developed the habit of smiling suddenly, disconcertingly. It was a dangerous smile that focused on nothing at all. She let the days pass, opening herself to all around her. She heard the partridge's call, listened to the shepherd's pipes and the bleat of flocks. She watched mules drag thick pines down from the mountain where they grew. She knew it took twenty such to make a boat, for she was of a seafaring race. She crouched beside the first yellow crocus, not yet unfolded, and touched its furled petals.

The festival of the joy-god Dionysos was upon them. Five days of theater, dancing, poetry, and all manner of drinking contests, knuckle-bones, trials of strength, and revelry. A messenger from the priestesses would come, as they had for two years past, asking her to lead the chorus with new works, and she must be ready. She wandered alone in sacred groves. When she had drunk in the world, the world would spill out again—the pale ash, the round silver leaves of the beech, the aromatic scent from lentisk and samphire.

She wished it were still possible to mingle with the gods as in the days before the quarrel between Zeus and Prometheus. She would seek out the Muses, those nine daughters of Zeus and Memory whose hearts were set on music and poetry. If she could speak to only one, it would be Erato, who sang on a golden lyre of sweet lyric love. It seemed to

Sappho that lyric poems, more than any others, said your inmost thoughts.

Toward day's end she plunged into the river like a naiad. Then, drying her body with the soft cambric of her robe, she hurried home. There was a man lingering by the whitewashed stones outside the city gate. She walked faster to her house and locked herself in her room. Once inside, she forgot the man.

She communed a few moments with herself and then made earnest supplication:

> *Hither now,*
> *tender Graces*
> *and lovely-haired Muses*

They descended, and Erato pressed these lines into her senses.

> *Now the Earth with many flowers*
> *puts on her spring embroidery*

She made it firm in her memory and went to sleep. The man she had seen by the whitewashed stone appeared to her as a kentaur, that half-man creature. She smiled her unexpected smile as she slept. So simple-hearted were her verses, so dangerous her smile. Kentaur or man, she recognized him even in her dream as a servant of Pittakos.

The next morning she did not leave her chamber. In preparation for the ode she would write to Dionysos, she thought of the world as it had been before he or any god inhabited it. She closed her eyes and, after a while, looked into an unmeasurable abyss. Darkness with Chaos brooding her bore two children: black-winged Night and Erebus the unfathomable, in whose bosom was laid a windblown egg. From this the Seasons rolled, and the Seasons created Love, who, holding within her Dionysos and Aphrodite, made Light and banished wild confusion.

With greater effort, looking closer, Sappho saw the disk of Earth divide into equal parts. Beyond where it flowed was cloud-wrapped mystery.

Some things were known. There were always seven wise men in the world and they told that at the back of the North Wind was a blissful land where Hyperboreans lived. To the South, Ethiopians held joyful banquets in their halls. The blessed dead lived by Ocean's sand. But the fearful Kimmerians lived no one knew where, and day was never there—so it had been told and sung to her. Therefore, not priests but poets were closer to the beginning of the world and the meaning that ever emerged.

It was Dionysos himself who showed her these things. Within her small frame a great cauldron spilled sentences, seemingly calm, but when you looked hard, the words seared; not raging, but rage invoking. Her lips formed what the young god dictated:

> While the full moon rose, young girls
> took their place around the altar.
> In old days Cretan girls danced
> supplely around an altar of love,
> crushing the soft flowering grass

Sappho swayed with abandon, repeating the verse. This year, too, she would lead the choral dance of Arkadia.

The message Sappho had been expecting came to her from the priestesses of the caves. It was brought by a young novice, a graceful girl of Sappho's age, with delicate waist and shapely ankles. Sappho delighted in looking at her and offered her a cup of Pramnian wine and grated goat's cheese into it herself with a bronze grater, while a slave threw in barley meal. The girl, lovely, virginal, and shy, kept her eyes down as she drank, only gradually daring to look at Sappho.

She is not used to a great house, Sappho concluded, and spoke kindly to the girl, who, for all that she was a novice of the powerful sisterhood, was still a simple country maid. "Come, have another cup of the wine I have prepared for you. Then you will tell me your message."

The wine brought a flush to the girl's face and courage to begin. "I am come . . ."

"Yes?" Sappho smiled.

"I am come . . ."

"Ah, it is the great festival of Dionysos!"

The girl darted a grateful glance at her.

Sappho continued to spare her shyness. "They, the priestesses, wish me to compose a verse."

"Yes, oh yes."

Sappho laughed. "It is difficult to talk with someone who knows me, but whom I do not know. Tell me your name."

"Doris. It is Doris."

"Well then, Doris, the verse is written. Shall I teach it to you, or am I to instruct the chorus?"

"The initiates, the holy priestesses of Dionysos Zagreus, son of Zeus, wish you to instruct and lead the chorus as you did last year."

"And," Sappho prompted, watching her, "these priestesses of Dionysos, what do they say of Sappho?"

"Those who listen to the joy-god whose heart All-Father Zeus swallowed to produce him anew, that he might destroy the Titans by lightning and from their ashes create man . . ." This litany, recited in a small, clear voice, left Doris short of breath. She began again, hands folded in her lap. "They say there is witchery in your words. That to produce them you enter into divine madness. They say you are our sister."

"Ah," Sappho breathed. She shared her mother's fear of this society of women who alone knew how to appease the powers below, the Khthonians, Lords of Death. "Actually, you see, it is all very simple with me. That is, crickets sing at noon and I sing back. Or I see a garden of cyclamen bordered with red-flowering oleander, and I stand outside myself and in joy grow with them. Do you see?"

The novice nodded her head. "It is ever so. Do you think she at Delphi knows the words that pass her lips? The sisterhood say your utterances are so passionate they are made in flames."

Sappho looked at the serene young face, unshakable in its knowing, and wondered if indeed her words struck so close.

She heard a zither, the strains floating up from the street.

Standing by my bed
In gold sandals
Dawn that very
moment woke me

She stretched her arms above her head and her heavy, well-molded lips curved with inward thought. Dionysos the spring-god signaled the time of year for his festival, when the long days begin, when animals are in foal, the earth newly bedecked, and the vine puts out young shoots.

I long and I yearn

The words were spoken aloud in furious joy, a hymn to herself. This was the first day of the celebration. Theater was part of it, and she, a participant, was temporarily a holy person, a servant of Dionysos. She savored the importance of it: Dionysos, master of magic and illusion. Last year he caused a vine to grow from the penis of the statue of a senator in the public square. It was a pompous statue, and as the vine lengthened the laughter grew.

Sappho's coan robe, made for the occasion, was purple, that most costly of colors, with circles of saffron. Even at this early hour slaves were searching for roses of the same hue for her hair. She remembered to give thanks to the poet Arion, who first costumed the chorus.

She sprang from her bed and rang for it to be removed, impatient to see the traditional masks: the supercilious young man, the scheming slave, the old man. She longed to melt into the crowds that followed the phallic symbol raised in honor of procreation and birth, all the while chanting the ancient chants. How wonderful this first day was!

Sappho set out for the baths with three of her women. In the street strolling bands of musicians recounted the exploits of the joy-god. Tales of his beauty filled all ears. Over pipes and flutes the human voice rang out—how he had turned the pirates who captured him into dolphins. Sappho loved the story—she loved all stories. She passed beneath Aeolian columns, and the owlish eyes of their decorated capitals watched as her maids took her robe and she slid into the Paros marble of the bath. Other girls were bathing, for it was their time at the pool. They chatted of plum cakes and caraway confections, of perfumes and the fine things their mothers took from their women's chests for the occasion—pale gold ornaments from Sardis, silks of Kos, scented Athenian oils, and from Thrace silver statues of griffins, herons, creatures combining man and lion, and many representations of the dolphin.

Listening, Sappho found their voices sweet and their merriment beguiling, but the observer in her did not allow her to be totally part of this or any gathering. She preferred to luxuriate in the clear warm water, handle her firm breasts, stretch her legs, wriggle her toes. She passed her hands over her belly, flat as a boy's, admiring the aristocrat's ankles. Though small, I am well made, she thought with satisfaction. She signed to her women to dry her body, which they rubbed to rosiness and covered with a single garment.

On the way to the villa their path was blocked by cavorting, caroling youths, holding bunches of grapes. She was not permitted to pass until she had plucked and nibbled some from their mouths.

At home her slaves waited to remove her robe and prepare her for the ceremony. She was handed a mirror of polished copper. She giggled with the girls at the handle in the shape of the male organ. One of the slaves went on her knees to shave the swelling mound between her legs and another her armpits, for when she led the dances, the diaphanous coan must show her statuelike through its draperies. From a milk-white glass container, spikenard of Tarsos was taken to lave on her breasts. Egyptian metopion was applied to her legs, and the palms of her hands received the scent of roses of Amathos. Her lashes were touched with gum ammoniac mixed with mastic to stiffen them, while her underarms were made sweet with marjoram, her loosened hair brushed with incense, and a comb of ivory from the Indies set in it with eight jeweled pins.

Next from her woman's chest came small alabaster boxes. The first held a white powder obtained by treating lead with vinegar. This preparation lightened Sappho's complexion. From another box came red ocher, which was brushed softly on her cheeks. The tinting continued: her lips and the aureoles of her breasts were rouged, and the outline of her eyes drawn in black fard.

Sappho looked intently at this created face. When she smiled, her women relaxed. "I will have the horns of my yearling heifer gilded. Run to the flower merchants," she told one of the servants. "I want her garlanded and beautiful. Each day, the flowers must be fresh until she is sacrificed."

The young woman nodded and disappeared. The decking-out continued. Massive bracelets of silver chiseled in bas relief with tiny seed pearls girded her arms; rings worked with gold thread were placed on fingers and toes. She slipped into sandals with tinkling bells, while ribbons of many colors were tied above her calf. It was time now for the coan chiton, gossamer, revealing. Two silver anklets emphasized the extreme delicacy of her limbs. Sappho waved away the amber necklace and instead bowed her head to receive a double garland of iris.

The servants stepped back and regarded their mistress with exclamations of rapture. Viewing herself from all angles, Sappho put away the mirror. "I will show myself to my noble mother." And she went on twinkling feet past the newly painted frescoes on the walls. Trimmed with gold leaf, they depicted the dolphin cresting sea waves. It was lovely.

Kleis was still in the midst of preparation. For a woman past child-bearing years, there was more foundation work. Before cosmetics could be applied, a compound of egg whites was used to eradicate wrinkles and scytharium wood to blonden her hair.

"My Sappho," she exclaimed at seeing her, "you are beautiful today. It suits you to have left off the amber chain and chosen simple flowers."

"I want you to be proud of me."

"You shine with an inward glow. Many young men will look at you today. Remember, my daughter, the erotic arts are seven: the gaze with eyes cast downward and glancing sideways are the first two. Try not to look straight into the faces of those you meet, like a boy. All the fard in the world will not help you then."

"I will remember."

"If any become amorous, call to mind the secret of the bite: just graze the skin of him you wish to encourage."

"So far," Sappho replied, "I have never had to use this technique."

"It is because of your tongue. It is too much to the point. But today you may need to remember the various body clasps . . ."

"Mother, I am in no hurry to find a husband."

"The movement of the body," Kleis continued, ignoring her daughter's comment, "the caresses that bring a man to fullness . . ."

Sappho sighed; she had no intention of bringing any man to fullness.

"Glottism," her mother went on, "if it occurs either by mouth or hand, you must tell me of it immediately. That man is a suitor."

"You've named only six," said the meticulous Sappho.

"You've been counting!" her mother exclaimed. "Any girl who can keep track of numbers while love is being discussed, I despair of. The seventh is the kiss. But what's the use? It will never get that far."

"I have observed," said Sappho, "that when a woman catches herself a husband, that is the end of her."

"Sappho, Sappho, what are you saying? Then children come—it is the beginning."

"My children are winged words and the rustlings of thought."

"You might as well go wash your face," Kleis said bitterly, "if those are to be my grandchildren."

Sappho put an arm around her mother. "Today is the first day of Dionysos, a happy day. Do not be cross with me."

Resignedly Kleis patted her only daughter. "I worry what is to become of you when I am gone. We have lived until now from the rich patrimony of your father's house. But it is almost spent. Your brothers will follow the honorable family business of tending vineyards and trading the famed wine of Lesbos. But you are a woman. I would not want to see you sit in the corner of a brother's house."

Sappho laughed. "Such a picture you have of me! That forlorn creature of your fears is not your Sappho. I have received true property from the golden Muses and when I die I shall not be forgot."

The mother could always be persuaded by the daughter. She was convinced by those luminous eyes that saw where she could not. Sappho kissed her hands and fairly danced through the house to drink in the bustle. The threshold of stone was freshly washed; the doors, double and high, gleamed with scrubbing. Slaves were polishing the carved tables with their feet of cyamus. Sappho began to sing: "Gold knuckle bowls, gold knuckle bowls . . . ," for in them they would dip their hands between courses of flesh and dishes of fruits, both preserved and fresh. From the kitchen came the aroma of baking cakes of poppy, honey, and barley. They would feast like joyous gods; ambrosia could not be sweeter.

Incense was lit, myrrh from Ethiopia, frankincense from Somaliland. Rose petals had been scattered in the fountain at the center of the garden. Panther skins and cushions were spread everywhere. "Gold knuckle bowls," she sang, "gold knuckle bowls." For the optimum moment to trap Pittakos had just occurred to her.

She went in search of Alkaios to confide her plan. She found him under the colonnades of the stoa, playing dice with Pelops and his friends.

When Sappho approached, Alkaios left the game and, throwing himself to the ground, clasped and kissed her knees. "Beautiful Sappho, like Aphrodite, always different in your guises."

"I see you have started your drinking early."

"Wrong. I haven't started . . . never stopped."

"Listen with as sober a mind as you can. It is on the fifth day we will bring down the Tyrant and his cur Pittakos."

"The fifth day?" Alkaios was suddenly sober. The fifth day of the festival was terrible, and during the other four was not even thought about.

"Yes, when the Earth is full of evil, and the air crowded with calamity and death, and, maddened by their thymos and aphrodisiac, women girded with swinging phalluses rush through the sacred grove deflowering young maids."

Alkaios stared at her. "Then?"

"Who will be guarding the body then? We will dig it up, fling it in the center of the agora, and set up a great cry. Everyone will rush to see."

Alkaios looked at her intently. Sappho's white-pigmented face was expressionless. It did not even belong to her but was an invention of her slaves. The sensuous line of her body glimpsed beneath the sheer garment, the reddened teats of her breasts that seemed to break through the material, were not lost on Alkaios. "Sappho," he said on impulse. "I need not be half charlatan, drunkard, spendthrift of my time. If you would have me, I would toss away the boys and the drink—"

"And the jokes and laughter too. No, thank you, I will have no reformed character on my hands."

"The tongue of Sappho says one thing, but her eyes beam a different message."

"Believe the tongue, and be my dear friend."

He laughed unhappily. "All that is left, then, is to agree to the fifth day."

She kissed him on the cheek as the boys summoned him with pretty chords on the lyre.

Sun had made his journey eastward when Sappho hurried to the sacred grove, where, before the temple, an altar to Dionysos had been erected. She strapped on her cothurnis, the high, cork-platformed boots, Lydian made, which all participants wore. She loved being raised for this brief interval above the crowd.

The games were in progress, a mock war in which attack, defeat, and death were mimed and sung. Sappho took her place leading the mystic chants of the women—a chorus of youths answered. Garlanded sheep and oxen were herded in and sacrificed before each episode. A group of youths dressed in fawnskin, horns, and tails, created a diversion, throwing bunches of grapes and singing as they made the stamping motion used in pressing out wine. Alkaios tumbled into their midst, scattering them, for he was a sight none had seen except on painted vases. He had done himself as a silenos, a mythic creature both horse and man who lusted for the flesh of women. His feet ended in cleverly wrought hooves and he had a splendid bushy tail and movable ears, which were attached under his costume to his hands. When he neighed, the ears stood straight up. He pranced about, reciting with mock-serious intonation that only two things made human love higher than the coupling of animals. He demonstrated by seizing a pretty girl from the audience whom he made part of his act, kissing her and taking other liberties. She struggled under these public attentions, to the delight of the throng. The bolder Alkaios became, the more they roared.

"You would push and shove to get in the first row, my love," he said to the abashed girl, then continued his lecture. "The kiss and the caress, these are human inventions. Animals do not know of them. Perhaps some of you also need instruction?" He peered quizzically at the crowd, which exploded with laughter mixed with jeers. As his caresses grew more intimate, the mood changed to one of sensuality.

"A bride for Dionysos!" The chant was taken up by a thousand voices. The silenos moved to the final position above the now screaming girl, as Sappho entered the stage with her maidens, making a living curtain. Their appearance was calming, the flow of iambic meter soothing. Sappho moved like a statue. With her verse the first day ended and the feasting began.

Day two: everyone drank Cretan wine, watching buffoons and jugglers, judging contests of lute, lyre, and zither. A straggling group of drunkards holding one another up were shooed from the arena. The chief priestess of Dionysos led her women, her feet nimble even on half-stilts. "The young king," she sang, "bearer of Spring." The cantata continued with a recitative of the chorus: "Thebes, pearl among cities where this son of Zeus was born. Most beautiful was the princess Semele. Ravished of the All-Powerful, she bore a son divine."

"A son divine." The line was repeated to kettledrum and flute. The priestess's eyes flared like torches, the expanded pupils shut out reason. She approached the freshly painted joy-god. How beautiful he was in all his limbs. Raised upon her clogs she pressed her mouth against the cold marble of his perfect flesh, offering him her breasts, cupped in her hands. And when he would not have them, she pressed her throbbing body against his, calling out a poem in praise of his prowess at love. She reached the length of him and, taking the jewels from her own neck, placed them around his. Nor would she climb down from him. The god possessed her. The crowd did not move, they did not breathe. Sappho, leading a section, no longer sang.

She, too, watched.

The votary mounted the sculptured penis and rhythmically roused herself against it. The audience clapped in time to her wilder and wilder gyrations—an orgiastic virgin, receiving climax after climax as the gift of this great god. She fell back sated and fainting into the arms of her women, who covered her still-shuddering body with kisses, taking with supple and darting fingers the hot moisture that lay in the three most intimate folds of her body. When she was stretched full-length upon the grass, Sappho came to her and raised her head so that she might sip rose-colored wine from a chrysolite goblet. The priestess opened her eyes, slowly coming back to her own form outstretched there before the multitude. When she heard how the god had honored her, a virgin, she was content.

The third day of Dionysos there were games of chance, trials of strength, more feasting and drinking contests. Naked boys hopped about, running races with one leg in a wineskin. Revelers costumed as nymphs and satyrs held hands, winding through the crowd, a confetti of petals sprinkled on them from horse-whipped chariots.

Sappho watched her brothers at dice. Khar's throw; it came up Kios. She clapped her hands and laughed. It was the worst throw in the game. Eurygyos did better. But it was young Larichos, calling on Zeus, father of gods and men, who won when the knuckle bones came up Aphrodite. Her brothers invited her to join in the play, but she shook her head. She liked to gamble, but not with money.

That night, initiate youths danced to tunes in a trance. Suddenly snakes turned on their arms, flowed upon their necks and shoulders. A boy was bitten. Convulsing in every limb, he writhed on the ground before Dionysos, who smiled his serene smile as he looked upon mortal perishing. When the youth was dead, everyone dropped a flower upon his body until he was covered by a hill of multifarious colors.

The feasting went into the fourth day. Prisoners were released with a great clash of cymbals, bedecked animals were constantly slaughtered to the gods, and libations were made. That day, too, continued into night, and for the fourth time torches were thrust into the arms of statues and slaves.

With the final dawn, which was the fifth day, a subtle shift in the atmosphere hinted at heightened tension. Everyone was drinking satyrion, an aphrodisiac saved until this last day to madden the women. Sappho drank with care. She was not thinking of the performance still to give, when neither her feet nor her tongue must falter. No, she was thinking past it to the digging up of the body of Melanchros.

She leaned back upon cushions, surrounded by her brothers and several youths of noble family. Serving men poured water over their hands, and from mixing bowls of wine and water their cups were filled. Sappho's goblet was of rare craftsmanship, with a dove perched upon it for a handle. Each in turn cast wine upon the mighty blaze that roared before them, roasting the flesh of boars on a five-pronged spit, bellies slit and stuffed with young kid and capon, garnished with savories of wild onion and spices. Polished tables were brought, and a carver placed platters of flesh on gold-worked plates, while slaves passed among them pouring Kios from leather bottles. Female slaves serenaded them as they dressed their hair with fresh flowers. At a signal everyone had to show how far they had emptied their cups.

A shadow fell across Sappho. She glanced up. It was Pittakos. A flower had dropped from her hair. He stooped to pick it up and, smiling, held it out to her. A flush spread beneath her tinted face.

"Sappho," he said, "of ravishing words." This overture from Pittakos caused a stir in the great hall.

She reached for the flower but knocked it from his hand. Could it have been an accident? But Sappho was never clumsy.

Pittakos bowed stiffly and moved on; the laughter at her table resumed, only now there was a caustic edge in it. She sipped again at the satyrion. She no longer cared; somehow she would get through the Arkadian dances and accomplish what the gods willed. The men were singing skolia, waving their cups. To each table was brought a woman, naked from the waist up, whose breasts had been dipped in wine. The guests took turns suckling her, and between times the paps were redipped. Sappho climbed into the lap of the woman and suckled as her brothers and the young men had. The breasts were deep and soft; she nuzzled and bit gently.

The group at her table left together for the sacred grove, arriving in time to hear the *Overcoming by Dionysos of the Minos of Crete* recited. No sooner had they seated themselves than Alkaios sprang up with a poem:

> *I bid them summon the beautiful Menon,*
> *if I may have him for an additional joy at my*
> *drinking party*

It was well known that Menon dispensed his beauty for a price to anyone and that Alkaios, who had taken him up, was mad with jealousy. The applause was mixed with good-natured laughter.

A stout man guffawing in the front row had a fig thrown at him. It hit its target, entering his mouth and sticking in his throat. He choked. Friends pounded him on the back. His face became purple, his eyes popped forward, and he fell over. They could not revive him.

"Flute and bells, flute and bells." Sappho listened to the familiar meter and stepped in intricate, sinuous patterns. The chorus followed her fleet feet and when her voice was raised, theirs were silent. She sang the song she had composed in her chamber:

> *While the full moon rose, young girls*
> *took their place around the altar.*
> *In old days Cretan girls danced*

supplely around an altar of love,
crushing the soft flowering grass

The priestesses surged forward, god-intoxicated, to fall upon the knoll. Feeling the entry of the god, divine madness overcame them. They mimed the positions of love, hips raised, thrusting forward.

Faster. Faster.

A handheld drum beat the rhythm, urging them on until they sweated at the edges of their hair. Sweat laved their armpits, while between their thighs another moisture washed, mingled with perfumes. Their tormented cries turned the mood to one of ill omen. A god who loves with human passion is subject to the terror of the human soul and body. The women on the ground gasped and collapsed, seemingly lifeless. Hysteria seized the spectators. With aphrodisiac alive in their veins, they broke like a wave upon the prone women.

The priestesses feigned exhaustion to lure their victims. On their upper legs were phalluses, which they now brandished. Others used pinecones, leaping up and charging like Erinyes after joy and blood. Some employed the thyrsos, a long ornamented rod. They fell upon the girls and sodomized the boy children.

Men watched the rape and themselves grew rods. But they were immobile as the priestesses rushed past, each swinging her phallus, bringing down and penetrating any they found. Titans had torn Dionysos's still-living flesh. So they tore flesh. The screaming and the suffering and the blood were his—the lust belonged to the Titans. The priestesses gave chase through the forest and the hunt continued in thickets and behind walls.

Sappho shuddered, her own body tingling with maddening desire and sick revulsion. She was protected by her high station and the holiness of a participant. However, while the atrocities lasted, she must act. Cautiously she left her place, backing away from the smiling, brilliantly waxed god. Alkaios and Khar waited for her. Together they fled until the cries were faint.

They did not pause until they were outside the gates of Mitylene. Breathless, they leaned against the whitewashed stones that marked their city.

"Here it is," Khar said. "This is the place marked."

Sappho nodded agreement. It was the place.

A shovel had been secreted nearby, and the men began to dig, taking turns.

Sappho paced nervously. Why was it taking so long?

"Ah!" Alkaios shouted.

"Shhh." Sappho turned away to study the night.

"Come look."

She went to the edge of the grave. Five feet down, a form wrapped in strips of cloth with clods of dirt adhering. "It is Melanchros," she said. "Bring him up."

Khar jumped into the hole and, as though this were a signal, night became day, bright with the light from a dozen torches. Not one of the three moved. It was a tableau. The circle of soldiers narrowed about them—Pittakos's private guard.

The captain stepped forward. "What have we here?" he asked almost jovially.

The white mask of Sappho's face turned on him. "The murdered body of Melanchros."

The captain and his soldiers laughed. "Melanchros is in exile. Everyone knows that."

"Melanchros is in this grave, butchered by order of Pittakos."

There was no laughter now. "These are serious charges."

"Bring up the body. You will see."

"Step back then." Going graveside, the captain yelled to Khar. "Out of there. Give him a hand up," he instructed. Khar landed beside his sister.

Sappho turned to the soldiers. "You are witnesses."

Alkaios whispered. "It is unwise to speak so to those in the pay of the Tyrant."

"Why?" Sappho demanded. "Are they not citizens?"

The shrouded object was raised. There was something odd about its shape, even obscured by the winding sheet—it was too short. Had the body been dismembered? Was this but part of the torso? Was the head at some other site to make identification impossible?

The sheet was unrolled and the carcass tumbled out. Sappho peered to see. She gasped. It was the remains of a large dog.

She heard Alkaios groan, saw him tear his tunic. They were betrayed. Atreus had bargained for his life with theirs.

Sappho felt Alkaios's anguish, but there was no comfort for him.

Khar's sandaled foot kicked the dead cur. Sappho drew back from the stench.

"Follow me," the captain said. "You are prisoners."

"For what crime?" Sappho demanded.

"Plotting treason."

"We were teasing about Melanchros," Sappho said. "Everyone knows he is in Rhodes. This is my good dog. How does it injure Mysilos or Pittakos if I bury my faithful dog?"

Khar grinned. But the soldiers closed ranks and marched them quickly through the city. Every doorpost was smeared with pitch to keep off wandering shades and ghosts from upper air. The frenzy of the death of Dionysos had passed, leaving the populace subdued, lethargic, worn out from the excesses of days of celebration. In the quiet of their houses, each family did honor to their dead. An intimate feast was decorously eaten as tribute to the joy-god, the tragic god, the only god to experience death. Wine jars, seed jars, and funeral jars, which had been opened to allow the spirits final hours of freedom, were once more bottled. In the morning the houses would be vigorously brushed with buckthorn to chase away any lingering shade. All would be born again in new crops, new stock, and new infants. The Earth replenishes itself and man has his part to play, in life and in death.

Past these shuttered houses the prisoners were marched. All Mitylene would hear of it and enjoy the joke: betrayed by the putrefaction of a dog. Claiming they were digging up the murdered body of Melanchros! What shame! For Sappho, the ridicule was worse than any punishment.

They entered the town hall, where Mysilos and Pittakos waited. These judges of her life were seated on high-backed chairs, their faces passive and unreadable.

The accused were led forward. It was Pittakos who spoke. Naturally—it was he who baited the trap. "I am sorry indeed to see you three before me again. Apparently a warning was not enough, for you are here on the same charges—calumny and plotting against the city. In particular, you persist in the belief that Melanchros was murdered, and tonight made an attempt to dig up the body. Tell me what you found."

There was silence in the hall. For once Sappho had no words either sung or spoken.

Pittakos continued, "The gracious Tyrant of Lesbos cannot permit this seething atmosphere of suspicion, slander, and false accusation. You chose to disregard my counsel. You, Kharaxos, and you, Alkaios, and you, Sappho, have not desisted. You still plot. The body of the cur will be dragged to the main square and the story told. I am sorry. I am sorry, too, that sentence this time must be pronounced against you." He nodded to a henchman, who read from a scroll that obviously had been memorized, as his eyes remained on the same spot. After a few words the meaning was clear: banishment.

"Excellent Lords," Alkaios cried, "consider and grant—"

Sappho interposed her will against his. "Ask nothing."

Sappho smiled suddenly at her two judges, and they shifted their eyes uneasily from hers.

The decree of banishment set her free.

She could almost have laughed in Pittakos's face. The pleasure he took in his small triumph, and the certain knowledge that Atreus had been tortured for his private seal and then killed, changed her life.

Had Pittakos buried the dead dog himself, or only thought of it? It was the kind of conniving his plodding mind would conceive.

Wonderful words formed new verse as she stood before him.

I begin with words of air
yet are they good to hear

The nine Muses had adopted her. And no man would again occupy her mind or keep her from song. In exile she would sing.

They were not being sent to the elder Kritias of Athens, or to Gamon in Syracuse. Or even into Egypt. Slowly the ramifications of what she must endure were borne in on her: she and her comrades were to sit out an indefinite sentence in high Pyrrha. The exile was more a mockery than true banishment. Only 140 stadia from Mitylene, Pyrrha by reputation was nothing more than a great crag on the Gulf of Kaloni, manned by a few poor huts and rude peasant folk. No one visited there. For what? A scrub pine or two, perhaps a stunted olive or lightning-struck oak. This for her, who loved the bright jonquils, the violets hidden under their leaves, the crimson wild rose, the streams and sacred groves. Things of beauty fed her poems. But she and her little band of fools were to rusticate with only Prometheus perhaps to visit them. Who knew, it might be his rock!

Their exile was a joke, as the dog was a joke. Men would laugh over it in the taverns as they raised mugs of mulled wine. But it must be borne.

Sappho's secret shame was that she had ever known feelings for and wasted thought on Pittakos. Love can make a poet out of a boor, she thought distractedly, or perhaps it is the other way around—love can imagine a poet even in a boor.

Pittakos ordered their immediate departure under guard from their homes. They were to take with them only those items that could be carried.

The daughter of Skamandronymos was allotted a single serving woman. "He is shaming himself, not me," she told her mother. "A single serving woman or none, what does it matter?"

"I can understand that prankster, that tippler, that idler Alkaios," their mother said, "but you, Kharaxos, a responsible and renowned young man of highest station, and you, Sappho, a girl only, the daughter of a proud and honored father. It is unthinkable. In any times but these it could not have happened."

"Nevertheless it has happened," Sappho said.

Kleis stopped crying long enough to ask, "And how long is this indignity to last?"

"The sentence is indeterminate." It was difficult for Sappho to be patient with the lamentations. There were no tears on her face, for it occurred to her that, though freemen might indeed laugh in the taverns and take sly pleasure in their disgrace, in the great houses of Mitylene there was bound to be anger. And anger could possibly accomplish their purpose.

Kleis and Tyro tore their hair and asked piteously which of the gods they had offended that the two eldest children of the house were publicly humiliated.

But there was no time for introspection or invective, and hardly any for good-byes. The guard at her side reminded her that Pittakos's schedule did not allow for delays.

"I will take Niobe with me," Sappho decided. Turning to her favorite slave, a girl her own age, she asked for a warm cloak, "and whatever is necessary from my woman's chest. Also my flute."

"Baskets of bread, smoked flesh, and fruits," Tyro ordered the servants. "O my Sappho, you have been a daughter in this childless house."

"Khar, Khar," Kleis broke in. "Do not ask what will become of the laughter, the songs, the flute playing. And what will the boys, your brothers, think? What are we to tell them?"

"It will not be necessary to tell them anything. They will hear it all," Kharaxos said, and to relieve his mother's mind promised, "do not worry. I will look after Sappho."

A twist of a smile appeared on Sappho's lips.

Kleis clasped brother and sister in her arms. "Look after each other." Tyro embraced them in her turn. Baskets of food and clothing were handed to Niobe.

"She cannot walk such a distance like a packhorse," Sappho said. "We will divide the bundles."

At this unseemliness, the women were again overcome. "It is the times," Kleis moaned. "No man or woman has seen such times as these. Exile! May the gods help us!"

LETO

*W*HEN THE STUDDED BRONZE DOORS OF HER HOME clanged behind them, Sappho's heart clanged with them on a doleful note. All things spoke good-bye: the harbors and piled rocks of the breakwater, the fishing boats and merchant fleets. Tyrian, Sicilian, Kypriot, from Egypt and Corinth, the ships rode at anchor, their painted eyes bobbing over the swells. "Eurynome," she prayed, "daughter of the ever-encircling waters of Ocean, help me keep my courage." For she was leaving everything she knew.

Even the rocks jutting into the sea she knew: the eagle, one wing spread, the other drooping as though hit by a stone from the slingshot of some god when he was young. And there was Hera's profile, severe, proud, cut into the rocks above the jetty. Was she looking for the last time at the arcade of the agora with its raucous, seething, colorful crowd and wares from exotic ports? Her glance lifted to the acropolis, from which Zeus watched over them. Maliciously? With amusement, compassion? She did not know. Perhaps they wanted her to drink a cup of bull's blood and be done with her life. But this she did not intend to do.

A fresh thought occurred to her. Perhaps the guards had orders, once away from Mitylene, to kill them? The possibility that she might be hacked to pieces by soldiers terrified her and she moved closer to Khar.

Mitylene's cascading gardens and terraced vineyards were left behind. The delicate swaying iris, the half-hidden crocus, the oleander dripping its clusters over the walls—she felt her parting from each. How many times she had joined her women at the washing stones, as they spread garments on mulberry bushes and rocks for Sun to dry. She fixed her eyes now on the thick tussock grass, on roots of scraggly olive trees. The orchards were already distant.

The piping of a solitary shepherd carried through the clear air— Iton, mother of sheep, give us help—for they were now walking in strange groves and she had never made offering to the nymphs that haunted them. When the sounds of the shepherd's pipe died away, civilization ceased.

Shadows were already long by the time the soldiers stopped for their evening meal. Sappho observed them with hidden glances. If they meant evil toward them, it might happen now. But they seemed intent on unwrapping cheese and swilling from goatskins.

The three prisoners sat a little apart and were served by Niobe. Khar ate with good appetite and whispered plans for escape. Sappho shook her head.

"How can we escape? Lesbos is an island."

"Eat, Sappho," Alkaios urged, for she had stretched out on her back to watch the clouds swim the sky.

"Some things will be with us in our exile," she said. "All-Mother Earth will be under our feet. Sky and Sea, who were her first offspring and with whom she mated, will follow us, and the clouds I watch now will be before us over Pyrrha."

"What is your meaning, Sappho?" Khar asked.

"We will be with strangers. But some things that we have known we will continue to know."

"Me, now," Alkaios said, "I like to travel. But I prefer to choose my destination." He smiled at his comrades with cheering bravado, and put into song what he had just said. Sappho answered his music with her own:

Not though my heart within me . . .

The guards stopped masticating to listen.

The understanding gods evoke tears . . .

Although she sang them low, the words were painful as a sharp wind stinging the face. The soldiers, to cover their emotion, were unnecessarily rough in getting them to their feet. "We can travel a long way before night," one of them said.

Already weary, Sappho had thought this was their camp. The desolate overhanging crags depressed her further, for there was no color or any tint that was soft. What was left to sing about? Could one carry the Muses, and the children they had fathered by the Moon, the lovely Graces, into such inhospitable surroundings? It was a drear land, steep and gray. They passed a pillar set over the tomb of someone who had gone this way before them and died of it.

As they turned a bend, a flock of daws startled and flew upward. It was a portent, if only she had the wit to unravel it. She pondered— the birds were small, she was small. They ascended; she, too, toiled up, up, up. What did it mean?

She turned her ankle but went on without saying anything. Sun had long ago slid behind the hills; all she could see was cast in a filtered blue light, eerie and unreal. She was thinking now, not of the Muses and their offspring, but of lions and wild boars. Instinctively the captives pressed closer to the armed men.

"Ida, mother of wild beasts, many a lay I have sung you. Do not let your creatures eat alive my songs. Think of the garlands I have left at your altar, fragrant and of many colors . . ."

Sappho stumbled. Alkaios took her hand. "It is growing too dark to see," he called to the soldiers. They did not answer, but a torch was lit, and by the way they swung it around, it would seem they were looking for a place to stop.

Camp was made by a large slab of rock, against which they could lie with their backs protected. Moss and branches and pinecones heaped together started a small fire. It was the soldiers who performed this menial task, for their captives were nobles. Niobe laid her robes before the blaze. As she lay down to sleep, Sappho found Alkaios on one side of her and her brother on the other. "I am the one. I am responsible for this," she whispered.

Each assured her it was he alone. She tried to wrap her small hands around their larger ones. It could not be done, so she squeezed them both. "Brother," she said. "Friend." And to cheer them repeated a verse she had told many times. It began:

Moon hung in a hollow night . . .

The Pleiades rose, and bold Orion. She watched the Bear turning in one place because an angry goddess decreed he could never rest.

If Pittakos had ordered death, it would come this night. The other two either had no such thoughts or left it to the gods, for they slept. Sappho remained wide-eyed, remembering Night's offspring were Sleep and Death. She recalled a verse sung at a happier time:

The night closed their eyes
and poured down black sleep
upon their lids

She wished for it, even if she never woke. "If it comes, Father Zeus, let the stroke be merciful."

The Pleiades set; the Bear kept watch upon Orion.

Sappho opened her eyes. The fire had gone out. Night moved in ebb flows. She heard it move, saw places more shadowy than others that shifted with wind, with rustling leaves, with the spirits of this unknown place. At least she knew, looking at the sleeping forms of the soldiers, that there were no secret orders. They were to live.

Rosy-fingered Dawn scattered the forces of Night. Starlings twittered above her head. Yesterday each step that took her from Mitylene was agony. Today it was a journey. Her early journey as a child from Eresos she scarcely remembered. And this was but the second time in her life she had ventured into unknown regions. Yet her father had been a trader and a rover. Khar too, spoke of buying a ship to sail and, in his turn, finding markets for Lesbian wine. But, as a female, she seemed destined to stay at home. As poet and rebel, however, she was considered dangerous enough to banish. Why? Because she mocked Pittakos? Or was it because he found her ideas uncomfortable? She laughed silently.

Then as a woman traveling among men, she turned to the shelter of the bush she had used last night to let out the accumulation of her body. She made ablution in the cold stream, catching the spray in her fingers before it drained away. Splashing her face, she waded with numb ankles to a rock where she could sit and watch the water braid itself. The several sounds set up a murmuring as, passing over stone with a deeper gurgle, the stream formed a pool. Sappho picked a reed and blew through it, making a soft tune. Later she would put words to it. She thanked the Muses for making the journey with her, for not deserting her. Her lyre had been too heavy for the trip, but she would send for it. Meantime her flute was tucked in with the food Niobe carried. She brought the gift of music and poetry to high Pyrrha. If she did not at first find beauty there, she would seek it out. For nature fed art. And if beauty were totally lacking, she would look into her own young heart.

In her were banked fires that had never flared. She feared the time that would happen. But so contrary was her nature that she knew she would welcome the conflagration even if she perished in it. She desired greatly—but what? That the gods love her? But they loved only beauty, and she was ugly. Yet not always. She knew this, too. And not to some.

Tradition said her people, the Danaans, came over the northern mountains. There were great sanctuaries along the route, in Dodona, Olympus, and Olympia. The Danaans had been an untamed lot, blond and tall, with a history of conquest. They swept down in their strength upon the Aeolean coastal valleys and onto the island, overrunning the more civilized Aegeans, whose main culture was in Crete. In the agora of Mitylene she had seen painted pottery from that island. And the maidens they depicted might have been herself: black hair that did not need to be plaited at night for curls, and high-bridged noses giving them the same look of hauteur which was a part of her visage. And she guessed that in those early days a blond Danaan daughter had bedded with an Aegean in her father's fields, and when she found herself growing heavy, quickly married, having no peace until the birth, for fear the child would betray her by its swarthy countenance. But she had not exposed the infant, for it was as herself and her people, blond and beautiful. There was, however, a seed within that none knew of, until her own birth generations after. For no one resembled her, only maidens on a vase.

She was roused from reverie by a clear, sweet whistling. Alkaios threw himself down on the bank of the stream. "A night's sleep and the world looks different! At least in this ignominious exile, I have the honor to be the companion of lovely Sappho."

"You will miss your pretty boys," she teased.

He grinned impudently at her. "There are pretty boys everywhere."

"You are incorrigible," she laughed.

He laughed back. "Only because you will not take me in hand."

"It is too large a job for me."

"What were you piping so prettily into your reed?"

"I was thinking of our people of ancient times, and wondering who they were."

"What a strange, unknowable girl you are. You should be thinking of breakfast, as I am. The brutes of soldiers are up, and cakes of barley cooking."

He led her back and they poured to the gods, and again ate in separate groups, Niobe moving between them.

The party climbed briskly all morning. Sky looked benignly on them. Sky possessed secret knowledge and could give oracles even to Zeus. Sky would know Pyrrha, for his vastness spread over all alike. The pines they passed here were knobby and stunted, the soil sparse and light. Their midday meal of figs, cheese, and bread was eaten by an olive orchard, the first sign that they approached a village. The soldiers and Alkaios played at odd-even, Alkaios having the sense not to win from them.

The captain ordered Niobe back to pick the wild asparagus they had passed growing in a cluster. Sappho sat and blew softly on her flute. When she looked up, the captain was not there. Her heart beat fast. He had gone after Niobe. Why?

She glanced at the others absorbed in their game, then got to her feet. Keeping to the periphery of their vision, she sauntered until she rounded a boulder, then quickened her steps. In a few minutes she came on them.

The asparagus had fallen onto the rocks. Niobe with small, strangled, hiccupping cries, was attempting to beat the man off. She lay naked under her attacker, who had wound her chiton around her head and face so she would not be heard. His member was swollen to enormous size and he was attempting to thrust it into the crimson slash that heaved under him.

"Hold!" Sappho's voice was terrible. It was also unexpected.

The man froze, his bared buttocks collapsing. The girl rolled from beneath him, pulling at her chiton. Her eyes fastened on Sappho. She hiccupped in earnest now.

"What are you doing with my slave? Mine, I say. Have you purchased her from me that you take such liberty with my property?"

Pulling his clothes straight, the man tried to regain a semblance of dignity. "It was nothing, an innocent frolic," he muttered. "Nothing to make a fuss about."

"If another such innocent frolic occurs, your superiors in Mitylene shall hear of it."

The man knew her high connections and said again, "An innocent frolic." Then buckling on the sword that had been cast aside, he recalled his status in captaining this small expedition. "You've wandered far. My orders are to keep you close. However, O daughter of Skamandronymos, each small infraction need not be reported."

"I understand you," Sappho said. Niobe crept to her for protection. "You have nothing more to fear," Sappho assured her. But the maid walked in her mistress's footsteps the rest of the way.

When they returned, the others were finishing their game and ready to start out.

"Where is the asparagus?" Alkaios asked.

Later in the day they came to washing springs. There were women at work who stared at them in amazement. Alkaios gave greeting and would have stood in talk, but a soldier prodded him. As he left, he set up his sprightly whistle and the girls and women gazed after him.

The exiles and their guards encountered a wagon, pulled by broad-browed oxen, on which were strapped great beams, wending downward the way they had just come to the ship-builders in Mitylene. Oh, if she could hide among those timbers!

On the floor of Zeus's palace, they say, stand two amphorae with double handles, one heaped with evil gifts and one with good. At first sight, Pyrrha seemed to have been forged from the urn of evil. Its steep terraced sides reached up to a wall built on a rock promontory austere and forbidding. Sappho's hopes dissolved. Life would be hard here. Even Alkaios's whistling faltered.

The soldiers motioned them to wait outside the gates and went in before them. They were gone a long time, and the day began to wear away. Their story, Sappho supposed, was being told to the Archon, or the council, or whoever ruled these desolate heights. Perhaps they were eagles and not men at all. Boys came out to look at them, mouths open at the sight of strangers. Sappho returned their scrutiny. She was not particularly attracted to children, considering them simply people shorter than even herself.

Presently the gates opened. The first thing Sappho saw was a small girl playing with a top. This was such a common sight in the streets of Mitylene that she was somewhat reassured. The walls and houses were mostly limestone, and the roofs wood rather than tile. There were some villas of imposing size with large walled gardens. They were led past these into the countryside, along a crooked lane that had been cobbled but was now overgrown. They stopped finally before an abode of wattle, extended by the addition of a porch, which was built on a windy, unsheltered spot.

The master came out. "You're late," he said by way of greeting, then spoke with the soldiers at some distance. It looked to Sappho as though they were haggling over money. When the householder was satisfied, he came over to them and nodded to Sappho. "You are Sappho of Lesbos?"

"I am Sappho."

"You, with your woman, are to stay here."

"But my brother . . ." she said in sudden panic. It had not occurred to her they would be separated.

"You and your woman," the householder said firmly. "The price has been paid."

"It's all right," Khar said. "I'll get word to you where I am."

"And I." Alkaios grasped her arm reassuringly before the soldiers marched them off. Sappho stared after them. How childish and ridiculous seemed the plottings that had brought them to this.

She turned to face her jailer, who said crustily, "I am Didymus, son of Thestes."

"What are your instructions regarding me?" Sappho asked.

"That you are not to think of escape. It is impossible except by boat. Our boats would overtake you, and the outcome would not be a pretty one."

"No such thought is in my mind," Sappho assured him.

"Come, then, enter and we will talk further."

The room was poorly lit and it was with difficulty she discerned two women. Didymus followed and then Niobe. "Well then," Didymus said. "This is my wife and daughter. We are simple folk. We do not know or care about the ins and outs of politics in Mitylene. You and your brother and the other young man are out of favor with the Tyrant there. It puts a few drachmas in our pockets, and by next spring I will buy another mule. What we have is yours to share, neither more or less. I can see you are a fine lady and it will seem less to you. But we manage very well. You will be expected to help the women, taking your turn at spinning and washing. If you don't know how to cook, your slave will do that under my wife's direction." It was apparent the speech was a long one for him, and when he was done he went outside.

"Where is he going?" Sappho asked.

"He is the master," the wife said reprovingly. "It is not for us to ask."

The daughter giggled. "He is gone to play knuckle bones, of course."

Sappho looked at her. The light from the dying sun flamed in at the window and she was touched with a glow that transformed her into a golden girl, her light hair falling down her back. Even the coarse robe carelessly belted seemed of shimmering gold.

"What is your name?" Sappho inquired.

"Leto."

"After the mother of revered Apollo," Sappho said. "Pyrrha is not without beauty, and flowers do grow here."

The mother expressed her cantankerous feelings to a pot she scoured vigorously, not daring to reprove the lady herself a second time. Instead she instructed Niobe that she would sleep in the hay piled in a corner, and told her to spread in the niche by the fireplace whatever personal things the lady Sappho had brought.

Sappho realized for the first time there was no other room in the house, that pallets were spread about at night. She was appalled there was to be no privacy. This, for her, would be the most difficult to bear. How could she compose? How could she sing new songs and retain the old, without privacy?

The girl, Leto, brought Sappho a mint-flavored drink. Sipping it calmed her. "Thank you, it's very good."

"Not what you are used to," the girl demurred.

Sappho smiled. "If each day were to bring what one was used to, why bother to open your eyes?"

The girl was too flustered to understand the words, but she recognized the kind tone in which they were spoken.

Sappho added, "May Father Zeus watch this house," a formula in general use when one wished to retire. Niobe brought her comb and mirror, shook out a chiton and placed a second pair of sandals for morning. Niobe whispered, "It is a very poor house. I do not know how to bring my mistress comfort."

"Bring water, Niobe, and a tub. I suppose they have one, and I cannot go to bed a second night without a proper bath."

There was a commotion, as Sappho's request involved heating water. Sappho paid not the slightest attention. She had stated her wishes. She applied herself to her bronze mirror, sweeping her heavy hair high on her head, while Niobe blew fire into dead coals. She decided that in the morning ribbons of many colors should flow down her back.

When the water was ready, Niobe dragged a wooden tub into their corner of the room and filled it, making many trips between it and the hearth. The washing sponge, fortunately, was among the items that had been gathered in haste. Sappho let her tunic fall and stepped into the tub.

Leto turned to her own corner and unrolled her pallet.

"Gentle Leto, do not sleep," Sappho whispered. "Talk to me." Niobe squeezed the warmed water continuously over her, letting it cascade down her body. Sappho saw that Leto was too shy to speak, so she began in an intimate tone that made the girl a confidante. "It is strange being here, yet I am not distressed. I feel I am a homely Helen or plain Penelope, caught by those spinning women, the Fates. I can almost feel the tautness of Clotho's thread, for Lachesis is laying out the pattern."

"I am glad that you do not feel too bad." Leto spoke softly so as not to rouse her mother. "It must be hard to be exiled."

"It is one way to learn about other people." Here she stretched her arms above her head so that the drops of water on her skin glistened. "For instance I have heard that among the Barbarians nakedness is a sin and they are shamed by it." Laughing, she stepped from the tub and allowed Niobe to rub her skin to a glow.

Leto gained courage to raise herself on her elbow and ask, "Are you the Sappho who sings? Are you that Sappho?"

"Have you heard my songs then? How, I wonder, did they climb to this craggy place?"

"We must seem very poor to you," Leto said.

"Well, I do not think I am in the palace of King Alyattes of Lydia, or among the Pharaohs."

This made Leto laugh.

"Which bed is mine?" Sappho asked as she slid into a sheer gauze sleeping robe.

Leto stared at it, then recollected herself. "The guest spot by the fireside, and the gods grant you rest."

Sappho went to the designated place. "The gods give you sleep, Niobe."

"Mistress," the slave murmured, withdrawing to spill the bathwater and settle herself.

"Have you always had someone to wait upon you?" Leto asked from her covers.

"Not someone. Many."

"How alone you will feel here!" the girl exclaimed.

"No, my brother and my friend are with me . . . and others." She breathed the last words to herself.

In the morning Sappho volunteered to go with Leto to the washing springs, certain she would learn from the gossip of the women where her brother and Alkaios were lodged. Niobe attempted to accompany them, but Chloris, the woman of the house, had other plans for her. She did not order Sappho about, for who is out of favor one day may be in favor the next, and she was a great and powerful lady, though small. But when in her life again would the Fates provide her with a slave? Didymus, who had come home late, still snored against the wall when the young women left.

Balancing her basket of clothes on her head, Leto asked, "Do the girls of Mitylene look like you?"

"No. For the most part they have light hair and are taller."

"I think it would be nice not to look like everybody else."

Sappho smiled. "I am accustomed to being Sappho. Tell me, do you have any idea where my brother is? He and Alkaios?"

"My father said they board with the hewer of wood. He is a rough man, but the gods gave him a good heart."

"It will be all right then. My brother is a lord who tolerates no one over him."

"No need to fear. I'm sure they were up half the night at odd-even."

They were on the main street of the town now, and people turned to look after them. Sappho had changed into a fresh chiton, adding a cloak of finespun wool, for it was cool in high Pyrrha, even when Sun was at his brightest. It was a respectable city, not the bare rock Sappho had imagined. Leto told her it was terraced to the sea and had a port and thriving trade.

Sappho seized on this. "There is a way to the sea?"

"You must not think of escape," Leto warned her. "They will not stop at killing, and a bad death it will be if you enter their boats."

"I do not think of escape, Leto. I have a love of the sand shore and the sea. Perhaps it could be a meeting place."

"Let a day or two pass," the girl advised, "and you will not be so closely watched. I can get word to your brother and, when it is safe, guide you to him."

"Then you are my friend, Leto."

The girl took the basket from her head and dropped to her knees, kissing the hem of her cloak. Sappho, glancing quickly around, lifted her up, but they were by now in forested country and quite alone. They kept walking and soon heard the laughter and chatter from the washing springs. This at least is not different from Mitylene, Sappho thought. But as they drew near, the women fell silent. Their eyes took in the cut of Sappho's garments, the rich material, the studded sandals. Nothing escaped their scrutiny. They did not need to know her history to see she was of a great house.

The soldiers had made a good story during their drinking and dicing the night before, and everyone knew of the feud with Pittakos and the circumstance of the dead dog—everything, in fact, leading to the exiles being among them. What seemed most strange was that a *woman* should be famous among poets, and at the same time a rebel banished with men.

Leto set down the bundle of clothes, gave greeting, and knelt at her accustomed place. Sappho would have knelt with her, but Leto prevented her, saying, "This is work not meant for you, Lady." Then shyly, "I noticed you wrapped a flute under your cloak."

Sappho took it out and undid the fastenings. She sat and, with a prayer to the Nine, began to play. It was a pleasant tune with the familiar sounds of morning in it. The women continued their work, but they listened so they could say, "I heard Sappho play."

She sang:

> *Though few,*
> *they are roses*

A spell was cast, an enchantment. Her vision was so sure that she made the roses bloom. The women murmured their thanks and went their way to tell of it in the village. Sappho, too, gave thanks to the Muses, who won her this sympathy. And when Leto laid out their simple meal, she set aside a tenth part, and spilled a tenth part of the wine.

Three days later Leto whispered, "Do not sleep tonight."

Sappho pressed her hand, and when Chloris drowsed off and the father had gone to the tavern, the girls got up and left.

Leto flitted like a shadow and Sappho after her. Finally, with their feet on the path, they raced down to the sand shore. Her brother caught her around the waist and lifted her into the air.

"Oh, Khar, Khar!"

"My turn," said Alkaios, stepping forward, and they laughed.

Leto kept watch while they talked. Khar prevailed upon Alkaios to recite his most recent poem, dedicated to Pittakos the Shuffle Foot, whom he referred to as "a lute without charm."

Sappho laughed until tears stood in her eyes. "Oh, if he could but hear this."

"He will," Khar said. "We worked half last night making wax impressions with a pointed stick, then sent them down this morning along with the timber to be delivered to a friend of Alkaios who will see they are copied and hung in the agora."

Again she was overcome with mirth. "Poor Pittakos! He cannot be rid of us even here."

They exchanged news. Alkaios composed and sang in the tavern, while Khar played games of skill and chance. They were treated as guests and had been invited to the villas lining the main thoroughfare.

"We are instructed to bring you. Everyone is anxious to play host to Sappho."

Sappho shook her head. "My hosts take their role of jailer more seriously. But I have a friend in Leto, and if we can meet like this now and then, I will not feel alone."

As the months of exile passed, Sappho expressed in a poem what her friendship with Leto meant to her. She called it "A Blossomy June." Like two children, they bathed in icy streams and afterward combed and plaited hibiscus into each other's hair. Sappho showed her how to stain her toes with the petals of crushed geranium, and found surprises for her among the many boxes of precious things that had been sent from Mitylene.

It was still blossomy and still June when Sappho said softly, "Come beside me and I will show you what I have under my cloak. See—a wonderful perfume. Lean forward and I will place the scent between your breasts."

Leto exclaimed at the beauty of the small alabaster jar, and again when Sappho, removing the stopper, passed it under her nose. "Musk," Sappho told her, "from the land of the Persians. It makes the skin breathe with desire."

"Desire? Desire for what?"

The question was troubling. And she had been troubled by it. Just as she was troubled by Leto herself. Why? Why should a simple country girl become the felloe around which her thoughts turned? Leto's glance, her touch, her voice, her presence determined how her own day went, whether it was happy or sad or both. When happiness and sadness intertwine, then great confusion occurs.

Sappho lowered her head so nothing of what she felt could be read in her face and ran the perfume stopper between Leto's wide young breasts and under them. The girl closed her eyes and shivered in delight. "Musk is like a whole garden, a field of flowers!"

Sappho handed her the jar. "Now you do me." When Leto bent over her, she caught her breath and held it.

Leto laughed at the contrast of their skins, hers so fair, Sappho's even more bronzed by the summer sun.

When Leto finished, Sappho placed the alabaster container in her hands. "It is for you."

"I couldn't," Leto protested. "It is too dear."

"Are we not friends? You know we were from the first minute. And there is nothing that belongs to one friend that does not belong to the other. Take it from your friend."

Leto still hesitated.

"I will share it with you," Sappho reassured her, "by resting my head against your breasts and breathing the fragrance. Is that not fair?" Settling herself against Leto, she felt happier than she ever had. "Your breasts are soft, yet beautiful and high. Do you use a breast band?"

Leto, who had been revolving the problem of the alabaster jar, suddenly brightened. "I could perhaps accept the perfume of Persia as a wedding gift."

Sappho did not move, yet life seemed to run out of her.

Leto must have felt a difference, for she asked, "Are you not betrothed?"

"No." The word was brought out through a welter of pain.

"But a lady such as you—"

"I said no."

Leto sought for a way to restore the easy companionship that somehow had been rent. "Will you sing today, Sappho?"

Sappho drew away. She felt cold as a corpse. Everything within her had turned sere. It was a moment before she could ask, "Who?"

"Who am I to marry? Smerdis. You must have seen him looking at me in the market. He always manages to be there when I am."

"I want to see him," Sappho said abruptly.

"I will point him out to you the next time we are in the agora."

"I want to see him now."

"Now?" Leto was astonished.

Sappho was already on her feet and dressing.

"But I do not know where he is at this hour."

Sappho sat down again. "Of course," she said. Leto watched her with a concerned expression.

"Describe him," Sappho said.

"I hardly know—"

"You know," Sappho snapped. "Is he tall, short, dark, blond?"

"He is tall," Leto said unhappily.

"Go on."

"He is blond."

"From your description he is a regular Apollo. Why did you not speak of him before?"

"I don't know. We have been betrothed since I was seven."

"But the marriage time draws near?"

Leto nodded. "At the harvest, so Hera will send us luck and many children."

"I see."

"I was going to ask you for a wedding song, but I thought—it is too much. A song from Sappho, it would seem as though I thought myself some fine lady. I know I am only Leto."

"Stop it, Leto. You shall have your song."

Leto embraced her knees. Her thanks was blinding pain to Sappho. "Go to Niobe. Tell her I want the lyre of the symmetric horns that was sent with the other items from Mitylene." She would start to work at once. The Muses would help her; something familiar—music, song, poetry—would bring her back to herself. "The wedding lays will be the most beautiful any girl ever had," she promised.

Leto's smile broke with radiance. "Then there is nothing wrong between us?"

With great effort Sappho returned Leto's smile. "Why should there be, my Leto?" She waited a moment for control before continuing. "Only . . . you must know that when the Muses are with me, no other can be present."

Leto's smile died. "You will not come to the washing springs anymore, or find a spot to bathe with me anymore?"

Sappho could not speak her reply but shook her head that it was so.

"You will not braid hibiscus into my hair?" She said it simply as though to make herself understand.

Sappho threw a flower at her. "What look of sadness is this, Leto? You will be the best-sung bride in all Lesbos!"

With Khar and Alkaios, Sappho began visiting those homes that previously she had been content to avoid. It was good, she told herself, to go about once more, and while the company did not compare to the scintillating, sophisticated circles of Mitylene, still there was talk of the philosopher of Miletus, one Thales, who returned from travels, and, after much study, made the startling declaration that the earth floated on a sea of water. "All that appears to contradict this," Alkaios explained, "he claims is only a seeming, that actually all things are of a wholeness. In fact, all is water."

Sappho laughed. "Then why aren't my feet wet?" But it was stimulating to hear what was being debated in the greater Hellenic world. For too long her thoughts had been confined to this rock. She told herself she missed the stimulation of cultivated people. How could I have allowed myself to rusticate? she wondered.

"Did you hear the latest on your friend Pittakos?" her host asked.

Sappho shook her head.

"We all know that what rankles him most is his own common origin. So what does he do but find himself a bride of impeccable family!"

"Pittakos is married?" How easily she could accept it now.

"Wait until you hear. He had to go as far as Thrace to find someone who was both of noble birth and would have him. I understand the woman was brought to Mitylene with great pomp."

"There is more," Sappho prompted, delighting in the gossip. "You are not telling it all."

Their host laughed. "It is rumored the lady is not as young as she might be, or as beautiful. Breeding Pittakos wanted, and breeding he has."

Alkaios knew instantly who the lady was and instantly rhymed a ditty:

She has been hammered by lovers,
as any old ship's bottom

As an afterthought he added that lead and vinegar did not lighten her leathery skin, that red ocher on her cheeks failed to give the bloom of youth, and that her lamp-blackened eyebrows always managed to appear smeared. Whites of egg mixed with mastic could not help her sagging throat. "I tell you, she could hurry a coffin into the ground. What is our Splayfoot about? O poor horny Yellow Toes! What are you thinking of? At what cost have you bought yourself a bloodline?"

Sappho laughed with the rest, but she no longer had any interest in Pittakos nor cared that he made a fool of himself. "There is to be a wedding much closer to us exiles," she said, changing the subject. "Leto, daughter of Didymus, in whose house I live, is to be married."

"Yes, quite soon, I believe. On Hera's day," their host informed them. "Smerdis comes of an old family of freemen. The union will unite their farms, both small, but together it will make a good parcel. The match is well conceived."

"Have you been asked to make an epithalamion?" Alkaios wanted to know.

"I will make one, of course. She and her family have been kind to me."

"Such wedding songs are the pearls of your poetry."

"I will not only devise the wedding hymenaeus but also train the girls." She sought the old excitement such doings roused in her in the past.

"And I," exclaimed Alkaios, "will sing with the boys and beat them into a chorus. It will be something to do." Immediately he was all apologies to his host. "Not that the time has not passed pleasantly. But no exile is sweet."

Sappho had stopped listening. The next farm. They grew some kind of coarse bean. She had seen it from a distance, and watched the ploughing. How could Leto have been so confiding with her, yet not mentioned . . . Aphrodite presides over the deceits that girls employ. But Leto the golden-haired was surely not deceitful. It was a matter she did not consider important; that was why she had not mentioned it sooner. This explanation did not satisfy Sappho. When is a girl's marriage not important?

She left the party early, and Leto, already in bed, roused to blow her a goodnight kiss when she entered. But Sappho was obsessed with Smerdis. She would have no rest until she'd seen him, judged his beauty, both of face and body. On the girdle of Aphrodite is embroidered all the goddess's wishes—if I had such a girdle, it would be worked with one name, Leto.

She turned restlessly from one side to the other. Some god has maddened me, she thought as she lay awake listening to that nocturnal bird, the iynx. Some thoughts she guided: I will send to Mitylene for my Erythraean stone earrings as a wedding gift. Other thoughts burst from her without control: She must not marry, she must not!

Finally she confronted it. She could not bear Leto in the arms of some farmhand.

Sappho slept in tumbled hair and dreamed she fell from morn to morn. When she woke, it was as dark as when her eyes were closed, but she was thinking clearly. She was twenty years old and had no desire to marry. "I shall remain eternally maiden," she spoke aloud to Night. It was a solemn vow. And having made it, she knew it was time to consider her peculiar virginity. She thought sometimes, because of the force within her, that she was a female in whom a man's soul slumbered. Could such a thing be?

She loved the beauty of her own sex. Their voices were sweet to her ear. And she found their soft, pliant bodies comely, their ringed fingers delicate and pleasing. She liked small feet and the pretty turn of a slender ankle. Narrow waists and swelling uptilted young breasts seemed to her incomparable loveliness. She took pleasure in going to the baths, in watching the voluptuous attitudes into which the maidens fell. She had thought all women experienced the same joy. Now she wondered. Did any other of Leto's friends feel torment, know restless agony?

It occurred to her that Adonis, favorite of Aphrodite, was double-sexed. Had the same gift been granted her? Gift? It was a curse, if true. Yet what of Alkaios and the other men with their lads? Men, of course, had love-friends of their own sex, young boys to pet and write odes to, even march into battle and fight beside—but a woman?

Was it so strange if the same longing, the same passion seized a female? Sappho knew herself to be a divine instrument. But what god was it who compelled her to write wedding songs for a wedding she did not want to take place? The sentences her mind formed were certainly no part of a wedding lay, but surely had been sent by Eros in revenge for her vow of chastity:

> *For whom curl my hair,*
> *for whom perfume my hands?*
> *Since I go not to . . .*

She broke off. Why was it she could not stand the thought of Leto's secret night with her bridegroom? Or think of his kisses on that full mouth? Why did she find such pain in it?

She twisted and turned until light, then lay pretending to sleep while the household rose. She joined them for breakfast, watered wine and barley cakes. She could not eat and only brought the cup to her lips to moisten them. The mother of the house set Leto and Niobe to spinning.

"I am going for a walk." Sappho avoided Leto's glance, for she usually waited until the girl was free.

"Where are you going?" Leto asked.

"Nowhere, anywhere, to think on someone's wedding." She took the footpath to the neighboring farm. On the pretext of gathering flowers, she went close. A young man followed the plough, steering an ancient ox. He ploughs straight, she thought, and drew nearer. His hair, she saw, was blond as a sheaf of wheat—why must mine be black as a goat's? She felt despair at his finely wrought body. It gleamed with sweat as though oils of great cost anointed it. And what height he had, like an oak of Dionysos.

Tears made a veil before her sight. "O Hephaestus, you god beside the forge, give Sappho courage. Like me, you were born dark and ugly and, besides that, lame. It may be you can understand my heart where I cannot."

Smerdis saw her and, resting a moment, called, "Greetings, Sappho, poet of Mitylene."

"And to you, Smerdis, son of Lycurgus."

"Do you return to the house of Leto?"

"I do."

"Will you give the blue-eyed daughter of Didymus tender greetings from Smerdis?"

"I will," she called and, turning, tripped, because she could not see the path. All her flowers were scattered.

Sappho kept to herself. Any visitors she told curtly that poems were not born out of the air but must be worked over as a potter spins his vase or a master in marble hews his sculpture. The first wedding carions were from the heart:

O bridegroom, never was there another girl like this!

And:

> *Bride, full of rosy love, desirous bride, the most*
> *beautiful ornament of Aphrodite of Paphos, go to your*
> *marriage bed, go to the marriage couch whereon you*
> *shall play so gently and sweetly with your . . .*

She stopped and added, reluctantly, "bridegroom."

Hera, goddess of wedlock, how at this moment she hated her! From her unhappiness came an extraordinarily lovely little melody:

> *O beautiful, O lovely! Yours it is with rosy-ankled*
> *Graces and with Aphrodite to play!*

Leto was not happy, even though the songs were in her praise and did her much honor since Sappho of Lesbos composed them. She would rather have back their rambles, their talks, their confidences. If Sappho took her lyre to the porch, Leto found tasks to busy herself there, weaving or carding. Then Sappho would enter the house. Leto soon found an excuse that brought her inside.

Sappho turned on her like an Erinye. "What thymos keeps you continually at my side? If you think it is easy to compose a molpe, make your own!" And out she flew, angry that she spoke angrily.

—Hecate, who combines the attributes of the fifty daughters of Nereus, and intercedes for humankind, help me! Monstrous and unruly violence has me by the throat. My thymos chokes me, the deepest desire for evil seizes me. I see myself dead at the foot of the wedding couch. Or I see *him* there, the bridegroom, doubled up with subtle poisons. How can I find my way? Help me calm my mind as the ruffled sea is calmed, that I may once more sing Aeolian rhymes.

But unruly thoughts kept pace with her. Though she had forbidden Leto to come with her, she *was* with her, her image consuming and ravishing her. Had Leto's soul passed into hers?

Sappho had wandered far from the house. She did not know where she was, but knew she was other-directed.

Climbing a knoll, she stood with the wind blowing fresh off the sea. The hum of insects was in the air. Women in a terraced field below weeded pulse. Their regular movements might be dactyls based on the balanced moment between long, short, quick, slow. She sang out:

> *Raise the rafters! Hoist*
> *them higher! Here comes*
> *a bridegroom taller*
> *than Ares!*
> *He towers*
> *above tall men as*
> *poets of Lesbos*
> *over all others*

With this poem came new knowledge. The poems she made—made her Sappho. They were not only central to her life, they were her life. The songs were more important than the wedding, more important than herself or Leto. Her in-dwelling Muses had shown her this. Now she dedicated herself to the Nine. In return, she was to be among the undying. Her songs would live, and she herself through them. In thanks her feet trod out the patterns the poem dictated.

In a few days Sappho had assembled the young virgins, while Alkaios took the bachelors of the village in hand. Sappho rehearsed her chorus well, finding comfort in the familiar, almost forgetting what it led to. One would not think these girls were spinners, dyers, beekeepers, threshers—they were holy nymphs performing ancient rites.

The event being upon them, she, with Khar and Alkaios, draped both the bride's and the bridegroom's houses with branches of evergreen. Her fingers, though they had gone numb, wove wreaths of flowers, and arranged armfuls of foliage in the bedchamber of the groom's house. Somehow she managed to laugh with the others even as the sleeping couch was brought. She found she was able to perform all the tasks. She soaked the bed with her own exotic perfumes, even those of Persia. Tapers in their brackets spread incense of their own, and Sappho felt weak in all her limbs, as though she were about to crumple on the floor.

Alkaios glanced at her curiously. "You're taking a lot of trouble for the wedding of a couple of farmers' children."

Sappho tried to straighten her disoriented world. "They have been my hosts. This must be as fine a wedding as Mitylene ever saw. Promise me, Alkaios."

"Oh, I have done my part."

"He has." Khar laughed. "Wait until you hear his verses."

She nodded, shaking the vertigo from her head. "Alkaios, see that the bridegroom is bathed in holy water and dressed in white garments. Khar, make sure his beard is curled and scented. Pick flowers for his hair and garlands for his chest. And by the Cloud-Compeller, please look to his fingernails!"

"You'd think it was your own marriage," Khar said. "So much fuss."

"What else is there to do on this cursed rock?" Alkaios asked. "We'll show these bumpkins how to put on a wedding!"

Sappho willed strength into herself. It was time to prepare the bride. As she hurried to Leto's house she ran her tongue over her lips and tasted blood. She had bitten them through. Feverishly she sought among the linens in her chest and brought out the lightest of cambrics cut after the newest fashion.

Leto's mother protested. "It is too much for you to do."

Sappho smiled. She knew it was the sheerness of the material Chloris objected to.

Leto, entranced, threw her arms around Sappho and kissed her. Sappho went rigid and the breath seemed stopped in her. Seeing her friend so white, Leto grabbed her hands and began chafing them.

"Sappho, how cold you are. You seem to have no more blood in you than a shade."

"I stayed too long in the heat picking flowers." She withdrew her hands from Leto's and began to plait roses in her hair.

Niobe painted the bride's face from her mistress's paint box. Chloris gasped to see her daughter's glowing countenance become the white mask of a high-born lady. Ocher and fard were applied, and many scents, each sniffed first by Leto. "I wonder," she said, giggling, "if my Smerdis will be overcome. He may smell me and pass out. Then what will I do?"

"That Adonis you are marrying will not pass out," Sappho assured her, and hung on her ears the priceless earrings that were her final gift.

Leto was ecstatic. "I can't believe this is me," she exclaimed gazing enraptured into Sappho's copper mirror. Niobe was putting the finish of red polish to her buffed nails. Sappho put a finish to much more.

The first feast took place at the home of the bride, to which the bridegroom came at sunset. He was driven in a chariot drawn by two rose-bedecked horses and accompanied by his friends and best man, a noisy crew. When they had passed under the bower of greenery, they were met by a circle of girls holding hands and singing the welcome Sappho had prepared.

Smerdis could not take his eyes from Leto.

"He's not sure it's me," Leto whispered. "He thinks he is marrying not a girl but a goddess."

Pyrrha was noted for its shellfish and wild duck. These were the main courses, served on the porch with sardines wrapped and fried in fig leaves. Then came delicate and dainty breads, which Niobe had instructed the women in baking. The wine of Lesbos was strong and the toasts to the pair many.

The best man quoted: "Get yourself first of all a house, a woman and a working ox."

"You misquote Hesiod," Alkaios laughed. "He said, 'Don't buy the woman, marry her. Then she will follow the plough.'"

Sappho monitored the merriment, the ribaldry, the jokes; it was all according to plan, in all respects a Lesbian wedding.

Once it had been her delight. Now she watched as one looks at distant mountains over which a gauze of mist descends.

The guests washed their hands and received their torches. Leto was driven to her bridegroom's house sitting between him and his best man. Sappho joined the others following on foot with a taper, singing:

> Your figure of loveliness,
> your eyes of tender look,
> O bride, and love spread over
> your beautiful face
> Aphrodite has indeed done you honor . . .

When the procession halted, the bride and groom were pelted with grain and confetti. The wheel of the cart was burned so the bride would have no way to leave her husband's home. The groom's mother took Leto by the hand and led her to the altar of household gods. Sappho sang the hymn, at the end of which she called out in a loud voice: "Hail to the bride! Hail to the bridegroom!"

This was the moment. Smerdis seized Leto in his arms and dashed with her into the wedding chamber. The cry that Sappho swallowed spread through her like a poison. It was with difficulty that she remained on her feet. The festivities were in full swing and no one noticed. The best man fended off the girls who made a pretense of rescuing their friend. But the door was firmly bolted from inside. So the girls contented themselves with taunting the young men. "Why," they asked in chorus, "have you failed to win some dainty maiden for yourselves?"

The boys, coached by Alkaios, answered song with countersong. "We have heard a bad wife roasts her husband without using a fire."

"Oh, so it is lack of courage that keeps you single! Imagine! By the looks of it, you are bigger, taller, stronger . . . but looks must be deceiving since we frighten you so."

Much laughter on each side. "Trust a woman! Trust a thief!" "You're safe enough with that bright red hair! How far down is it red?" "In *Works and Days* it is said, 'Don't let a woman make you lose your head over her bedizened rump!' "

"Bedizened!" The girls laughed. "Where would anyone get such a word? It must come from Mitylene."

"Come, girls," Alkaios insinuated, "why don't we imitate what's going on behind the door?"

"We don't give ourselves to the first who comes along. Ask those boys who were our playmates." And they stamped their feet and clapped their hands as Sappho had shown them, upbraiding Hespereus, the evening star, for bringing a night on which Leto must give up her virginity.

Sappho's eyes saw through the door. Smerdis had unveiled his bride and together they tasted the quince she had placed by the bed in token of future sweetness. Now he stripped the chiton of rainbow hues from her and Leto stood naked before him, as Sappho herself had seen her many times entering her bath, frolicking in a mountain freshet, splashing, chasing over pebbles until the water rippled around knees and thighs. The limbs of Aphrodite could not be more rounded or more perfect than Leto's. She remembered drawing the perfume under her breasts, high half-moons, soft and white, their centers like the stamens of twin flowers.

At that moment the door was flung open and a bloody rag waved at the revelers. Smerdis's triumph was complete. He had desecrated the shrine at which she once worshiped. Must love take such violent form? She continued to drink with Alkaios and Khar but felt worse for it, not better.

All night through her dreams Smerdis ploughed his field, and when he came to the mound of Aphrodite the ground ran red, the cries and strangled groans could not be heard for the lewd jests and laughter.

The next morning Niobe drew Sappho a face that did not match her own. They gathered again at the groom's house and the wedded pair appeared briefly to listen to the aubade, which asked Aphrodite to ensure a productive union. Afterward they received gifts. Leto looked like Leto—but it was delusion. All was different, changed, ended.

The second night, the banquet was prepared by the bride, but, according to tradition, she herself did not attend. Libation was made, the guests helped themselves from the many dishes and partook of wines that gladden the heart.

Sappho, asking the Muses to breathe into her their divine spirit, sang the final song. She chose the old epic form such as Homer used in telling the tales of Ilium. She began her tale:

> It seems that once long ago in the house of Didymus,
> flaxen-haired Leto dwelt . . .

The season of harvest passed and Sappho still lived with the parents of Leto in the wattle house. When summer came again, there were ill tidings from Mitylene. Three black eagles had been observed swooping and diving over the city. A shepherd tracked them to an entrance in the cleft of a certain cave. Now it is well known that Cholera, Smallpox, and Plague are three daimones who live in just such a cave. One of the evil sisters awoke and breathed her foul breath over the town. It caused bowels to loosen and food could not be kept on the stomach. The fever god consorted with the hag of death, unsparing, striking with the suddenness of the lightning bolt which the Cyclops gave Father Zeus.

Those who sickened first—infants, children, old people, and lepers—were shut out of houses. They died in the streets and were torched. Hekatombs were offered, with every house giving the best from among its flocks. Libations were poured, priestesses consulted. But the evil ran rampant; there was no assuaging it. Now the hale and hardy were struck down, the young and beautiful. Fear bred unrest, and anger filled the hearts of the people. They blamed themselves, they blamed their neighbors. And they blamed their rulers.

Mysilos of Leanex, Tyrant of Lesbos, flanked by soldiers, visited his barber in the deserted agora. His counselors did not consider it safe because of contagion, but there was no one about. The stalls set up on the long finger of land that separated the two harbors presented a desolate scene. The white stone bridges were swept clean of people. The melon sellers were gone, gone the dice players. Neither Mycenaean artifacts nor old Lydian coins were displayed. There were no red clay pots with geometric black designs readied for export. Sponges fished from the sea, once hoisted on long poles, had disappeared. None tended to the mending of sails or the forging of iron. Nor did women dip their wool in heated vats for dyeing, nor sculptors work the winged gryphon with his lion's body and spiral of curls.

The tailor shop was shut down. The barber alone remained open by command of Mysilos. The Tyrant posted bodyguards to either side and sat, somewhat overflowing the chair. Mysilos gave directions as to the styling of his hair and beard. He was particular about the cut, the curling, and especially the pomade.

The barber nodded obsequiously as he was given these detailed instructions, although he attended the Tyrant routinely and knew exactly what unguents, lotions, and oils to use. As he laid these articles beside the curling iron and scissors, an arrow out of nowhere hit the Tyrant in the jaw under his ear. It cut his tongue in two. Mysilos clutched the chair and hung forward, blood splattering the swept earth under him. Something gelatinous oozed from his eye as from the center of an egg.

The barber hopped helplessly about, calling on the gods to witness. "I am an unfortunate, an innocent, a bystander!"

Soldiers dashed to the body that had toppled out of the chair. They ran in and around the deserted stalls, returning once more to inspect the body. Since the murderer could not be found, it seemed best to convey the corpse to its residence.

When news of the murder was brought to Pittakos, he went to the people. In the main square he talked to those willing to assemble, and asked them what he should do. It was suggested the Oracle at Delphi should be consulted. Pittakos dispatched a priestess on this mission.

Also put forward by members of the nobility was the suggestion that the raging of the gods against Mitylene could be due to the banishment for a year of two sons and a daughter of ancient Lesbian lineage. Pittakos agreed to their release. It was the first act of clemency by the new Tyrant of Lesbos.

In high Pyrrha, Alkaios was jubilant at the news, and composed a ditty for the occasion:

> Now is the time to
> get drunk,
> the time to
> make love,
> now that Mysilos is dead

Laughingly he turned to his friends. But brother and sister looked thoughtfully at each other. Mysilos's death had lost importance. A year ago they had been angry and involved. Now it was their new freedom that concerned them. Certainly it was not without danger. Suppose on their return the plague did not abate? Suppose it grew worse? They sent up fervent prayers.

By the time the trio reached Mitylene, the fever no longer blew its hot breath, the last of the dead had been burned, and a fresh wind came from the sea.

The city was grateful to Pittakos, who offered public hekatombs to the gods and, in preparation for the coming of his old enemy Alkaios, strengthened the laws against drinking. A proclamation lettered in wood and hung in the main square announced that this edict would be strictly enforced. Alkaios laughed. "Well, well, a personal greeting, you might say."

They were given warm welcome by their families, who, except for Sappho's aunt Tyro and a few retainers, had remained miraculously untouched. With Sappho's house in mourning for Tyro, and indeed the entire city mourning, no public show of their private rejoicing was made.

Pittakos vowed he would hunt down the murderers of Mysilos and bring them to justice. He was convinced it was a conspiracy. For one thing, Lydian gold was being passed in the public houses and in the street of women.

He proclaimed: "The guilty must be found and dealt with if the gods are not to bring back the foul death that sucks life from the body."

The populace shuddered, but Sappho paid little attention. She was happy to be home, to find her mother as before, Eurygyos matured, and Larichos grown into a young lad of great beauty. She cried with her mother over her aunt Tyro and listened gravely as Kleis lamented how thin she and Khar had become.

Actually both were hardened from the coarse, spare diets and plain life they had led in Pyrrha. The simplest things now seemed to Sappho luxury beyond measure—her baths, her handmaidens, the oiling of her skin, the massaging of her supple limbs, the dainties served at table, and the wardrobe of coan dresses she had almost forgotten.

Small, informal gatherings took place nightly and friends begged for her latest songs. One they found hard to make out; it was a song in praise of gold:

> *Gold is the child of Zeus,*
> *neither moth nor worm devours it*
> *and it overpowers the strongest*
> *of mortal minds*
> *For gold is unspotted*

"What does it mean?" the guests asked uneasily, thinking of the Lydian gold.

"It means what it says." Surrounded in Pyrrha by rough materials and utensils of the peasantry, Sappho thought often of gold and wove its gleam into a song, for it meant the things she was used to, the many rich objects familiar to her touch.

Attaching no importance to the song of gold, she played and sang another devised since her return. It was of crickets:

> *And the clear song from*
> *beneath her wings does rise*

when she shouts down
the perpendicular blaze
of outstretched sunshine of noon

That night Niobe stopped her before she could enter her quarters. "Lady"—her voice broke—"I know not how to tell you. Someone has been in your chambers, and what they searched for I do not know. Your jewels were left untouched."

Sappho hurried to look and saw at once that her woman's chest was in disarray. "And my jewels are all here?" she asked Niobe.

"Yes, Lady. And a quantity of gold besides."

"Gold, you say? A thief who gives rather than takes," she said musingly.

Niobe blamed herself; she had crept into the great hall to hear her mistress sing. Sappho assured her she was not at fault and sent her to fetch her bed. Almost immediately there was a scratching at her door; Niobe had returned without slaves or a bed. "Pardon, Lady. Your brother, the lord Kharaxos, is here and would speak with you."

Sappho motioned her to let him in.

Before saying a word, Khar took her hand in his.

"Sister," he spoke in a rapid undertone, "we have been denounced. Alkaios is waiting. We flee to Egypt. It seems while Pittakos rules, there is to be no truce."

Her heart, like a netted fish, floundered before resuming its beat. "Why denounced, and by whom?"

"For the murder of Mysilos. Pittakos declares it to have been paid for with Lydian gold. Tonight you sang a song in praise of this metal, so our apartments were searched. And caches of gold were discovered, hidden by Pittakos's agents. It will be said, while sitting above suspicion in high Pyrrha, we ordered and paid for the Tyrant's death."

"All this because of my song?"

"Come, Sappho, get your things together."

"But it is so mad an idea . . ." She could hardly orient herself to this fresh disaster.

"There is a ship waiting."

"Ah, there are troubles in our house." She took several turnings in the room before facing him. "You are right to go, and Alkaios. But I will stay. I will face my accuser."

"None live long who strive with gods."

"Since when is Pittakos a god? May Zeus destroy his might, not ours. Hurry brother," she urged Kharaxos. "For you it is the ordained time."

"And for you, sister? Think carefully."

"My mind is firm, Khar."

They clasped arms as comrades. They had shared much, and now Khar was being torn from her. In such a way she had parted from her father. Hastily, to nullify the unlucky thought, she said, "May Poseidon of the blue hair watch over your craft and bring you safe into Egypt."

"I will send a token, my ring."

She kissed him on the cheek, and the next moment was alone. What thymos drives Pittakos to wrong my house in this manner? she asked herself. The song of gold had been innocent, and she was innocent. She was also young and inexperienced enough to believe that would save her.

The populace was roused. They demanded that Sappho the poet be questioned, for her brother and Alkaios had taken ship by night and quantities of gold were believed to have gone with them.

Sappho was composed when they sent for her. She now looked on Pittakos with Alkaios's eyes. Yes, he had a slight potbelly, and his feet were certainly unsightly, in fact, splayed, just as Alkaios sang. They surveyed each other. It was a long hard look on both sides.

"Sappho, Sappho, daughter of a mighty sire, it grieves me that no sooner are you returned than new controversy swirls around you."

She drew her perfumed mantle close.

"Your brother Kharaxos and your confederate Alkaios have fled to Amasis in Egypt."

"They have gone to trade. Since when is that a sin for a merchant family?"

"I have heard the song Alkaios made when he learned of the murder of the good Mysilos. Do you know it?"

"If you mean Mysilos the Tyrant, I know it well. We were sitting on a rock in Pyrrha when he composed it. It possesses a nice cadence, don't you think?"

Red anger crept up the man's neck, but he mastered it and seemed to speak casually. "There was another song sung in Mitylene last evening. I am told its theme was of gold."

"A worthy theme."

"You must think so, for you, Sappho, were the singer."

"What you say is true."

"Why did you sing that particular song?"

"Who can say? The Muses put it into my mind."

"More likely it was Hermes, the mischief-maker, who is enough like you to be your twin."

Sappho said simply, "At the close of the year when we place our sins on a scapegoat for sacrifice, I will not require the rite of purification for any crime. Can you say the same?" She studied him with a look that appeared to be candid but in fact rendered judgment.

He had to remind himself that it was she who was here for judging. "The gold was seen," he told her.

"Naturally it was seen. By those who placed it in our rooms."

There was a pause as Pittakos strove for a judicious tone. "If only you had not put aside the womanly role that is rightfully yours. Surely you do not think it gives me pleasure to send you once again into exile? For I am of the same race as yourself."

Sappho's lips twisted. "Hardly," she said.

"There is grave suspicion that you are implicated in the murder of our beloved Tyrant. You must leave Lesbos."

"Yet my heart is like that of a child."

He regarded her from beneath heavy brows. "You should have gone with your brother."

"Why? To please a Tyrant who perverts justice?"

"Pyrrha taught you nothing."

"It would have pleased you had I fled, as when a lion attacks a sheepfold, the sheep panic and smother themselves in piles."

"You are banished from Lesbos."

"You are a small man for all your size, Pittakos, blown about by small winds. I will go, since I must. But I will go as befits the poet of Lesbos, with my servants, my eunuch, and my female slaves. You will look mean-spirited before the world if you deny me these decencies."

"It is seemly. You are no longer a child. I grant your request."

"It is not a request. I stated to you what is my due. I request nothing—not a pardon, because I am innocent, not forgiveness of sins I had no part in—nor do I apply to you to stay in Lesbos. But I tell you this: brother will not be dear to brother as in the old days."

"Are you threatening me?" Pittakos bellowed, half rising.

"I make no threats, just a prophecy. My eyes cannot always see—but my art sees, my songs see. Farewell, Pittakos."

He got up from his high-backed chair. But Sappho was not yet done.

"As for the one who placed Lydian gold to be found in my room, may terrors grip hold of him. May he become the slave of strangers! For he is the murderer."

Involuntarily Pittakos's hands clenched.

Until this moment Sappho had concealed her suspicions. But there could no longer be doubt. It was Pittakos himself.

The servants had slaughtered, the sacrifice been made. Sappho studied the entrails as they fell. Much could be foretold in this manner, not only by the shapes but by the color of the offal as well and what parts lay next to one another.

After conferring with Kleis, Sappho decided to journey to Corinth and be the guest of Arion, the poet whose birthplace was Lesbos. He came from the same small village of Methymna as her mother did, and Kleis knew his family well.

"No less a man than the Tyrant Periander is his patron. You will be received by Arion for your sake and for mine. And for my part, I will not feel I am casting a daughter upon the sea like flotsam, to end up the gods know where."

Sappho was still studying the entrails. "Earth-encircling Lord Poseidon, grant a fair passage for Sappho! And you, Nereids, children of Doris the Ocean nymph, who dwell at the bottom of Sea, Amatheis of the lovely locks, dark-eyed Halia, Galatea, sisters all, I pray you keep your realm calm. And Clymene, shapely offspring of Ocean, intercede with the tides. Let them be peaceable for this daughter of Lesbos, unfairly sent from family, home, and friends."

This brought fresh tears from her mother. "Perhaps it would be better if you went to Athens; at least it is a city of the Hellenes."

"They keep their women too strictly, Mother. I would have no freedom to go about as I chose."

"But to take ship across the pathless sea to the land of the Barbarian!"

"The Attic tongue is spoken everywhere. Besides, I bring greetings to your friend, the good Arion, inventor of the dithyramb, who costumed the Dionysos chorus."

"How you can be serene in the face of another exile, I do not know."

"O Mother . . . I long and I yearn!"

"So you have sung. But for what, Daughter?"

"The world, Mother. Nothing less. If I had not been sent, I would go. I want to see strange people and places, to know new customs, taste exotic foods, see the apparel of the women."

"You speak like a boy. A young man might feel as you do, but it has never been a woman's way."

Sappho shrugged off the familiar words.

"Be that as it may," her mother continued, "I have a gift for you, to go where you go. I brought it with me when I turned my face from Eresos. It is your father's soil and patrimony. See, it is wrapped in rags, but the bare roots will flower. Wherever the gods take you, these vines of home go with you."

Sappho, much touched, hugged her mother, clinging to her now it was time for parting.

Her fifteen-year-old brother, Larichos, said, not for the first time, "If only I could go with you."

Sappho smiled at him. "Your time will come. You are still very young."

"But your mother is not young," Kleis said, "and I have a presentiment that the vines I give you are more fortunate than I, that I will not see my Sappho's face again."

"You will, Mother, you will. Pittakos will not be in power forever. The rule of his predecessor was short enough. Politics have a way of changing. I will come home, and Khar too."

"It is hard," her mother lamented. "Two children gone, and one a girl."

"Girl? O Mother, I am tiger, Minotaur, nymph, poet! The Sappho that you see and touch is only what binds me in a skin. I am so much more—and many."

"You are not my Sappho?" her mother asked, bewildered.

"I am she, too!" And with that she kissed both her and her brothers. And sang them words she strung together a year ago in Pyrrha:

A murmurous blossomy June

For such it was when she turned her back on Lesbos. It was to be an exile of nine years.

KERKOLAS

*I*RIS, GODDESS OF THE RAINBOW, STRETCHED HER IRIDES-
cent mantle of many colors across the peninsula, from the harbor to
the shore of Asia. The fleetest ship in mooring was a high-prowed
Phoenician. Sappho and her small retinue stepped aboard the merchantman bound for Corinth. She pressed a silver double drachma into
the captain's hand and was shown to the tent set up in the waist of
the ship. Cushions and pelts had been spread for her, a bed improvised
on sheepskins and fine linens.

She ordered a goblet of Lesbian wine. Niobe, who had followed
her into this exile too, motioned the other servants away and poured
for her mistress. But Sappho dismissed her and drank alone.

Her mother did not have the heart to come to the dock. And of
her friends, young people with whom she had played and sung before
Pyrrha, not one came. It was dangerous to be Sappho's friend. But it
hurt her that her middle brother, Eurygyos, did not stand with little
Larichos on the dock.

There was motion under her feet, and water opened between herself and Larichos, between herself and the quay. She watched it slip
away, grow small and smaller. What was distance, that it could erase
things as though they had never been? Was it another god, perhaps,
one that sailors knew of? The bravado she felt when she stood by her
own hearth with her mother and brothers evaporated. For the first time
she was utterly alone in an unknown void, sailing between two inverted
domes, Sky and Ocean.

The craft hugged the shore as they passed Chios. When the island was sighted, the captain, by prearrangement, informed her. Here was where her father died, in these waters. Little Pebble it was who undid a flower from her hair and tossed it to the undulating surface.

A secret companion traveled with her, Erato, the Muse who loved poetry best. She whispered it was ordained that the daughter of Skamandronymos journey to far places, bringing her songs to strangers.

Sappho became used to the pitch and roll of the ship. She held the rail for hours while the lovely Muse helped her compose an ode to the portals of heaven, which were kept by great clouds piled as temples and colonnades on one side and on the other by the Seasons where Apollo played his harp. She brooded over the lines, trying and discarding words. She wanted to create a perfect work. For the young Sappho was left behind, and the poet in her was more forceful than before.

Journeying toward foreign lands, she swore always to sing in her native Aeolean dialect. She thought in it, and her emotional life was lived in it. She would make the Lesbian accents ring from bronze threshold to bronze threshold where Night and Day meet.

The painted eyes of the vessel found their way through the unmarked water. The ship reached the eastern port of Corinth on the third day without incident.

Corinth, city of fine craftsmanship, city of Periander. The small party disembarked, and her eunuch managed to engage a covered cart. She sent runners ahead and proceeded to the gates of the villa of Arion. For this meeting she reminded herself she was Sappho, whose fame was here in Corinth as it was in all places.

Arion came out to greet her, and his words were winged. "Sappho, of inspirational mind, who catches the bird as it flies, the flowers as they open, the dew on the leaf and in the heart—my joy at this meeting is indescribable. Before you leave, I beg that you teach me your songs. For not since Homer has there been one who combines the simple with that which is most profound."

Sappho smiled. His reference to her departure indicated there was not room in Corinth for two poets. However, she was grateful for present hospitality, and also for his graceful manner of speaking, which made things clear and confirmed her secret desire—to continue her journey west and settle in Syracuse, that colony of the Hellenes noted for its pleasure-loving sophistication.

Arion's slaves showed her to a sumptuous suite where a bath had been readied. The soothing warmth of perfumed water, the tonic of oils upon her skin dissipated the effects of the voyage.

A feast had been ordered in her honor. She dined and drank and was persuaded to offer up a song. Afterward there was talk of the direction her wanderings should take.

"Yes, yes, of course to Sicily." Arion did not hesitate in his concurrence. "There are many flourishing cities there. If it were I, my choice should be Sybaris. It is an Achaean colony on the Gulf of Tarentum. For a woman alone, however, Sybaris is perhaps too notorious. It is the town to which we send our best-trained prostitutes. I agree that Syracuse might be preferable. It was founded a century and a half ago by Corinthians, very civilized. They know how to live, believe me."

Sappho did believe him, for she could see he was an indolent man, perhaps ten years her senior, fond of luxury and soft living. Only the piercing eyes assessing everything that passed before them betrayed the poet. He and Sappho were much interested in each other. She had studied his style, lyric like her own but with a softer, almost oriental alliteration. It was he who had turned the feast of Dionysos into theater.

"Yes, I can recommend Syracuse to you. All the arts are cherished there. Especially the poetic."

"That is what led me to think of it. And your words have settled my mind."

"The only thing . . ."

"Yes?"

He seemed not to know how to begin. Arion had been so fluent until now that Sappho listened with unusual care. "As a poet who is sung wherever the Aeolic tongue is spoken, which as you know, my dear, is everywhere . . . as Sappho, you will be freely admitted, in fact courted, by society. But as a woman, well, your sex has not the freedom to come and go at will."

"It is like Athens then! Thanks to the gods I am Lesbian born. I shall take my customs with me."

"I hope it may be so."

She was aware of the dubious, dissenting note.

Periander, the Tyrant, having heard that Sappho the poet was in Corinth, invited her and her host to a banquet. The villa lay on the sand shore, and its pools were half indoors and half out, falling with a tinkle in miniature waterfalls. The walls were a mixture of colored marbles, from veined salmon to lavender, while the colonnades were purest white.

At this time Periander, once of powerful stature, was already portly, with a hint of sagging in his jowls and about his knees that made him look older than his forty years. Still, he was a great ruler, one of the seven wise men of the known world, and he did Sappho the honor of coming forward, pressing her hands in his.

"Spellbinder of Lesbos" was his greeting. He had wine of Lesbos in readiness and, after pouring libation, thanked Earth-Shaking Poseidon for bringing this jewel of worth in health and safety to his land.

The first tables were brought. But the main course served that evening were the songs of Sappho and Arion. She sang his, and he replied with hers. It was a glorious exchange. Periander himself had made, by his own account, some two thousand verses and maxims, but in such company he could not be prevailed upon to recite them. "What, when I have here the two most famous bards of Hellene! They do not name me wise for nothing," he joked.

Arion began one of Sappho's sweetest lays:

I have loved delicacy . . .

In lines of Arion's, she carried forward the same meter. Periander was enchanted.

Slyly, Arion gave her description of Pittakos:

Crabbed age and youth cannot together live!

The whole company laughed.

She replied with a verse of Arion's in her conversational style, and in their local Lesbian Aeolic dialect. It was irresistible.

Then Arion sang her famous dove song:

But the heart of the doves became cold,
and they drooped beside them their wings . . .

Toward the end of the evening Periander asked, "What, O golden-tongued Sappho, is the relationship between a poet's life and his works?"

"It is all one, Lord. My song is an expression of my life, which has been bitter. Many times on high Pyrrha I watched the dove and understood her."

Arion saved until last the verse that was known throughout the colonies of the Hellenes and further:

> *Though few*
> *they are roses*

Periander and his court applauded, insisting that now Sappho render her own songs. She opened herself to the sublime rhythm of the music. Her body was only half seen as she bent over her lyre. The unseen part was felt in her words. Mad with passion, her witchery spun itself in the hearts of her hearers.

Periander, builder of temples, architect of the portage across the isthmus of Corinth, richer than Midas by reason of the tolls collected both entering and leaving his domain, spoke to kings and princes, saying: "Sappho of Lesbos sang me her verses."

When the next merchantman heading for Sicily put into port, news was brought Sappho and, saying her farewell to Arion, she installed herself and her retinue on board.

The first day's sail was through the straits, past high land on either hand. They sheltered in the bay east of Ithaca before trusting themselves to the six hundred stadia of open sea. In preparation for the crossing they proceeded north to Leucas to take on fresh water. The winds were notoriously uneven in this passage, and they were close to being blown upon the terrible cliffs, which seemed a bridge from Sea to Sky. Joining her at the rail, the captain recounted the story of the many criminals who had been thrown from the pinnacle of the Leucadian heights.

Sappho shuddered. "What a dreadful fate."

The captain shrugged. "Only for the guilty, for great birds were tied to their shoulders, and they say the innocent descended gently into the arms of friends waiting in boats below."

Sappho shook her head; the tale was not credible. Small boats would surely be dashed against these perpendicular granite sides. In fact, their own much larger craft seemed to her equally at the mercy of gusts that could easily drive and splinter it against that great white rock. The captain assured her he had put in here innumerable times, and he guided their vessel into the small harbor without mishap. By noon they were securely anchored, and Sappho set out to visit the scene of the executions. Her excuse was that the same spot was known for its shrine to Apollo.

She climbed for the colors above her in the tinted clouds, and for the wildflowers hidden in rock crevices. She climbed for Apollo—the loveliest pair of children descended from Father Sky were Apollo and his sister, Artemis. She thought of the prisoners and their savior birds, and wondered if they had said their last prayers at the shrine. But mostly she climbed because she must, for she was driven by a strange compulsion.

At the top was a series of colonnades of a type she had never seen. Their capitals were carved with great marble leaves in recurrent design. The Harpist willed her past these to the highest rise, where Sea and Sky mingled. This must be the death spot. A wind colder than any she had ever felt swept her. The deep band of Sea seemed all that held the world together.

She turned quickly and laid the wildflowers she had picked on the altar. "I hope you are not lonely here," she whispered to the god and ran back down the steep path, not pausing for breath. She did not know why the place affected her so strangely.

In spite of the threatening appearance of Sky, the captain refused to delay sailing. Word of their crossing to Sicily must have reached Aegae, that impenetrable place beneath Sea where winds are born and hurled in all directions. Sky had reason to be angry and periodically vent his rage in terrible fury and storm, for had he not been castrated by his own son, Kronos? At times he tore himself open to pour down rain, which beat so that human eyes could not open against it. The ship wallowed in troughs and was hurled to mountain crests. Sappho had no doubt that they were about to be engulfed, that she and all on board were to perish, swallowed by the wrath of Sky.

She did not wish the end to come upon her crouched with her women, the tent blown in on them. Rather, she stood alone, holding to any support she could find, lashed by Sea, shaken by Poseidon, struck by rain, harassed by winds. She did not pray for mercy. She did not pray at all. Deep in her there danced a madness that reveled in the deeds of these gods. It was a splendid end, to go with the crash of a thousand cymbals, to drink the fatal spume. She lifted her face to the might hurled against her.

When the worst of the raging had worn itself out and she stood wet and shivering, she noticed the other passenger. He had come aboard at Corinth but kept to himself. Her women said he was the owner of the ship, a merchant prince of a princely house. She looked at him with curiosity, for they had ridden out the storm together. His dark eyes watched her with the same intensity as the gale they had just weathered. He made a single comment: "You loved it."

She laughed, shaking herself like a wet dog, shaking the seas from her lashes and hair so she could see him more clearly. She knew his face—he had been among the guests of Periander. In a moment his name came to her. "Kerkolas," she said.

He bowed and, being as thoroughly wet and bedraggled as she, presented so comical a picture that she laughed again.

The next instant her women crept out of hiding and led her to a draped tub. They had managed to heat water with charcoal, and when it washed over her, her eyes rolled back into her head and her limbs loosened. Niobe fed her drops of wine, a gift from her fellow passenger, and rubbed her body until it coursed again with its own hot blood.

If Delphi was the navel of the world, Syracuse was its heart. The harbor greeted them with saucy red Samian craft riding lightly at anchor. They slipped past vessels with painted sails, Kypriot and Tynan, sleek Sicilian and stately Egyptian galleys. The narrows connecting the harbor to the mainland were heavily bridged, and from the mighty citadel in the heights of Ortygia, the Syracusan acropolis guarded the city. Kerkolas appeared and arranged that Sappho and her retainers were the first to be put ashore.

"I claim the right of guest-friend," he said to her, "for we shared a feast and six hundred stadia of open water that too nearly turned into the River Styx."

Sappho gave him her most charming smile; she had intended that he ask. It would give her time to find a suitable villa. Her people were busy storing chests in the small boat, and she herself carried a wrapped bundle.

"May I?" Kerkolas asked, offering to take it from her.

"No." It was said abruptly, with no charm at all. Then, relenting, "They are vine slips. I know there are no lack of vineyards in this land, but these come with me into exile. They are from home."

"Gentle Sappho," he murmured, "are you really a threat to great Pittakos?"

She decided that, when dry, he was quite handsome. It was an observation only, devoid of interest, except that she liked handsome people and things in preference to plain ones.

On the thronged mole she heard for the first time the tongue of Barbarians, as well as Attic speech. The town faced a lazy southern sea. Awnings of many colors stretched across the main thoroughfare to shield passersby from the summer sun.

"The patron goddesses of leisure reign here," Kerkolas told her, "and of them all Cotytto is foremost."

Sappho said nothing; she was taking it all in. Cotytto was goddess of sensuality, and this was indeed her city. In Mitylene the statues were mostly draped, but here young Apollos were free-standing, naked and sexed. Dionysos leered, as did accompanying satyrs with pointed ears, from a frieze in which ungarbed women playfully retreated. Male organs fashioned in terra-cotta were sold as ornaments and as charms. Men with the hindquarters of horses gazed at her from colonnades and as small votive images in bronze. The marble flesh surrounding her seemed more alive than her own.

Women went about accompanied by slaves, but in fashions more extreme than she was acquainted with. She gaped at the eupygia, false buttocks—for certainly Nature had not so fully endowed this area of the female anatomy. She saw Amokgina made clothes seemingly woven of air. Ladies draped themselves in silk from Assyria and Kos, and wore Tarentine veils of coan. The peplos was damp-pleated, clinging to the body from one shoulder, revealing the breast fully.

"They are called wet-garments," Kerkolas said, following her eyes, "and the ladies wearing them are quite respectable. The prostitutes you will know by the Thessalian gold trim embroidered with flowers. It is their mark."

Sappho was startled to see apes led through the streets by ribbons, and a dwarf with bells on his cap who capered about doing odd little dance steps. Thin, long-legged hounds were held by chains. "They come," Kerkolas told her, "from the island of Ibiza and are found as far away as Egypt where the Pharaohs are so fond of them they have them carved on their tombs."

In Lesbos they had neither the Egyptian vault nor the Babylonian arch; here, she passed under both. She saw again the columns she had seen at Apollo's shrine. "How are they called?"

"Doric." And he went on to explain the ratio between the height and the space between the axes. The leaf design was as on Leucas, chiseled into the capitals.

In the stalls of the stoa, wreath makers with dextrous fingers wove lovely ferns and flowers. Across the way palm oil was for sale, while in the next booth were displayed softest plumes of exotic African birds. She paused before Persian sapphires and Egyptian emeralds, wanting to linger, but Kerkolas signaled a cart pulled by matched Arabians.

"It is hot and you will be wanting your bath," Kerkolas said.

She agreed, hoping she had not seemed too provincial, but the wide-wayed city of Syracuse was overwhelming. For art, for wealth, for the exotic population that inhabited its streets and squares, there was nothing that compared with it. Mitylene seemed a village. She was glad she had come here. A poet needed to know all that was in the world. And if it was not in Syracuse, she was sure it was nowhere.

Kerkolas's villa was on the sand shore. The structure of the far-flung house was of harmonious proportions, being quarried from rock and in some sections two-storied. The approach to the estate was hung, as she had seen in the city, with gaily festooned awnings. Three-tiered walls of limestone dazzling with mica enclosed the main edifice, from which gardens blossomed on all sides, except where it lay open to the sea. Pomegranates, apple trees, and a flowering pear scented the air, as did deep beds of cultivated flowers. She met Apollo the archer again standing beside a splashing fountain, and Artemis faced him on her pedestal.

"I am fortunate to be the guest-friend in such a home as this," Sappho said as they stepped inside.

"It is I who am fortunate to have captured the legend of Lesbos. Today you rest, tomorrow a feast of hospitality."

"And then I must set about finding a place of my own. Not like this, of course, a small house will suit my needs, but I would like it to be by the sand shore, for I was born in Eresos."

"Eresos? I know it well. It lies on the west coast of Lesbos."

"Yes, west even of the islet of Hera."

Kerkolas nodded. "I am from nearby Andros. It was in those waters that I learned to sail."

"But this is now your home?"

"Once one has discovered Syracuse, it is hard to live anywhere else."

Sappho admired the marvelously woven wall hangings that gave warmth to the spacious rooms and stopped in wonder before a harp. It was the first of that size she had ever seen.

"I brought it back with me my last trip to Egypt," Kerkolas said.

He called, and a servant woman led Sappho to the women's side of the house. This was a novelty she did not care for. In the home at Mitylene rooms belonged to all alike. The suite assigned her looked toward the sea and off it opened a smaller room containing a terra-cotta bath around whose sides nymphs and goddesses cavorted. She dropped her cloak and pleated chiton to the floor, where they were retrieved by Niobe. Then the dainty Lydian shoes of which she was proud were lifted from her feet. She had seen all manner of fine dress, but another pair of Lydian shoes she had not seen.

She slipped into hot scented water that gathered an azure hue from inset turquoise stones. It was good to stretch and soak off the weariness of travel. How far she had journeyed! Was she to live her life among strangers? Her mother's presentiment weighed on her. Suppose Kleis were to die—she might not even hear of it in this land—or Khar, trading wine for gold and slaves, that their house might prosper and she be kept, though an exile, in a way befitting her? Eurygyos had spoken of returning to Eresos, replanting and harvesting the vineyards and pressing the grape. Only young Larichos would remain at home. She recalled his diminishing figure as he stood and waved. Would she see him again? And Alkaios? What trouble was he in now? Had he stayed with Khar? Wherever he was, Alkaios would be playing his songs somewhere to a lad with sloe eyes—while his comrade, the Little Pebble, was washed up on an unknown shore.

A eunuch was sent her, an enormous black. She was afraid of such large hands, but they kneaded her indifferently. She felt she was being deboned like a fish. Essences she had never smelled were rubbed into her skin until she glistened and her limbs were jelly. A bed was brought and swift sleep descended, dreamless.

If it is possible to sleep hard, as they say one exercises, that is how she slept. When at last her eyes opened, Helios had been chased to the exact position he'd held when her eyes had closed. She lay without movement, taking in the rich chamber. Furs were scattered on the floor, thick, luxuriant; a tapestry depicted Athene of the flashing gray eyes commanding Hermes, guide of the dead, messenger of the gods. Sappho's clothes had been laid with care on an ivory clothes stool, and a high-backed chair inlaid with mother-of-pearl set near. Through the archway the sea rolled gently without making an advance. Heavy hangings had been tied back to bring this vista into view. How perfect the moment—to lie like a goddess, every wish attended to before she thought of it herself.

She got up quietly so as not to bring a servant to her side, slipped into her chiton and walked past the marble portico toward the sand, to touch with a toe Aphrodite's foam. A small Maltese puppy chased after her and she found a stick to throw for it. The tiny creature brought it back obediently, tail wagging. "I like you better than those lean Ibiza hounds," she said, picking it up. It was soft and well-tended—like everything here, she thought.

She set the little dog down and waded into the warm water. It washed so delightfully around her ankles that she decided on a swim. Leaving her chiton on the shore, she raced into the sea and stroked toward the jetty on her right. She swam with a school of small yellow-banded fish. A transparent organism trailed by, propelling itself with the opening and closing of an attached parasol. It, too, was not larger than her hand. She turned and floated, kicking her feet lazily, to rest before making the swim across to the far side of the jetty. She was enjoying the rhythmic motions of her body when she was attracted by a commotion on the pier; people seemed to be signaling her. She swam closer and could see that she was being waved back.

Then she realized—she had left the women's side, that part of the sand and sea, those rooms and baths reserved for women. She had trespassed. She was not free to swim where she chose, or wander as she wished. This knowledge came as an unpleasant shock. Even in Pyrrha she had come and gone freely, finding her own spots for solitude in which to work at her songs. Periander of Corinth had called her the songbird of Lesbos, but here in Syracuse her wings were clipped. She had failed to understand that the women were jailed in their side of the house. This was untenable.

Treading water a minute longer, she decided not to understand the signaling from shore but continue her swim. She passed wide of the jetty and the comic figures jumping up and down. What a scene she had raised by infringing on the men's beach. She deliberately struck toward this shore that was off-limits to her, coming in naked.

Kerkolas himself had been summoned. He stood with his servants, one of whom stepped forward with a cloak in which she could both dry and cover herself.

She approached Kerkolas and smiled fully into his face.

He did not smile back.

"What a delightful swim." She found she panted slightly.

Kerkolas motioned the servants out of earshot. "Sappho," he began, and began again: "Sappho, are you sea nymph or woman?"

She laughed, shaking water from her dark hair.

"Sappho," he began for the third time.

He is uncomfortable about saying it, she thought; good.

"Did you notice the women in the streets of the city had slaves at their side? In Syracuse women, even married women, do not go abroad unaccompanied."

"Very picturesque. I am fascinated by quaint customs."

"I think, Sappho," Kerkolas was gently reproving, "that you misunderstand me on purpose."

"Oh? You mean this in some way applies to me? But surely not. I am a visitor."

"You left the women's section in your adventurous swim and have landed yourself on the men's beach. Something, I might add, that has never happened before."

"And what is my punishment for this social blunder? My head on a platter?"

"It is, Lady, with your permission, that this evening at a small party I am giving in your honor, you play some of your compositions. I was never so enchanted as the night you sang in the house of Periander, which I have visited many times before and found quite unexceptional."

"I will sing in your house tonight. And now swim back with me."

He smiled. "I cannot. You see, I know the rules. I am not a visitor."

"But it is your house!"

"I'll swim straight out with you. Then you will go to your side and I to mine."

She dropped her cloak and dashed into the sea before him. He left his himation with his thrall and plunged after her. "You swim well," he said, "like a boy."

"I swim well," she laughed back at him, "like a girl."

"I have heard the women of Lesbos are brought up in a very free manner."

"We are not slaves or servants, if that's what you mean."

"Are other Lesbian women like you?"

"No one is like me—I am Sappho. But their lives are not bounded. They come and go as any other."

"And swim where they will?"

"We may not have the organs of men. But we have arms and legs. And heads on our shoulders. Now I will go back to the women's side and try to behave myself." With that, she jumped on him, pushing him under, then got well away so he could not return the treatment.

He came up spluttering.

She dived and broke surface too far away for further conversation.

Poles had been rammed into the sand shore and awnings stretched across them to keep off the sun, and there she dined, Niobe bringing honey cookies, fruits, and chilled wine. Her childhood by the sea came back to her. She remembered her swing in the garden and her little cart pulled by a pair of nanny goats, and that she left it all to search out shells and stand on the spray rocks. It was a different sea in Eresos, one that gathered with passion to dash itself against the shore. But the smell of brine-encrusted tangles, Poseidon's ropes, was the same, with berries inedible for humankind but from his deep kingdom. She picked up her instrument.

> Come, holy tortoiseshell, my lyre,
> and become a poem

Half-remembered things kept coming to her mind, and Niobe allowed no interruptions while she sang. So Kerkolas, coming to the entrance of the women's quarter, was obliged to wait. When Sappho laid aside her strings, she was told her host was detained outside the doors. Kerkolas bowed as she waved him in.

"You are so tall," she complained, "it seems you are bending down to me."

"I? Condescend to Sappho?"

"Tell me," she asked pertly, "are you allowed on the women's side?"

"When I am invited."

"I do not invite you then. I wish to see the other side."

"It is my intention to show it to you. All houses here are laid out in much the same way. You will notice that they face south for sun in winter. While in summer the colonnades outside provide shade. Essential things we store, the produce from the fields my servants place in jars, while fish is smoked and hung. The coolest spot is reserved for wine."

"Do you press your own?"

"Some we press. But for the most part it is imported, as you shall see tonight. The wealth of the home is in its fine vases, sculptures, and tapestries, so they are placed in the most secure room."

She exclaimed at the collection of musical instruments: an Egyptian sistrum, a large sambyke—and on a simikion she counted thirty-four strings. She touched a kithara with tentative finger, wondering what notes could be coaxed from it. Pausing again before a barbitos lyre, she was more bold and plucked a resonant sound. Partly hidden, leaning against the wall, was a santir encrusted in gold.

Kerkolas, following her glance, said, "From Persia, perhaps beyond."

Not large or imposing, its proportions appealed to her. Trying it, she made a face. "It badly wants tuning."

Moving ahead of him to another part of the room, she came upon a stiff stone figure about which there was much power. Standing before it, Sappho concluded, "This is made by some older race." Her attention was caught next by a battered sea chest. "And what does this hold?"

"Parchment scrolls and a book bound in iron." He opened the chest and she looked inside, reverently lifting the book, the first she had ever seen. She was familiar with lines impressed on a single sheet, but never bound together. She studied the words that were in columns, but did not know them.

"It is written in some strange tongue."

"And what do they write down?"

"Who knows? No one here can make it out."

Sappho continued thoughtfully to examine this wonder, noticing how the semitransparent papyrus was pasted together, and puzzling over the mysterious words run on without demarcation. "It may be the work of some great poet of whom we know nothing."

"Most likely it is a farmer drawing up his accounts."

She laughed, placing the book carefully back in the chest.

"Sappho," Kerkolas said impulsively, "I do not want you to hurry in finding a suitable place for yourself. I hope to keep you as long as possible as my guest-friend."

"I thank you, Kerkolas of Andros. Then I will follow our Aeolian custom. You shall give me dinner this night. Thereafter during my stay I shall provide for myself and those who are with me."

"And you will not hurry to find a villa?"

"It is always nice to be settled, but I will not hurry." She gave him her hand in friendship, and he clasped it with ardor.

It seemed Kerkolas invited all Syracuse to meet the exiled poet of Lesbos. Her songs were a craze here. Everyone had been repeating them for months, and each arriving ship brought new ones. That she was a woman they looked on as a strange miracle. The gods, who are ever capricious, had put genius into a female, and who could say why?

This female Homer did not write in the old-fashioned style. Her words revealed her, and through her they knew themselves. Through her they saw not the gargantuan world of heroes and monsters, but a natural world. Sappho described accurately what she saw, and she knew how to look. Nature was her teacher, Nature and her own untouched heart. Her virginity surprised everyone and was the subject of endless debates. How did one who had not known a man know such passion? Had she secret lovers? What about Alkaios? It was said that he was willing enough but she would not have him.

Kerkolas was congratulated on all sides on his good luck in making the crossing with her and securing her as a guest-friend for his house. It was rumored she was very wealthy, others said she was quite poor. Some said she was a revolutionary who had plotted the overthrow of Melanchros, that she and her brother had a hand in the murder of Mysilos, former Tyrant of Lesbos. The allegation was brought up that she, her brother, and a co-conspirator had paid for the deed with Lydian gold.

A dangerous woman, one they would not allow their wives to consort with, but whom they looked forward to meeting themselves. They would boast of knowing her, although they agreed that an intellectual woman could not be completely respectable. Her swim to the men's side of the pier was already talked of in the city. Some thought the act one of bravado, others of defiance. "She is determined to prove that artists are not subject to rules." A few voices pleaded her ignorance: "She does not know our customs." But what were customs to a revolutionary who sang so prettily of flowers?

Sappho had no desire to be the baffling personality she was. Opposing forces had always dwelt in her. Sometimes she listened to the fastidious side of her character. At other times she was seized by some dark, unfathomable being, and gave song to it because there was no resisting.

To prepare for her presentation into Syracusan society, she spent the afternoon in the complicated rite of toiletry. She must look as splendid as possible for the sake of Aeolian Lesbos. She was bathed, hennaed, oiled, perfumed, pedicured, and manicured; flowers were braided into her hair, bracelets snapped around wrist and ankle. When all ministrations were done and her women stepped back, she consulted her mirror. She remembered her mother's comment—"You have a sweet smile." Beautiful you are not, she told herself, adding—but you are Sappho.

She had little idea of the idolatry in which she was held. She knew her work was known, but the craze for it, and for glimpses of herself, was something as yet unimagined.

When she entered the great hall it was light as day. A fire blazed, on which flesh would shortly be spitted, and perfumed torches flared from brackets on the walls. Many of the artistic objects she had seen in the afternoon had been brought into the room, including curved marble benches on which several persons could sit. The guests, all male, lounged both indoors and out. An oboe player, a girl of perhaps fourteen, was being carried naked on the shoulders of one of the company. Sappho had heard about this game in Corinth. He who outdid the others in the number of trips back and forth claimed her for the night.

But even the man with the oboist stopped where he was, the babble of voices died away. It was she, she of Lesbos.

Kerkolas was immediately by her side. He made no attempt to introduce her, he simply announced her and led her to the hearth where the sacrifice stood, a boar with feet shackled in gold whose horns were gilded and garlanded. Kerkolas cut the bristles from the animal, as he began his oration to Zeus, then expertly slit its throat. Slaves drained the blood and it was poured out. The carcass was bound to the spit and turned. Lesbian wine was brought and as Sappho drank from the cup extended to her, she found her name and one of her poems inscribed. She smiled over the rim at Kerkolas.

As she lounged on pillows and panther skins, cups were raised to her and her name called out thrice before any drank. "I thank you friends," she said loudly, looking at Kerkolas, "and would that every exile knew happiness such as this."

There was foot-stamping and hand-clapping approval of her remark. Then the first tables were brought, salt fish from the Black Sea, and oysters piled high, with nuts and fruits sweet as nectar. After wine and before the next course, slaves brought the santir she had admired. "It is yours," said her host.

Sappho inclined her head, accepting it, but she called for her lyre, which had seen the first exile with her. Her hands knew its strings, which seemed extensions of her fingers. She spoke to the nine sisters: "Daughters of Zeus, I greet you. Add passion to my song."

It was her intention to meet the most damaging rumors boldly by singing the song that led to her exile. All was hushed as she sang in her low, clear voice:

> Gold is the child of Zeus,
> neither moth nor worm devours it
> and it overpowers the strongest
> of mortal minds

Wild applause erupted in the hall. For this she must wander the wine seas and the world? Pittakos was an old woman to think a girl like this was implicated in murder! These sentiments flew from table to table.

Now that she had set before them her statement, she plied them with:

> *It was summer when I found you*
> *in the meadow long ago*
> *And the golden vetch*
> *was growing by the shore*

Her poetry shed radiance on whatever it touched. The Aeolian dialect, soft and exotic to the ears of her listeners, and the manner, reticent and unaffected, caused each to feel she sang to him alone. As always her body crouched against her instrument, while voice and string were one sound.

The wine passed yet another time, requests were called out: "Though few . . . !" "Upon what eyes . . . !" "I yearn and I seek . . . !" "O sweet tongued . . . !" "They say that Leda once . . . !"

Her instrument quickened with the assault of her fingers, and her voice accentuated the intimate meter. Singing of Leto, she recalled not the girl, but the pain she had known then. Line by line she offered up what she had and what she was. Yet, like herself, it was elusive. One thought one had hold of it, only to have it slip away. Was it her phrasing that made it unique, or the abrupt changes of mood? Sentences striking like the flick of a lash sent an amorous quiver through the guests, yet the next instant she called to mind such ordinary things that they wondered if they had heard correctly. She wove patterns of sound that entangled emotions. At times she questioned, and the answers leapt from her in flame. Finally she put by the lyre, bending her head to remove the silken sling.

There was silence. Sappho had sung. An hour before they had been interested in her dress, her diminutive stature, the way her hair was done, her ornaments, the expression on her face, and the face itself. Now those were externals. None of it mattered. Sappho had sung.

They had experienced something intangible, Sappho with her simple words, her soft enunciation, had reached these sophisticated hearts, for it was part holy religion. They felt both purified and strangely stirred: purified of old sins, yet desiring to find such passions as she knew, who was neither maid nor woman. Her eyes had the look of one who has drunk poppy juice, the pupils swallowed the iris to the rims.

They looked and saw. "Divine madness overcomes her," they whispered. "She is a treasure," said one official to another, "an acquisition for our city."

Over the next several days a number of people busied themselves on her behalf. Sappho was told of a villa on the sea, which was surprisingly inexpensive. She did not question her luck. Sappho never looked too hard at luck. Taking ceremonious leave of Kerkolas, she moved her small retinue.

Her new home was neither as large nor as richly appointed as the one in which she had been a guest, but it lay not too far distant, and the exposure was the same, the courtyard joining the sand and the sea fringing the edge of the property. She twirled through every room, her arms thrown over her head, calling on her sisters, the nine Muses, by name to share her home.

The first day she took the bundle of rags into the garden and knelt on the ground with a small digging tool. A pergola, she decided, would be erected here for her vines to climb. Perhaps after several harvests there might be enough grapes to press.

In the midst of her digging, she reached out suddenly with one hand for support, and the trowel fell to the ground. Homesickness gripped her so that she saw the double harbor of Mitylene, the long agora on the peninsula, the steep climb past groves of olives, the winding path leading to her aunt's house and garden. The entrance to Heaven guarded by the Seasons seemed not as good to her. Her tears spilled onto the earth.

It was for no fault! For no fault! She remembered her mother's premonition. What if something should happen? She prayed to Demeter that her mother would clasp her in her arms again. Aloud she spoke to Kleis: "Mother, I know I have been a difficult daughter, stubborn, willful, and unwed. But the gods will reunite us. They will. They must!"

The outburst over, she retrieved her tool and tamped down the earth firmly, her dainty nails that her women worked over grimy and black. Surveying her planting, she was satisfied. Now the small Aeolic island would be part of her, she would stand here as her vines grew, looking across the sea toward Lesbos, remembering how it lay in the crook of the Ionian coast, remembering the five cities, remembering . . .

Once the whole family made a journey traveling north to the hot medicinal springs of Thermae under the patronage of Artemis. She had romped with her brothers, splashing, swimming, diving. And there had been a pretty festival of animals—so long ago, so lost.

Gifts kept arriving—from Kerkolas, the magnificent Egyptian harp. She set it in a place of honor and worked an hour tuning its strings until the pitch pleased her. The Archon sent furniture, a bed, chairs, an Arabian ottoman worked in leather. There were silk hangings and Meletus wool for her women to spin. Carian honey was brought by black slaves, sponges from Rhodes for her bath, saffron too, sweet oils, scent of musk, Corinthian pottery, figs, raisins, an assortment of berries. Large and small, all were tributes to her singing at Kerkolas's party.

Her favorite gift was the little Maltese dog she had played with on the sand shore. Yet in a way it disturbed her. Eyes were always on her; she was forever observed and her actions reported, her preference in scent, her pleasure in the puppy.

She knew it was meant kindly, and the presents were princely. I am fortunate beyond women, she told herself. But she was conscious of a curious resentment. She felt keenly the loss of privacy. Another irritant was the isolation from her sex.

In Syracuse the ladies did not dine with the men. They were kept secluded, as in Asia and Athens. Sappho was in an odd position. Though a lady born, and of a family and breeding equal to any, she was as segregated from wives and daughters as the naked oboe player. Had she lowered herself by entertaining? Was she considered no better than a courtesan, a wandering bard? Did they not know whose daughter she was, Skamandronymos's, of the house of Orestes? She was being put on a par with successful gladiators—idolized, lionized, but not invited into homes unless the women were first shut in their quarters, well away from where the men caroused and played backgammon or Cottalos. In this game the contestants threw the dregs of their wine at a target, pronouncing the name of the one they wanted to sleep with that night. "I throw for . . ." was the cry. And the one who made the bull's-eye got his wish, either youth or courtesan according to his pleasure.

Another favorite pastime was to heat a small area of the floor by brazier and push naked slaves onto the spot, fastening them with ankle chains. At first they hopped and jumped about, then they brought each

other down, the stronger lying on the body of the weaker. Strenuous copulations took place as the one whose buttocks burned strove to fling off the form pinning her. Sappho recalled the tears of merriment in the eyes of the spectators.

When she complained to her friend Kerkolas that she was invited to such spectacles, he replied solemnly, "I suppose, Sappho, that you are considered too brilliant, too famous, too unique, to be respectable."

"But I am respectable. There is no blot against my name, and my lineage is as old as any. I find the constant company of men coarse and their amusements revolting. I long for the gentler companionship of my own sex. What must I do to be accepted by them, Kerkolas? I ask you to advise me."

He gave the matter thought. "Well then," he said slowly, "do not go about unaccompanied. Make sure always to have your eunuch with you, and a slave or two. And accept no invitation at which Cottalos is played. I will inquire and tell you which functions you may attend. Even so, you will be the only woman. That in itself is cause for talk."

"Kerkolas, the first time that I ever saw Cottalos played was in your home."

"I was at fault," he acknowledged.

She shook her head. "It doesn't matter. There is no way that I see. I am marooned from my own sex and may not even talk with them, or watch them twine flowers in their hair or hear their pretty laughter. I feel at times no better than one of your apes on display."

Kerkolas pondered what she said, but did not answer her. Several days later he addressed the issue, adopting an offhand manner. "There is a way," he said casually, "by which you can gain acceptability among female society, and that, of course, is to get married."

"Married! You would have me bind myself to free myself?"

Kerkolas's languor deserted him; he seized both her hands and spoke quickly, as though afraid she would not hear him out. "I have loved you, Sappho, since the day that Sea and Sky contended and you stood in the waist of my ship, your hair streaked and plastered against your face, sea and rain hurled against you. And a look about you I can neither describe nor forget. It wasn't defiance of the elements, but more a joining with them. Your eyes mirrored their fierceness, your lips spread to them as to a lover.

"I have not mentioned marriage for fear it would cost me your friendship. But as my wife, you could have the life you want. You would no longer be an outsider."

His voice dropped softly, persuasively. "And I would cherish you as though a goddess had agreed to mate with me." He did not relinquish her hand but drew her close to him.

She listened to all he said, rehearsing her reply in her mind before she spoke. "I do not know how to answer you, for I have not had your thoughts, Kerkolas. But I will think on what you have said and consult my Muses. Until you have my answer, you have my thanks for the honor you have done me."

"How well you speak," he said somewhat ruefully, "like a young sage. It is for me to thank you. And I do, Sappho, that you consider being my wife." He left quickly and gracefully.

He was a man of breeding and culture. Yet her heart felt nothing and her mind was not troubled over him as it had been over Leto. She liked looking at him. He had the body of an athlete and the easy assurance of position and wealth. He was, she knew, much handsomer than she. His eyes were a dark blue and well spaced. But it was not of his eyes she thought. Rather she continued to brood, feeling keenly her removal from other women; she missed the dulcimer sound of their softer voices, the gaiety and the lighthearted confidences that passed between them.

She revolved Kerkolas's proposal from every angle. It seemed odd to her that freedom should go hand in hand with slavery. Yet, unless one bound oneself to a man, one was regarded with suspicion. With no protector, one's name could be bandied about with impunity. To be a wife among other young wives seemed good to her. She decided to regularize her position. It would be a challenge to discover if a man could rouse her. Until now she had channeled her needs and longings into art. But she knew herself to be unfulfilled and restless.

As Kerkolas's wife, all doors would open, and her own she intended to fling wide. She would make their home a gathering place for poets and philosophers. Artists of all description would be welcomed as guest-friends. On thinking it through, it seemed to her the best life she could attain, with maximum freedom, was as a married woman.

When she saw Kerkolas next, it completely slipped her mind that she had neglected to inform him of her decision. He spoke to her of the arts of navigation and astronomy, then, without sequence, lectured on Samian marble carving. "It is the finest ever seen, the statues are turned on lathes like column bases . . . Sappho!" He fell on his knees before her and buried his face in the folds of her robe.

She looked at him, stunned, then she recalled. "Oh, the marriage. Do get up, Kerkolas, how can you prepare for it in this ridiculous position?"

He bounded up, his arms enfolding her.

"Gently," Sappho said, pushing him away. She smelled him under the scent; it was the smell she had recoiled uneasily from when the tattered Lesbian troops came off the first boats to take possession of their homes, their goods, their cattle, and their wives—it was the strong smell of the male.

She thought she should explain herself to him. "I will not be called 'wife of Kerkolas' as the custom is here. I must preserve myself. You understand that I am Sappho of Lesbos. You do understand this, Kerkolas?"

"You are unique and precious. If I had a diamond, would I call it 'stone of Kerkolas'? I would say diamond."

But she was not satisfied; his strong embrace had unsettled her. "I am twenty-one years old. And I have prized my virginity, although it is perhaps a peculiar virginity."

"Peculiar?" He stepped back from her.

"No man has violated it," she assured him. "Yet from the time I was a child, slaves massaged the mound of Aphrodite if I cried or was out of sorts. There is no part of me that has not been stroked with sweet oil."

"Is this your confession?" He laughed. "Do you think it is different in Andros? We Aeolians are half Asiatic."

"How can you say that?"

"We share with the Asian their sensuality. It could not be otherwise. We know their headlands and shores as well as the fingers of our hands. Standing on any Lesbian hill, one can see the Lydian coast."

"It is so." A sudden wave of nostalgia made her feel very close to this man from her part of the world.

The almighty gods look down and for entertainment watch the human spectacle below. It was not an Olympic or a Pythian year, but it was the year Sappho, she of Lesbos, took a husband, Kerkolas the Andrian, whose single vessel brought him 1,640 talents annually, and he owned a fleet of twenty.

The citizens of Syracuse made the wedding an excuse to outdo their neighbors, the Sybarites. That famed Achaean colony on the Gulf of Tarentum had never been festooned with such exotic flowers as now Syracuse was. Bowers stretched across the arcades, doors, and archways in honor of the wedding.

Sappho was concerned to send a missive to her mother. She busied herself with a wax tablet which she impressed onto papyri transparent as silk, and this she sent to Mitylene by one of Kerkolas's sleek ships. It pleased her to think how happy the news would make her mother. To marry into a princely house was her mother's dearest wish for her, and one poor Kleis had often despaired of.

When the appointed day arrived, Sappho was as ice. She sat statue-still while Niobe twisted her hair into long ringlets using heated irons. Even as Athene is armed for battle, so Niobe arms me, she thought, looking at herself in her glass. Immediately she wondered why such a simile occurred to her. Can it be that I still desire my maidenhood? But she could not remain virgin forever. The vow made in high Pyrrha was unrealistic. At twenty-one she was as close to the age of many widows as to most brides.

It was her wedding day, and her thoughts returned to her mother. If only Kleis could be here for the ceremony, could see her house ablaze with flowers of every hue. Sappho herself had attended to their arrangement.

. . . the hyacinth's brightness blinding to the eyes

She loved to handle flowers, bury her face in their sweetness, touch the fragile petals, place them where each showed to advantage, so that your heart caught in your throat at their perfection.

Kerkolas's much larger and grander house, she was confident, would not match these garlands of hers. One has to know and love flowers before they respond to you. She tried to keep her thoughts on the preparations, on the beautiful epithalamion she had composed, the lovely aubade to be sung by the chorus of girls.

She would not let herself think of what must follow. She called for the wine pourers a final time, instructing them again how much water should be in the mixing bowls. The wedding guests would remain sober, at least at her house. And at Kerkolas's villa there was to be no vulgar nonsense of waving her bloodied undergarment at intoxicated revelers. Kerkolas had agreed that crushed berries should be placed in the bridal chamber. He could dip into that as much as he pleased.

She captured her thoughts once more, pulling them into the present, but they would not stay there. She felt much as she had when Leto married. Except now, *she*, Sappho, was to be the sacrificial lamb.

It was a ridiculous comparison, and she knew it. Why did her thoughts keep sliding beyond her control? The way of her people was to seek the mean, the middle path, especially where the emotions were concerned. This ideal was needed by a passionate race, who, like Thales, wanted to think all the thoughts in the world—and, like herself, invent new ways of saying them. She prayed to the gods to steady her:

> O Hecate, gold-glittering
> handmaiden of Aphrodite

But she could not keep on with it. Her thoughts tended to scatter like startled birds, taking a dozen directions. Yes, the epithalamion was a pearl. It was worth getting married to have written it. She began to hum it under her breath, then remembered that was bad luck and stopped in dismay. She recalled an early poem that was so much part of her:

> I long and I yearn

Was it for this day she yearned? Her heart fluttered with some secret knowledge it did not impart to her. Had Leto felt like this before the wedding feast? Had they all? All the small white faces to whom she had sung? Were they frightened and alone, separated from their childhood companions at the spinning wheel and washing springs, from their friends of the lute and the dance, from their garland-weaving playmates?

She reminded herself that she was making a new life with Kerkolas, her friend. It had all been thought out with utmost care. Her reasons for this marriage were sound. She was no flighty girl, but a woman who, facing the inequities that bound her sex, traded freedom for freedom.

If only Khar were here to lead the young men of the chorus, if only Alkaios had written the nuptial songs . . . Surely some god or daimone had possession of her—this loss of control was not like her. The splendid bridal raiment was girded about her; it fell sheer, the popular wet look in rainbow hues. If it was a daimone, why had not the bath in holy water sent it from her? Niobe was plaiting roses in her hair. It struck her that Niobe had been silent and withdrawn during these preparations.

Am I to worry what my slave thinks of my marriage? Sappho asked herself distractedly. The three bells above the arch of her door began to ring with much rope pulling. "Hymenaeus! The bridegroom draws near!"

Sappho waved her women back and, without glancing at Niobe, went alone to the entry threshold. When Kerkolas dismounted—his hair in a wreath, his white mantle falling to golden sandals—he looked a young god. Her fears fell away and she welcomed him to her house.

He responded with the traditional "Hail to thee, O bride, O Sappho!"

"Hail to thee, Kerkolas, son of noble Archias. Hail, O bridegroom!" And she continued the ode she had composed to honor him:

> To what, dear bridegroom,
> may I rightly liken thee?
> To a slender sapling
> do I most rightly liken thee

Her phrases dazzled the company. It was true elegance, yet deceptively simple, even as the bride herself.

The wine-mixers poured according to their mistress's orders, and the drink that makes glad the hearts of men flowed. Sacrifice was made. Kerkolas caught her eye and smiled his approval.

Everything was tasteful beyond criticism. There had been more lavish feasts—his own would be—but none was more correct, or served with more grace. Between the bringing and taking of tables there were ewers of water for rinsing the fingers, and slave girls knelt before the guests, offering their long perfumed hair as towels.

Toward sunset Kerkolas led her from her home. She stepped into his bedecked chariot, whose matched bays with cyclamen-braided manes pranced and danced. The dancing horses of Syracuse were famous. But Kerkolas confided to her, laughing, that they were an embarrassment when ridden into battle. Wedding torches, scented and flaming, formed a path to Kerkolas's villa, where they alighted, passing under a canopy of rare herbs and twisted ivy. A flute sounded, confetti fell on them and strains of the Hymenaean were taken up:

> *Hammer up the rafters now*
> *At the wedding.*
> *Raise them high, carpenter-men,*
> *At the wedding.*
> *The bridegroom is as tall as Ares,*
> *At the wedding.*
>
> *Far taller than the tallest men,*
> *At the wedding.*
> *Towering as does the Lesbian poet*
> *At the wedding.*
> *Over the poets of other countries,*
> *At the wedding.*

As they approached the traditional household gods, the maidens held hands. It was the signal. Kerkolas seized Sappho in his arms and carried her to the wedding chamber. Although he flung the lock quickly, the pounding commenced at once. Kerkolas set her down and they stood on either side of the door. It sounded as though the merrymakers intended to break it down. But the girls began the song she had coached them in, a tribute to virgin girlhood, the young men answering that it is better far to be a wife and mother.

A bed had been placed in the chamber, heaped like a shrine with softest petals, the silken underdraperies touched with royal perfume. Candlelight flickered from a discreetly placed wall bracket. Outside, the girls began a new song:

> *And we maidens spend all the night at this door,*
> *singing of the love between you, blessed bridegroom,*
> *and your bride of the violet scented breast. And*
> *when the dawn is come and you arise and depart, may*

the great god Hermes direct your feet
whither you shall find no more ill-luck
than we tonight shall find sleep

Kerkolas took a step toward her and removed the coan veil, letting it fall to the floor. The quince had been prepared and in silence they each took a bite. In a golden cage two sparrows hopped, symbols of fertility, birds sacred to Aphrodite.

Kerkolas reached to unfasten her peplos. His hands were very large. She had never noticed how large his hands were. They undid her dress. Her small person was before his glance. There was no hair on her body, and the points of her breasts were rouged. At sight of this, he divested himself of his bridegroom's white, and unruly desire swelled his organ. The phallus carried in procession during the festival of Dionysos, the phallus as ornament, as votive, was one thing, but the flesh raised to pierce her was enormous, a weapon of horn.

"You madden me." He pressed her against him, and she began to struggle. Cyclops and Enceladus of the Hundred Arms had hold of her. Sky collided with Earth and brought her down. Sappho beat with small ineffectual fists. Sky smashed upon her in a battle that caused hot blood to run down her legs.

It was rape. He forced his organ into the center of her body. She battled frenziedly, pushing at what she conceived to be a he-ass, the most lustful of all creatures. The agony of her penetrated hymen coincided with the sobbing notes of a nightingale. Or was it herself sobbing in fury? Her hips attempting to swivel away excited him further; he thrust deeper. She could not believe this terrible invasion of her person, this ramming, this humiliation, legs spread, blood everywhere. Her dignity was gone. He had mastered her.

Outside the door she could hear the young voices:

Come dear girls,
let us cease our singing,
for day is nigh at hand

Even as she was violated, she swore to keep her mind and her thought virgin, never to allow them to be trespassed against, never to share them. He thought he had found and ploughed and made the very core of her his own preserve. He had not. Sappho bloodied was virgin still.

Her husband fell back beside her, breathing hard, well pleased. His proud organ shriveled. It was laughable. He had spent himself on her, and she was not spent at all, only wounded. Women, in this moment, were stronger than men.

"Wipe yourself with your chiton, Sappho, that I may toss it out the door."

"Have we not in the chamber an infusion of red berries for that?"

"You think I want to be a laughingstock? You think men cannot tell the difference between juice and a girl's maiden blood?"

Sappho got up as though to obey him, but instead poured a ewer of water over her extremities.

"What have you done?" Kerkolas cried out in protest.

"I have washed."

"Oh, very well." He ripped a bit of linen that had been under her and, opening the door a crack, waved it. There was a resounding cheer from the males. The rite was accomplished. The penis, the life-giver, had subdued the poet Sappho.

She did not close her eyes that night. She was on fire against this bull, this he-goat that slumbered in a state of unconsciousness beside her. She looked directly into the gleaming eye of Selene, the moon goddess. Sappho spoke to her, mind-to-mind, saying: "I see now that I am not as other women, or the race should have ended before this. I cannot endure such profanation. I cannot, I who value all that is delicate and dainty since my childhood, cannot tolerate the violence of this weapon upon my flesh. It must be that I am other than woman.

"I see the gods made only one of me as an experiment—poet I am, who finds my own gentler sex more fair, more graceful, and more desirable. Yet I do not wish to play the part that a man does. But I confess, I have tonight a longing for my Leto, to caress her with tender fingers, to kiss with my lips the swelling of the apex, to bring her joy and fulfillment, while receiving her pink tongue into my mouth and bestowing touches that bring not a bloody night, but a moist warm one. . . . Only by now Leto is a wife who wallows in the thighs of the wheat-haired peasant and does his bidding and is whacked on her backside in passing. A child pulls on the roseate teats and drags them down, no round, soft swelling now, but bags. And when her man has made her old and ugly, he picks up with a pretty boy.

"Passion was given me, the gods know; it goes hand in hand with Erato, violet-wreathed Muse of Poetry. But coarseness and crudity and the invasion of my body seem the grossest kind of love. I dream in another manner—of an insinuating hand, a light stroking, lips pressed . . . everywhere!

"This is why it is called the Night of Secrets. For not until you have experienced your wedding night do you know what kind of love it is you long for. And then it is too late. For what can I do now? I am trapped as surely as any small creature caught in a cruel snare. Sing woe! Sing woe!"

Gradually Sappho gave up her fantasies. She knew now, having gained entrance into the Syracusan society she so longed for, that she would never be at home in it. She became acquainted with the unmarried girls, whom she taught wedding songs. But they were a tightly bound group, having known each other since childhood, and it was hard to find a place among them. The matrons, on the other hand, were busy with young families. They chattered of cutting teeth, how to reduce swelling in infant gums, of colic and first steps.

She realized reluctantly there was to be no close attachment with her own sex. As before, she attended parties given by her husband. Too often, cocks and quails were set at each other, fighting until they were torn into remnants of still-living flesh. It is true that her husband's Persian cupbearer offered the goblet charmingly with three fingers, but during the same evening a stammerer, as a forfeit, was made to sing, and a bald man mimed combing his hair. Sappho found this adolescent humor so boring that, when they brought out the wicker baskets of dice, she would wander into the room that held the carved chest. Very often she removed the iron-bound book, touching its petal-thin pages.

Kerkolas's ships returned laden after a voyage to Kyprus, and he gave a feast to which the Archon was invited. This was the first occasion since their marriage two months past that Sappho was invited to hear her own songs. Kerkolas did not feel it proper for her to perform them. "That puts you in the position of an entertainer."

"An oboe player?" she suggested.

"It is more seemly," he replied, "to let others sing."

For the most part her verse was adequately presented by a professional bard. But this evening the cadence was delivered faultily. Although her lips did not move, Sappho had been repeating the poem along with the singer. At the failure in accuracy, she broke off.

Despair filled her. Everywhere in the civilized world her work was sung, but how could she be assured it was done correctly? She was obsessed by this thought, tormented at dependence on any wandering minstrel.

Then it occurred to her . . . Kerkolas kept accounts in writing, carefully recording the talents of gold and the worth of items from each voyage. And physicians frequently wrote out remedies, nostrums, and treatments. Why not use writing to set down her songs as she sang them? Alkaios had done so from high Pyrrha. Even Pittakos had written out his laws, impressing them on wood for all to read. Would not poetry be a better use of writing? Why not a book of poetry? The thought was surely from her nine sisters, and she rose from bed to spill wine to them.

She had insisted on a night chamber separate from her husband's. How glad she was of that now. There had been times in her loneliness when she wished that the desire to visit her would come more often to Kerkolas. But he was occupied with his pretty cupbearer. She wanted not Kerkolas, but any distraction. And now suddenly there was a secret purpose to which to dedicate herself. And for it she needed lonely and unsleeping nights.

She went to the room that held the chest and, setting aside a tray containing her husband's accounts, carefully removed the stylus. She had last used it in preparing the wedding message for her mother, and had an understanding of the technique. It would be a simple matter to transfer a poem onto rolls of papyrus.

She set everything up as though she were a marketplace scribe and pressed out her latest verse:

Love, the wild heart

Hours later, when she crept into bed, sleep leapt on her.

Now that she had found herself again, it was time to broach her long-cherished plan to Kerkolas. She made a treaty with her husband. "Kerkolas, I want to say something to you."

"Speak then, Sappho."

"It is these endless parties. You waste your time at them. You are a distinguished man in Syracuse. We could make our home a center of culture, a waystation where poets and sculptors, philosophers, persons of far-flung fame come as guest-friends. I dream of holding converse with the great minds of our time. Would this not be a better use of your leisure, husband?"

"I suppose so. Yes, of course. But I cannot give up old friendships."

"I see that, and it is reasonable, indeed loyal, of you. But let there be less cockfighting and gaming, so there can be more poetry and song."

The bargain was struck. It gratified Kerkolas to think the famous and celebrated would flock to his door. It pleased him, too, that his wife was a magnet to attract world luminaries.

The invitations left on the next vessel and, as the wait would be long, Sappho set about to regain the friendship of her husband. She rhymed for him a song of his untold riches, writing of the things beyond price that came from his vessels:

> *I love delicate living,*
> *and for me*
> *richness and beauty*
> *belong to the desire of the sunlight*

She grew impatient. How long was it possible to wander cultivated gardens and sit by splashing fountains? She sang softly to herself.

> *Never, O Peace,*
> *have I found thee*
> *more irksome!*

The poet Alkman was the first guest to respond to her invitation. Alkman was a Lydian, born at Sardis, who migrated to Sparta and wrote love songs to a golden-haired girl named Megalostrata. But that was many years ago. When he visited Sappho, he was a fat, jovial, obscene fellow—and what was worse, the servants came in consternation to tell Sappho that her guest was full of lice. Alkman fit better into Kerkolas's parties than hers. After his third goblet of wine, he unwrapped his himation and, belly jiggling, danced "The Feast of the Naked Youth," which he had composed twenty years before and which the young warriors of Sparta still chanted. His capering was so odious that it was impossible to imagine the beauty of four hundred Adonises. Gone with his dignity was his love. Megalostrata, he confided, had grown as fat and unlovely as himself. Nevertheless, he had a treat for Sappho, the latest paeon circulated by Alkaios:

> *He doesn't love me, you say?*
> *I don't suppose fish or wine love me either,*
> *but I take pleasure in them all the same*

Sappho clapped her hands and was about to kiss him when she remembered the lice. "Yes, that is Alkaios," and she gave thanks to whatever gods protected him, allowing him love and laughter and the visitation of the Muses. How close to him she felt.

Another poet arriving from Sparta was Polymnatos, who was also old, obese, and originally Ionian. He was a fine musician. Composing for flute, he worked with semitones and used the enharmonic scale with great effectiveness. He was director of the music school at Sparta, as Terpander had been before him. Terpander was an idol of Sappho's because he added the high octave string to the seven-stringed lyre.

"I grew up playing it," Sappho said, thinking of home.

"Did you know," Polymnatos went on, "that Hermes invented it, using a tortoiseshell? He taught Orpheus to play, and when Orpheus was killed by the Thracian women, his lyre along with his head fell into the sea. . . ."

Sappho finished the tale: "And was washed by the waves onto Lesbos, where a fisherman found it and brought the lyre to Terpander. I often wonder if he brought him the head too," and she laughed, but almost immediately grew serious.

"Did you know that Terpander was from Antissa, the town nearest Eresos? He died the year I was born."

"Why do you suppose it is," Polymnatos asked her, "that so many great poets have come from your tiny island of Lesbos?"

"Freedom," she answered without hesitation. "When it is lacking, we Lesbians go into exile . . . or are sent," she added.

They spoke of Thales and his island, Miletus, everywhere dubbed the Isle of Thought. For he continued asking strange questions. Instead of accepting his fellow man, he asked, "What is man?" as though he were more than the sum of his parts.

The poet Stesichoros of Himera, who wrote in the style of great Homer, also came to visit. But he extracted a moral from everything, and Sappho found him tedious. It was Stesichoros, however, who told her of a young pupil of Thales, one Anaximander, who had set about to draw a map of the world.

This seemed to Sappho an incredible idea, and how one would go about it she had no notion. But what she heard of the young philosopher fascinated her. Although she was scandalized by his calumny of the Moon goddess, who, he claimed, had no light of her own but borrowed light from Sun. It seemed he gave no credence to mighty Atlas, and did not believe the world was held up by anything. Anaximander didn't even espouse his master's thesis that all was water but instead envisioned a substance he called the unlimited, which was in all things, with each part moving while the whole remained unchanging and unchangeable. In the beginning, according to his theory, hot and cold were one. Then they began to separate, forming a moist center of cold. This gradually hardened to become Earth, showering out particles which became Moon, Sun, and Stars. He also preached that human life began in the sea, human infants having once been nurtured by fishlike creatures who acted as nannies.

Sappho nodded. "Men are ever inventive. However, what he says about Selene the beautiful is surely unjust. Her soft light is hers alone, nor would she steal from another. As for the rest, perhaps some god whispered into his ear. I never did think we floated on water."

Adroitly, she managed that the elderly Stesichoros return home, for she was planning a summer of fun, and was eager to dispense with his presence.

Sappho was the unquestioned social leader of Syracuse. The parties of the Lesbian songstress were famous for being based on novel ideas.

It was she who introduced forfeits into the ancient game of blindman's bluff.

No one guessed that at night she worked with waxed wooden blocks to press her poems onto sheets of papyrus. Soon she would have her book, bound even as the book from the sea chest was bound.

Polymnatos told her that he had once seen Homer written down and that Hesiod, too, had been transcribed. But he was rather disapproving: "Such a static thing as writing should be left for ledgers of business. Poetry should fly on the human voice alone."

"But if the human voice falters? Or the singer misremembers? We are at the mercy of hundreds unknown to us. How can we trust their ability or memory?"

Polymnatos was not interested in the work of scribes. He spoke of the early lyric poets, Eumelos of Corinth and Olympos of Phrygia, whose songs were still sung.

One day Kerkolas had fresh news from his captains, who had recently put in at Corinth. "It seems," Kerkolas told her, "that there was a defection in the ranks of the nobles against our late host, Periander. So, being a Tyrant, he sent a messenger asking a neighboring Tyrant to visit. The guest—I will not mention his name, other than to say he is from Asia Minor—talked long and earnestly with Periander, who told him his problem and wondered aloud how to deal with it. It seems they were walking through a field of rye and the visiting Tyrant with his walking stick flicked off the heads of the tallest tassels. Upon his visitor's departure, Periander beheaded all the leading nobles of Corinth."

"Periander?" Sappho gasped in horror. "With whom we made so merry? Who could not do enough for our comfort? Before whom I sang my brightest songs?"

"The same."

"What thymos possesses the human spirit?" She was quite distracted, for Periander was among the seven wise men of the world. But Kerkolas simply shrugged.

The dog days arrived, Sirius shone bright, and the heat was such that the nobles of the great houses removed to the caves along the shore. Awnings of bright colors were stretched overhead.

Before Sappho could enjoy the cool of the caves she had to be assured there were neither snakes nor priestesses in them, that these practices were not known in Syracuse.

In this informal setting Sappho was permitted to sing, and many gifts were laid before her in thanks. One she prized was a coin minted over two hundred years before in Lydia. It was of gold and silver mixed, with the figure of Pegasus skillfully executed on it. For even in ancient times the finest artists were employed to design coins.

A favorite picnicking place was among smooth diving rocks, below which the outline of a long-vanished city could be discerned through waving kelp. Sappho and Kerkolas, at home in the sea, swam down hand over hand against the still-standing remnants of a wall through which fish swarmed. Wide streets shimmered before their eyes; broken columns were moss-covered perches for barnacles and clustering sea anemones. When they came to the surface, Sappho said, "One never thinks of those that went before. They walked those streets, Kerkolas, lived as we do, knew the same pleasures, the same pain."

Kerkolas shook his curls from his eyes. "It is thought to be the abode of Eurynome, daughter of the ever-encircling waters of Ocean."

"I do not think so. I think people like us lived there, that they displeased the Earth-Shaker, Poseidon, who tumbled the city into the sea, and all the people with it."

She was quiet all day, pondering what she had seen.

The men were drinking and singing skolia. Kerkolas attempted to arrange a boar hunt but was voted down. It was too hot. They decided to award prizes to any who could devise a fresh amusement. The winning game involved sending for doves, whose wings they clipped. These were collected overhead in golden nets, while before them the loveliest of the slave girls were stripped naked, and when the net of birds was untied, it was their task to catch one. If any succeeded, she was to have her freedom. So the girls scrambled over the rocks, slipping, jumping, stretching, tumbling their fair bodies in ways delightful to see.

One of Kerkolas's friends handed Sappho a wonderfully wrought cup, and when the wine was drunk she saw incised on the bottom a nude male mounting a female. The young man smiled across at her, but she returned him his cup. Many guests had slipped away, some catching the slave girls before they caught the doves. Others lolled with young boys. The same youth who had given Sappho the goblet was telling her that prostitutes trained their daughters in their art. "The most gifted teach their female children through three and four generations."

She looked about for Kerkolas, but he was temporarily absent; so, too, was the Persian cupbearer. Sappho moved to another group, where the talk was of navigation, a skill which the gods had secured for man.

On the way home from this outing, Sappho rode with Kerkolas, who, anxious to be back, lashed the horses. It happened that a man darted in front of them; their chariot wheels struck him and passed over the midsection of his body. Sappho heard the rib cage give way and, looking back, saw him writhing in the dirt. "Stop, Kerkolas, stop!"

He did not so much as slow. "It was a slave. I will inquire tomorrow who the man belonged to, and make recompense."

"But he can't be left like that, he . . . turn around, Kerkolas. Surely we can do something."

"What?"

"Take him to our servants, who will look after him."

"You can be so strange at times, Sappho, that I scarcely understand you. The man was a slave."

"But he feels his pain as any would."

"There you are mistaken. One is born a slave because he has the blunted feelings and inferior mentality of a slave. They do not, I assure you, feel in the way you and I do."

"I will not ride with you again." She spoke angrily.

When they were home, she sent her people to the spot where they had run over the man. They reported he was dead.

Kerkolas made due reparation to the man's owner, and the matter should have been at an end. It wasn't. It was like something undigested in the bowels of Sappho. She barely thanked her husband for a carpet from Persia of blue and gold, which he had been at much trouble to procure for her. Almost feverishly she etched her poems at night. The characters were written in columns to be pasted together and unrolled. Several poems were in the shape of ellipses. She liked fitting the layout of the calligraphy to the mood evoked by the individual poems, and hummed as she pressed the wax. It was a task she had come to love.

———

Once again Kerkolas's sleek, high-prowed ships anchored offshore. Their cargo was evil tidings, for runners brought news that her mother was dead. As oxen receive the blow that stuns them, so Sappho stood. She was mute. She did not cry out but sank slowly to her knees.

Her women ran to lift her, but she got unsteadily to her feet and walked to her rooms. She shut herself in, locked the door with a leather thong, cut a strand of her hair, and proceeded trancelike into the garden. Standing a long moment before the transplanted vine of Eresos, she broke off branches and wove them with her hair into a funeral wreath.

When Kleis clasped her that final time, her presentiment had been true. Sappho's organs knotted together and spasms passed over her. —Mother, never in this life to feel your arms about me. Poor wandering shade, bloodless, lifeless, gone to join All-Time. Wrapped at the last in a flaxen mantle. Who closed your eyes? Was it one of my brothers? Or have they all taken to the roving life of the hollow ships?

She returned to her room and sang dirges and threnodies. She did not take food or share her grief. Her women wailed outside the door. She would not let them in. Sobs choked her as she thought of her sweet-faced mother, bewildered by such a child as she. Yet Kleis had only shaken her head and left her to be Sappho.

Sappho knew that only her Muses rescued her from oblivion. "Some, I tell you"—she raised her fist to heaven—"will remember me hereafter."

Her songs would be handed down. Long after she had ceased to be, people would repeat her songs in places unknown, in civilizations that had not happened. But Kleis was just a woman who had lived, and lived no more. Sappho took up her kithara:

> *Night rained her*
> *thick dark sleep*
> *upon their eyes*

Was that what it was like? A sleep from which there is no waking?

During these days of loss the gods set before her a revelation. She was with child. She pressed her hand against her hard belly. Her womb was vital with life, yet that which had nurtured her was no longer. Kybele, mother goddess of Eresos, sent by Kleis, whispered it was a daughter.

She hoped it was so. But this was something even the seven wise men could not predict. And what did they know, since she had heard that Pittakos was among their number. He with the gross manners and uncut nails who persecuted her, drove her from her mother, was called a wise man—and now her mother was dead. Sing woe! Sing woe!

She bent herself in two and, when Kerkolas hammered on the door, would not open it. This was her grief, hers! The same was true of the child. She was not ready to share that either.

Some person lodged in her. Who? The gods sent this trespasser to show her she was a woman like any other. This was what happened to the women gossiping at their spinning; loose bowels and vomit, the inability to digest certain foods—this was what life had shrunk to.

She refused to submit. It was an imposition, an invasion. She was Sappho, poet of Lesbos. And her concerns would be as they had been, to recount the sturdy quality of a wildflower, to praise the daintiness of a young girl, slender of ankle, delicate in her movements.

She emerged from her quarters seeming to be as she had been before. Kerkolas knew better than to condole with her, or so much as mention Kleis. Instead he took her to a discus-throwing contest in which only the few sat in chairs to watch. She was among these.

It was a lovely sight as the gleaming bodies bent and poised for the throw. The custom here also was to pull the foreskin over the member and tie it off.

She watched the umpire run out to mark the distances. Kerkolas wagered entire ships on a single contest. It was at these games, amid garlands of laurel, many-colored ribbons, and much gold and iron, that she heard talk of Solon of Athens. He had broken the debt tablets and decreed that no freeborn Athenian could sell himself into slavery. Furthermore, he decreed that those who had done so were once more free men. "Ah," said Sappho, "Solon will have to flee Athens and tend his farm after passing such a law."

Kerkolas laughed. "He already has."

She did not think overly well of Solon, because he gave a low place to women. He felt a husband had the right to take his wife's life if adultery were proved. A woman's rights were confined to being kept with child. Toward this end Solon ruled the husband's duty was to sleep with her once weekly. That was how justice between the sexes was rendered in Athens. And that was why she had not journeyed there.

She did not tell Kerkolas of the child she carried because she had become convinced it was a girl-child. When it was born, a bunch of woolen ribbons would be tied to the door, and crowds would gather in the streets, for though a girl, it was hers, Sappho's.

The sickness of the first months passed and a feeling of well-being gave her confidence. So when her husband spoke of a merchantman lying off Crete, a prize waiting to be taken, she was excited. Many of the treasures in her home had been won at spearpoint, and she knew Kerkolas would send a ship against this richly laden trader. She did not know that he intended to command it himself. He kept this from her until the last.

Sappho did not protest. If Kerkolas wanted his old freewheeling adventurous life, why scold like a wife? Better to abet him, be his companion in the planning of his route and the provisioning of his ship. His long, slender finger traced out the littoral sea, showing the way he would travel. And when he met the Cretan, lying lower in the water than his own light craft, he would dance around her and circle in.

They laughed together, and Sappho permitted him her body. Her mind, as always, she sealed off. He was a little drunk. He was always a little drunk when he came to her. He did not know what a small part of her was present, and yet he did.

"You are like a statue, Sappho. If only you would melt to my love, which is hot for you, I would not go to the street of women, or to oboe players, or bother with cupbearers, but it's as if . . . as if . . ." He stopped. He did not know how to express what he felt, because he did not know in what manner she was not with him. He tried again. "Your eyes are dark with passion. Your mouth as sensual as I've ever seen. Your songs speak of desire. Why do you not love me?"

"Be content, Kerkolas. Your seed within me bears."

"It is true?" And he began to kiss her body. In ecstasy he nibbled at the mound of Aphrodite and suddenly she wanted the frenzy but not the long, hard rod he inserted. His genitals were large and she was small; there was always pain and a slight disgust at the procedure. The fact that he was dominant over her was part of her distress. She was sorry she had told him her body's secret, and received him with the stillness of death.

That he had impregnated Sappho of Lesbos excited Kerkolas, and he didn't care that he took his pleasure alone. In fact it pleased him.

Later in the night when he lay passively beside her, his arms behind his head, he instructed her to drink the sap of thistle. "This will ensure a boy. We will call him after my father."

Sea put on its sparkling look the day Kerkolas sailed. Sappho and her household went to the harbor. The sprightly vessel danced against its chains, and when the sacrifice to Poseidon had been made the rowers took their place.

"The brother of great Zeus guide you on the pathless way," Sappho said.

"I will return with gold and iron and wonderfully wrought things," Kerkolas vowed.

When he was aboard she took a scarlet sash from her waist and waved it. The rowers saluted with uplifted oars. At her husband's command the boat nosed past other shipping and, once free of the port, the sail was raised. Sappho continued to let her red sash fly, remembering as she did how her youngest brother, Larichos, had run along the quay when she left Lesbos more than a year ago. She realized Syracuse was no longer exile. She still proudly used the title "of Lesbos," but since her mother's death Lesbos seemed far away, and of her brothers she had been close only to Khar. The land of Egypt was distant, and he had promised to send his ring as a token that he lived. If it had been received in Mitylene, it had not been forwarded.

Of Alkaios's fate she was more confident. He had never been one to put himself in danger, and every now and then a poem of his was sung, telling her that somewhere he lived and prospered. She smiled in memory of their little band. Pittakos, she had heard, was rearing a son to succeed him. Not even at her mother's death had he relented, nor sent word that she was free to visit her homeland.

Kerkolas's ship was now a dancing toy; she turned away and gave her mind to a verse she would make on the subject of leave-taking.

For a week or more she was pleased to be alone, then a restlessness seized her. She plucked the Egyptian harp. The song didn't come well.

A wind had sprung up, a strange wind blowing not from the water but toward it, which made evenings hotter than before. She felt the west wind and the south wind clash.

Blood fell from Sky. She woke; it was rain.

Kerkolas died within sight of the island where he was born. The messenger knelt before her. "A reef, it was. We ran aground."

Sappho looked intently at him. "Unsay what you have said."

"Lady . . . that I could."

"I call on Zeus, I call also Earth, Sun, the Erinyes who dwell below, and Eurynome, daughter of the ever-encircling waters of Ocean, that I will have out your tongue if you swear falsely."

"The great Lord Kerkolas is dead."

"You saw him die?"

"The mast crashed down on him."

Her eyes wandered from the face of the messenger. There was only her child and herself now, and she did not want the child of a dead man.

She jumped to her feet and began to pace as an animal paces a too-small cage. "Such a host of ills some god has sent. Must I tie my hair again into a death wreath?" she asked Niobe. But her expression was so fierce that Niobe feared to answer. Kerkolas, strong, confident, young, had yet been sent into the night of endless length.

"There is no harbor for my misery," she cried, and her maidens began to moan.

> *Young Adonis is*
> *dying! O Kytherea,*
> *what shall we do now?*
> *Batter your breasts*
> *with your fists, girls—*
> *tatter your dresses*

Words had not come readily at her mother's death. She had lain as at the bottom of endless Tartarus in dreadful numbness. But when she thought of her husband's death, it was with words. She picked up her lyre: "Wrap me in sand, gather my bones in silt!"

Then, throwing the instrument from her, she ran outdoors and with both hands scooped up dust and let it settle on her. She tore and rived her hair, cried to her maidens to make loud lament, did everything in fact that was proper. Yet she didn't think of him as dead. She thought of the dining club he had joined that made a point of meeting only on unlucky days. She remembered their summer under gay awnings stretched before caves by the sea, the wine during hot afternoons, how they had danced the Cordox, gradually in time to a tambourine, removing their clothes. He called her "goddess of my body."

Why, oh why had she disliked his touch? His favorite dishes came to her mind—pig stuffed with lark, ramplios, a purple fish born in sea foam—what did all that matter now? "There is no escape once you are born. Clotho spins, Lachesis lays out the pattern, and cruel Atropos cuts the thread." No mortal yet had broken the loom, destroyed the distaff and thrown away the shears! Had she been playing her songs or bathing in the marble pool while Hermes guided her husband past the river of fire, Styx of unbreakable oath, and across Lethe, river of forgetfulness?

Had Kerkolas, being struck down, come to himself in the water, to struggle? For he was a strong swimmer and loved life. She hoped he had not wakened until he reached Erebus, the anteroom of Tartarus. She prayed to the elder gods, to Hades, Lord of Death, and his wife, Persephone, and even to dread Thanatos himself, that they deal kindly with this young man who in his strength and beauty came to them. But what did the immortal gods care for man? Ichor, not blood, flowed in their veins! She remembered the account of the Shade given by Homer:

> The sinews no more bind together the flesh and
> bones, and so soon as life hath left the white bones,
> the spirit of the man flies forth and hovers near

Was Kerkolas near? Walking past her wailing women, she went to the sand shore. She remembered the night the west wind and the south wind clashed. Was it then?

Facing the bay was the Arethusa spring. It was icy cold because a chilly-hearted nymph chose to be changed into these waters rather than submit to the advances of the river god, Alpheus. As Sappho approached, her steps dragged and she repeated sadly:

> To what, dear bridegroom,
> may I liken thee?
> To a slender sapling
> do I most rightly liken thee

In what other times were those words sung!

Sappho slipped off her chiton and plunged beneath the icy spring, exposing herself to its cleansing. From all her body she washed off death. Niobe, who had followed her, brought from under her robe a vial of costly myrrh. When Sappho stepped out, her servant anointed her and dressed her in a fresh garment of quince color dyed with the juice of boxwood.

"It is over," Sappho said. She meant she was free of him. Niobe nodded; she understood.

There were countless things that must be seen to, and a feast to be got together. "We'll want roasted almonds and wine. Heap our finest plates with figs, apples, mulberries, and have cakes of wheat and cakes of poppy. Eel and other exotic things we will serve from Sea, since Sea took him from us."

She felt she had been spared, for when a corpse was available the wife inserted a feeding tube into the moldering jaws and poured liquids down. No one could remember that any had been revived by this means, but it was the custom here.

She could not wrap her dead in herbs and honey and burn his remains to fine ash, so she ordered a miniature terra-cotta sarcophagus with Kerkolas's likeness sculptured on the cover. Her way of meeting death was to hang perfume flasks from pegs inside the coffin, place beside it a lock of her own black hair, jewels that he liked to handle, a favorite ring, a goblet of gold, and she herself would fill the casket with flowers and the bridegroom poem.

It was three weeks since the night of the great wind. It was fitting that all be expedited and a mound erected on the grounds where the casket could be burned and interred.

At the appointed time mourners appeared shrieking and wailing. Friends came and sobbed on her breast. Sappho herself acted more hostess than widow. There were no tears. Her face was without expression. And this was remarked by the relatives of Kerkolas, especially his mother, who was supported by servants.

Sappho waved her guests to pillows. Libation was made and prayers offered before the small, replicated coffin on its raised dais. The guests exclaimed at the workmanship and swore it was the perfect likeness of a perfect lord, the faultless Kerkolas, merchant prince, true comrade and leader of men.

Tables were brought and food, both steaming and cold, while the wine was of a vintage that makes men travel to a land that never was. The dirges grew louder as the miniature casket was carried ceremoniously to its designated spot in the garden. Resin was flung, and in seconds a blaze leapt skyward. The family of Kerkolas threw locks of hair upon the fire. Others dashed wine or tossed dainties. The keening was redoubled until it seemed the flame was carried by the sound.

They returned to fresh tables ladened with poppy cakes. Bitter and sweet relishes were passed. Kerkolas's aunt leaned toward her.

"How bravely you bear your loss," she said with an arch smile.

"One bears it as one must," Sappho replied, not knowing if it was said in spite or as comfort.

Naked acrobats appeared, both boys and girls, performing dangerous tricks with swords and spitting fire from their mouths. After this entertainment the guests went a final time to the garden to throw flowers and sprinkle perfumes on the smoldering pyre. The professional mourners in the background cried to Sky, tore their hair, rent their clothes, and scratched their faces until blood ran. More wine was thrown to douse the fire, after which the company repaired once more to the dining hall. In their absence floor tiles had been removed, revealing a deep pool. The guests seated themselves around it. What was this new diversion peerless Sappho had devised?

A naked Adonis appeared among them and dived into the water, followed by an exquisite maiden. The guests understood they were to witness a struggle between the Life Force and all-powerful Death. During an underwater dance-inspired undulation, the male was to penetrate the female. The danger was that, in accomplishing this feat, one or both would drown. Acrobatic swimmers that they were, entangled in each other's bodies they could not rise to the surface for air during climax. When the male succeeded in parting the plucked arrow of the mermaid, not only his body but his face contorted. Bubbles streamed from his mouth, his eyes bulged.

The audience clapped their appreciation, for as the man's living seed replenished the girl, his organ fell from her and dropped flaccid, wizened and dead as he was. The orgiastic female, trailing triumphant blood, carried the body to the surface and draped the lifeless form on the floor.

"The girl performed well," Sappho the widow spoke without emotion. "Give her freedom in honor of my husband."

"And the man has freedom of another sort," cried an excited guest as they sprinkled the corpse with parsley and sweet herbs and dragged it to the funeral fire, which was rekindled.

Syracuse was enraptured by this small, restless miracle of a woman, who as widow of the prince Kerkolas entertained now in her own right. Gamori of their city and Kritias, Archon of Athens, dined at her table. The poet Arion and many others were her guests. None knew better than Sappho what to serve, what to sing, whom to invite and what tableau or mime to obtain as entertainment. In death, it might be said, Kerkolas was more famous than in life, for news of his funeral feast spread throughout Sicily and carried back to Mitylene. Sappho's genius had long been acknowledged, and herself acclaimed as the greatest living poet of the lyric style. Now her personal charisma was demonstrated.

She wasn't sleeping well. In fact she dreaded sleep, for a recurring dream lay ready to take possession of her. In it she thought the dread goddess Circe spoke to her, saying, "The Muses have often talked to you, and told your name will be remembered down echoing time. This is true." Here the goddess bent close. "But only partly. Proud Sappho, I say you will be remembered for ill and not for good, your very name an abomination."

The dream, like a chorus, repeated in her head. And she woke dripping sweat, her body arched in spasm. "It's a lying dream," she said through clenched teeth, "for how can poetry and music bring evil?" This did not prevent the dream from recurring the next night.

She had taken a new fancy. She began breeding and racing horses. It seemed swift Boreas, from whom all great horses descended, had lent these his prowess. And Nestor, the first lord and tamer, had bestowed special favor, for Sappho's stables bred the finest animals. And though she was large with child, she rode to hunt like a second Artemis, bringing down a boar unaided.

Such actions caused an undercurrent of gossip. Kerkolas's relatives openly disapproved, saying that participating in such things as men do she might abort the child which was Kerkolas's immortality on Earth. What would these same wagging tongues say if they knew she had eaten the root of the cyclamen to achieve this very result, and that Eileithyia had punished her with the sharp pains she sends women? But the child clung to her womb and would not be dislodged.

Criticism of Sappho was mixed with the general praise, as one might add a dash of pepper and the dish be better for it. Nothing could dim her celebrity. Coins were minted in her likeness, busts of her sculptured, and her whole figure worked in Parian marble.

She did not take a lover and she did not marry. Kerkolas's family hinted that she choose another of their sons. But she let it be known that her husband was still vivid in her mind and heart. She caught Niobe's speculative glance and confided to her later that she was not glad he was dead, but relieved he was no longer present.

No longer present? About this she was wrong. He made his presence known one night after the last guest left, the last perfumed torch spluttered and went out. As Sappho lay alone upon her couch, Kerkolas found his way up from beneath the three rivers. He came to the edge of the bed and surveyed her with reproachful eyes.

"Why do you attempt to murder my child?"

She shrank from the dripping figure and dared not answer.

Kerkolas raised his hand over her and blood fell on her breast. She screamed herself awake. But none heard, so she got up and poured herself a goblet of Lesbian wine.

Gradually, as her time drew near, her attitude toward the life within her underwent a further change. She began to think of the child as an ally of her house and lineage. She gave up riding to the hunt and jumping horses; she even wrote Pittakos, asking if she might return to Lesbos.

His reply reached her in her eighth month: "The time is not yet auspicious."

What did all her fame mean, if her child must be born in exile?

Her swollen body was troubled by more than its persistent heaviness. She shivered with a torment she refused to understand. And the song she sang was this:

> *The moon is set and the Pleiades gone;*
> *it is midnight, and the time is going fast,*
> *but I lie alone*

She remembered her still-vivid dream of Kerkolas and shuddered. She tried to sort out what her feelings for her husband had been. Though kind, he was too often befuddled with drink. One thing was certain, his carousing friends no longer had access to her house. Neither did his family. She did not like the way their eyes roamed her possessions, estimating and evaluating. It was her house now, and everything within it. And there was a good deal within it.

Many times in the night she got up and unlocked the treasure room, to wander for hours. She would sit and play the strange instruments and touch the fine raiment, unfolding and holding it against her, fragrant with rosemary. She lifted small gold votives, turning them so the light of the tapers revealed their craftsmanship. There were barrels of drachmas, ancient Attic coins, oisbrophoec from Asia Minor, obolos and the Babylonian milna, all the finest work, though in miniature. Jewels for the fingers, toes, nose, and ears; pendants for the throat; snake-twisted silver bracelets to enclose the upper arm and ankle—she tried them all.

I am wealthy, she thought, remembering her mother's fear that she would be a pensioner by a brother's fire. I and my child, she added thoughtfully. Through most of her pregnancy she had given it every opportunity to leave, yet it grew to enormous size within her body. And now she was glad. It had fought for its life and won. She knew her time was close, which was why she humbled herself to Pittakos. But the child would be born here, to know Lesbos only in stories.

She could not escape Kerkolas. The hour always came when she must go back to bed. This night he took the form of a black raven and used his beak to enter her. The pain was such she thought she would die of it. This time her women heard her screams.

On her knees was the way a woman brought out a child. No poems marshaled now in orderly array, but wildest cries, as her too-small, too-bloated body sought to pass its burden. She tried to call Llithyia, daughter of Hera, the special goddess of childbirth. She tried to tell her that her innards were being pulled out of her along with the child. Then she forgot it was a child. Torture! The ultimate torture—for her pride, for her neglect of the gods. Sweat fell into her eyes, tears fell out of them. She stuffed her whole hand into her mouth. But the screams kept coming as though from a door improperly closed.

"Push down," Niobe commanded. "Harder."

She obeyed. She obeyed her own slave. Her living flesh was torn apart. Poor Dionysos. Poor Sappho. One could not be sundered like this and live. "Mother!" She held out her arms. Her mother on the other side would help her.

"The head has been born," Niobe said. "One final effort and the child will leave you."

Sappho expelled the infant with all the strength remaining to her. It came in bloody trappings and the trailings of afterbirth. Before she looked at the squalling infant's face, she looked between its legs. A girl.

"Kleis." A life had been given for the one taken. The agony was forgotten in unexpected joy. Memory, mother of the Muses, gave permission to bestow the name Kleis.

The child was carefully oiled, wrapped, and placed in her arms. A beautiful baby. Not like her at all, long and blonde with blue eyes shading to black. Did she look like her namesake? Like her brothers? As Sappho peered intently into her daughter's face, Kerkolas looked back at her.

"Take the child," she said abruptly to Niobe.

ERINNA

ERIANDER, TYRANT OF CORINTH, MURDERED HIS WIFE, and then, to prove his innocence to himself, had intercourse with the corpse. He owed her nearest male relations some pittance for her demise, as the offense under law was not against the woman, but the family.

When it was related to her, this episode caused Sappho to ruminate on her own situation. She was a woman alone, and eight-year-old Kleis a girl-child. If anything happened to them, Kerkolas's nearby kinsmen would inherit. The family had given up hope that she would marry someone from their house, and since that time were openly hostile.

There were other suitors as well, whom it took a great deal of tact to discourage. She knew she would not marry again and have a lord over her, a man to whom she was accountable, a man to run through the fortune that should go to Kleis. She had thought her renown protected her, and her position in society. But that had been no help to the wife of Periander.

To dispel the fears the evil news engendered, she watched the child on her swing, the ropes freshly woven with violets. Kleis was laughing and her blond hair flew out behind her. Sappho took up her lyre and sang softly:

> I have a little daughter,
> like a golden flower:
> my darling Kleis,

for whom I would not take
all Lydia nor lovely Lesbos

"What are you singing, Mama?"

"Just a little song."

"A pretty song? About armfuls of chrysanthemums and golden buds?"

"Yes, child, yes."

"Tell me a story, Mama," and leaving the swing she ran to nestle against her.

"What shall I tell you? How great Zeus and his brothers drew lots for their share of the world?"

"Yes, that one."

Sappho teasingly handle-kissed the child, taking the little one by the ears. Kleis tried to grasp her ears in return, and they ended laughing helplessly.

Sappho picked up her lyre again and sang:

O beautiful, O lovely!
Yours it is
with the rosy-ankled Graces
and with Aphrodite
to play!

Remembering the terrors with which her own nurse filled her, Sappho was her daughter's only teacher. "Hercules had his home in Thebes. And Aphrodite was born of foam by the island of Cythera. And at night, galloping Pegasus, who skims the air all day, has his comfortable stall in Corinth. While Poseidon, that Earth-encircling lord, travels so swiftly in his chariot beneath Sea that he is never wet. He too has a home; golden and imperishable Aegae." Sappho's luminous eyes smoldered with passion. "And we have a home, which is not in this place."

"Lesbos!" piped the child. "On the main trade route between Attica and Lydia. The land to which the waves carried Orpheus's head and lyre."

"Only Treasure, you will wiggle your toes in its sand, and taste fruit from its orchards, apple and fig, and stuff your pretty mouth with grapes of its slopes."

"Why don't we go there, Mama?"

"Why? Why is a big question for a little girl. Someday we will. In the meantime, learn that the Lesbians were loyal allies of great Troy, as were the noble Pelasgians of Larissa, the proud Mysians, the Lycians, the Cardians, the Dardanian warriors . . ."

But Kleis's head drooped against her; she slept.

Sappho sighed. The child did not drink in knowledge as she had. Kleis could follow her mother as light-footedly in the dance, and her voice, though small, rang true. But she was not interested in accounts of Creation. She did not care that the gods were the grandchildren of the Titans. And the Phoenician alphabet came haltingly to her lips. She could not remember the name of the ever-flowing river which had streams that fell to Earth from Heaven, even the clear and wonderful Spercheius. Kleis was very like her father, a laughing daughter of laughing Aphrodite. She was bright and clever, but she did not care to know. And Sappho wanted to gobble up the world. Sometimes she thought if her eyes and heart could look into and really understand a flower, that all knowledge would open and everything in the lap of All-Mother Earth tumble out. This, she supposed, was fancy. For poetry is apart from reason and, she believed, above it. One can gather a bouquet of beauty, but not a bouquet of truth.

She thought often about Thales on his Isle of Thought, asking his strange questions: "What is man?" "What is the world?" Man of Nature, his students called him, Physis. She did not care for his verses, which were in a grand and lofty style. Not like mine, Sappho thought. The Muses breathed into me their divine voice. They sing to delight the soul, and so do I.

Sappho was to remember that lazy summer day, not for what happened, but because it was the last day in which nothing happened. For a week the wind had blown steadily from Sea, and her child's cheeks were pink with the flush of health. But all men know that the origin of disease is divine. From deepest recesses it is called to hang in the heat over a city, and there is no help in all of Apollo's healing shrines. Though it was hot past enduring, rain fell and tore and muddied the ground. And a mischief befell Kleis. Her throat was red and sore and the glands in her neck swollen. She tossed her head from side to side on her pillow, and her yellow curls were a tangle.

Sappho sent Niobe for an oracle, and kept vigil by the bed. Niobe returned to say that the hot water that came up from the vapor baths must be mixed with the blood of a white cock. Once swallowed, this concoction would weaken the sickness, and between times the child must ingest small amounts of snake blood and ashes purchased from the priestess and carried in a small bag.

All was done as prescribed. Sappho strewed the sickroom with laurel, sacred to Apollo, who taught men the healing arts. Kneeling, she pressed her lips against the child's burning face. Kleis slept fitfully and threw up both the cock's blood and the snake's. Fear ringed Sappho's eyes. She said endless prayers to all the gods she could think of, promising to set free her most beautiful slave on the day her daughter recovered. She asked Gello not to bend over her child too far, nor hold her too closely, or kiss the air from her. For Gello was a Lesbian maid who loved children but, dying before marriage, had none of her own; so when a child died, it was said Gello clasped too tightly until life was gone.

Sappho made sure Kleis slept, then went into the garden to pick jonquils so the child would have something glad to look upon. It would awaken in her the desire to be well and bloom like them. She hurried back to the sick chamber and placed her hand upon the silver door handle, then drew back. This punishment was visited upon her for not wanting the child, for eating root of cyclamen, for dashing so madly about on horseback. "But know, O gods, I love her well. Of all the treasures my husband left me, she is my chief joy." When she entered the room, Kleis would be better—or dying. "Groans then shall be my speech, nor will I afterward sing." She turned cold at threatening the gods and immediately placated them. "Let her stay with me and I will take her home to Lesbos. Not a hundred Pittakoses will stop me. This I swear. Or if you will, take me in her stead, or any other whom I love."

She pushed open the door and saw the child was wet from head to foot, the fever broken. The jonquils fell from Sappho's hands and scattered across the floor. She made hekatombs of thanks and freed the slave girl. She wrote once more to Pittakos.

While Sappho waited for a reply, a letter arrived on one of her own ships. It was from her brother Khar. He wrote from Mitylene. His news brought a great cry from Sappho, and she fell upon the floor. Her servants raced about for drink, for covers. Niobe chafed her limbs, which were as in death.

When she opened her eyes, it was to turn against the wall. In a terrible voice she cried them away. What had she done? Had meddlesome Hermes been passing as she made the great oath and, like the tale-bearer he was, carried it to Pallas Athene?

She had slain her friend. Alkaios was dead.

Time flowed darkly, and she could not think past it. With Alkaios deep in ever-receiving Tartarus, her own youth died. She mourned them both. The fine lines she had noticed upon her face this year came from being twenty-nine.

Gradually she allowed herself closer to her grief. For Alkaios she had been violet-haired, of hidden harmonies, always different in her person. They had plotted childish revolt, they had shared an exile. My dear friend, my dear friend—Sappho has brought you this sightless end.

She dragged herself to her brother's letter and read again the manner of Alkaios's dying. It had been without dignity, Khar said, for he had it on good authority that Alkaios, too, had been returning to Lesbos—and of course celebrating himself, and of course drunk. ". . . Like the ever-young god of flowing locks, when pirates boarded." According to Khar's information, which was from an escaped sailor on that same ship, Alkaios hid in a wine keg. When he came up for air, one of the invaders cleaved his skull and the wine turned a deeper hue.

Grief overcame her; she spoke to his shade. Even Alkaios's shade could not be too serious: "Remember when we slid down the mountain on our rumps?" And while the shade yet smiled, she spoke quickly. "My little girl is so small. She was so pitiable, you would have forgiven me. You would, Alkaios, I know it."

But that appeal made her feel no better. She could not bear to think of his wry gaiety expunged by some ruffian's sword. He, who had contempt for violence, to end so. The cask of wine would have amused him, though. He would have thought, not that it was undignified, as her brother wrote, but that it was suitable, an appropriate end, to imbibe wine with his last inhalation.

She looked again at the dreadful missive. She had to know how her brother came to be in Mitylene. She read that Pittakos's only son out of the well-bred sow he had married had died violently by an ax, intended no doubt for his father. Khar wrote that all Pittakos's hopes had been in this boy. With his death, the Pittakos they knew was no more. He cared nothing about old quarrels or old friends. Day was the same as night to him. He allowed all exiles back, declaring total amnesty in memory of his child. Sympathy welled up in Sappho for the boy with the ax in his head, and she sobbed again for her dear Alkaios, who always asked her to take him in hand but to whom she had handed Death, that Kleis might live.

For this crime she was to be rewarded. She was to go home.

Sappho returned to Lesbos like a queen. She and her daughter and her women rode on a ship with well-trimmed sails, followed by three wide-bellied vessels with holes cut into their decks to hold the casks of treasure.

Swift escorts with fighting men at the ready parted the seas on either side. For Sappho had emptied Kerkolas's villa of its ivories, its gems, its bags of lion-faced Samian coins, its tapestries of loomed vestments, its wondrous musical instruments. Nine years before she had left Lesbos in disgrace; she returned with wealth past counting and a reputation as the world's greatest living poet.

The rolled papyri of her work she carried in the carved chest. The collection, including the verse of exile, filled two volumes. She intended to have it copied and distributed among family and friends. The volumes contained lyric poems, cult songs, odes to marriage, and elegies.

When the ship passed craggy Chios, she put a flower in her daughter's hand to throw on the gleaming surface, saying, "Your grandfather died fighting here."

They hugged the shoreline and, as it grew familiar, Sappho's arm went around the child. "See how near to Lesbos is the steep Ionian shore. The entrance to Heaven is not more beautiful than the twin harbors of Mitylene. There before you lies the Aeolic island of my birth." She disappeared into the tent erected on deck to have herself prepared. Her slaves rubbed her face and body with sheep's fat that had boiled slowly during the journey, been collected and allowed to cool. Sun-dried, it produced a deep penetrating cream. Her skin was patted with a tincture of the roots of the almond tree. Over this her face was drawn, the face with which she was to greet her city.

All Mitylene crowded dockside. Khar she saw first; garlanded himself, he held a wreath for her. Beside him, Eurygyos—and was that handsome young man Larichos?

Sappho took Kleis by the hand and stepped onto Lesbos. Her three brothers embraced her and passed her child from one to the other. They spoke and laughed and cried the nine years. They tried to hug away the time that had devoured their lives. Droplets of news filtered through the exclamations. Larichos was cupbearer to Pittakos, a mark of great favor indicating he considered theirs the first family of Lesbos.

Eurygyos presented a wife, Antiope, a charming girl whom Sappho remembered having sported with at the baths. They had returned to Eresos, rebuilt the home of their father, and replanted the vineyard which now bore as in her childhood. Khar's plans were to sell his brother's harvest, putting to sea in a fleet of boats he purchased with his inheritance as eldest son. "I am by now too used to wandering," he told his sister. "I doubt I could stay long in any land." He invited her to live in their aunt's old home in Mitylene, which had come to his branch of the family.

Sappho replied gaily, "In far-fruited Sicily I made other plans. But since they will take time to carry out, Kleis and I will be your guests for a while."

The dark-fronted treasure ships were mooring. Her brothers were too polite to comment, except Larichos, who asked brashly if they held the riches rumor endowed her with.

"There are some fine things indeed from the estate of my late husband," Sappho answered him. They nodded, understanding fully for the first time their sister was wealthy as well as famous.

Friends and neighbors who hung back while the family greeted one another now pressed around the poet. It was a rare and splendid welcome. Sappho remembered her departure, with only Larichos jumping up and down, waving from the pier. Still, she was home and these were her people. She had brought her daughter to grow up among them. Sappho smiled and nodded. She was gracious, she was aloof, she was Sappho.

They were driven to her aunt Tyro's home, and the tablets of her mind were inscribed with the past. Her mother, now in sunless night, should be standing on the stone threshold, lifting her first grandchild, her namesake, in her arms. "She lives no more!" Sappho had to tell herself. For the rolling years were nine.

Sappho entered as a shade from another lifetime, throwing back her Sidonian cloak. Servants carried off her things to a different wing of the house, while she and her brothers and Antiope, her sister-in-law, spilled wine and drank.

"Are we permitted to know our sister's plans?" Khar asked.

"Yes," Antiope put in, taking note of Sappho's apparel, from her saffron-glowing sandals to the jeweled combs that flashed in her hair. "Those you spoke of."

Sappho looked at each face before saying anything. A dream had been whispered to her by her way-gods, the Muses, and she had hugged it to her. To utter it, release it to others, would make it seem perhaps mad and impossible. Yet she must try to explain.

"You have met my child, Kleis. My thought is simply this: not to leave her upbringing to others, but to teach her myself from Hesiod, Homer, the great poets . . ."

"Sappho too," Larichos laughed, rounding out their number.

She smiled.

"That seems an admirable idea, inspired by the gods," Khar said.

Sappho hesitated. "It has taken on new form in my mind since then, and grown somewhat. I thought, since I will teach Kleis, why not others as well?"

"Others?"

She could feel how alien her thinking was to them, but she continued. "Yes. I wish to build a school, where I will teach ritual songs and the festival dances of our city. I shall look for a suitable location facing the sea and build first a villa, and then cottages to house my students." Sensing their mounting puzzlement, she continued rapidly. "They will be young girls from the finest families. They will come to me to learn not only poetry, song, and dance, but something of philosophy, current thought, the unequal laws concerning women, the history of the Danaans, and," she added impishly, "how to weave daisy chains."

Her brothers laughed uncertainly and smiled shallow smiles.

"It is a new thing," Khar said cautiously. "There is no precedent for it. In Miletos wise Thales gathers young men about him for instruction. But when and where has one heard of a school for young women?"

Surprisingly Sappho's support came from Eurygyos. "Any maiden who has been trained by Sappho of Lesbos would be sure to make an advantageous marriage. After all, our sister has experience running a large household which she could pass on."

"I did not hear our sister mention the management of a household," Khar put in and looked at Sappho questioningly.

"I will teach that, too," Sappho said, "if it will win me friends."

"I think the project a sound one," Eurygyos reiterated, "and that our sister will increase her fortune."

"I do not need to increase my fortune. But I am very glad of your good opinion," Sappho told him. She was radiant. The long-cherished notion had not sounded foolish in the telling.

"You will be married again," her youngest brother quipped, "before you even lay the foundation of the villa!"

"No," Sappho said so positively that the four were startled. "I will not marry again. I will have my school." She had forgotten to add "an the gods will it." Wine was hastily spilled for this oversight, which could bring misfortune at the outset, even on those in whom it was confided. For great Zeus was willful and had sired a willful bunch.

The site Sappho acquired was removed from the main portion of the city on a sheltered, low-lying spit of land encircled by bluest water. It was from here she watched her brother's fleet of high-riding ships as they pulled toward the horizon. A trip such as Khar was embarked on meant more long years of separation. To stifle her pain she threw herself into the project of building.

On the chosen spot a profusion of wildflowers grew and blossom-working bees filled the air with their drone. Sappho grieved for each colorful head of sweet alyssum or crocus that fell beneath a workman's sandal or that must be uprooted to make way for the slabs of marble she had shipped. Yes, she elected to walk on marble.

But in recompense to the sacrificed flowers she sang:

> The wild hyacinth which on the mountainside the
> shepherd treads underfoot, and yet it still blooms purple
> on the ground

Many of the architectural features she had observed in Sicily were incorporated into her plans. She enclosed extensive gardens with a triple wall. The villa took a year and a half to build. People made excursions from Mitylene to see its progress. Her brothers reported that it was much talked of in the town. Some felt an academy for girls was a dangerous idea, since the students might imagine themselves capable of serious thought. Others believed peerless Sappho would make princesses of their daughters, or that a daughter-in-law trained by her would be an asset to their house. And so the controversy burbled along.

Meanwhile the edifice grew daily in beauty as the plan for it was transferred by the Athenian architect to stone and marble. She named it House of the Servants of the Muses.

Her Kleis, her golden-haired daughter, would grow up to have older sisters and wise friends. For if, as Eurygyos concluded, young girls boasting of her tutelage would make better marriages, they must be older than she had at first contemplated—young maidens, models for her daughter and companions for herself. She liked the idea of companionship. In her life, it seemed to her, she had been too much alone.

The completion of Sappho's estate coincided with an awesome event: the total eclipse of Sun. Both sides in Lydia's war against the Medes were thrown into religious terror at this sign of displeasure from the gods. The opposing forces came together and, bathing their hands in the steaming blood of ox and swine, swore a mighty oath of friendship. With the sealing of the peace, Alyattes gave his daughter in marriage to the King of the Medes.

And Erinna of Telos persuaded her parents she could now travel in safety to meet the esteemed Sappho, poet of the known world, and join her household for a time. When she arrived at the white stone pier of Mitylene, Sappho was standing alone without entourage or servants. This gesture of independence amazed Erinna, the Asiatic.

Sappho gave greeting in a low voice in which the modulations of a singer could be heard. Her smile, by some interior route, lit her eyes. They glowed with pleasure at meeting her first student. The girl was very slender, perhaps too delicate, but beautifully so. Her slight body seemed fatigued by large crescent breasts.

Sappho embraced her, called her guest-friend, and said, "Erinna of

Telos, I have heard your work sung. You speak in a new way of ordinary things and people. There are too many paeans to kings and heroes."

Erinna's boxes and chest were unloaded, for at a signal Sappho was no longer alone but commanded a dozen slaves who took charge of the luggage. A garlanded carriage drew near, and from it Sappho removed a chaplet. "I wove this for you," and she pressed tiers of blossoms on Erinna's head. She had to stand on her toes to do this and that made her laugh. "Perhaps you expected . . . more of me."

Erinna laughed too, suddenly glad she had come, intrigued by the quick-witted grace of Sappho. She had been right to feel that her destiny was here.

They mounted the chariot lightly, Erinna no longer feeling tired. What promise the dark eyes of Sappho held, what fulfillment of herself as an artist.

"Yes," Sappho said, as though she had spoken aloud, "we will work side by side, each an inspiration to the other."

"You are Sappho," Erinna demurred.

"And you, Erinna," Sappho replied. "You are young yet, your parents said only nineteen. In time your verse will shine equally with mine."

"You are kind . . ." Erinna began.

"No," Sappho said, "honest. I am honest."

"Do you think that is what makes a poet great?"

"It is an ingredient. Honesty must be present. But simply looking is a part also. And an interior looking, that most of all."

"You have had much experience of the world," Erinna observed.

"Experience of the world is something that comes by living in it," Sappho said somewhat ruefully.

"Are you not a better poet for it?" Erinna asked.

"I do not know."

They laughed together because she had been honest.

"I am already glad I have come," Erinna said. "You have made me glad."

Sappho installed her first pupil in quarters closest her own. If there had been no boxes at all, Erinna would have lacked nothing. Sappho had stocked her cottage with the best she had, given her slave girls to wait upon her, and placed musical instruments about so that if she wandered from one room to another and the mood took her, she could play.

The young women had great delight in each other's company. And ten-year-old Kleis adored Erinna. She was always clapping her hands in time to the new songs or tagging after when they strolled deep in conversation. It was she who gathered the flowers for their nimble fingers to weave.

Sappho sang the legends of great Homer and instructed Erinna in the art of finding on an instrument the pitch one wanted. She taught cult dancing and invented new positions and forms. She found she could discuss with Erinna the latest ideas from Miletos, Isle of Thought.

Interspersed with these studies were tales of her Syracuse days, of Maltese lap dogs and capering dwarfs decked out in finery, of pink flamingos, their slender legs stepping lightly against the splendor of the sea. She told of the dead city that lay in Poseidon's kingdom and of galas under stretched cloths with golden fringes. She spoke of the singers and poets she had entertained.

Sappho noticed, as though watching another Sappho, that she pruned her account, tailoring it to fit young Erinna's mind. Expunged, for instance, was the death of the sex-maddened slave in the sunken pool. She thought often of this incident, and the picture of his final rutting never failed to excite her. But she did not speak of it because of the puzzle. She recognized it as a puzzle of her own nature. In her mind she would place her dead slave next to Kerkolas's dead slave, the one he had run over. How upset she had been, frantic, that he would not stop. Yet as her own slave struggled, she felt merely a faster beating pulse as she wondered if he would gain the air or drown to complete orgasm. It was a betting question in which there was neither pity nor anxiety. Yet it was Sappho who experienced both episodes, the twin Sapphos, the two contenders. She could not reconcile her reactions, or know in advance what they would be.

When the Muses gifted her, they allowed her to encompass all that men knew. The good and the gentle were hers. But the intensity of feeling drove the other Sappho to depths she did not want to probe. She would like to deny her—but there was a dead slave with protruding eyes, wasn't there?

There were times when she searched her being. What had occurred between the incident of one dead slave and the other: the knowledge of her pregnancy, the death of her husband. But would not such events tend to soften her nature? She shook her head at the conundrum and the dark-chambered ways of her mind, recognizing that, though she sang like a goddess, the three sisters spun her fate as they did all.

The companionship of Erinna meant a great deal to Sappho. There was an air of tranquillity about the girl which she found soothing. The two poets took pleasure in dissecting the rhythms of Aeolic meters. Erinna was sensitive to the textures of sound, and it was a delight to explore with her the forces that drive language. The cool logic Erinna used to praise Sappho's conversational tone or the harmony of a rightly selected word was a joy. And the girl sang sweetly as she rested on mounds of clover or dainty anthrysc, on which cushions had been strewn. Erinna sang with the same detached freshness with which she untwined the scorching threads of Sappho's lays. Her songs, when she could be persuaded to sing them, held a serenity that reflected her own person, and repose stole over Sappho as she listened to the kithara of seven strings.

One afternoon when the singing was done, they became quiet. Silences were always easy between them. They were the anteroom to confidences. Soon they were telling each other of the dreams the gods sent them. And Sappho spoke in hushed tones from the nadir of her soul, laying before Erinna the dread prophecy that haunted her. "It began in Syracuse and has rung in my head since. What being put it there, I do not know."

"Tell me, for it may be I can separate lying words from true."

Sappho hesitated, yet she was eager for Erinna to discount the dream. "Always," she began, "I have known who I am. Long ago I accepted myself, my smallness, my darkness, my ugliness." Erinna would have defended her against herself, but she waved her to silence. "No, no, this is part of Sappho, just as the great gift the gods endowed me with. It was ordained that men sing my songs wherever the Attic tongue is spoken.

"But in dreams it was told me that indeed my name will echo through time, but not with praise. Circe it was who whispered that I shall be remembered for ill and not for good, that Sappho the Lesbian will be abhorred and my words erased from earth." She gripped Erinna in terror. "I beg you, can you see into the truth of these things? Can you tell if they will come to pass? And why I am so cursed?"

Erinna considered what Sappho said and was a long time answering. "The Songstress of Lesbos is held in awe the world over. How could your reputation be otherwise than what it is? Therefore, they are your doubts that speak to you, and not dread Circe."

Sappho allowed herself to be persuaded. Erinna's gentle wisdom convinced her. In a rush of grateful feeling she embraced her friend.

That night Sappho held a long imaginary conversation with Erinna, in which she said how strange it was that so young a girl could provide such solace. "I think it is because of your wonderful breasts; they are like a mother's."

And she had Erinna say, "If you would nestle against them, I would be content."

Whether it was by night, or at noon selecting a menu with Niobe, there came into her head thoughts of Erinna. It occurred to her that the girl should be sculpted. Immediately she pictured the artisan smoothing those deep breasts, going over them first with flint, then with his hands. "Ah," she imagined Erinna turning to her and saying, "if they could be your hands."

All summer days were lazy, filled with pleasant walks and talks. One such day Kleis left them to hunt in a glade for a flower of many petals she could not identify.

Erinna sat with her kithara in her lap. "Have you noticed that in your poems you locate your feelings in the organs of your body?" she asked Sappho.

"Where else?" Sappho responded. "They are my feelings."

"It is often as though you are speaking to yourself."

"Perhaps I am."

"Why? When I am here?"

Sappho's luminous eyes surveyed her, lingering on the luscious fruits that hung before her. She took the stringed instrument from the girl, lowering it to her own lap. Her imaginary conversations with Erinna no longer satisfied her; Erinna herself must answer. So she said, "I wrote a song for you. I vowed not to sing it."

"For me? But why?"

Sappho sang without taking her eyes from Erinna.

Without warning
as a whirlwind

Sappho

swoops on an oak
Love shakes my heart

She put by the kithara and reached with both her hands to the girl's shoulders, bringing her close so that their breath mingled.

Erinna closed her eyes and waited like a statue. Sappho let go of her, jumped to her feet, and stripped off her garments. She stood defiantly before the girl, all parts of her glowing, the rosy teats of her breasts standing erect.

"This is I, this! Is it enough? Is it enough that Sappho loves you? You see me here. There is nothing else. Yet these arms could hold, these hands caress. Would you taste my kisses? I could cover your whole body with kisses."

Erinna trembled and said nothing.

Sappho was breathing fast and angrily. "Very well, go back to Telos. Go in the morning. You can laugh at me with your friends. Tell them that the poet was awkward and foolish, that she was utterly mistaken. Sun-struck by your beauty, she declared her love. It is a joke at which the world can laugh. Go in the morning, Erinna. Some man there is, with the usual rod for loving a woman. And he will love you."

"No."

At that single word Sappho flung her arms about her and held so tightly that each memorized the other's body with her own. The sweet oils with which their skin was rubbed made the slightest movement an undulation. All provocative swellings and private declivities were felt out.

"Here? In the garden?" Erinna gasped.

"Why not in the garden?" And they sank down together among cushions. Later Sappho was to write:

I will put you to rest on soft cushions

And again:

You shall lie on cushions new

Her hands skimmed the girl at her side as though they could not come to rest.

"I would never have laughed," Erinna said, "or told any mortal."

"Softer than fine raiment," Sappho whispered as her hands cupped the full breasts—"daintier than rosebuds." Her lips settled there as though drinking nectar. "This will be a night without blood," she said softly as she bared the girl's thighs and found between them dewy response, and a clitoris straining with expectation. The girl opened all recesses to her as a flower unfolds. Sappho's tongue flicked and her fingers skillfully brought sighs, until Erinna twisted and lifted in a demand for the final ecstasy. Sappho rode her own desire like a horse when the bridle has been cast off. She had imagined this a thousand years ago with Leto, and yet she had not. The reality of orgasm, which she had never experienced, was like the limb-loosener of Death. So completely was she stricken that she, too, would have drowned to make the body she had pinioned yield the final, divinely maddened moment. Then, clinging to Erinna, whom she had ravished as completely as herself, she paid homage to her beauty with incoherent words:

With what eyes . . .

She began again but must stop to give pleasure-giving kisses.

"Which of the gods," Sappho murmured, "has set this wild love in my heart?"

Erinna nestled against her like a sated child. "Have you never before . . . ?"

"Never! Aphrodite, whose servant from this moment I am, put it in my mind to dream—but until you opened yourself to me, I have been virgin, though bloodied."

"I am trembling from your love, Sappho. I feel consumed by you. I would die for your kisses. So tell me, for I will never know, what is it a man does to a girl in his lovemaking?"

Sappho's slender body became rigid. "A man stares at your nakedness, not with joy as I behold you, but to examine the differences between you. His member swells with pride that you are defenseless against him. Because he comes into you, he believes thereafter that you are his toy, his creature, his!"

"Does a man give no pleasure?"

"To himself. And by the manipulation of your hidden parts he rouses you, then turns on his back and snores, while you ache and throb, want and desire. Come, Erinna, lie with me on my bed. I cannot be away from you, I cannot do without your touch." And she led the girl to the main house.

At supper they devoted themselves to Kleis, but could not avoid secret looks and outbursts of merriment, which they covered by demanding further accounts of her rambles. That evening she suggested Kleis retire early.

"May this night last for me as long as two." Sappho said it as prayer, as once more her small body demanded to reacquaint itself with her partner's.

Through the tumult of her senses she heard Erinna cry out. A goddess possessed her, the foam-born, who felt each quivering triumph with her. Like the shaft of an arrow Sappho slid between her lover's legs, abandoning herself to pleasure-giving. Then with a dancer's agility, she turned completely on the supple young body, spreading herself that her student might practice what she had taught. Pleasure grew to such dimension that it surpassed pain, equaled childbearing, equaled death.

Sappho could not stop. Exhausted, Erinna permitted her all, hardly conscious of what was done to her. As Dionysos knew flesh, Sappho knew flesh. As Dionysos was flesh, Sappho was flesh. Softly Erinna was nuzzled until once more she strained after delight. She found herself worshipping, not Dionysos, who had never performed such intimacies upon her, but Sappho, who brought the voluptuousness of her poems to her body.

Sappho, too, could not believe the miracle. "How short a joy!" she cried, and before morning teased desire into her friend yet again. And stretching herself upon the girl, melted into her flesh, for she knew Erinna's body now and was as expert with it as with her lyre. It was her pleasure to bring her to the point of climax, then pretend to sleep, while slender fingers stole over her, caressing in their turn. Sappho moved as in slumber, wantonly. The nether part of their bodies danced together, their breasts bobbed and swung. Then the play was done and Sappho fulfilled herself. Intent on orgasm, she lowered herself upon Erinna in every position Aphrodite bade her. Sappho bit tentatively; Erinna cried and Sappho licked the tears away. She investigated with finger and tongue, following out the threefold partings, and into each pressed a different scent, jasmine, quince blossom, the oil of lotus.

Getting up from the bed, she brought her box of jewels and laid the gems cold and blazing on all the places that excited her. And when she saw Erinna's body festooned, she could not tame the madness of her blood but must have again. The gems cut her flesh as she descended on them, climaxing them both.

The orgy did not stop with day.

Sappho sprang from the bed of love that they might bathe together and lay flowers where in the night she had placed gems. They rubbed each other's skin with sweet oils whose seals they broke. They perfumed once again the secret places where they planted kisses.

"I will die of ecstasy," Erinna said and teasingly ran away from her.

Sappho caught her ankle and brought her down.

Neither Sappho nor Erinna was pleased to learn that a maiden had set out from the city of Pamphlia in Asia Minor, and was aboard the ship which had been sighted pulling for their shore. "Some god has dealt us this blow!" Sappho whispered in Erinna's ear.

But a school she had built, a school she would have. The time had come to set in motion the many aspects of philosophy, mathematics, and astronomy she intended to make part of the curriculum.

She began with Kleis, telling the child of Thales, who believed Ocean was the father of all. He hypothesized a fundamental substance out of which everything derived and which appeared as a liquid, a solid, and a vapor.

She was able to prove to herself Thales' method of finding right triangles. Using thread and wooden pegs, she drew a circle in the sand, marked the ends of a diameter with two pegs, and deftly looped the thread around them and a third. "He was right," she said jubilantly. "No matter where I move the third peg on the circle, the taut thread forms a perfect right angle."

"Why should I care about right angles?" Kleis asked.

"Ah, but you must care. They are the key to geometry and make possible the design of temples and the building of ships. By them great Thales predicted the eclipse of Sun. The right angle was the first shape to come out of brooding Chaos, before the gods themselves."

Kleis escaped this lesson as quickly as possible.

"She is still a little girl," Sappho told Erinna that night as they followed the movement of the planets, those silent wanderers among the stars.

They speculated together about the eclipse that had stopped the war and enabled Erinna to journey to her. Erinna thought it was the gods who whispered this knowledge to Thales, but Sappho insisted he had learned the art of prediction in Egypt and that it had to do not with gods, but with right angles.

Erinna glanced apprehensively into the shadows in case Hermes the tale-bearer was at hand. Her friend, she felt, was too bold, too reckless with these new ideas.

At the last moment before the other girl came, Sappho led Erinna into her library and showed her the treasure in the carved chest: two books of her own work, pressed from wax tablets and transcribed by herself. Beside these were complete books of Homer and Hesiod, acquired at great expense.

Erinna could scarcely grasp what her eyes saw. "You are all of magic," she said to Sappho. "One never knows what you will think of." She too had a surprise for her friend on the final evening they would be alone. She sang for Sappho "The Distaff."

Sappho listened, hypnotized. Her eyes filled with tears when it was done. "I did not know your talent was so great."

> *I do not believe*
> *that any maiden will ever*
> *rival you in your art*

And she herself served the girl that night, bringing wine and pouring freely. Flesh and fruits she set before Erinna, and would not let a servant woman near. Out of respect, she did not touch her as a lover but waited upon her as a slave.

Later she asked again for the song.

Damophyla was a handsome girl, her figure of one piece, like a column. Her eyes had a bright, bold look, but fell away from a long appraisal.

Sappho welcomed her somewhat formally with a garland of violets and larkspur.

Damophyla clasped the flowers to her and began to repeat thanks, which she had memorized.

Sappho interrupted her, asking abruptly, "Why did you come to me?"

The girl seemed surprised and suddenly confused.

"Well?" Sappho asked again.

"Because you are the songstress of Lesbos and your fame is everywhere. Also . . ."

"Yes?"

"I heard a song." She picked up a lute and sang prettily:

Though few
they are roses

"Yes, yes," Sappho said. "It is an old song from other days, but I too am fond of it. You are an accomplished musician. Do you also compose?"

"I cannot make such a claim before Sappho."

"Speak, I wish to know."

"I have composed some slight hymns to Artemis and to Hera, but they are nothing."

"I wish to hear," Sappho said.

The girl bowed her head. "Sappho speaks."

Damophyla sang her songs well, but they were derivative and not of the quality of Erinna's. Sappho watched her musingly as she performed. The girl was tall and strong as a boy. Her breasts were small, not pendulous like Erinna's, and she had not the delicacy of wrist, waist, and ankle.

Why do I compare them? Sappho wondered, annoyed with herself. Damophyla is simply a girl whom I will instruct. And she planned how to keep her busy at her studies along with Kleis so that she and Erinna could disport themselves as before. Sappho did not intend to lose hours from love. It had come to her so late that she was wild for it.

She installed Damophyla in the cottage on the far side of Erinna's. Sappho then set her tasks with Kleis, so that for the next few weeks she and Erinna planned their encounters and giggled when they thought of the big girl and the small, working out dance patterns and memorizing verse under the tutelage of servants. Damophyla, while not original in her efforts, was intelligent and made a fair try at imitating Sappho's odes. Meanwhile she and Erinna managed their escapades, the chance of discovery adding spice to their trysts.

Sappho had spent what she considered a flawless day: the morning in frolic with Kleis; retiring in the afternoon for hours of solitude in which her own work flourished; then in the cool of evening, singing rounds with the girls, a light supper of toasted cheeses, radishes soaked in olive oil, and, afterward, ices. Finally she rose, bade the others goodnight, and returned to her apartment. Preoccupied with Erinna, she ordered her bed and went to her bath. Later I will go to her, she thought as slaves bathed her with sponges, rubbed her with precious oils, brushed her hair with incense. Sappho stretched herself like a cat, dismissed her servants, and went to her sleeping room, lifting the cover and slipping into bed. It was occupied.

Two strong, young arms were around her.

"What are you doing here? What god has stolen your senses?" she asked, recognizing Damophyla.

"I but follow the practice of your house."

"I do not understand you."

"You understand me, O Desirable. I want only my share of the love you lavish on Erinna."

"You have been following us! Spying!"

"Yes. She of the seafoam led my feet. It was by accident I stumbled almost into the very spot where you lay."

"And you did not leave?"

"I could not; the goddess held me. I could not breathe or move. How sweet it looked, you two. How passionate and intent you are, O Sappho, like a supple leopard. With such love you gathered her. I could not believe your face. I knew I had to have your touch upon me, and touch you in the same way."

Since she could not stop her by other means, Sappho pushed the much larger girl away, and got up from the bed. "This may be how it is done in Asia Minor, but here it is not tolerated to thrust yourself upon another."

Damophyla covered her face with her hands and was wracked by great rolling sobs. Seeing Sappho was not moved by this, she snatched up her chiton and ran from the room.

The night for Sappho was sleepless. She supposed the girl but followed the customs of her country, that it had not seemed an improper thing to her. Had she been too severe? But how else would Damophyla learn restraint?

Sappho spoke her thoughts to Selene as the goddess rose languorously against Sky. "You look on all, Lady. You know the sacred groves where the maidens of Asia Minor give their young bodies before marriage. You have seen the art they learn, know the wiles they practice. These customs are not strange to you, Lady. But for me it was unnerving—arms out of nowhere, unexpected kisses, love words issuing from the pillows."

Still, she could not help smiling to herself when she thought how she would relate it all to Erinna in the morning.

In the morning there were other things to do, and she did not say a word to Erinna. The day was spent listening to recitations, teaching the correct fingering for a zither, and how to tune the strings by geometry.

"There now," she said to Kleis, "you see how it all comes together, and that mathematics is first cousin to music, even to the Nine themselves."

But her daughter chased after a yellow kitten born in the compound, dangling wildflowers before its paws. Sappho, giving up for the moment, turned to the other two. Although she had been busy, she had been acutely conscious of Damophyla. The girl avoided her glance and spoke only with Kleis.

Looking at her, Sappho speculated: So those were the arms that had gone around her—strong, rounded, kissed by Sun. And the mouth that had planted itself so firmly against hers? Full, with the fullness of an open petal. She had been too hard on the girl. What, after all, had been her crime? Simply the desire to know her in love.

Was it not an affront to Aphrodite to have sent her away? She wondered uneasily why she had not told Erinna of the incident.

The two Sapphos contended. Her heart beat in anticipation that evening as she bathed and prepared herself.

When she returned to her bed it was empty.

She was relieved. She was disappointed.

———

It seemed to her nothing was as it had been; there was tension in the air, as when the strings of a musical instrument are pulled taut for tuning.

Damophyla still would not glance at her directly, and preferred looking at her feet. While Erinna formed the disconcerting habit of watching her from the corner of her eyes. Even Kleis seemed out of sorts. Reaching the conclusion that everyone was behaving badly, Sappho had the grace to recognize it was she herself, and laugh.

"Today," she announced, "we will have lessons of another kind. I will take you on a tour of the house and grounds, and you shall see the inner workings whereby the fruit is picked, the tables laid, the winter mantles spun. Tell me, would you like this?"

Kleis clapped her hands, glad to be excused from lessons. Erinna, too, agreed. Damophyla, as the newcomer, said nothing.

"Well then, I shall call Niobe; she above all knows how the House of the Servants of the Muses is managed." She smiled fully on them. "I must remember to tell my brothers we did this thing."

Niobe was pleased to have her domain inspected, and a large one it was, encompassing many sections which her skillful overseeing brought together. On the way to the kitchen, they passed outdoor clay ovens with wide flat boards protruding from fiery bellies. On them dough had been shaped into loaves. When those inside were done, the boards were shoved in a notch and the next batch baked.

Kleis was delighted when Niobe broke off a corner of one of the breads for her to taste. "It is the odor," Sappho said, "that I would eat." And she watched Damophyla help herself to a piece and crumble it in her mouth. A provocative mouth, ready on the instant to laugh or cry. She remembered how she had cried when she sent her away.

Sappho came out of her daydream abruptly, conscious that the eyes of Erinna rested on her.

Kleis rushed ahead of them, ducking under great slabs of smoked flesh, fowl and fish that hung by hooks from the rafters. "Look," she said, seizing a ladle and stirring soup that boiled in a large cauldron, "I am making our dinner."

"Wherever did you find such a pretty little slave?" Erinna asked, laughing.

"She was sent me by Selene, the Lady Moon."

The wine cellar had been dug into the floor, where a hundred bottles were stored, Niobe said, with a dozen others cooling in the well, ready for drinking.

Sappho knew in a general way how her household was run, but the details fascinated her. "You are beyond price," she told Niobe, as she told her every day for one reason or another.

Large rounds of cheeses were kept under damp cloths, and shelves displayed rows of condiments. Salt was stored, too, that precious gift of the gods, from the Kumju Trail in Africa, used in preserving the flesh that came to their tables. Beside this, fresh fruit lay in woven baskets. Again they were encouraged to help themselves, and Sappho watched as Damophyla, deciding between a pear and an apple, bit into the apple. Aphrodite's fruit, Sappho thought. The girl did well in her choice. Yet for all their high spirits, she felt things were not in balance.

The candle-dipping area was announced first to the nose by the perfumed tallow. The tapers themselves were piled in great mounds, for Sappho had ever been a lover of light.

"I will take you now to the stables," she said, "so you may see how the horses are kept."

But Kleis had opened a side door and peered in. A slave wearing only a loincloth sat at work upon the floor. His body gleamed with sweat as he hammered with a covered wooden mallet what appeared to be a large white mat.

Sappho had not intended that the papyrus maker be part of the tour. This was an encroachment on her private life, which was shared with no one.

"What is he doing?" Kleis asked. "And what are those plants growing from pots?"

Since it had been discovered, Sappho shrugged and explained. "The plants are papyrus, from Egypt. And very difficult it was to bring them such a distance. Being water plants, they had to be kept damp. This when the sailors themselves had no drinking water. Needless to say, the plants arrived in poor condition. Most died, but the few you see here were nurtured and brought to health."

"What is done with them?" Kleis asked.

Erinna had already guessed.

Sappho continued: "A most wonderful material is made from the pulp of their stalks. See that fibrous white stuff he pounds? Now look on this workbench, where at a later stage it lies smoothed. Its own gluelike sap cements these long strips, which the papyrus maker has cut. Other strips are then placed over them in a crosshatch such as you see drying. Eventually they are pressed into a sheet. Many sheets pasted together comprise a roll, which is what I write my poems on."

"You write them down!" Damophyla exclaimed.

"Yes, I preserve them. This slave was purchased for his ability, when I was yet in Syracuse. The amulet upon his chest is called the Papyrus Column, for it is in the form of this wonderful stalk, and its power makes his fingers nimble."

The hour was late. In dream, Damophyla roused her. But it was no dream. The girl had again slipped into her bed.

She leaned over her. "O Sappho, lady of my heart. I felt your glances today and I knew—"

"What did you know?" Sappho whispered.

"Your hunger." The return whisper was accompanied with a tongue-kiss. "I want to sleep with you this night in love. And if I can, to please you. Lie back, O Sappho of strange beauty and banked fire, and I will teach how we approach one another in Asia Minor. First, we anoint the skin." The girl drew out her vials, which she had secreted under the pillows, and began rubbing Sappho's limbs.

Sappho closed her eyes and gave herself to yearning. At last the swelling engorgement of her flesh caused her to pull the girl close. They discovered each other. Damophyla handled her aggressively, as Erinna never dared. Voluptuously Sappho arched her small body. The hands of love spanned it like a bridge. And something exploded—she herself.

The girl lifted her to her knees, for Sappho was light and fragile. On her knees she had given birth, and on her knees she had Damophyla. Unlike Erinna, who was too soon exhausted, Damophyla continued her assault on Sappho as she swayed insatiably in her arms.

Sappho's lidded eyes only seemed closed; she watched all that the girl did. How skillful she was in the arts of love, yet hardly more than a child, sixteen or seventeen, she guessed. Sixteen, she decided, as the girl rotated her on her lap, examining her as she would a toy. Knowing fingers caused the rush of anguish that precedes release.

When they were able to lie quietly side by side, Sappho asked, "Was it Eros gave you such skill?"

Damophyla laughed. "No. Practice."

"You are so young," Sappho protested.

"I earned my dowry in the sacred grounds of the temple. One learns quickly how to win the last drachma from a purse."

"I know the custom," Sappho said. She moved away in her mind, composing, but the girl did not know it.

Damophyla went on, "Men have done such things to me as we did, and more because of the way they are made—and less, because they do not know what drives a woman mad. Sometimes it is to hold without motion and let sensation reign until the last contraction.

"How small your feet are, Sappho, how perfect your toes. How elegant and dainty your hands. I cannot breathe; I think I will die," she ended because Sappho was again with her.

When she was able, Damophyla continued, "I have my dower, and all is ready for my marriage, but I want to stay with you. Say that I may. I wish it with my heart."

There was a cry, cut off, suppressed. Someone had lifted the silver latch. Someone had stood at the door of the chamber.

Seeing her lover so startled, Damophyla said, "It was the sound of a bird, a night sound." And she began once more to kiss her breasts. But Sappho had turned pale. She took Damophyla's hands and stopped them.

"So it was the other one," Damophyla said, "the top-heavy one. What of it?"

"I think Eros sent me trouble when he sent me you. Stand up."

"Why?"

"Do it."

Damophyla rose and Sappho also got to her feet. Hunting around she found the girl's chiton of many colors and tossed it to her. "Put it on," Sappho ordered as she, more carefully, dressed herself.

"Why?" Damophyla asked.

"You shall see."

The girl threw herself upon the floor. "Do not send me away," and in suppliant but sinuous ascent began to work her fingers up Sappho's leg to the division of her body. But her wiles could not deflect Sappho. She yanked her to her feet and marched rather than walked her through the house, into the courtyard, and to Erinna's bungalow.

Sappho did not call out for permission to enter, nor did she scratch at the door, but flung it wide. Erinna was crouched in a corner of the bed. She regarded them with mournful, questioning eyes.

Sappho, giving a dextrous flick of her wrist, threw the much larger girl between them.

Damophyla looked uncertainly from one to the other.

"She is here," Sappho said. "I have brought her to you."

"To me?" Erinna's voice was a harsh whisper.

"Are we not friend-lovers? Do we not share all things? I had her. Now she is yours."

"No!" Damophyla shrieked. "I am a guest-friend; I am not to be handed about."

"You handed yourself about in the sacred grove," Sappho snapped.

"That was different, honorable. It was for my dowry. I came to you through love. I loved your songs when I was a child, when I was grown I came to you as to a goddess. Then I saw how things were with you, I thought I too . . ."

"Could play Sappho's games? Oh no. Only I say who is to play."

"You yielded to her," Erinna said in reproach.

"Yes. The gods have made me weak when my own kind are near."

"Weak? And for your weakness I am to be a jest, a prostitute?" Damophyla cried.

"For your audacity," Sappho replied.

Erinna interrupted mildly. "Will neither of you ask or consider me?"

Sappho looked at her friend in surprise.

"I want none who come unwillingly," Erinna said. "I am happy in your love, Sappho, Lady of Art. I apologize for my tears and my jealousy. I do not wish my love to place bounds on you; I have no wish to fetter your pleasure."

Sappho's look was hard and discerning, then it softened. "You are a rare gem, my Erinna. Let us sit with you and have a glass of Lesbian wine, that which my brother cultivates in his vineyards. Will you pour, Damophyla?"

The girl did as she was asked, handing the first cup to Sappho, who gave it to Erinna. "And where is yours?" Sappho asked Damophyla.

The girl began to cry. "You both hate me. I am odious to you and to myself."

"What nonsense. Some god has surely run away with your wits. No thing of beauty is odious or hateful to me. I loved your love. There is no reason to deny it, since Erinna saw. But Erinna"—she turned to her friend—"the girl is a gift, full of delights. Can we not, as friend-lovers, all three lie upon your couch? My husband, Kerkolas, told me many times that he and his friends did this both with boys and girls. He did not ask me to join him in such games, as he knew my heart was not toward him. Come, we three will compare the beauty that together Aphrodite has given us. And I will praise her and you in a wonderful song that is already in my mind. Come, lie with me. Disrobe if you wish, I shall."

And she, childlike in her nakedness, climbed upon Erinna's bed. "What do your feelings tell you, Erinna? Does this sharing not seem to you a good and a pretty thing? And you, Damophyla, look with tenderness and wonder on Erinna's breasts. One can bury one's face there as in one's mother. And observe the extreme slenderness of her body, like a delicate reed. Spread balm upon her, feel with your fingers the coolness of her flesh. Allow it, Erinna, for her fingers knead all tension from you and leave you powerless to overcome the ardor of her caress."

And so, coaxing, Sappho induced both girls to her, one to either side, and both reluctant.

Quick as a sacred Egyptian cat, she extricated herself from the center and tumbled them together. She had them laughing now, and with both heads upon her lap, gently stroked each, dipping her hands into Erinna's alabaster jars for tinted oriental oils and delicate creams.

Erinna leaned over Damophyla to lay the scent of ambergris behind Sappho's ears, then with the smallest hesitation performed the same service for Damophyla. Damophyla was intoxicated with the way Erinna's breasts swung against her. She touched and then suckled. Erinna, smiling at the girl's adolescent sucking, caressed her.

Sappho stayed still, fascinated as passion swept over them like lava flowing hot from a crack. The girls wound around each other, legs entwined; Sappho felt her own blood surge as their four arms lifted her, head and breasts hanging. Damophyla held her pelvis, Erinna her shoulders, and Sappho swung in air as Erinna's passionate tongue felt out her lips and mouth. Damophyla took possession of the long scarlet opening, and Sappho cried in frenzy. Inside the skin of her secret recesses the fingers of her lovers almost touched. Sappho knew she had been born for this ultimate voluptuous moment. Their heightened sensual play lasted until light stole under the door.

The girls carried her to the spring, where they floated her indolently, murmuring gently. She clung first to Erinna, then Damophyla. They were no longer rivals, but one in passion and in love. And Sappho made sacrifice of a garlanded lamb.

It was typical of Mitylene society to hold back, judge the success of Sappho's endeavor, before entrusting their own daughters to her tutelage. It took the arrival of Euneika from Salamis, near Athens, and Anaktoria from Miletus, and especially Gorgo of royal lineage to convince the first families of Mitylene. They no longer hesitated and a group of young women from Lesbos itself appeared at her door: Kydro, Atthis, Dika, Megara, and Telesippa.

Letters sent a year before also brought dainty Timas from Phokaea to the House of the Servants of the Muses. She was tiny like Sappho, but with a merry nature. The others treated her as their doll, cajoled her from her lessons, petted her, and fed her sweets.

Hero, a supple little maiden, arrived from Gyara, near Andros. Her family had known Kerkolas. She informed Sappho that her husband's relatives were incensed at her taking the treasure in the counting house, all the stores, and what ships and men were in Syracuse harbor.

Sappho shrugged. "I left the villa. I could not think how to get it onto the ships!"

Their laughter formed a light but friendly bond.

With such an influx, Sappho had each girl stand forth and tell of her home, and what was the state of art there, and philosophy, and the status of women. "For know," Sappho lectured them, "that Athene was born from the head of Father Zeus. Therefore, she is all intellect. And the gods in their councils listen to her words.

"When I was young," she went on, "I was rash enough to think because women kept Mitylene and ministered to the people and their problems during the ten-year war, that they should continue to do so. But two exiles taught me that only at times may we succeed in softening the laws that not only strip women of property but make them property themselves. And toward this end the House of the Servants of the Muses will fit you." It was a heavy promise, and she felt her responsibility.

From the outset Sappho decided the "initiate" alone could know her favors. The rest knew her as teacher, as patron, and did not suspect Love was the god she and her small inner group worshipped. For was it not in the act of uniting with another that the gateway opened to that elemental force which created the gods themselves and all Nature and whatever worlds filled the void? In that implosion one is lifted out of self and joins the All, the great mystery. And she understood Damophyla's temple prostitution. It is at such moments one reaches the ultimate and becomes it.

From among the newcomers she chose little Timas for their intimate romps and frolics. To love her three friends was natural to Timas; her innocence was genuine, and it was her delight to give pleasure in new ways.

Timas danced naked on a net arranged over their bed. The dance ended when they caught her little feet and pulled them through widely separated holes. In this position their snared bird was tickled, fondled, and caressed. Next they made a swing for her in the walled garden, and not once did she swing alone or with clothes on. She had not known play could be so exciting. Sappho she adored as a goddess, squeezing in next to her when the time for learning songs came. But she loved them all and was so winning and of such a happy nature that they spoiled her outrageously.

"What a child you are," Sappho murmured, as, like the yellow kitten, Timas curled against her.

During the second year of her academy, Sappho's hetaerae performed at the Mystery of Dionysos. She had them learn new songs while she pounded out the meter with a stave. Erinna's verse was sung with her own, and the girl's name became known.

With the exception of her brothers, with whom she occasionally dined, Sappho lived once again in a society without men. It was pleasant to see the maidens going arm in arm, hear their laughter, see their heads bend toward each other as they gave and received confidences. Sappho loved the sweet sound of their voices, calling, murmuring. How the gods had blessed her, for they made much of her Kleis, including her in all their sports and in their daily walks and baths.

Kydro of Lesbos was physically the most perfect of the young women. Her hair cascaded long and blond to her waist; her features were as though carved by a master sculptor. She was nicknamed "the Beautiful," and this she accepted, for she thought so, too. Damophyla transferred her allegiance to the Beautiful, and Sappho was secretly glad. She had always found Damophyla lacking in refinement, but had not been able to withstand the onslaughts of her affection. As for Kydro, she was somewhat slow in learning steps and her memorization was faulty.

Sappho's glance fell often on Anaktoria, the sultry maid of Miletus, who had arrived at the same time as Atthis. Sappho had first seen Atthis as a small child clutching a bouquet of jonquils. She had dropped one and Sappho retrieved it for her. She remembered singing then, "What a dainty little girl!" And she still was. Sappho noticed that the two had become inseparable. They walked together, took their places beside each other, studied on the same instrument, and even sang as one. How lovely they are, Sappho thought, how they complement each other, like figures fired on a vase. Whenever they were near, she stopped and talked to them. Atthis was their spokeswoman—the clever one, Sappho judged.

Kleis, who was sometimes shy among so many older girls, was particularly fond of Gongyla, who had come from Kolophon. Round, soft, and white-skinned, she was called by the girls "the Dumpling." When the name got back to her, Gongyla only smiled.

At eleven, Kleis was an accomplished child. Sappho was proud of her, especially of her beauty, which combined the best features of her own house with the chiseled look of Kerkolas. Recently, however, there had been an upset with Kleis. At first she complained that Sappho had favorites among the girls. "When lessons are finished, it is always Erinna and Timas you go off with."

"Erinna has new songs, and I like to go over them with her."

"Then why does Timas go with you? Why not me?"

"Darling, you know you haven't the patience for yet more lessons."

"You might at least ask me sometimes," Kleis said petulantly.

"I will, pretty one, I will." And Sappho resolved to take her daughter on a picnic, just the two of them as in the old days. But she was busy and, before this could happen, a more serious incident occurred.

Kleis, not satisfied with her mother's explanation, feeling passed over and left out, followed her and removed a stone from the wall of Sappho's small private garden. There she saw not lessons or lute playing, but Timas swinging naked. Her mother and Erinna were naked also except for flowers in their hair.

The two made a game of sending Timas winging, and indicated, with whispered instructions, what places she was to kiss on their opponent. There was much laughter as she complied and, with a push, was sent off again with a fresh commission.

Kleis had seen enough. Clambering on top of the wall, she threw the stone into her mother's garden and ran away.

"Kleis!" Sappho cried in dismay, for she had sprung to the gate and opened it in time to see her daughter racing off.

Sappho did not know how to make up with her. Later that day she suggested they have their deferred picnic, but Kleis said she did not feel like it. Sappho next proposed they go down to the sand shore and search for agates. Kleis said it was too hot.

Sappho was glad when Gongyla was able to entice the child with promises of songs from her homeland. But rebellion simmered in Kleis and broke out during the daily lesson. Sappho was going over a theory of Anaximander. Kleis misquoted his words and Sappho rebuked her, but gently, saying, "You must listen with more attention, for this man's thoughts are caught in the curious current of creation itself. He has written and put together a book, not of poetry but prose. Therefore, be attentive when he tells us that the world is infinite and the nonlimited pervades all things."

"If it can't be seen," Kleis objected, "how do we know it's there?"

"Anaximander tells us while it itself can't be observed, yet it holds the world in balance and flows through all Nature."

Kleis tossed her head. "I don't believe in things I can't see."

"You believe in many things you can't see. You believe in love, for instance, and you can't see that. You should think into things a bit, Kleis, before making foolish remarks."

Kleis flushed. "You're always finding fault with me. Because I am your daughter, I have to be perfect, better than anyone else. It isn't fair."

Sappho was at a loss. "I don't understand you, Kleis. When I was your age, I was greedy to learn. I stretched out my two arms for knowledge."

"I am not you, Mother." Her tone implied, And I thank the gods that I'm not.

Sappho recognized that Kleis was passing through a difficult period, and that part of the blame was hers, but she refused to be judged by her own child. She is my daughter, she thought, and things are not easy for her. She supposed it was natural for children to pull away from parents and find their independent selves. In the meantime, with Gongyla and her many fair companions, Kleis need never be lonely or alone, except by her own wish.

Since Kleis had stumbled on their lighthearted games, they had all but stopped. The serious Erinna, she suspected, was secretly pleased, but Sappho had been awakened to mad, exciting ways that had been withdrawn. Although little Timas still danced for her and Erinna played her songs, Sappho was not entertained for long but restless and dissatisfied.

Niobe was dressing her hair with ivory pins when Sappho asked suddenly, "Do you have a husband? I inquire because I see you are pregnant again. You were pregnant last year, too, were you not?"

Niobe said quickly in apology, "I tied the stomach band as tightly as I could."

Sappho laughed. "I don't mind. I just wondered what you did with them, your children, I mean."

"I find them places with the priestesses."

"How many have you?" It was odd, all these years she had not realized Niobe had children.

"Five."

"Five! Boys and girls both, I suppose?"

Niobe nodded.

"And your husband, did he come with you from Syracuse?" For she knew a head slave had power and could arrange these things.

"I have no husband, Lady."

"What, only children?"

"My oldest was born in high Pyrrha."

"Pyrrha? As far back as then? I didn't know." Unbidden, Leto was before her. Leto, whose hand she had held on the way to the washing springs. Leto, whose soft wide breasts she had outlined in exotic perfumes. Leto, a farmer's wife with a brood of children. Annoyed at this unbidden picture, she lifted her polished mirror and examined Niobe's work. "Tell me, Niobe, what do you think of men?"

"I put up with them. What else can I do? I am a woman."

"Does it seem strange to you that I have no husband?"

"Sappho is Sappho" came the swift reply.

"I dreamed last night," Sappho continued aloud, but to herself. "I dreamed of the city under the sea. I walked its streets. Broad, empty except for jeweled companies of fish. Its great columns, porticos, and entablatures lay in massive ruins at my feet." Conscious again of her servant she asked, "What do you suppose such a dream portends?" But her attention was diverted. Someone was in her garden, her private, personal sanctuary. She got up to investigate and was amazed to see one of the hetaerae, Gorgo, the daughter of kings. She was even more amazed that she was twining the ropes of the swing with flowers and ivy.

Gorgo turned. "I had hoped to surprise you when it was all done," she said.

Sappho was put off by the girl's bold assumption that she was free to trespass. "How did you know there was a swing in my garden?"

"Kleis told me."

What else, she wondered, had Kleis told her? Aloud she said, "This garden is my retreat, Gorgo. I come here to be alone."

"Then who pushes you in your swing?"

"I push myself."

Gorgo laughed. Her teeth were sharp little seed pearls. "I heard otherwise. And I've come, O esteemed Sappho, to join in your games."

Sappho caught her breath sharply. "No games are played here."

"But I heard that little Timas . . ."

"I can't help what you heard."

Gorgo's dusky cheeks deepened in hue. "I thought to please you by decorating your swing." And, as Sappho said nothing, she continued with more assurance, "The girls say that among us you have special friends. I want to be such a friend."

Sappho regarded the girl appraisingly. She had a premonition about Gorgo. The other hetaerae complained of her, saying she was proud and arrogant, with a tendency to show off her fine possessions. At one time Sappho had reprimanded her, "Do not be so conceited over a ring." And while she did not want to quarrel with her, Sappho felt she must be dealt with firmly. "In my position, Gorgo, I must be careful to appear evenhanded and not rouse the serpents of envy."

Gorgo, being of royal descent, made no effort to hide her displeasure at Sappho's reply. "You are my teacher, O Sappho, yet you yourself must learn how to receive gifts. You have ruined mine." She threw the flowers and the ivy into the dust. "Would you have my friendship lie there too?" And she left with her anger.

It was not finished with Gorgo. Several days later there came a scratching at the door, and the girl burst in, her attractive face flushed and distorted. "There is a thief among us! I have been robbed of my Egyptian necklace, the one of polished onyx set in gold filigree."

Sappho held up her hand. "Certain it is that there is no thief in the House of the Servants of the Muses. Think a moment—not the lowest slave would take such a costly ornament. Where could she wear it? How display it?"

Gorgo's finely arched brows drew together. "I had it yesterday."

"Then it is mislaid behind some pillow or other."

"I tell you it is gone. And it was my grandmother who gave it to me."

"It will be found," Sappho said firmly, and called Niobe to bring her jewel case.

Niobe obeyed and, kneeling, held the casket out to her mistress, but Sappho shook her head, indicating it was to Gorgo she should present it. Gorgo looked questioningly at Sappho.

"Take something that pleases you from my box."

Gorgo drew herself up. "Sappho is generous; there are beautiful pieces here. But you did not accept *my* present."

Silently Sappho asked whatever god was near to help her hold on to her patience. But she was tried further, for it was apparent that the necklace was a pretext. Gorgo had come with a purpose, which, as she spoke, became plain. "My bungalow lies so far from yours, O Sappho. If I were closer, I would feel more at ease about my jewels."

"As you know, the bungalows are all occupied."

"But a word from you and someone would trade with me."

"I cannot give such a word. The assignment of bungalows was made long ago."

"But you could change it, esteemed Sappho."

"Perhaps, but I have no intention of doing so."

It was morning and Sappho brought together her hetaerae. They sang with handheld drums, experimenting with rhythms and meters. Erinna was again absent. Many days she kept to her quarters with some indisposition or another. Sappho sent a slave with flowers to inquire after her. In the midst of these lovely girls, she felt lonely. She was uncomfortable around Gorgo and purposely did not go near her.

Her eyes, wandering the pretty group, came to rest on Manasdika, whom they called Dika. An imperious girl of fine family, although not royal. Her dress of Lydian work blended in an array of colors harmonizing with her tawny hair.

> As for me
> I am conscious
> of this . . .

That morning Dika had chosen hyacinths to wear, the flower Sappho loved better than any other. Did Dika know this when she wove them together with anise? Did her preference guide the girl's choice?

It came to her that she had never properly assessed Dika's loveliness. How could she have failed to notice the perfection of her profile, the delicate modeling of her lips? She was charming.

Dika became conscious of Sappho's gaze and turned her head away. Sappho set her hetaerae to discovering new chords. Later in the day she looked for Dika and could not find her. Had word of her wild affairs come to the girl's ears? Did her hetaerae know that she had taken lovers from among them? She didn't think they would care, but their parents might if word of such doings were to get out. Worry jumped on her like a cat from a tree.

Work, she decided, would cure her mood.

What came to her? The following:

> But you, Dika, plait with your delicate fingers a
> wreath of sprigs
> of anise
> upon your lovely hair;
> for very sure it is that the blessed Graces
> are inclined to look

with favor
on anything decked with pretty flowers
and to turn away from all that come to them
ungarlanded

The gods had shown her what course to set. She sent the poem by the hand of a slave to Dika's bungalow.

She waited.

She poured wine.

She dined.

There was no response from Dika. Sappho spent a night of fragmented dreams. Dika invaded her sleep. Dika in her many-hued gown, Dika *on* her many-hued gown.

Sappho threw off her cover and sprang up from bed. Night had not ended, but she decreed an end to it. For its coldness seemed to burn more severely than the heat of noon. Sappho moved about the apartment collecting stylus and wax and the stele to hold impressions. Aphrodite, on her right hand, whispered that the proud Dika would require assurance of being first in her affections, that old loves must be forsworn. Dika would demand renunciation. After a struggle in which she reminded herself of Erinna's recent coldness, she wrote:

Manasdika is even lovelier
than the exquisite Erinna.
Never did I yet meet, my sweet one,
a more disdainful beauty
than you

She reached for the bell that brought her servant, then stayed her hand. Pale, delicate, intellectual Erinna. She would always love her, but her body no longer throbbed at the thought of her. A sister, that is what she was to her—so she rationalized, she who had never had a sister.

Sappho called her slaves from sleep to bathe, anoint, and dress her. "Go back to your rest," she told them when they were through. And to herself whispered, "Golden-slippered Dawn has not yet come." She went out clutching the poem.

She could not stop herself; Aphrodite herself compelled her. She hurried toward the building that housed Dika, knowing that the outcome was far from certain.

Sappho scratched tentatively at Dika's door. The girl slept on. Sappho opened it, arousing a slave whom she motioned to leave.

Dika slept deeply, her lips parted, her wonderful breasts exposed. Sappho knelt by her, drinking in her beauty. No facet of face or body escaped her. She waited without stirring until the girl woke.

Dika gasped at seeing her.

Sappho spoke softly, "Lovely Dika, I have brought you a morning gift." And she laid the poem upon the bed between them.

Dika did not touch it. "Why are you here?"

"To bring you the gift."

"A poem? Why not send it by a slave, as you did the other?"

"This morning I am the slave, your slave, Dika."

"I do not understand you."

"You understand."

"You do not know me, Sappho. I am not second in anyone's affections."

"Read, I pray you, the poem."

Dika picked it up and read. "It is very pretty," she said. "Thank you."

"I did not bring it for a thank-you. Dika, you are too much for me. Pity me, for your beauty is too much. I am overcome like a warrior on the field. Let me touch your hand, let me kiss just the rings of your fingers."

Dika hesitated. "Is it true, am I more pleasing to you than Erinna?"

"I swear it." Her hand spanned the girl's ankle and the amulets tinkled.

"What of the others?" Dika asked.

"Only you." Her hand insinuated itself along the calf and pressed the young thigh.

Dika removed herself from Sappho's touch. "What of Damophyla?"

"It is ended."

"And Gorgo?"

"There has never been a Gorgo."

"Timas?"

"Timas!" Sappho jumped back from her. "Would you take little Timas from me! Must I despise everyone but you?"

"Yes," Dika said.

"Your words disturb my soul. Yet I must do as you say." Sappho kissed the pretty foot and fondled it, but it, too, was withdrawn. "O Dika, what lies have you listened to against me? I think you do not know my heart at all."

She became conscious of the slaves stirring in the compound. The household was awake. Hastily she said, "Tonight, Dika. I'll wait for you in my rooms tonight."

Dika did not reply.

During the day the girl paired with other friends, and Sappho watched her covertly as she spoke to her hetaerae of the Heavens and the star charts Thales drew. As soon as possible, she retired to her rooms and threw knuckle bones to see if Dika would come.

Unable to settle to anything, Sappho finally snatched up her lyre and went to sit on the steps. If she sang from there, Dika might hear; even though it had grown late she might yet be persuaded.

In the morning there was a commotion among the girls, for it was discovered that Dika's cottage was empty; her toiletries, clothes, gems, and slaves had gone in the night. The hetaerae whispered among themselves and stole pitying looks at Sappho, who must bear it. Erinna's look, however, was not of pity but of reproach.

Did I deserve this? Sappho asked herself. Did she deserve the awful hollowness that spread through her whole body?

She went inside and beat herself with her fists and hit her head against the wall. "I drove her away," she mourned. That little foot, that high-arching little foot—she had held it like a bird.

So the woman grieved.

> *Zeus does not give to all men*
> *their heart's desire*

So the poet spoke.

Shortly after the defection of Dika, Sappho's younger brothers came to see her. Sappho rushed to give greeting. She had seen them but rarely.

The demands of her poetry and her teaching kept her from outside contact. But her welcoming words were checked as she encountered stiffness in their replies. Drawing back, she attempted to read their countenances. Young Larichos was grim, Eurygyos equally cold.

"There has been ill news?" Sappho cried. "Has the blue-haired brother of great Zeus not spared our brother? Tell me quickly, is it Khar?"

"Lead us to your villa that we may speak in private."

Sappho immediately regained her composure. "It is no word of Khar that has brought you." She took them without further speech into the gardens of her home. "Will you have wine or food?"

Larichos turned on her. His handsome lips writhed. "Whore!"

Eurygyos put out a hand to restrain him, but the boy was filled with bile that could not find release except in direct onslaught. "It is not my word," Larichos said. "It is what I hear of you, and worse. 'Slut' is too good, from what I hear. The House of the Servants of the Muses belongs on the street of women. Except no men are welcome here. You are the man here, and these your concubines, who serve you in every shameful way you can devise. 'Husband-hating Sappho' is how you are called in town. By the gods, I cannot figure out what it is you do. But even in the great hall—where I have the honor, as you know, to be cupbearer—there is talk since Manasdika returned so unexpectedly."

Dika? Had Dika spoken against her? What had she said? O Dika, belovedest of girls— A spasm of the heart caused her to bring her hand to her bosom.

"Of course, everything is innuendo," Larichos said, "so that I cannot pick up a spear and challenge them. It is all obliquely put. But I believe it to be true."

Eurygyos spoke to calm the situation. "We will have the wine you offered, Sister, and accept what refreshment you have, which we could not do if these vile reports, these calumnies which have so upset Larichos, had substance."

Sappho put by the pain caused by Dika. She inspected her brothers. She had taught them to walk; they had taken their first steps to her, and babbled out first words. But now she said, "I fear you must go away from my house parched and hungry as you came." She spoke with severity to hide the sick anger. Her brothers judged her as they would their wives. They did not recognize that she was Sappho.

Eurygyos could scarcely speak. "You are saying it is true? That you prostitute yourself here among your women?"

Sappho considered her words. "I make account to none. By self-made laws I rule myself. But since you are of my blood and brothers, I say—should I take a girl in love, she would be dearly held by me. There is no prostitution here." Then with that maddening smile that bode no good for any, she asked gently, "Do you object to the love the gods set in the hearts of man and maid?"

"But you," Larichos cried, "are neither one or the other! What do you use upon them? The pinecones of a Dionysos night?"

Sappho went pale. "This is a house dedicated to the Muses—no brutal thing happens here. The lyre sounds here, the high-arched feet of maidens beat out our ancient Aeolian dances. The poet Sappho composes verse, as does the poet Erinna. If Eros or the goddess born of foam finds a way to us, is this an evil? Is this a reason for breaking in on a sister with accusations unloving and unkind?"

Eurygyos said slowly, "We came, I from far Eresos and Larichos from Pittakos's hall, that you might deny the rumors that fly about. They are an embarrassment to us both, I in my business, Larichos among the leaders of men. We were prepared to defend you, for you are our sister."

"Atlas in the West bears the pillars of Heaven and Earth upon his shoulder, and his home is in dark Cilician caverns. He is my brother . . . and Khar."

"Then it's all true!" Larichos sounded as though he had been run through and disemboweled.

"It is true and it is not true. I have no way of making you understand." The three looked at each other with great misery. "If I were a brother," she asked them, "would you be here?"

"Of course not . . ." Larichos began, and stopped.

"Spit your venom on the ground!" Sappho could no longer yoke her anger. "Have I not knowledge of oboe players, Larichos? Such is not done here. And none is here except by her own will. Speak to any. Ask them to leave, beg them to leave." She smiled into their faces. Though small, she was dangerous. Dangerous and willful.

Eurygyos shook his head. Larichos rent his clothes in a gesture of despair. They went away. They knew of old they could not change her.

After this visit, Sappho wrote:

> *Pain penetrates*
> *me drop*
> *by drop*

Pain sewed a line between her eyes. Pain pierced her vitals as though she were spitted like some sacrificial beast.

She made an attempt to work. The work did not satisfy her. The distant strains of a waxed reed gave no pleasure. She recalled dread Circe and the prophetic dream. In her mind she made answer: Love, like poetry, cannot be an evil. Does not everything that has life sustain itself through some means?

And what did she have? Only love. Love sustained her art, and her art in turn sustained her. She needed to give and receive it. It was necessary to her. Still, it was impossible to reason away Dika's desertion, the rebuke of brothers, the shadow of a dream.

Let them censure her for her lovers. She had not changed from the child who *wanted*, the young girl who *desired*. Was there evil in this, when she gave herself completely, without stint, to each friend-lover? Poetry, knowledge, laughter, tears—she laid them at the feet of the loved one.

What account had Dika given of the House of the Servants of the Muses? And of herself? It could not, she thought, be as bad as her brothers made out. If so, the citizens of Mitylene would have ordered their daughters home. Neither Kydro, Atthis, Megara, nor Telesippa had been sent for, which meant her brothers listened to gossip that did not reflect the general esteem in which she was held. Surely it was her critics they should attack, not their sister. For they were Argive, even as she. Were they not to blame in lacking loyalty?

Another thought tormented her: Would Khar, had he been home from his voyage, have sided with them? Would she have read the same contempt in his eyes? She shuddered and put her arms about herself, as though they had been Khar's arms. She could not lose Khar.

And what of Larichos, the little boy who had run along the pier until exile took her from sight? How vitriolic he had been! Surely Hermes, that mischief-maker, inflamed his mind. Could any love she pursued in the three-tiered garden of her home damage his position or career? As the brother of Sappho the poet, he had won distinction. Was that what was behind it? Did he dislike owing anything to her?

As for Eurygyos, he had never understood her. It was his contention that she brought misfortune on herself.

Did she?

And Kleis? Since the episode in the garden, how much did her daughter know or guess? She thought of her as still a child, but . . .

On impulse, Sappho left her chamber. Taking a dusty footpath she set out for a statue that had always had special meaning for her. It was of a pretty girl-child of seven or eight who had, in days gone by, been sacrificed to the fiery torch of Artemis to bring honor upon her house. Recently the statue had troubled her. It reminded her of Kleis when Kleis had been all hers, in the Syracuse days when she braided flowers in her hair.

She came upon the marble figure surrounded by cyclamen and knelt to it, knelt to her own fears. For she realized, gazing into the marble face, that it no longer resembled Kleis. It seemed while she turned her head, Kleis had grown up. This grown Kleis no longer broke into hoydenish shrieks of laughter, no longer whispered confidences. This new grown Kleis made judgments and, like her uncles, rendered verdicts.

Clasping the feet of the statue, Sappho wept. Not only had she lost her brother, she was afraid she had lost her only child. Last night they had dined together. She had been at pains to have Kleis's favorite dishes prepared, each course served with flowers. But the old intimacy was gone.

Sitting at the foot of the statue, Sappho made a poem:

> I am a little girl and voiceless,
> and yet, if any ask,
> I cry aloud with this voice at my feet

She put the poem by to finish it another time. The price for being a woman was too high. From this day on she would be not woman but poet only. Poetry shed radiance on her life, while love—all love—was a torment.

Gorgo waylaid her. "You are avoiding me, O Sappho."

"Yes," Sappho said briefly.

"But why? Have any spoken ill of me?"

"No one has spoken ill of you."

"Then why? Surely Dika is not worth such sorrow?"

Sappho reacted angrily at any mention of Dika. By what right did Gorgo prod and question her? But because she was beset by many sorrows, she answered with restraint, "Have you never felt the need to be alone? I must have wide swaths of aloneness about me."

"Let me bring you comfort in your grief, O Sappho. Together we could touch Sun."

Sappho shook her head. "I do not look for another love, Gorgo."

The girl's eyes darted the fire of an anger she did not speak.

That night Sappho pressed into wooden tablets the question

> *Why does that daughter of Pandim,*
> *the heavenly swallow*
> *weary me?*

For it was certain that she was weary of Gorgo's constant importuning. What did she think? That Sappho replaced one toy with another? But it was herself she was most weary of. Oneself one cannot so easily dismiss.

She was aware finally that little Timas crouched on the floor by her bed and cried softly.

From her lethargy Sappho reached out a hand to her. "Dear little Timas, you alone come to me."

Timas cried harder. "I do not wish to be here. I wish it, but not to say what I must."

Sappho sat straight up. "Cry woe! Cry woe! There is more—tell it, though it tie up my bowels and stop my heart. What misfortune? Sweet little Timas, I would rather hear it from you than any I know."

"Gorgo! She is also gone."

The strength of anger flooded Sappho's voice. "Gorgo? Do you know where she is?"

"It is known. Dika only left because of Gorgo's advice. And it was Gorgo who helped her. She thinks someone told you what she did, so she has gone to hide herself with Andromeda."

"Andromeda? Who is Andromeda?"

"No one, really. Just some country woman, who, hearing of the success you have made, has set up a school on the same model . . . or so she claims."

Sappho was astounded. "There is some person who is imitating what I have done here, and no one told me of this insolence?" Anger brought color back to her face and fueled her body. She jumped to her feet. "I want to know about my 'rival.' " She used the word with sarcasm, for who could rival Sappho? "Is she a poet?"

Timas laughed. "I do not think she understands either meter or song. She is without accomplishment . . . except . . ."

"Go on."

"I have heard she is versed in witchcraft, that she sells potions for love and nostrums for sickness."

"It is the same thing," Sappho said tartly. "What else have you heard?"

Timas hesitated. "I do not know if it is true. But I have heard her women patronize the maker of leather."

Sappho laughed scornfully. "You have completed the picture. Gorgo shall have no punishment from me; she has arranged it for herself."

And because Timas was the only one she could speak freely to, she went on. "How the gods must laugh at our folly. There are women, Timas, who consider themselves inadequate men. They imitate men in all ways, even to the buying of the leather phallus which they strap to their thighs and use on their sisters. But this is a Sybarite evil. You see before you Sappho, a woman, who makes songs. And I tell you this, I love being female. I am not an inadequate male. I am inadequate at nothing. I am not jealous of the build of a man, nor his dangling accoutrements for love. No, in my person I am complete. And my way of loving is complete.

"My own sex stirs me deeply, for we are delicate of limb, fond of laughter, of music, and gentle with one another. We do not wish to be heroes, going into battle to make ourselves great by taking the lives of brothers. We abhor violence and live graciously, surrounding ourselves with flowers, with friends, with sweet play, and our kisses grow from affection to the madness the gods and goddesses procured for humankind. And which they envy, for do they not take our shapes to lie with mortals and taste the sweetness of our love? Then comes some monstrosity like this, this . . . what did you say her name is?"

"Andromeda."

"This Andromeda, who takes it into her head to behave as a man. Oh, this is a great sin against our sex, for violence is against our nature. I have only pity for Gorgo, even though she took my Dika. At least Dika had the sense to go to her parents. Still, I mourn her, and the manner of her leaving—by stealth, Timas, as though I would have detained her."

"Dika did not trust herself, Sappho. That is why she left."

"She was afraid to love me?"

"Gorgo told her she would be cast off."

Sappho frowned. "None is cast off, not ever. Any girl I have lain with, I love always."

"But lie with others."

Sappho bit her lip. Timas was allowed impertinences she accepted from no one else. She considered the complaint, then said, "There are many ways to love, little one. When one candle is burned out, another is lit, so there is always the blessed light which all love. Every one of my hetaerae, my dear companions, live in the light of this calmer love."

She fell silent, but her curiosity was not satisfied regarding Andromeda. She guessed the woman would accept any for a fee. To test this she sent a serving maid, who, asking admittance to the society, learned all she could and reported back to Sappho.

"Describe this Andromeda," Sappho ordered.

"A countrified woman who gives herself airs and does not even know how to drape her peplos."

Sappho was unbelieving. "How can Gorgo, of royal family, bear it there?"

"She is taught many odious things—how to overcome a rival, and . . ."

"And how is that done?"

"One way is with footprints. You put your right foot into your rival's left print and your left foot into her right print and say: 'I am trampling you. I am above you. I shall triumph over you.' "

Sappho laughed incredulously. "Can they really be so childish?"

"This is serious business for Andromeda, Lady. For this spell she receives a loaf of bread, salt, a drachma, and seven obols."

"She is paid all this for such nonsense as footprints?"

"And there are other spells. For a faithless loved one, a bowl of watered wine is brought and an item of her clothing to bewitch her back. With sulphur and salt the old hag then starts a burning in the water and summons her by terrible oaths."

"More nonsense."

"I learned that the most expensive incantations are done with molds of Thessalian birds and wheels. Wax is melted, to melt the heart of the one who will not love."

"And the wheel?"

"To grind her into the Earth if she does not come back."

Sappho nodded, her picture of the woman borne out.

"And it is true," the slave continued, "that she uses self-satisfiers on herself and her girls. They are made in Miletus by master cobblers and can be wielded by two girls together, who sometimes make an entertainment of it and ride upon each other naked as though they rode a sow. Also, they are not fastidious, but dip the monstrosity in a bowl of hiero, which oils it well, then use it again."

"Enough! I have heard enough. I do not wish this woman or Gorgo or their vile practices mentioned in my house again."

That night little Timas crept into Sappho's bed to kiss the palms of her hands and dampen her hair with sweet-smelling oil of crocus. Her innards, still burning for Dika, were soothed by the curling and uncurling of the rosy body burrowing into her flesh, kissing where she dared and then kissing where she dared not. Dear Timas, sweet and tender, could not put out the fire.

Sensing this, the girl tied her favorite purple-dyed kerchief on the sculptured curls of Sappho's finest statue, a Syracusan Aphrodite that watched over their bed. On discovering it in the morning, Sappho exclaimed, "A gift from a precious giver!" And later pressed her thanks into her stele, making the transfer, as always, in secret and at night.

> *And the purple*
> *handkerchief,*
> *arranged over both*
> *thy cheeks, which*
> *Timas sent for thee*
> *from Phokaea, a*
> *gift from a*
> *devoted giver*

But even the devotion of Timas could not help her find joy. Though she slept by the warm body of the little one, she was not warmed.

"Let us be happy," Timas begged. "Let us have a feast or a contest."

Sappho reminded her that contests had been popular since ancient times, when Hera, Pallas Athene, and Aphrodite disputed which was most beautiful. "And you know how that ended—with the unfortunate judging by Paris and the Trojan Wars."

"Ours will be a little contest among ourselves, and we will be the judges, for the goddesses will grant us divine vision."

"Perhaps later," Sappho said, for she still brooded. Not only had Dika fled from her, Erinna had guessed the reason. Without giving voice to her grief she simply withdrew. Even her daughter stood to one side regarding her quizzically, and found no time for a private word. Sappho could not endure silent disapproval from those she loved.

Enough! Enough! She told herself Timas was right to demand a diversion and in the morning went out to her hetaerae. It was as though she returned from some far place. The girls rejoiced and played, chasing one another and throwing chains of flowers. Even Kleis smiled at her, though somewhat distantly.

For the noon repast Sappho ordered wine and cakes, and a large platter of pistachio nuts, which Timas adored. It was so easy to make the child happy. Why could she not succeed better with her own daughter?

But watching Timas's enjoyment lightened her mood, and she whispered to her that she could announce the contest. The hetaerae were delighted at the novelty and went to the baths to wash and make themselves ready. Afterward they gathered at the fountain, at first throwing baubles onto the water, then dashing wine on those they wanted to sink, for the owner must pay a forfeit. Much laughter and mock groans accompanied their misses.

As a prelude to the judging, Sappho had slaves carry in a naked Aphrodite and lay the statue beneath the water. She was their new target. They threw jewels at her breasts, her thighs, the perfect mound, so that their own parts would be enhanced by the goddess and made more beautiful. Then Sappho indicated they were to withdraw to the courtyard. There before the statue of Hera their embroidered robes fell, wafting down one upon the other in flaming red, pear pink, saffron, purple from Tyre. Sappho picked up her lyre and strummed an Aeolian rhythm as the harmonies of the maidens were revealed.

First to stand before them was Diomede of Lesbos, whose skin was pure alabaster. The girls formed a ring around her and the aulos piped shrilly as they gave her marks for the tilt of her breasts, the slenderness of her ankles, the high aristocratic instep, the delicate shell closeness of her ears, the heavy loop of hair, the wide setting of her eyes, straightness of nose, fullness of lips and buttocks, flatness of belly and length of leg, for the taller were most admired. Then Euneika, the bubbling, merry girl, even now laughing and making silly poses in imitation of a fawn or a statue. Her complexion was of coan transparency and her charm was in her movements, her lively eyes and quick-wittedness.

Hero was shoved forward to the center of the ring. She was a runner from Gyara, muscular but beautifully formed. All her features were pleasing, and she herself pleased.

Telesippa from Lesbos, stately, with gray eyes like Pallas Athene, born from the head of Zeus. Also from Lesbos was Megara, with luscious mouth of berry red, and glorious hair that caught the lights of Sun. She was a languorous girl, made for love, with heavy-lidded, sleepy eyes.

Atthis was pushed out next by her friend Anaktoria. Her hair fell in a thick plait over her shoulder, reflecting many shades from copper-gold to the yellow of a jonquil. Her body was slender of waist, wrist, and ankle, but womanly and full. Her eyes mirrored the sea, a tempestuous, changeable blue-green. And her legs were shapely, with rounded calf and thigh. She was given many marks for her beauty. And Sappho thought her beautiful, but with the kind of beauty that disturbs, for it was not harmonious or ideal. Somehow her features were at odds with one another.

They were now judging Anaktoria, who was as dark as Atthis was fair. Her eyes were blackly lashed, her hair thick and curly, and her navel a deep, inverted goblet in which Atthis playfully placed a purple bud that she might win the contest. This made the girls laugh and give her a high score.

The judging continued. There was the young and sturdy Damophyla, whom she and Erinna had once found pleasure in, but who paired now with Kydro. It was Erinna's turn. She was made to stand reluctantly at the center, so delicate, so graceful, and with the most sensual of bosoms, two doves with deep aureate blooms that hardened under the gaze of the girls and under Sappho's. Her light eyes were lowered, but how willowlike she was on her long, slender legs. And her fingers were most fragile.

She and Erinna disporting together without restraint while Cotytto, goddess of sensuality, looked on—Sappho remembered it all: how they played in the stream, caught each other's ankles until they lay, their bodies happy islands against which the current rushed: through their fingers, between their toes, across their legs, making a dash at their high breasts. Erinna was singing poems then, and Sappho knew that of all the young women that had joined her coterie, Erinna alone was visited by the Muses. But days give rise to new suns. Erinna no longer sang and was very distant with Sappho.

Sappho, to hide her hurt, found only formal words for her friend. She was conscious of loneliness even here among her maidens. She had turned thirty-four, and her companions seemed young indeed. Recently she searched her mirror for signs of the years. They had not yet appeared—still a cold fear flowed along the pathways that carry blood in the body and are its many rivers.

She made an effort to focus on the contest as Kleis, being too young herself, led Gongyla to the judging. Sappho looked casually at Kleis's special friend. The Dumpling was no more. Three years had formed the adolescent plumpness into shapely breasts and an enticing rump. Her thighs, still heavy, were well shaped.

The judging before the shrine of Hera of the glancing eyes was at an end. Sappho followed Gongyla's movements as she dressed. Kydro was acclaimed the most perfect. And with this Sappho agreed, but her perfection was unanimated. It was the overly rounded thighs that pleased her most in Gongyla.

Sappho thought of another reason to be pleased with the girl—her memory for songs and for sums was excellent. A girl like this could be helpful to her in keeping her accounts, and she convinced herself that that was why she went out of her way to speak to her.

Kleis stood chatting with her friend, discussing what to their minds had been the merits and demerits of the contestants, when Sappho approached them. "Next year, Kleis, you will be ready for judging as well. And I don't know which of you should win. But," she went on,

"I take this opportunity to speak of more serious matters. My black ships have once again returned. In the past I have allowed slaves to tally up their wares, and I believe I have been defrauded of a fortune over the years. Since you are so quick with numbers, Gongyla, I thought you might help me oversee this enterprise."

Gongyla looked startled. "I don't know that I am capable."

"Oh, you are capable. I am your teacher and I know. But perhaps such serious business would keep you from your diversions?"

"If I could assist in any way . . ." Gongyla began.

Sappho smiled. "You can. And I will call on you."

"You didn't have to agree," she heard Kleis say as the two girls walked away.

Borrowing her friend for a few hours each day will not inconvenience Kleis too much, Sappho told herself. After all, she has many friends to play with. Still, she was uneasy that Kleis would not see it that way. But a twelve-year-old would be quickly diverted, she concluded, and she put it from her mind.

Her black ships roamed the seas even as they had in Kerkolas's time, bringing booty of gold, spices, and slaves. In spite of the expenditures incurred in the maintenance of her sumptuous villa, the far-flung grounds, and the lavish style in which she provided for herself and her hetaerae, she was richer now than even in Syracuse. It was like tumbling downhill—wealth begot wealth at an ever-increasing rate.

She was grateful, for these riches protected her. She knew in the town there was resentment at the conspicuous style in which she lived. Her people reported to her what was said: a woman alone, knowing such freedom, administering a fortune, managing a shipping empire— it set a dangerous precedent.

Because she was Sappho, she could ignore this subterranean hiss of disapproval. Because she was rich, she paid the eunuch army that defended her house a handsome wage. She was secure. She was safe.

In her dealings with sailors and captains alike, she was generous and her crews loyal, boasting that they sailed in her service. It was a small inconvenience that now and then she must spend a few hours assessing the fruits of their journeys. She congratulated herself in thinking of Gongyla. The girl was always ready to laugh and would make the drudgery easier.

In fact, there was no drudgery, only a few guilt pangs at taking the girl from Kleis so much of the day. But in all probability, by now Kleis had filled the gap with other companions.

Sappho's head and that of Gongyla met over a single scroll of papyrus, as they scratched off another bundle of sticks representing bales of silks. She found herself glancing tenderly at the curve of cheek and swelling of breast, at the milk-white shoulder.

Sappho attempted to curb her thoughts. But Aphrodite willed that she imagine herself framed by those heavy thighs, imagine the girl's breath against her and the flick of her pink, pointed tongue. The madness inflicted by the gods entered her.

Can I still desire? her wearied heart asked. She thought of Kleis and sent the girl away.

At the door Gongyla turned back. "Have I done something wrong? Where is my mistake? Show me and I will do it over."

"There is no mistake. My head bothers me. I will take a walk to clear it."

Still Gongyla lingered. "May I come with you?"

"No." The word rang out more sternly than she intended and she called after Gongyla, "It is only a small walk to the orchard. Come if you like."

The girl was at her side in a moment. If she was surprised that Sappho had changed her mind, she did not show it. That was one of Gongyla's attractions. You did not know what she thought behind her wide-spaced eyes.

Sappho led the girl deep into the orchard, aware of how freely she moved, for she prized freedom in walking almost as much as in the dance. Grace was given of the gods; it could not be taught. When they stood among the bearing trees, Sappho said, "Pick me an apple."

Gongyla looked puzzled; surely Sappho could pick her own apple. But she hunted among the branches for a perfect one while Sappho sang:

> Like the last red apple
> sweet and high;
> high as the topmost twigs,
> which the apple-pickers missed.

O no, not missed
but found beyond their fingertips

She broke off and said to Gongyla, who had selected one, "Toss it to me." Catching it, she laughed, and Sappho's laugh was very sweet. Many lights came into her eyes. "On holy Mount Olympus, where the gods dwell, the apple is the symbol of love. Did you know this?"

Gongyla nodded.

"Don't you see? You have thrown it to me and I have caught it. That has significance. It means there is something special between us."

Gongyla remained impassive. Sappho's heart beat in her throat. Had she chosen another Dika, who would not love her? She could not go through such misery again. So she hazarded everything. "You know me as Sappho the Aeolian poet, teacher, singer of songs. Could you know me in love?"

Gongyla was quite motionless and her expression did not change. She could have been rechecking and tallying the cargo of the black ships.

When she spoke it was formally. "O Sappho, O great teacher," she began, and Sappho's bodily organs cringed and tightened. "O Sappho, there is none among us who do not love you and none who are not proud when you notice us, speak to us, fling us a garland, or allow us to sit beside you or at your feet. But Sappho's love is scorching love. I am afraid to change my status. I would rather you look on me kindly sometimes as you pass than ascend with you in a flame. Only gods can drink fire. And yet if you are angry and shut me from your presence, I cannot imagine worse pain."

"Listen to me, Gongyla. Erinna is all intellect, my sister in art. Damophyla has found another friend. Dika went back to her parents without knowing my touch. Gorgo I turned away, and because of this she did me much harm—" Sappho broke off. What was she saying? It was as if she were in Dika's bungalow, pleading. Would Gongyla leave her as Dika had? Trembling with dread, she waited for the girl to speak.

"You name so many, Sappho. And this I understand, for all run after you and would be noticed by you. And I also," she added softly. "How can I explain myself? I have a dream—perhaps foam-born Aphrodite put it in my mind, I do not know. My dream is that on this

Earth there is one who will love me and whom I will love to the edge of time. O Sappho . . . I fear suffering. You cannot help it; you will make me suffer."

"As you now make me!" Sappho turned away from her and from the orchard.

Yearning followed where she went. By day it was present in her, and in the night would not leave her. She analyzed and agonized over each word of Gongyla's. It was true that constancy had not been a strong point of hers. But that was a thymos from the gods; they had made her so that even the way a girl slipped on a thonged sandal could stab her with longing. But all this was before Gongyla, who now took up all her thoughts. She entered the garden with her barbitos, for it was with its lower, more poignant voice that she would make an ode to Gongyla. She called it "Ode to Aphrodite":

> *Throned on many colors, undying Aphrodite, child of*
> *Zeus, weaver of wiles, I pray you do not with anguish*
> *nor with torture break down, Lady, my heart,*
>
> *But come hither, even before at any time you have*
> *left your father's domain, the golden, and have come*
>
> *With yoked chariot, toward the dark Earth the*
> *strong pinions of your two swans, fair and swift, have*
> *drawn thee, beating down from heaven through the midether.*
>
> *Quickly then you came, O blest Lady,*
> *with a smile on your undying face and quietly did ask*
> *what now had upset me, why I called*
>
> *And what thing it was that I so much wanted to*
> *accomplish in my mad heart. "Whom now must I*
> *tempt to give you her love? Who is it, Sappho, that*
> *hurts you?*
>
> *For even if she fly now, she soon shall follow; if she*
> *spurn the flight, yet shall she give; and if she love*

not still shall she soon love, though she be not
willing.''

Come to me now! Loose me from cruel trouble, and
accomplish for me that thing which my heart desireth
to be accomplished: yourself be my assistant!

As always, composing restored Sappho's confidence. With the en-
chantment of this eleven-syllabled meter she would besiege her love.
She did not go herself but sent the poem by the hand of a slave to
Gongyla. Prompted by the nine golden-crowned sisters, the girl came
with her own slave, and stood uncertainly, clutching the parchment.
"You have written it down," she said.
"Yes."
"It is wonderful and strange, so simple and yet each word chosen
with precision and care."
"It is so," Sappho acknowledged.
"May I sit and listen to your glorious art?"
"We will sing together."
Gongyla had brought her Lydian lyre and she played on this while
Sappho beat time and sang. Slowly Gongyla gathered courage to sing
with her. Her voice was a bit unsure, but there was sweetness in it, as
in all she did. Imperceptibly Sappho signed for the slave woman to
withdraw. She gave Gongyla a lesson, but the girl ended by laughing
at her own effort.
How sweet a sound her laughter! She talked to Sappho of her
home, Kolophon, one of the many Ionian strongholds which held Lydian waterways.
Gongyla was coaxed into giving an account of her house and of
the meals they ate. Kandaulos was a favorite, prepared from boiled flesh,
thickened with cheese and breadcrumbs into a gravy to which grapes,
pickles, honey, hard-cooked eggs, and a dash of aniseed were added.
Another famous Kolophon sauce was the spicy kakuke.
"No wonder you were called the Dumpling when you arrived,"
Sappho teased. "However, my women will prepare these wonders, and
later we will feast on them."
"But if I return here tonight Kleis will . . ."

"Miss you? And if you do not return, I shall miss you. Kleis will miss you with a child's heart, for a moment. Then on to other things." Sappho touched Gongyla's small foot and drew its arch lightly with pearl-shaped nails. "I shall miss you in the deepest recess of my being."

Gongyla said softly, "In the poem you have Aphrodite say: 'Who is it, Sappho, that hurts you?' "

"And you want to know who that person is?"

"Oh, don't let it be me!" And Gongyla threw herself on Sappho's breast and wept.

Sappho comforted her with a stroking of her hands both languid and intimate. Gongyla was very like Kleis, an unawakened child.

Sappho's hands slipped down her chiton and caressed the wide immature breasts, turning the nipples hard. Gongyla seemed to notice only now that her servant was gone. She jumped up and pulled her garment about her. "If I come back tonight, it will be worse pain for you, and for me, too!"

"Come tonight," Sappho said as Gongyla ran from the garden.

Sappho smiled, for Gongyla had left behind the lyre of Lydia. She went into her kitchen and ordered a menu that included the sauces of Kolophon.

She waited, but not long. Gongyla came in hesitantly by the gate. The gods had granted this.

"Sit on my lap, beautiful one, facing me," Sappho said. "My hands will be at your shoulders to support you, and you shall lean back and dance for my delight."

"Dance in your lap?"

"Even so. You shall tremble in the embrace of my knees. But first remove your chiton that I may make your body glisten and gleam with rich oils when the torchlight falls on you." She began with her hands a slow movement, well away from the centers of love. "When I was a child," she whispered, "my slaves from Ethiopia were black and shone like ebony, and they anointed me in other ways."

"How?" The word was long in coming.

"Close your eyes. Pretend I am your lover."

"I have not had a lover."

"That is an offense against Aphrodite. In Syracuse mothers slit their girl-children with a ritual knife to win favor with that goddess.

But I do no such thing that is violent, for I love all things delicate. I practice an ancient art, learned from slaves who taught well."

"Teach me." Gongyla scarcely breathed.

"You must not cry out, though you think you will faint."

"Is it painful then?"

"Past pain. Past anything." She spoke against her ear, pushing back the long silky hair. "Begin the dance."

Gongyla swayed against Sappho's hands, one of which roamed her heavy thighs, which were on either side of Sappho's hips. Sappho slid to the door of pleasure, and the girl opened like a pearl shell. The song in Sappho became deep. "I worship at the very apex of the mound of Aphrodite. Ah, know you madden me. Your delta hides a flower of crimson, full of honey that I must taste." And she raised her to her feet. "See, it opens fully to me."

Sappho felt Gongyla's rhythmic contractions as her own, and, changing places with her, she experienced the ultimate more times with Gongyla than ever before. How often her body had gone rigid she no longer knew. At last she laid the girl gently down and stretched beside her.

Gongyla said, "It is past anything."

"Yes."

"But tell me, Sappho, did your slaves not dry you?"

"They did. For then, like now, there were drops between my legs."

"Then it is the same with you? O Sappho, do we love?"

"We love, my Gongyla. Every night I will fasten my lips against your third teat and suck as though you were my dam. This I will in these darkened chambers, and also in the blessed light that floods the meadows. In rushing streams we will mingle and know ecstasy."

From that moment on, over the following days and nights, Sappho and Gongyla bathed, fed, and dressed each other, poured out wine and sipped together, clasped gems upon each other, braided flowers and tied fluttering ribbons on willing thighs, for the gods had laid a fascination on them.

Kleis, observing her mother and her friend while seeming not to, fed her anger. Sappho had and was everything—great poet, wealthy patron, adored teacher, mistress of the hearts of all, with the admiration of Hellenes up and down the world. This same Sappho, her mother, who had all this, had taken from her the one thing that was hers—friendship with Gongyla. Now that she was of an age to take her place among the hetaerae, it seemed to her she had grown without distinction. Her face and body were pleasing enough, except in the company her mother kept around her, where she was much outdone. Her singing, while tuneful, was not outstanding. No particular talent was hers, and certainly not the one her mother possessed of making all who knew her, love her. This ability she considered a more important asset than her fame as a poet, not understanding that the two were one.

Kleis walked proudly by herself, and when Gongyla remembered her and had some small word in passing, she turned away as though she had not heard. Soon, she consoled herself, her mother would weary of Gongyla, and then her friend would turn to her for comfort.

It did not happen. And the resentment and jealousy bottled up in Kleis's small twelve-year-old being became a poison. It overflowed; she could not contain it.

She went to Gongyla's bungalow and found her preparing to go out. "Don't let me keep you. You haven't time these days for your friends. Only for her. She has bewitched you as she did the others."

"I don't know what you're talking about," Gongyla said, flushing.

"I'm talking about my mother, and so is all Mitylene. My uncles no longer speak to her or associate with her. She is notorious for conducting love affairs like a man. There's a name for it, an ugly name—tribadism—and some say Lesbos itself will become synonymous with her corruption. How you can lend yourself willingly and indulge her in her practice, I do not know."

"If you do not know, keep silent. You are still a child, Kleis. All those with any sensitivity revere your mother as peerless among singers since great Homer. You must not listen to the small-minded. Your mother is all-burning flame; she needs love as others need air. It kindles her, it brings the Muses to her side. Without love, Sappho would not be Sappho."

"Sappho, Sappho, Sappho! Must everything be sacrificed to her as though she were an immortal, and we goats or pigs to have our throats slit? For you, Gongyla, have cut out my heart."

"I did not mean to hurt you, Kleis. You are my friend, but also a child."

"Does that mean I have no feelings? Neither of you so much as thought about me. You are a false friend, Gongyla, but you have met your match in Sappho. She will tear you apart and not notice your suffering. Look at Erinna, if you want to see Gongyla. And do not come to me then."

There is something of Sappho in her after all, Gongyla thought, for even if sprawled bodies were left lying, Sappho would speak as she was minded. Gongyla hastened to suppress the thought. As for the rest of Kleis's outburst, it could be laid to a spoiled and jealous child. Besides, had not Sappho sworn a dozen times to love her always?

But Gongyla was disquieted. Had she known where Kleis was off to or suspected her rage, she would have run after her.

Kleis went directly to her mother's well-proportioned house of white stone, passing the watchdog eunuch from Chios, who sat cross-legged and asked each their business. But the question was not asked of the daughter.

Sappho had spent the morning on the sand shore looking for agates and letting the scalloped prisms of foam wash her ankles. Now she stood contemplatively in the unroofed courtyard before the stone water clock, to see what hour its markings showed as it slowly and predictably drained.

"Kleis." It was a glad note at the sight of her child. But there was a certain warning in the way the girl strode up to her. Instinctively Sappho drew back. "Have you come to share the midday meal with me?" she asked, knowing she had not, knowing all was not well, but unprepared for the savage torrent that poured over her.

Kleis addressed her with a curse, a terrible prayer to the Moon goddess: "Deprive my mother of sleep. Throw a firebrand into her. Punish her with the unrest of madness. Scatter her songs like leaves." Even this did not satisfy her— "Take the breath from her nostrils!"

Sappho felt behind her for the support of colonnades. "What are you saying?"

"I am cursing you, Mother. I want your life to wither. I want what you touch to shrivel and die. I want the Muses to desert you . . . and Gongyla, and all you love. I want you to grow old and be ugly and alone."

Sappho fell to her knees. "Kleis! My Kleis, what god so hates me as to seize your tongue and speak such things with your voice?"

"No god, Mother. It is I, Kleis, whom you brought forth from your body. It is your only child who hates and despises you. I say with my uncles that your life is an abomination, and that is how you will be remembered."

Sappho let her head touch the stone flagging. She could not rise.

Servants found her there. But with all their skills they could not undo the rigidity of her limbs. Gongyla was summoned. She was appalled and would not leave her side. "Some fit has seized her to keep her so unmoving."

But when Gongyla was told of Kleis's visit, she began to understand. She stroked Sappho's burning forehead and murmured to her: "Will you let a bad child, a naughty little girl, make you ill? She has forgotten her words already, I know she has. And you must forget them, too."

"You don't . . . know . . ." Sappho's speech faltered. She began again. "You don't know what she said."

"Do not think of it, sweet Sappho."

"She wants me dead, Gongyla."

"No, no she doesn't."

"And worse. I cannot tell even you."

"And you will oblige her? Will great Sappho lie down on the command of a twelve-year-old and give up her life that has brought light and beauty to the world? I never knew you to be lacking in sense, Sappho."

Sappho strove to sit up, and pillows were placed behind her. "Bring me my mirror," she ordered hoarsely. She gazed into it a long time, and touched her skin and examined around her eyes.

"What are you doing?" Gongyla asked.

"She wanted me old and ugly. I would rather be dead."

"You are pale, it seems to me. But you are she whom we all love and honor."

"She said the sacred nine of Pieria would desert me, my songs be scattered like leaves . . . She echoed a dream that once . . . She used the words of a dream. Gongyla, how can that be?" She clutched the girl with hot fingers. Could it be true that her songs would be forgotten and she herself remembered for ill and not for good? Could a daughter's curse do this? She had never meant to hurt Kleis. What other child had she? Surely she could have found another friend.

Some of this she spoke aloud to Gongyla, but Gongyla would not listen. She took it on herself to call slaves, have water heated, to bathe, oil, scent, comb, and dress the distraught Sappho, who gradually calmed under these ministrations.

"You are right," Sappho said at last. "It would be odd indeed if Sappho allowed herself to be governed by a child. And yet, Gongyla, I cannot face her. Not yet, not for a while."

"There is no need. She has gone to Gorgo's old bungalow."

A trace of irony crept into Sappho's lips, but she would say nothing against her daughter. Instead, fearing that Kleis would not eat well or be taken care of properly, she sent slaves and servants to her.

No songs were in her head, only the curse. She could not tap into her strength, or will herself to be as she had been. The hetaerae were told only that Sappho was ill, and they tried to cheer her. They made snares to catch grasshoppers, and came singly to bring her little treasures—a comb worked with gems, earrings of emerald, a girdle richly braided, perfumes, wines as tonics. With each gift were flowers. Sappho smiled wanly, accepted listlessly. She noticed that in the tumble of gifts there was nothing from Erinna. In an odd way she was closer to Erinna than any. They were sisters in art. Erinna should understand and forgive her. At one time Erinna had said she would not put herself in the way of her happiness, but her thymos had her by the throat. Sappho felt alone—and lonely.

The girls begged her to weave garlands of celery with them, but she said her head ached. When they left without her, she was sorry she had stayed at home for there was nothing she wanted to do.

Gongyla had gone with the girls, and even had she stayed Sappho would not have been satisfied. For Gongyla was still solicitous of her health and would not indulge her or allow her what she craved.

She drew her knees up to her chest in a womb position and addressed the goddess with whom she was most intimate. "You, O Aphrodite, had a sea birth, and my father and my husband sea deaths. You sprang from foam; *they* drank it as their last drink. Therefore have I followed after your ways, O goddess. Now I beg, release me. Your servant Sappho will tie up her hair with pins of bone and metal. Do you, O immortal beauty, forget me? From this time, Daughter of Zeus, pass me by."

She woke in the morning, remembering her prayer of the night before. Terrified that Aphrodite would do as she had begged, she immediately set about making things right with her by explaining what her body wanted and her soul needed:

> Be kind to me
> Gongyla; I ask only
> that you wear the cream
> white dress when you come.
> Desire darts about your
> loveliness, drawn down in
> circling flight at sight of it
> and I am glad, although
> once I, too, quarreled
> with Aphrodite
> to whom
> I pray that you will come soon

Certain it was that Aphrodite knew her heart better than she did herself, and would not withhold love, though she asked it. If only she could lie at Gongyla's side continually, sip wine, let each day reach its zenith, listen to the girl's harp. For this she had come back to life. And now she must convince Gongyla she was well.

She began by selecting half a dozen maidens—Timas, Telesippa, Anaktoria, Atthis, Kydro, and Megara of the shining hair. With these girls Sappho made her first foray out of doors. She had not chosen Gongyla, though Gongyla was the reason for the diversion.

She heard the swallow, glimpsed the scented white violet beneath its furry leaves, reached for a sprig of thyme, parted myrtle branches. The girls ran beneath the olive trees and stopped to pick oleander, which they wove together with bloodred windflowers. They gathered honeysuckle to the drone of bees, who more than once drove them from the drooping, heavy-burdened bowers. The world was festooned with wild beauty, carpeted in anemones, arrayed with myrtle, and she had lain as one dead. "Mother Earth, you greet me with your wonders." And she stretched out her arms. If only she could hold some portion, however small. Sappho hid the purpose of this walk from her hetaerae.

The girls debated animatedly which glen was best for the lunch their slaves carried. They decided to dine by the stream, and the slaves unrolled mats for the sweetbreads, figs, dainties, and wines of two colors. Little Timas put her head in Sappho's lap and asked for songs.

Sappho smiled and recited:

> *Golden chickpeas*
> *growing on the seashore*
>
> *Earth of the many chaplets*
> *puts on her embroidery . . .*

She ended for the day with:

> *I love that*
> *which caresses*
> *me. I believe*
> *Love has his share in the*
> *Sun's brilliance*
> *and virtue*

The songs heightened Sappho's longing. Her pulse kept the rhythm. The whole day, the entire charade, was solely to enable her to pass by Gongyla's bungalow and leave a poem inscribed on a transparent scroll, tied with ribbons. She brought it out and added flowers, threading them through the gaily colored ties.

"What are you doing?" Timas asked.

"Oh, it is nothing. We pass Gongyla's presently. It is a small gift for her, for her goodness to me when I was ill."

The girls exchanged glances. They were not deceived, but Sappho didn't care. The poem would ensure Gongyla's coming. Aphrodite would oversee it.

> *For you came to my house the other day and*
> *sang to me, and for that reason I am come. Oh, speak*
> *to me! Come down, and give me freely of your beauty;*
> *for we are out walking and are near, and well you know*
> *it. But as quickly as you can send your slave girls away,*
> *and let the gods give me whatever they have for me*

That night she murmured into tangled curly hair that shared her pillow. "You scorch me . . ." The rest of the sentence ended in kisses. She pressed a golden-ankled drinking cup into Gongyla's hands. They sipped from it as one. Spilling drops, they laughed.

"It is not an Olympic or a Pythian year," Sappho whispered. "It is much more: it is the year that Gongyla loved me that is the most important year of my life." And she kissed the palms of her lover's hands. "Surely Erato, loveliest of Muses, watches over our night. Answer, and tell me—do you love me, Gongyla?" She must hear it again and again; nor was she ever satisfied. She adored all parts that made up Gongyla, and murmured, "You are dowered with beauty by the gods." And Sappho gently traced the pretty belly and the three folds of Kypris.

To amuse her, she sang new songs:

> The yearning-voiced messenger of spring,
> the nightingale . . .

And when Gongyla wearied of songs, she told stories of Syracuse and of her travels.

"Did you love your husband, Kerkolas?" Gongyla asked unexpectedly.

Sappho took some time in answering. "The Graces do not lend such prettiness to a man as to you. When girls love and lie together, the patron goddesses of leisure, enjoyment, and happiness are present. But to accept caresses from a man means more likely than not that one must tie too tight the band across the stomach, and know much pain. There is no pain here . . . only delight."

Sappho was wrong. But prophecy was not her domain. She did not know the air was crowded with calamity, so crowded that there remained not one chink into which to push a blade of grass. Death, hovering in a cloud over Mitylene, descended swiftly. The houses became dark-chambered sepulchres for pestilence to enter. Acolytes began pilgrimages to the healing shrines of Apollo, but silent-footed Thanatos traveled with them. Father Zeus gazed in another direction, and was absent altogether. "Sing woe. Sing woe."

Sappho called on her hetaerae to purify themselves by ritual ab-solution. After which:

> *The moon rose full and the maidens took their stand*
> *about the altar . . .*

She herself sank to Earth, calling on Persephone to spare this house dedicated to song. For she believed the poet, not the priest, had greatest influence with Heaven. She prayed also to gray-eyed Athene to make her words winged and well received: "Let not the soaring eagle of death sweep down onto the timid hare or lamb. Spare these gentle girls." And she promised hekatombs:

> *To thee will I burn the rich fat of a white goat*

They staked out a scapegoat onto which they piled their own sins that they might be left pure and the gods protect them. They made further sacrifice, pouring wine, scattering flowers and perfumes, burning sandalwood, and singing odes to the undying. It had been fifteen years since the daimones of plague were released from the hideous wrinkled declivity in which they had been shut. In the city they said that a dog urinated at the entrance to that dread cavern, and shortly after a man relieved himself at the exact spot. Furious, Disease leapt out.

Even those who had not seen a stricken person knew the symptoms: the extremities became cold, the urine brackish; the ill person wan-dered in his mind and vomited blood.

Sappho closed the wooden shutters against Sun's rays. She and her girls would hide until the scourge was past. Who knew? The pretty beams of streaming sunshine, the bright motes themselves might be messengers sent to seek out fresh victims.

The stillness from the city, the absence of its sound, reached them. No business was conducted. Only Death was busy. A slave with her fore-head pressed to the floor trembled before Sappho. So lowly was this thrall that Sappho had never seen her. She must have been sent from the bow-els of the kitchens, the most menial low-born that could be found.

Sappho stared at her misshapen ugliness, gross body and shriveled limbs. She seemed the personification of Disease itself. "Who are you?" Sappho gasped. "Why are you here?"

"I was sent, O high-born . . . I have to tell you . . ." The woman choked in terror.

"Yes? Yes? Tell it!"

"The poet Erinna . . . she . . ."

"No more! And never let me look on you again!"

The creature crawled away and the world closed around Sappho.

Erinna, whom she had injured, neglected, almost forgotten, first in her passion for Dika and now Gongyla, was to punish her with her death. Erinna was not strong, that she knew, but she would not let this happen! "Artemis of the bow, Lion among women . . . give her strength." To her servants she called, "Bring armfuls of sweet clover to the chamber of Erinna, and dainty anthrysc." Snatching up her lyre of seven strings, she crossed the compound, taking a way she had once used so often. Her mind was filled with strengthening broths. She would order goat's milk and duck eggs, she . . .

When she saw Erinna, she knew it was too late. None had dared tell her until now. It seemed a Titan had smashed a great fist upon the creature in the bed. She was like one caught between colliding Sky and Earth in the night of Creation. It was the shell of Erinna that lay there, her hair braided with sweat. Sappho stood motionless. The many times she had braided those same locks with hyacinth and violets.

There was a gurgling sound from Erinna's mouth, and from her nostrils red drops rolled down. Sappho was terrified. She forced herself to the bed. No strengthening broths, no eggs of duck or peahen, no milk of goat, nothing could call this pale shade back. She had begun the long march toward the land of the dead. But those eyes, those ringed sockets moved, they looked on her face.

"A priestess of Apollo will come presently with healing herbs." Where had she found voice to utter this lie? "You will be well and sound of limb, O Erinna. Together we will go to the black sand shore and search for moonstones and agates, as we used to do. Remember?"

Those terrible orbs regarded her without change of expression. Sappho raced on, hardly thinking what she said. "And we will sit before the scrolls where our work jointly lies, and recall the times we scratched letters with the ivory stylus. Your words are deathless, Erinna. Such philosophy you found in the spinning, twirling distaff. You called it the twisting thread of Destiny. Humble things grew fresh dimension when you sang of them."

She fell on her knees beside the bed. "We will analyze meters. Your preference was for the Ionic, yet how skillfully you used the alcaic and dactylic . . . O my Erinna, forgive your Sappho. Some thymos descends on me. I do not know what happens. I follow after a fair face or comely form. But with no one else did I ever speak as I did with you. We shared the melodious sweetness of the Muses, and I have never shared it since with any other. You thought yourself forgotten. But it was never so. I cannot explain, I was distracted . . ." And she was distracted now, for she bent so close that the mold of the sickness and its stench almost made her faint. Her hands tightened on her lyre; she commanded her lips to smile at the widening black sockets of the eyes that pierced her. She began to sing. Erinna's gaze clung to her as though she were the only thing in the cosmos with which she still had contact.

Sappho's voice came uncertain and wavering.:

> *Upon the eyes*
> *Night's dark slumber*
> *poured down . . .*

It was the old lullaby. Did one sing a lullaby to Death? Sacred Muses, she begged, help me to go on.

The accursed children of Night were moving in Erinna, a film was spreading over her eyes. "Erinna, I will give up Gongyla. I will not see her more. Only live, live and do not leave me alone!" Then seeing that she was losing against forces no mortal could contend with, she wiped the blood from her friend's face and whispered, "It is the agony of the struggle that reveals the person. So they say of the great Olympic contests. And what can be greater than the one you fight? Erinna, a word, a gesture, so that I may know you have forgiven your friend, your lover, your Sappho."

The air carried to her two words. "Kiss me . . ."

Sappho drew back.

Erinna's fixed irises reproached her. She wanted to offer the final endearment Erinna craved, she wanted to give this proof of love. But in that moment of hesitation a dam broke somewhere in Erinna's head, the flood poured over them both. Sappho screamed without sound.

Her women came to her to pick her up. She looked at them with a countenance so terrible their wailing filled the air. Sappho clutched and pulled down her hair, tore at her clothes and lacerated her flesh. Like an Erinye she ran to the house of Gorgo, where her daughter lodged. For the source of this hideous death, this not-to-be-borne misfortune, was plain to her.

She broke in upon Kleis, who sat with another girl before a meal. Sappho in a frenzy dashed the raised cup to the floor. The dishes she hurled at the wall, screaming imprecations that sent the friend gliding from the room like a shadow, as though she had never been there at all.

Kleis was transfixed. Was this dread Circe in her mother's guise?

"She is dead!" Sappho screamed at her. "Erinna, without forgiving me. A daughter's curse did this thing. A curse my only child laid on me, my life, my art, and all who love me. No dog's pissing, no man's urgency laid low the city of Mitylene, but *you* have set the many to mourning and lit the funeral pyres one sees at night. Now I tell you this: I, who gave life to you, want never to see you. Keep away from me." And Sappho raised her arm and struck her child, who cringed against the wall and fled into the night.

Sappho lifted her voice in lamentation and beat her breasts that had given suck. It was a mercy from the gods when she crumpled on the floor.

As so often happened with her, her mind was double. She was stomach-sick for her words to Kleis, her golden little daughter whom she cried for even as she did for the statue of the stone child in the garden. But the other Sappho in her remained hard, and her eyes were dry.

When the second death happened, none dared tell her. Not the lowliest slave could be beaten into going to her. But there was no need; somehow she knew. The walls themselves seemed to breathe and whisper "Death."

Hermes came to her in a dream, and she said, "O Master, I am utterly lost. Your coming I take as a sign, O Blessed One. And I swear if my girls are spared, I will go with you to the lotus-covered banks of Acheron."

It was Gongyla who roused her, speaking gently. "It is Timas. This time it is little Timas."

Sappho became very still. "Some say the souls of the dead live again in flowers. Do you believe that, Gongyla?"

"I do not know. I hope it."

"Yes, I hope it too." She struggled to get up, but Gongyla's hand held her back.

"You cannot spare me, Gongyla. I must look on her. I must say good-bye."

Gongyla saw she could not dissuade her and so helped her to her feet. Sappho leaned heavily on her friend, but did not know she did. The loss was too big; too much had been swept too suddenly from her world, her world where garlands were strung and conch shells sought on the sand shore.

Timas was not the piteous sight Erinna had been. She was washed, her limbs laid straight. The body was oiled and perfumed and her fair hair caught back with ringlets escaping, just as always. She looked like Timas sleeping as she had seen her many nights.

Looking down she made an epitaph:

> *This dust is little Timas,*
> *who having died before marriage,*
> *was received into Persephone's*
> *dark bridal chamber, and though*
> *she faded away from here,*
> *all her fair companions*
> *cut off with the knife*
> *the lovely hair of their heads*

She motioned to a serving woman, who brought the ceremonial knife, and Sappho cut a lock of her own hair, laying it on Timas's breast. "In death," she assured the small, still form, even as her mother had assured her, "there is a happy place."

"She died asleep," Gongyla whispered.

Sappho nodded. "Slain by a silver arrow shot by Artemis, who gives a swift and painless death to women she loves. And who could not love precious Timas? Do you remember the gift she gave my statue? Her purple handkerchief she tied around the head." She laughed at the recollection. But Sappho could not long indulge her memories; she was mistress here and there was much to do. "Set out the death jars that all may rinse and purify themselves. Then bring the bodies to the sand.

The ashes of little Timas shall be returned to her people, yes, to Phokaea, the northernmost city of Ionia, and those of Erinna must to
Rhodes and on to Telos."

Called together, the hetaerae followed in a long line of sorrow,
wending their way, letting the death hymns rise:

> *When for them*
> *Night long overtakes*
> *their senses*

They stopped where the waves seemed not to break. All things
were suspended in time, as though the world died when the poet Erinna
and the little Ionian maid were laid at their length.

Slaves had built twin funeral pyres, and each girl was placed before
the one that would consume her. Lovers and friends passed silently,
weeping, and on each laid a lock of their hair—dark and blond, chestnut and black. Straight and in curls, they clustered on the breasts of
the dead.

Sappho worried about Timas, she was always getting mixed up
about directions. "The water of the Styx is the tenth stream," she
whispered, wanting her to find her way and not be frightened. She was
so easily frightened. Sappho looked a last time; and piling woe on woe,
she passed to the form of Erinna.

The agony had been erased from her face and form with special
preparations. Sappho had no last word for her because of the way they
had parted. She knew she was not forgiven. And the sight of the deep
bosom in which she had so often nestled, but which was covered now
with the locks of the girls, brought unbearable pain. She laid a lock of
her own violet-black hair with theirs. She was afraid to say "I love
you, Erinna," although it was true. She was afraid of the shade of the
poet.

It was an honorable cremation. Many sheep and oxen were flayed.
From the two-handled jars, honey was scooped out and unguents sprinkled before the fire that burned with the fat of the sacrifices. The young
corpses were carried by slaves atop the twin pyres. In moments the gay-
colored material of their dresses caught, making a brighter blaze.

The bodies shriveled to ash, the bones were collected in ossuaries of gold, covered with embroidered cloth, and the last embers put out with wine as each girl spilled a cup to her dead friends.

Sappho tried to soothe the grief of the hetaerae. "Noble Homer tells us Death is 'the divine for which all men long.' Our pain is much, but we should believe him. At Dawn's coming, my black ships shall leave for Phokaea and for Rhodes."

"Sing woe! Sing woe!" wailed her companions as they followed up from the sand shore. Each was bathed before her bed was brought.

The night of the cremation, Erinna of the deep breasts and slender ankles appeared. "I come to you, O Sappho, from the mists of far shores. There I stand like a beggar at the gate."

"Why do you not go through the gate, O Erinna?" Sappho asked from sleep.

"Because you have not put Gongyla from you as you swore to me you would. Until the deathbed promise is fulfilled, I must stand outside. Do not betray me a second time, O Sappho."

Sappho started and woke to an empty room. "I would I were dead . . . because of my pain."

The next day, before the boats sailed, Damophyla clasped and kissed Sappho's knees before the hetaerae. "I return to my home, O Sappho. On the coast of Asia Minor I will sing your songs, even in Pamphylic where I was born. I will gather my own hetaerae around me and tell happy tales of our life here with glorious Sappho."

"You earned your dower. Will you not marry?"

"After this life, I am desirous of living in art and love—I will follow your light. I will love you always, O Sappho."

And so they parted. And the proud galleons, one for Rhodes and one for Phokaea, left with three of her hetaerae, and only one living.

When she was alone, Sappho took out her mirror. A woman looked back at her, more handsome than the girl she had been. She sighed. She was no longer young. She felt, but did not look, old. They are falling away from me, my hetaerae.

For another day, and then hour by hour, she put off sending for Gongyla. When finally the girl was before her, Sappho took a step toward her but restrained herself.

Gongyla looked at her expectantly and smiled.

"It may no longer be," Sappho said quickly.

The girl paled, but could not understand. "Sappho, what is it?"

Sappho shook her head and spoke as from a great distance:

> O, *what intense desire your beauty evokes*
> *No one could but tremble at its seduction!*
> *And I rejoice*
> *for it is she herself,*
> *the Kyprian goddess, who has made you so.*
> *She whom I blame, I invoke in prayer*

Her voice broke.

"Sappho," Gongyla cried in alarm, "what is your meaning? Speak!"

"I can no longer . . . we can no longer . . . it is Erinna, she cannot enter in at the entering gate until we part. Her shade can have no peace. I know. She talked to me and told me."

Gongyla sank to the floor, tears on her face, a suppliant. But Sappho would not hear her and sent her away.

The instant she was gone, Sappho cried:

> *Come you back, my*
> *Gongyla,*
> *in your milk-white tunic*

Then distractedly, "It is you, O Kyprian, it is you I blame. You have done your worst to me. I now fear no god."

The words were heard.

At least they must have been, for with the words came fresh desolation. Niobe told her, none else dared. "Lady. Kleis is gone."

"Gone?" Her emotions were used up. She spoke flatly, trying to recall anger and indignation, which once she knew well.

"She was not at the cremation," Niobe said.

"How would she be? She was afraid to face me."

"She was already gone, although none knew it until now."

"I do not wonder. She could not look at what her curse brought. Where is she, at my brothers'? With Larichos? Eurygyos?"

"Lady, she is gone to that witch, Andromeda, purveyor of evil. She is gone to Gorgo. Now you know, Lady." And Niobe bowed her head.

"I do not grieve, Niobe. As you see, I am past it. Do not fear, I will bring her back. The honor of my house demands it. But my heart has lost the ability to feel. If it were left solely to me, I would stay here and never rise. For what? For whom? But I know my duty. We will go together, Niobe, to this Andromeda who tangles with Sappho, and I will bring back the child of woe, born of a dead father. What could come of it? And yet she was a fair child."

"You must forgive her, Lady. She is of your flesh."

"There is no forgiveness in me, Niobe. I am empty."

As Sappho left the house, Gongyla stepped from shadows. "Gentle Sappho, one thing I ask."

They had not spoken since that cold, sere morning, and Sappho steeled herself for fresh calamity. "Say it then."

"Do not send me away. Let me be where I can see you. I will not speak to you or touch even your hand. Only let me continue as a hetaera. I will ask nothing more of you."

Sappho nodded. "It is well, too many have left . . . one way or another. Stay, Gongyla, I love you well, and we will try to be as friends."

She hurried on, Niobe following, and in a few moments sighted on the horizon those ships carrying the ossuary jars. They had hoisted anchor and were distantly silhouetted against Sky. A final farewell rose in her for Timas. But to Erinna she murmured, "You have made my world as dark as yours." She turned abruptly, making for the house of Andromeda. A lizard drowsed against the stone of the walls, the heavy blinking eyes followed them.

Once Sappho spoke. "There are such sorrows in my house, where formerly all was laughter, song and love." And again she cried out: "Why does my daughter go where she will humiliate me?" Her cloak caught on a thistle, she pulled it off in disgust. "I, who have loved daintiness and dainty things, must rescue my child from a coarse woman who deals with a leather-maker." She wrapped her mantle more securely around her. "I feel as though I am about to enter the House of Hades."

"She is only a countrified woman who has no power at all," Niobe assured her mistress.

"She had power to pull Gorgo to her and now Kleis. O, Niobe! Those harm me worst by whom I have done well."

Niobe nodded agreement. "It is ever so."

The way was steep, the day turning hot, Niobe opened a parasol and held it over her lady's head. It was rude farmland and the base of olive roots obtruded, running along the ground in gnarled shapes.

The wall they came to was of heaped stones and, where they had tumbled down, there they were left. They were within sight of the main house now, which was also in disrepair.

Sappho felt many eyes upon her, though no one was to be seen. She hailed the house. A figure she knew well came out—it was Gorgo. Gorgo of exalted lineage who had turned Dika from her. With exaggerated courtesy Sappho addressed her: "Many greetings to the daughter of many kings."

Gorgo flushed. There was a smell about the place of the ass, the bull, and the goat, all lustful, rutting creatures, thralls of their own low natures.

Sappho stood apart with her nine Muses. "I have heard a certain Andromeda is mistress here. I would have a word with her."

"I will see if she has time to see you," Gorgo answered insolently.

Sappho's eyes smoldered. "Tell the woman Sappho is here."

Gorgo entered the house, returning with a person who looked "like a worn-out dishcloth hanging wet," as Sappho afterward described her. To wear a peplos at the knees was extravagant, but above the knee was indecent.

Sappho was so struck by this ungainly form and figure that she stood mute.

Gorgo spoke, and her words were full of venom: "The notorious Sappho seeks audience with you, O skilled Andromeda."

This audacious speech brought Sappho's wits back. "Sappho does not seek audience with any such as this. I come for my daughter, Kleis, child of the prince Kerkolas of Andros."

Andromeda surveyed her critically as though she had not heard. "She is smaller than I thought," she said to Gorgo, "and of a more swarthy complexion."

"Small I am," cried Sappho, "but a name which fills all the world is mine." She approached the pair. "She-dog! Bring my daughter."

"And if your daughter does not wish to go with you?"

"She will come. Fetch her, Gorgo."

"I am no longer one of your hetaerae to do your bidding."

"It is not by my wish that I am standing here in a place that stinks of the barnyard. I have come for my daughter, and you shall give her up, for I did not come alone, but in company of those I pray to, even the holy Nine. If you wish curses, then will my sisters put them on my lips and all your life be withered."

Gorgo could not withstand Sappho's fury. "Of such things talk not. Kleis is here."

But Andromeda stayed her and spoke directly in a bold voice to Sappho. "You wear a chain of amber and gold. Some things can be traded."

"And some cannot. My patience is done. Give me Kleis."

Her daughter walked out, with clothes dirtied and hair uncombed. Her hands at her sides were clenched as though she did battle with herself. But her expression was disdainful; she might be wearing coan and exquisite trinkets instead of a smudge across her face.

The mother's heart in Sappho foundered at sight of her child, and she rushed to her. "Kleis, have any here mistreated you?"

Gorgo whispered, "Do not answer."

But Kleis had the clear intention of bringing pain upon her mother. "I am no longer virgin, if that is your meaning. I was bloodied, but by no man."

Andromeda laughed and poked between the girl's thighs, where caked streaks of dried blood still adhered. Niobe threw her own cloak around Kleis and led her away.

Sappho stared steadily at Andromeda. "May you burn in the Lemian volcano, from which Prometheus stole fire, and may wild dogs dig out your bones."

None dared longer dispute with her, for her anger was greater than she, and it was clear a god had hold of her.

Sappho turned and motioned her daughter to follow.

"Walk five paces behind," Niobe told Kleis. "None may touch you until you have been given a ritual bath."

Kleis began to cry. "They were all laughing at me."

"I do not wish to hear," Sappho said.

"They told me if I did not bring them joy, they would rub me with bitch's blood, tie me in the courtyard, and let loose the hounds."

Sappho did not answer her daughter, but from the rise stood a moment and called Andromeda in that same terrible voice. "You shall suffer for what you did to me." For at that moment she made no distinction between herself and Kleis. It had been done to her.

Within the walls of the House of the Servants of the Muses Niobe tended Kleis. When she had been cleansed in each crevice and fold of her body, when her skin glistened with sweet Athenian oils and her hair shone and was bright with flowers, a tunic of white was put over her body and she was led to her mother.

Sappho regarded her sadly. "You are no longer a child, and I can no longer protect you. Neither can I clasp you as a daughter. We have done each other too much hurt. But my home is your home. And when you marry I will dower you handsomely. When we meet we will speak to each other with comfortable words. It is seemly."

"I understand," Kleis said calmly.

But I do not, Sappho thought when she was once more alone. No matter which way I turn, it is toward pain. What happens to love, the overflowing love for the infant at one's breast? How can the grapes of one's own vineyard poison one? "Hide me," she begged the All-Father, "in a thick mist that I cannot be found!"

She wandered halls from which joy had departed, desolate without Gongyla, grieving for her daughter. "Man's fate," she cried, "is decided on his knees."

She rededicated herself to the Muses and kept to her room. In these melancholy, hopeless days, she sang some of her sweetest verse:

> O, evening star, you bring
> all that the blithe dawn has
> scattered wide;
> You bring the sheep;
> you bring the goats;
> you bring home the
> child to its mother

But it could not be. Kleis was lost to her, though she saw her every day.

Atthis

*N*EWS WAS BROUGHT THAT HER BROTHER KHARAXOS sailed with his fleet for the Lesbian port, being returned from the Egyptian city of Naukratis, where the Nile ran in a hundred tributaries. It had been an expedition of five years, during which she had not seen his face.

His vessels with their stiff sails and many rowers had been sighted, and were no rumor, but a rumor accompanied them. It was said that with him was no other than Alkaios the poet—the same she had consigned to death rather than give up her child to Gello, that shade whose famished kisses drew the living breath from the very young.

The possibility that Alkaios was alive and sailed with her brother was more than she could absorb. For years she lived in the belief that she had caused his death. Now she was afraid to let herself hope. Her old companion, dear, irreverent Alkaios!

She rushed up and down the stairs of her home, giving orders that everything be put in readiness to receive guests. They would be showered with flowers and walk on cloth of purple to the steps of her home. She devised tempting and exotic menus of caviar, oysters, lobster, crab, and cuttlefish. Snails and anchovies fried in condiments were laid out, highly spiced cheeses, sausage and onions, all strongly salted to arouse the wish for wine. Slaves would cool the foreheads of her guests with pomade, tightrope performers balance above them, oiled and naked.

Jars were handed up from the well so that wine bars and seafood bars might be set up. Giant candelabra and fish bladders overhung them filled with tallow, waiting to be lit.

And Hermes had been kind, for without special reason, so it seemed, a Persian dress was already woven, glinting with beads of gold, and a strap of fair Lydian work was in readiness to cover her feet. In the midst of these preparations, Sappho stopped short. Would Khar go first to Eurygyos and Larichos? What tales would they tell of her? Would he hear that his sister had become a whore? All her body seemed to knot in one great spasm. She took a cult bath and prayed the gods to tell her what to do. And as she prayed, it came to her mind to go herself to the quay, be the first to speak, and afterward let slanderers say of her what they would. If the battle was to be one of words, Eurygyos and Larichos were already defeated.

Joyfully she sang:

> *In my prayers*
> *I looked into the*
> *vaults of Heaven*

She went by chariot with many servants and slaves to the mole. Her two brothers were also there. She had not seen them in three years. They bowed toward their sister for the sake of public opinion. How stiff they were, like puppets! She inclined her head, but no word passed between them.

Dark-prowed ships hewed of sturdy poplar, oak, and pine rode outside the breakwater. At a signal, all sails were furled and laid on the decks; the forestays and masts were also lowered into place. The boats themselves seemed to grasp the intent of the captain. The oars on each ship were lifted from leather loops and raised in salute.

A great cry rose from the mole, answered deep in the throats of the sailors, as they set the curved ships to the shore's breeze and rowed into harbor. Kharaxos held the rudder of the lead ship. There was born wave after rolling wave that helped them beach and drag the boats high.

Alkaios, a portly Alkaios with a potbelly, managed to reach her first. Looking into the porcelain blue of his eyes she saw they still danced with mischief. He grabbed her upper arm in salute. She was too moved by the sight of him to say anything but, turning over his hands, kissed the palm of each.

"Sappho of the glancing eyes. How little you have changed."

"It is a seeming only, Alkaios. I am a woman who has known much. But you, I see, are still attractive to both sexes alike."

"It is your fault, tantalizing Sappho of the inward gaze. You never would take me in hand."

She laughed ruefully. "I have enough trouble with myself." And then, "O Alkaios, I have grieved for you, burnt incense, said prayers, for these many years I thought you dead."

"Sappho, your words have a way of reaching the gods. For after all the adventures and misadventures I have undergone, I would surely not have survived without them."

Kharaxos was striding toward them. His upper lip was shaved and his beard neatly trimmed to a point. He clasped Sappho to him, and she kissed his head and hands. To hold and be held by her brother again so confused her senses that she cried instead of laughing. "Is it you, brother, or some god?"

"Poseidon guarded me from the two winds that spring in fury from Thrace, north and northwest. It was a miracle, for the seas were roaring and the timbers of the ship are rotted. But we are here and in the holds of my boat are great prizes, clinquant copper, many slaves, furs, exotic perfumes, and innumerable spices. The whole world, it seems, wants our Lesbian wine."

"I prayed every day of your voyage to the beautiful Nereids, the fifty daughters of Nereus, eldest son of Sea, and to Doris the Oceanid, who is their mother."

"They are indeed a group of gracious influences that helped see us safe, although many times we were in danger of falling into Poseidon's palace. . . . But here are our brothers come in greeting!" And he embraced them warmly.

Only Alkaios noticed that Sappho stood to the side. When the welcoming was over and Kharaxos had seen to the laying of the rollers on which his ships were mounted, Sappho spoke in a voice at once innocent and happy. "Come, my brothers, and Alkaios, to the House of the Servants of the Muses, for everything is in readiness. There you will rest and bathe and make offering to great Zeus and his brother of the blue hair, after which I have ordered up refreshment, the best my house can provide."

Kharaxos's tanned face was smiling with the pleasure of his homecoming, but Larichos said stiltedly, like a man unused to speech, "It has been three years since we set foot in the establishment of Sappho."

Kharaxos looked at them, startled. "Why? What is this?"

"You have been away a long time," Eurygyos began.

"And he does not wish," Sappho put in quickly, "to hear on his first day tales of pettiness. Put aside all that, brothers, I beseech you, and in honor of our eldest brother, who has returned to us, let us gather for prayer and feast."

But the two kept their eyes fastened on the ground. Kharaxos looked in puzzlement from them to Sappho. "What is this estrangement between brothers and a sister? Lay it by, for I am home and we will joy together."

Eurygyos said with unpleasant innuendo, "Surely you know there is excess in greatness? And too aptly does Sappho demonstrate this."

Kharaxos, commander of men, waved an angry arm. "I go to the house of my sister who bids me welcome. Come all others who would."

By prior agreement, it seemed, the two brothers held back.

"I return to a family divided? What churlishness is this? Do you not know the duty a brother owes a sister?"

"Or the duty a sister owes the reputation and good name of her house."

"Do you not take pride, as I do, in the fame Sappho's songs have brought our land? I understand you not."

"You have been away too long."

"Enough. I want no talebearing, nor do I wish to stand squabbling on the docks. What I do want is my family around me, to celebrate my safe return after my life among the Egyptians and my many trials."

Eurygyos and Larichos conferred.

"If you come in joy and gladness, you are welcome," Sappho said.

Larichos grew angry. "Do not try to make our brother's return an occasion for forgiveness and the condoning of your licentious deeds." He shrank back, for Khar was about to strike him.

Alkaios from the chariot called, "Why are you dawdling? I am parched, hungry, filthy, and in need of the hospitality of peerless Sappho."

Sappho cast him a grateful glance and, taking Khar by the arm, left the other two arguing and guided him to the waiting chariot. The horses tossed their flower-braided manes and stepped proudly.

Bystanders and sailors alike cheered Kharaxos as he passed. Like a god he was come with much treasure, bringing the renowned Alkaios with him. The city of Mitylene gave thanks and offered hekatombs for the return of its sons.

Sappho, distressed that she had not been able to persuade Eurygyos and Larichos to come, said with bitterness, "As you see, my brother, fame is not peace."

"Am I to know what those black looks and ill words were about?" Khar asked.

"They do not approve my life. To them I am not Sappho, the Lesbian poet, but a sister they feel free to criticize."

"Well, well, let it wait. I have not crossed the trackless wastes for a family quarrel. Wherever I set foot I was asked by all, 'Know you fair Sappho, the Lesbian songstress?' And when I answered with the truth, they would fall on their knees to me simply because the gods willed we share the same parents. How long I have looked forward to this day and to being your guest."

Sappho sighed with relief. "Your words coincide with my wish, Brother, that we will have time together to learn the people we have become. Very dear you were to me in days past. We shared a childhood and an exile when we were young. Tell me, do you find me much changed?"

"The years have given you dignity. And there is magic about you, so that one would suppose one was in the company of a goddess."

"And the wrinkles, Khar?"

"I see none. You are as when I left."

"I fear age, Khar, more than death. You see, I dwell with youth and beauty. I am an example to my hetaerae. But were I to grow old, they would leave me or, if they did not, I would send them away."

"Why?"

"Why? Because the joy I teach them is all of beauty, and I could not bear to be other than lovely in their eyes."

Khar laughed. Renowned though she was, his sister had her share of woman's foolishness. "Your fame sets you beyond such thoughts."

She shook her head, but smiling now. "Let us talk of you, Khar, and all you have experienced."

"I have experienced heat and battle, luxurious living and rough-running tides."

"In my home slaves have drawn a scented bath. You shall be anointed, and you shall sleep. Then we will close the years with good talk and confidences."

The taut face of her brother relaxed.

At the villa Sappho took Khar and Alkaios along the flower-strewn purple cloth to an anteroom and herself removed their sandals and, bending over them, washed their feet. "I had word of your death, Alkaios, while I was yet in Syracuse. Khar it was who wrote me." She did not speak of the bargain she had made.

"I did not know myself he lived, until just before sailing from Naukratis. My joy at finding him was muted by the anguish I caused you to live with these many years," Khar said.

Alkaios turned it off as a matter of no consequence. "I was on a ship that was, in fact, boarded by thieves. They wanted my gold. I offered my latest songs instead. They settled for both."

"I thank great Zeus for your life. And for the life of my brother who braves the changing seas."

"And you say it is called the Fort of the Jew's Daughter?" They breakfasted on wine poured into water, on honeyed cakes and eggs in a rich batter.

"Yes." Alkaios took up the story. "Egypt, with thirty thousand Hellenic mercenaries, marched into Palestine. And Nebuchadnezzar of Babylon made an alliance with the Medes, slaying all the princes of Judah at Rublah. When his army broke down the walls of Jerusalem, they say four thousand six hundred souls were carried into Babylon. The Jews mourned as their palaces and strongholds were destroyed, even the gates of their city sunk to the ground.

"Among those to survive was a madman whom none dared kill and a nobleman of the house of Judah, together with his daughter. They made their way to Daphnae, where they were given asylum at the fort. This Jewish daughter was beautiful beyond women, and the place where she stayed was renamed for her."

"How greatly the Jews must have sinned against the gods to be so chastised," Sappho said.

"They believe otherwise," Alkaios replied. "Their belief is not in Father Zeus and his offspring, but in one god only."

"What? Only one?"

"And they say it was for the sin of forsaking Him that their temple was destroyed and they brought low."

"How know you this?" Sappho asked, for she dearly loved a story, even a preposterous one about a single god.

"I spoke to the mad prophet himself, one Jeremiah, who thought the Lord walked with him and scourged him. For he had been a laughingstock when he prophesied doom, and his own people stoned him. He foretold that Mount Zion would lie desolate and jackals prowl over it."

Sappho said pensively, "The madness of a priest is very near that of a poet."

"I heard in Daphnae, on the Pelusiac branch of the Nile, a most beautiful and sad song," Alkaios continued. "It drifted down from the fortress carried by a woman's voice. I believe it was the Jewish Princess herself, for the song originated, as you will hear, in Babylon." Alkaios picked up his lyre and sang in his moving voice:

By the waters of Babylon
there we sat down, yea,
we wept when we remembered
Zion.
We hanged our harps in the midst
thereof.
For they that carried us away
captive
required of us a song,
and they that wasted us,
required of us mirth,
saying sing us one of the songs of
Zion.
How shall we sing the Lord's
song
in a strange land?

"There was more to it, but I have forgotten."

"As you say, it is both lovely and sad." Sappho took the lyre from him, repeating the verses Alkaios had remembered. "One god only. What a strange people. It is no wonder that all the other gods visit vengeance upon them."

Wine was once more poured. Her guests feasted and reclined to the sound of dulcet music, watching the scent curling musk. It was then Khar spoke. "It is time, I think, to tell me, Sister, of the quarrel with our brothers. Why did they refuse to come? Tell me, for the gods know all."

"Amatheia of the lovely locks, dark-eyed Halie, and fair Galatea, daughters all of Nereus, those sea-nymphs who dwell at the bottom of deepest waters, brought you safe to me that you may hear and judge."

"Judge! I do not sit in judgment on Sappho!"

"I swear by those of our family beneath and above the earth, Brother, that I am not deserving of the ill treatment I receive from Eurygyos and Larichos. Since I am a weaver of fictions, let me begin with an old story. It is about Love, which is the author of all human happiness and enables us to live in harmony.

"We humans in our physical bodies have undergone many changes since time stood at its beginning. Originally there were three sexes, male, female, and another, which took of the nature of both the others, the hermaphrodite. Now all three types were completely rounded, having a double back, which formed a disc, four arms, four legs, and two identical faces upon a common head, which looked in opposite directions. These creatures had two organs of generation as they had all else. The male was born of Sun, the female of Earth, and the sex that was both male and female came from Moon.

"Now their strength and vigor were great. Also their pride, so that they attacked even the gods. Father Zeus debated what was to be done, for he could not allow a race of god-fighters, nor could he bring himself to kill them as he had the giants. At last Zeus thought of a solution: he would cut them in two. 'And if they continue so arrogant, I will bisect them again and let them hop upon one leg.'

"So saying, he cut the members of the human race in halves. Apollo healed the wounds and gathered together the skin like a purse so that we have bellies.

"Now it happened that each severed half yearned to find its other self. Those who were Sun-born desired other men. And women who were halves of a female gave their affection to women. While the parts of the hermaphrodites sought the opposite sex. Not only are we possessed of these physical demands, but the soul has a longing to complete itself which it can express in no other manner."

There was a pause when she finished. "This is indeed the way of it," Alkaios said, and then perceiving Khar's stern countenance, stopped.

"I understand your parable, Sappho," her brother said. "And it is certainly usual that men and women copulate and men with boys. Many such lovers have I seen march into battle together. Yet I did not realize that women were capable of an equal passion for each other. However, I find no evil in such a practice, except that it leaves fewer women for me."

His lips relaxed into a smile. Alkaios was delighted to laugh with him.

Her brother continued, "And you, Sappho, as a poet of great stature, perhaps require a more dominant role in sex than the female is generally granted. Tell me, for I have seen lovely girls here in your home, are they all inclined toward their own sex?"

"Only a few have girl lovers. Most leave to marry."

"It seems to me," Khar said, "a paradise has been created in this house where I hear only laughter and music. And certainly I can think of no reason why the pleasure of your own sex should be denied you. As long as all are here by their own will and not carried off from the town . . ."

"No, no, only about a third of my hetaerae are Lesbians. The others come from islands close and far, from Athens and Lydia."

"And our brothers are against your pleasure?"

"They find it unseemly in a woman to find such fulfillment. They say of my life that it is licentious, and that I bring disgrace on them as though I were a common whore. They do not come to my house, nor am I invited to theirs."

"They set themselves up as second Solons, then. Even the gods have body parts and must satisfy them. It is reasonable that you have needs beyond other women. One must feed art even as the gods subsist on hekatombs."

Sappho clasped her brother's knees and laid her head upon them.

Alkaios, much moved by the scene, took care they should not know it. In a loud and jovial voice he proclaimed, "This Kharaxos, this captain who commands both Sea and squadrons, who urges men with whips and blows, is soft, unfired clay in the hands of this sister."

Sappho exclaimed, "Let me send to the flower merchants in thanks for your support. Recently I have endured such conflict of passions. Like a great cauldron of soup I am stirred one way and then another. Sometimes I thought myself a perverse and evil person in whom all the storms of the human heart gathered."

"That can happen when wave chases wave and the sea breaks on a lonely headland."

Sappho smiled tenderly on her brother. "Your mind and my heart are not strangers, Khar."

Alkaios, never one to be outdone, said, "Let me tell how night after night Khar guided us over the pathless Sea by the Pleiades and the Bear, who turns ever in one place. Your brother does not lie at anchor nights as others do, but continues with Orion ever on his left. Consequently, his ships are filled with prizes, both earned and won. Your house has trebled its fortune."

"The gods grant, Brother, that now you will rest at home in Mitylene, and find yourself a wife."

Khar shook his head. "The sea is in my blood, as it was in our father's."

"Then you will pursue your quest like the mighty Odysseus?"

"I have scheduled a return trip to Naukratis. There will be time later when there are white threads in my beard to think of wife and fireside. And you, Sister, perhaps you will be making a water journey of your own."

"I? Oh no, I am done with travel. Twice noble Poseidon protected and spared me. One must not trespass too often on the domain of gods."

"But I am bearer of a special message. It comes from Iadmon, Prince of Samos. He is owner of the slave Aesop, whose parables you have often related. Iadmon is holding a great ceremony at which your presence is most urgently sought, as the occasion is the setting free of this man of genius, the storyteller Aesop."

Sappho clapped her hands at the news. "How fitting! For no prince, no matter how powerful, should own art. Art must be free; I have always believed it and believe that only in Lesbos could I have sung. Perhaps you are right, Brother, perhaps I should travel to Samos. Would I be Iadmon's guest-friend?"

"He will have it no other way."

Sappho did not wish to make the trip to Samos. The reason was hidden in the words of one of her old songs:

> *For whom curl my hair*
> *for whom perfume my hands?*
> *Since I go not to . . .*

One saffron-robed morning a name had come unbidden to her mind—Atthis.

The stars had gone forward many times since then and always the girl was at Anaktoria's side. Yet even at the gate of her dreams the nymph of the braided tresses stood. In her dreams Atthis walked alone; there was no Anaktoria. "Her soul has passed into me." Sappho cried nights into her pillow, for she would almost rather die than love again. "I will hang my wreath on Aphrodite's sacred tree and remove the ribbons from my legs!"

But the disorder of her pulse did not steady. She asked as she had in the past:

> *Which of the gods*
> *set this wild love*
> *in my heart?*

And she sang bitterly a truth she had learned:

> *Aphrodite's*
> *daughter, you*
> *cheat mortals*

But she didn't care, and many times she put herself in Atthis's way. The girl always smiled at her, but kept her arm around Anaktoria's waist. To Atthis she was a revered teacher, nothing more. While for her Atthis became the focus of her thoughts.

The sight of Atthis and Anaktoria, playful as two colts, throwing a ball to each other, combing each other's hair, whispering, their heads close, tormented Sappho. Atthis's voice was particularly sweet, and she liked to sing softly into Anaktoria's ear. Pictures of the two came between Sappho and sleep. She had a desire that grew day by day so great that she wrote:

> *I would commit follies for that woman . . .*

When Atthis merely passed by she felt she had drunk nectar subtly mixed with fire. The air itself seemed to scorch her as she saw Anaktoria take Atthis by the hand or the ends of her peplos.

To Aphrodite she breathed:

> *Many's the time*
> *I've wished I,*
> *O gold-crowned Aphrodite,*
> *had luck like that*

She sang a new song:

> *Love coming from Heaven*
> *throws off*
> *his purple mantle*

Unruly desire let her think of nothing but the girl, and she devised lawless plans for being rid of Anaktoria. Then Atthis would turn to her. Sappho persuaded herself that she had always loved the girl. Had she not sung of her even before her first exile?

She wrote in the night:

> *Is it possible*
> *for any maid on earth*
> *to be apart*
> *from the woman she loves?*

When the queenly Dawn again showed Atthis hand in hand with Anaktoria, Sappho decided it was better for her, better for Atthis, better for Anaktoria, that she make the journey to the island of Samos.

It was not as a woman but as a poet she was valued. She knew the trip would enhance her reputation, give fresh impetus to the stories told of her. It was legend-building to depart on such a journey to do honor to art and the Muses she served. Besides, the auguries repeatedly fell out well, they promised seas as smooth as a mirror.

When Khar promised he himself would pilot the ship, she put by her reluctance and agreed. Her girls were delighted at this venturing and danced all in unison for her, her brother, and her friend Alkaios. The men leaned back against cushions and watched. The sacred figures of the dance, the heavy movements of the loins caused them to breathe more quickly. "The crowned Muses have descended," her brother whispered in appreciation, "even golden-haired Harmony."

Glancing sideways at him, Sappho said slyly, "If a maid in my house pleases you, Brother, and you would give up your roving ways . . ."

Khar only laughed. "I am a sailor, too rough for the arts of love they hint at."

Sappho smiled, for her hetaerae had indeed been well and delicately taught. However, she knew Khar would not choose a maiden trained by her. He was of her house and would train his own woman.

Alkaios leaned close to her. "Your poems are a breaking through and throwing off of restraint. It is as though you remove all pins, both of ivory and bone, from your hair and allow it to fall free."

"Hesiod taught, 'The holy gift of the Muses to man—is song.' "

"He also said, 'He is happy whom the Muses love.' Yet I see melancholy too often on your face."

Alkaios had always been penetrating, yet she denied his words with her old fire. "Why should you say this thing?" But this was Alkaios who knew her.

"What you speak is true," she admitted. "Do you know, I thought myself responsible for your death? Yes, I prayed Zeus to spare my child and take another whom I loved in her place. Directly after this I received news that you were murdered at sea. By this barter with the gods, you can see there is not one Sappho within me, but another who brings calamity by her folly. Is it she who sings? She who makes immortal words? I have never known.

"I know who I want to be, but only sometimes am. There is a willful, frightening spirit who at times inhabits me, inconstant in love, seeking always what she has not. I do not like this person. And I have never spoken of her before." She realized her brother was listening also. "I ask you, Khar, and you, Alkaios, is there a way to expel her by prayer or magic? Is it some curse the gods have laid on me along with being double-sexed?"

Khar shook his head. He was a simple man and his solution was simple: "A trip by sea will be good for you."

Sappho laughed until tears stood in her eyes.

But Alkaios said, "Your hurt is in comparing yourself with others. You must not do this. As for me, you did me no harm. As for your art, it lives by love. That you love easily is not an evil. You have an eager heart. Therefore your words fly up in flame. Do not mourn that you are Sappho, but send up hekatombs."

"Yes?" she asked tentatively, wanting to be reassured.

"It is as I say, you are a gem unmatched by any other. Sun, Moon, cloud-shrouded Day, the tapers of Night, each show a different aspect, reflecting some part of Sappho. The whole . . . none can know, not even you. But I agree with Khar. Perhaps the voyage will ease your heart and mind. As I see it, it is an act symbolic for all time, that Sappho of Lesbos be present when the fetters are struck and Aesop made free."

"And you will join me, Alkaios?"

"That I will not. I have had my fill of wandering. I will find a pretty boy to bring me comfort here in Lesbos. I shall not be missed from the Samian festivities. Besides, though it be a small matter, Iadmon forgot to include me in his guest list."

"He is the loser! And you, Brother?"

"My ships are even now being provisioned. I will take you to Iadmon's grand festival and then leave with a cargo of wine and olives once more for Egypt. I must return a final time with fine metals, hides, and matchless linens such as I brought this trip."

"And will it be a venture of so many years?" Sappho asked sadly.

"You quest in the mind, Sappho, I in strange lands and upon unharvested seas that produced Nereus, who never lies and is always true."

"May you find another such upon the Earth, call her wife, and settle down."

"Why do you want a settled life for me, Sister, when my blood courses hot as yours?"

"I fear for you, Khar. You are all I have left."

"What about my niece, your pretty Kleis?" He realized he had not seen her this visit.

"She is well. But mothers and daughters have difficulty understanding one another. She takes her uncles' part and stays here only reluctantly."

"I am grieved to hear this."

Sappho shrugged. "It is all one. She will soon be married, I suppose. She is coming to that age and is a well-grown girl."

During the next days Sappho helped Alkaios in the selection of a site where he planned to erect a villa, and left him immersed in plans and quarreling with his architect. With her brother she went to the quay and watched skins of wine and water loaded onto the ships. "When you return this time, Khar, you will be a member of the governing assembly."

But he did not hear. He lay on his belly to inspect the work of slaves, and kicked the fresh planks to test their soundness.

His sister smiled. He is like me, she thought, when I am seized by a poem sent of the gods.

At home she supervised her servants as they packed her woman's chest. Her finest garments were folded between scent, and there were gifts of much worth for her host and for Aesop. One would think her busy, but during this preparation she watched Atthis covertly.

> *The immortals know no care;*
> *yet the lot they spin for man*
> *is full of sorrow*

For the glad echoing voice of Atthis was lifted in happy song. And her happiness was in Anaktoria. Surely my brain is blighted, Sappho thought, and with relief stepped aboard her brother's vessel. Niobe had prepared a couch of rugs and pillows, and from its comfort she indolently watched Khar set his sail to the wind, cresting wave after wave as they were born.

At night she entered her draped tent, while her brother lay on coils of rope in the stern. Their curved bark went steadily on, for as Alkaios had said, Khar did not tie up at night as other captains. He watched the sky and constantly took soundings, so their journey was cut by half.

On the third day some god shrouded the land, and Sea was roused to passion. Her brother told her to sit by him and watch as the storm swelled. Calling on Poseidon, he fell as a reveler into a dance. No matter what partner Sea raised against him, he skimmed and tacked and bore lightly over her until by day's light he had worn her out.

Sappho laughed in glee at his prowess.

She discovered, after the storm had died, that the entire time of its churning she had been afraid. But the excitement of watching Khar turn into the troughs and leap to the peaks had hidden this from her. Now, exhausted, she made ablutions and fell into a deep sleep. Her tent, which had been torn apart during the storm, her women quietly erected again about her.

Samos was a dream island. Opening her eyes, she thought she still slept. It lay in striped water, the many shoals reflecting tan, the gouged basins a dark sparkling blue. The slopes of Mount Mylale were terraced in vineyards, and orchards perfumed the air.

A lookout had been kept for them, and welcoming crowds threw blossoms into the harbor, so that the oarsmen caught petals of roses on their blades. The most beautiful lads dived naked into the water and caught hold of their craft, laughing and pretending to pull the ship in.

On the shore maidens formed a procession singing Sappho's songs to the accompaniment of tambourines. Khar drew her to him before he let her go. It happened so quickly that she could not recall any words of good-bye.

Samos was a miniature Lesbos, being only 243 stadia across. A mole ran the length of the protected harbor, in which bobbed bright red triremes, the ships for which Samos was famous. The houses, too, were red-roofed and richly gilded. From the hills a temple shone, home of Hera, who gave special love and care to women.

On the quay Iadmon, her host, stepped from beneath a colorful canopy to embrace her and pour libation that Sea had allowed her safe passage.

Khar's rowers lifted oars in salute. It was a powerful sight. As each man in each ship hefted his oar simultaneously, there were wild cries from the shore. Sappho murmured a blessing under her breath as the fleet headed out of the harbor, and the boys who had gained the decks dived again into the water. Her gaze followed the lead ship. Khar must follow his path as she followed hers.

Beside the imposing Iadmon was a dark, ugly figure with a hunched back. Sappho could scarcely hide her horror when told this was the bard-slave Aesop, whom she had come so far to honor. The small, wizened creature hopped forward and croaked a welcome. Whereupon she was driven to the villa, a long procession of girls and boys winding behind. Those going before pelted her path with flowers.

They passed within guarded gates, and she exclaimed at gardens made bright with jonquils and fountains, and dazzling ornate birds who spread great tails covered with mock eyes. "It is the peacock," Iadmon told her, "indigenous to our island, the bird beloved of Hera."

Dismounting, Sappho followed her host up marble stairs along a portico supported by slender-stalked columns. Iadmon led her to an apartment reserved for her, and murmuring, "Divine Sappho, I and my house are honored forever," left her to the ministration of his women and hers.

From her bath she whispered to Niobe, "I would not have made the perilous trip had I known Aesop was a grotesque. I can hardly bear to look on him."

"Then do not, Lady. The guests are many distinguished princes and merchant princes, lords of far lands." She slipped a gossamer robe over her. "From Lydia they are here, and distant Rhodes. It is meant that Sappho shall reign over all in revelry and celebration."

"At what hour do festivities begin?"

"Upon the arrival of Sappho," Niobe replied and with utmost art fashioned a visage heightened by fard and tints of color. "There are slaves placed along the way to announce it when you choose to visit the large hall." She fetched the jewel-case from among the wrapped parcels.

"The amethyst," Sappho decided, and the single gem fell between her breasts.

In the great hall the guests strained to see this small but elegant woman with the figure of a girl and the bearing of a queen. There was a compelling quality about her, intriguing, withdrawn. She moved lightly, but her eyes were eyes one would do well to draw back from, for they saw where only gods looked. A glance from them and the soul was no longer hid.

Her host placed her at his right hand, where Hermes the god of good fortune stood and where the lucky Heron came when he visited men.

To the other side of Iadmon, where she did not have to look on him, was Aesop. Her aversion had been discreetly relayed. Sappho bent her head to receive a crown of cyclamen from her host. A cup of honeyed wine was placed in her hand and she was proffered a dish of wild pomegranates. The servants were naked girls and boys without blemish. The air seemed to breathe a strange exotic fragrance; when she asked what it was, she was told "Nardus from India."

Iadmon introduced her with lavish words. She nodded an acknowledgment, received her lyre from Niobe, and began with her usual invocation:

> Come now, my heavenly
> tortoiseshell; become
> a speaking instrument

To herself she murmured, Daughters of Zeus, I greet you. Add passion to my song! She lowered her eyes and began a chant:

> Come here to us
> gentle Gaiety, Revelry, Radiance
> and you, Muses with lovely hair

When the songstress was done, Iadmon motioned Aesop to stand forward. He had been festooned in gold fetters. With a jewel-encrusted sword Iadmon ceremoniously struck off the bonds. Aesop knelt in gratitude before him, then, rising, thanked peerless Sappho for making this moment of freedom even more memorable. "Honorable guests of my great lord and patron, mighty Iadmon, I stand before you—ugly, hump-backed, deformed in my limbs. As a child I was no prettier, besides which I was a slave. I despaired of myself. And my mother, seeing me so unhappy, one day stopped the work of her fingers and, drying my tears, said, 'Aesop, I tell you this: Be diligent to perfect the little tales you sing and if you please the Lord Apollo, who is a lover of poetry and paeans, one day he will come down from Heaven and give you treasure greater than beauty.'"

Aesop's glance rested on them. "This day my mother's words are made truth. For freedom is the greatest treasure of all."

Applause swelled in the room, at the end of which Aesop of the hunched back and shoulders approached Sappho. To indicate how greatly he was honored by her presence, he touched the hem of her gown. At that instant, the journey, the departure of Khar, the heat—all combined with the sensation of his little claws on her garment. Sappho fell to the floor in a faint.

Consternation prevailed, with everyone hovering about the fallen songstress. Each, while afraid to touch her, had some nostrum or remedy to offer. Niobe saw to it that she was carried to her chamber, where she chafed her hands and spoke soft words. Sappho's eyes sprang wide. "He touched me, that hideous apparition. He must have been forged beneath the roots of Aetna by Hephaestus the lame in his own image."

"Fear not." Both women were startled by the male voice. Aesop, out of concern, had followed. He did not enter, but stood at the door in shadow. "I myself do not look in a mirror, or my day is spoiled for me. I realized at once it was my hand upon your robe that made you ill. The others, being used to me, hardly notice. Wonderful Sappho, I must make amends. Having shown you the ugliest being on Samos, I have permission from my lord to bring you the most beautiful." And Aesop stepped aside, drawing into the room a statue of Aphrodite, except that her flesh had tints of life.

"She is Doricha, the White Rose, a young Thracian trained in the arts of love. She is yours for your stay—and may her beauty bring you forgetfulness of myself, so that when you think of Aesop in future, you remember only my thanks."

As he turned to go, Sappho called to him. "Wait, Aesop . . . I bow to your genius, which was touching tonight, and at other times has made me laugh. You were never a slave in your soul and it is right you are a free man." Then she sang:

> *He is fair in appearance,*
> *but he who is good*
> *will soon seem fair also*

Aesop smiled at her attempt and replied, "I honor you as no other mortal. Accept the White Rose and when your thoughts would stray to a vision of me, see her instead."

The beautiful child-courtesan smiled at Sappho when they were alone. Sappho inspected her with interest. "You are all white and gold. I see you shave the fullness between your legs, and that it is gilded."

"It is my treasure," Doricha whispered and swayed toward her.

Sappho sank back against cushions. "I would see your treasure closer up, to make sure it is not dross."

To approach her the White Rose slid to the floor and wriggled her body across the marble and spread herself. The long lips were filled with purple grapes. "The juice of this fruit," Doricha whispered, "is not like any other. It is hot with life. May I plant in your vineyard, Lady?"

Sappho was delighted by the novelty. The girl was so practiced that her touch alone roused, while the rosy tongue brought madness and the convulsion of utmost desire.

"You destroy me," Sappho cried when both were reddened by the crushed grapes. She held the reins of long blond hair, while the pony bucked and was wild beneath her. She had satisfaction and pressed a gold talent where there had been grapes.

Sappho became so intrigued by the Thracian that she sent to buy her from Iadmon, but he replied regretfully that he could not part from her.

"It is a lie," hissed the White Rose at their next tryst. She uncoiled herself from Sappho's arms. "He has already sold me to one Xanthes, who plans to take me into Egypt, to Naukratis, where garrisons of Hellenic soldiers are stationed. I am much afraid, for I have known the favor of Iadmon and his guests, and have not been the property of soldiers."

"You are too valuable, Doricha, to receive other than delicate treatment, for you will bring a fortune to your new master. Tell me, have you been with a woman before? How do you find it?"

"I love being at your side and having you remove my grapes with your mouth. Your passion comes suddenly like a storm. It shakes us both, as the leaves from the bough you sing of. I prefer men to women. But I prefer Sappho to any."

Sappho laughed. "Your words are paid for, but they are nonetheless pleasing."

So that her pleasure did not flag, Doricha brought one of the enormous peacocks with its oriental coloring of bright gold-and-blue patterns into the chamber; then, from a vial she poured and rubbed a certain scent upon her full crescent and inside the crimson slit. The giant bird, roused to orgasm by the preparation, flew at Doricha. Flapping his wings and unfurling his dazzling tail, he extended a huge organ that had been retracted in its body. Its wings beat wildly about the slave girl, fanning her nakedness. The White Rose gave the sexual cry of women; the shrill sound of the cock answered. It was like watching a god mate with a mortal. The bird lifted his dangling white burden off the ground. It half hopped, half flew, the girl hanging from its swollen member in the most bizarre sexual act Sappho had ever witnessed. The scream of two species mingled, and it was done. The cock shook Doricha from him and a slave led it from the room.

Sappho stared at the voluptuous child, who lay before her with flecks of blood upon her legs. "Lick off the blood," the White Rose begged. But the spell was broken. Sappho shook her head.

"Do you want to try it with the peacock?" Doricha asked.

"No," Sappho said in horror.

"Then let me show you what it was like."

Such was Sappho's visit to the isle of Samos.

During the course of her stay she met a young man who had journeyed from Sardis, in Lydia. He was the eldest son of a great house. "I came because I wished to hear famed Sappho sing. But also I look for a wife, and thought perhaps I might find one here."

"I have seen in fair Samos girls most lovely to look upon," Sappho replied. "Of course," she continued thoughtfully, "they are not trained in the gracious arts of song and dance as are my fair companions in the House of the Servants of the Muses."

"Can the maidens of great Sappho ever be persuaded to leave her?"

She smiled. "That is why they come to me. I prepare them to be wives in the finest homes, to go as princesses. Although it always saddens me to part with one of my hetaerae," she added.

"Perhaps there is one among them who is ready to become a wife?"

"I will give the matter thought," she told the young man. "Of course if I do think of an especially gifted friend, I would not want my name mentioned, lest any think that my school is something I do for profit. I make no profit, nor want any. We are dedicated to the Muses only. And no unseemly ideas should go abroad."

"If you could but call to mind one girl with a fair face and good disposition, who is versed in song, I would be discreet, and forever in your debt."

"I promise nothing other than what I said; I will think on it."

That night Sappho made ablutions. Aphrodite had surely sent this young man. And she called for a white ewe to be perfumed and ordered chains of flowers around its woolly neck.

The same ardent young man sought her out at the first opportunity, and she spoke with seeming reluctance of the prize among her hetaerae. "One Anaktoria comes to mind. She is the most gifted, coming as she does from Miletus, that Isle of Thought where great Thales and Anaximander rule by intellect alone . . . but the sweet nature of Anaktoria I could not do without." After a pause she conceded, "Of course, one so blessed in all her parts by the Kyprus-born herself cannot long remain a maid, and I know I must resign myself to losing her to some princely house."

When she was alone, she smiled, recalling the lines of Hesiod:

> I know how to speak many falsehoods
> (even as you)
> but I also know how to speak truth when I wish to

It was her wish now to return home, to see Atthis and be rid of Anaktoria. She made a prayer to Hera, patroness of women, to see her safely back across the sea.

When her feet stepped upon Lesbian shores Sappho cried in joy:

> *Come, Lady of Kyprus*
> *to hand round in golden goblets*
> *nectar*
> *mixed with delicate good cheer*
> *for these*
> *my hetaerae and thine*

At this greeting, her dear companions, who had gathered at the harbor, tied themselves, singing and laughing, to her chariot, lashing one another with ropes of flowers that broke, scattering their petals.

Her daughter stayed distant from her, Gongyla close. Nothing had changed since she had left. When she looked at Atthis and Anaktoria, her eyes were masked. She hailed both girls by name, and they, made happy by this attention, hugged each other.

During the gala homecoming festivities, during songs, dances, and the giving of thanks for a journey safely consummated, Sappho thought only of Atthis. The wanting in her created the opening line of a new ode:

> *Yet I could not expect*
> *to touch heaven with my two arms . . .*

Not yet. Not now.

But it was possible that in Sardis, Lydia, a princely family would soon inquire about a maid from Miletus who studied the art the gracious Muses had bestowed on Sappho of Lesbos. And if the young man spoke truly, a golden necklace heavy with rubies would accompany the inquiry. Then a parchment would come to Anaktoria from her parents. For it was a high connection their daughter would make.

While she waited for this to happen, Sappho stifled her impatience; she called on Eros, god of desire, most beautiful of the immortals, and begged him:

> *You are the charioteer*
> *in charge of the steeds of lust and reason;*
> *control them,*
> *make them move in harmony*

She needed a calm mind. But calm eluded her. Commissions for her work had accumulated in her absence; she did not attend to them. Her body was ready for love, while her girls thought her mad with music. Eros had not listened to her prayer, she was not in control of herself. She took a hyacinth from the water and threw it accurately and directly at Atthis.

Atthis looked at her in surprise.

Sappho laughed. "You did not expect it," she said, "and so I could not resist." But she must resist. She knew this.

Work.

Work rescued her. She busied herself with a wedding song:

> And many are the golden curls
> and the purple draperies
> which are the breezes'
> many-colored playthings;
> and countless also
> are the silver drinking cups and the ivory ornaments

That for others. For herself, she pressed not only into tablets but into her heart:

> Now I know why Eros,
> of all the progeny of
> Earth and Heaven, has
> been most dearly loved

Yet it was a torment. The constant sight of Atthis with Anaktoria increased both her misery and her longing. Why did the gods measure out time so slowly? In anger she strummed:

> I dreamed that
> you and I had
> words, Kyprian

She woke to pray, to sleep again. What if there were no message from Miletus? What if the young man, on returning to his homeland of Lydia, found a charming girl who had suddenly grown up, and forgot the picture she had presented to him of feminine perfections? Sappho found herself unable to work.

Suppose treacherous waters had closed over the ship from Miletus, and a message would never come? Suppose her hopes lay at the bottom of the sea? She sang softly to banish these thoughts:

> *When love comes down from heaven*
> *and throws off his purple cloak . . .*

She couldn't finish. Would she ever sing these words to Atthis? Sappho knew day by day what Atthis wore, which flowers she braided in her hair, the color of the ribbons that floated from her thighs, the piece of jewelry she momentarily fancied. She recalled the story of the girdle on which is embroidered all wishes and wants. Oh, had she such a girdle, one name, one name alone she would repeatedly stitch.

In the morning she wrote:

> *An embroidered sandal was hiding*
> *her feet,*
> *a beautiful piece of Lydian work*

And in the evening:

> *The very clothes you wear charm me!*

"I do not know what to do," she cried into her pillow. "My thoughts are double." If she spoke to her, she would drive her away. She knew it. Yet she could no longer follow the path of reason. She must touch the web of cloth that enclosed Atthis—she must.

To overcome this compulsion Sappho climbed the path behind her house daily, from the height of which one could see the line of Attarmeor, the port of Pergam. She willed the ships on the horizon to put in at Mitylene's twin harbors. But they held fast to their preordained courses.

When the longed-for message arrived, Sappho was busy with a flute she had just purchased. It was Athene's instrument, used by her at her festivals. The one Sappho had chosen had an unusual tone but needed working. She shut herself in her room to coax a sweeter, purer, sound from it. Diligently she cleaned the inside with a soft rod and adjusted her breath across the five finger-holes. Better, but it could weave more magic still, and she blew from the other end in case some particle still adhered. A shadow fell across her and she looked up.

It was Anaktoria.

Without a word the girl handed her a missive. The breath seemed stopped in Sappho's nostrils. She took the parchment without comment and read. It was a greeting from Anaktoria's parents, by the hand of a scribe, in which they expressed their wish that Anaktoria, beloved daughter of their house, prepare to depart Lesbos, and in joy hasten on the next available ship for Lydia. The holdings of a princely house in Sardis were then described, its wealth listed, enumerated were slaves, gold, iron, and orchards. The eldest son of this family was of a mind to marry and he wished an accomplished wife. Knowing of the maidens the peerless poet Sappho gathered about her and instructed in sacred song and dance, as well as on musical instruments, he was minded to have such as had undergone this tutelage, and he heard from one who recently had been a guest-friend in the House of the Servants of the Muses that of all the lovely flowers, none compared to Anaktoria of Miletus.

Sappho looked up from the document. "But this is marvelous, a proposal of marriage. An alliance with a notable house of ancient lineage. It must be you made an impression on my brother Kharaxos or Alkaios the poet; I can think of none other who has recently been a guest here with us."

Anaktoria held out to her a necklace wrought with rubies.

"What is this?" Sappho exclaimed. "He who is desirous of being your bridegroom has sent you a token? The chain is most dexterously made; with gems nestled into it as though they were birds. How rich, yet how tasteful. Your heart must contain great happiness that such a lot has befallen you."

Sappho reached to press Anaktoria's hands, but the girl put them behind her.

"I do not wish to marry," she said.

"Not wish?"

"No. I wish to stay here and continue as your hetaera. That is my greatest happiness."

"But surely every maid hopes to marry?"

"You are not married."

"But I was, and had a child. A woman is not complete without a husband and child."

Suddenly Anaktoria was on her knees hiding her face in Sappho's lap. "Lady, dear patron, poet of the world, protect me. Do not let me be sent away! I would stay here always. Throw over me the mantle of your command. Say that you will not part with me. And from this time on you will be as a goddess to me. I will make hekatombs to you and pour out libation. Only lend me your name, your rank and reputation that I am not made against my will to become a wife in Lydia to a man I do not know, whose ways and customs I do not know. You yourself have often inveighed against this. Help me, sweet Sappho, help Anaktoria. I cannot bear to be parted from my life here."

Sappho was touched by the sight of such distress in one so attractive. And it was true, she had often spoken against young girls being used as pawns in the acquisition of wealth and status. Now, however, she replied coolly, for she easily deciphered the girl's intent. She knew too well it was Atthis she could not bear to be parted from. And, like the living part of a shell, Sappho's nature closed over her pity. She had the girl sit beside her and patted her hand.

Anaktoria drew away. "I see you will not help me, Lady, and I must go to Sardis to dwell with strangers."

The door was flung open and Atthis ran to throw herself at Sappho's feet and clasp and kiss them. "I stood outside, and heard. I know I should not have, but I had not the strength to walk away from your words. O noble Sappho, surely you with your great power can intervene and stop this? Anaktoria loves you well, and her voice has ever been uplifted in our songs, while her fingers are clever with all manner of instruments. Besides . . ."

"Besides?" Sappho asked, observing that Atthis's eyes were heavy from weeping and wiped tears left a mark upon her cheek. How adorable she seemed, and how vulnerable.

"I cannot live without my friend. We are never separated. Have you not seen how one is never without the other? I should die! I would not want my life if it meant I should not see my Anaktoria."

"Peace, sweet one. Do not cry so. You must think of her whom you love. Would you fetter her with your affection? Stand in the way of a match that will bring her the joys of womanhood, a man of wealth, family, children? I know when you consider with a clear mind that you will not."

Both girls left her attempting to restrain their tears, to be worthy hetaerae, to live up to Sappho's expectation, to do the right thing. They knew it was the right thing because it made them so miserable, and the gods, though themselves forever enjoying nectar, ambrosia, and love, set a course of suffering for humankind.

Sappho let several days pass and then sat down with Anaktoria and helped her compose the dutiful letter her parents were expecting, and the more formal letter to Sardis, in which she, professing herself unworthy of such an honor, yet gave thanks to Father Zeus, Aphrodite, and Hermes alike, for her good reputation which had traveled even into the land of Lydia. Her dearest hope, Sappho wrote for her, was to be a model of womanhood, both as wife and mother.

Tearfully Anaktoria signed both documents. Sappho ordered her own servants, Niobe at their head, to see to Anaktoria's woman's chest, to fold her garments in layers of crushed mint, and to include presents of value from herself and the other girls, particularly Atthis. In this cause she sought out the girl, who lay in a darkened chamber, hair unbrushed and no word for anyone.

Atthis tried to rouse herself when Sappho entered, but the heart had gone out of her. She could not be interested even in a parting gift. "Do you choose something appropriate, Lady."

"Well, for a keepsake, what do you treasure that will have meaning for Anaktoria?"

There was a long pause. "Flowers," Atthis said finally, "but they wilt."

"Then let us find arm bracelets or earrings, or a rope of pearls that came on a time from Sea."

Atthis roused a bit. "Once, lying on my breast, she commented on the perfume I use; it is a blend of attar of roses. I will slip that into her woman's chest that she remember the day."

Sappho disliked the idea, but could think of no reason against it.

Love is
a weaver of fictions

and

a bringer of pain

She wrote this when she returned to her rooms. It was a torment to be close to Atthis and not touch even the shining hair of her head. Her women reported to her that Atthis cut a lock of this hair and laid it in Anaktoria's chest. This was the extremest grief. Anaktoria tied strands of her hair with Atthis's and so the friends separated.

Sappho composed a poem to Anaktoria and, armed with this, announced herself at Atthis's door.

She found the same listless and bedraggled girl. She longed to take her in her arms and comfort her. "Atthis, I have written down something that will make things easier. Will you listen?"

Atthis's head, heavy with tangled hair, bent slightly like a hyacinth on its stalk.

Sappho leaned across her lyre and chanted:

> *Some say cavalry and others claim*
> *infantry or a fleet of long oars*
> *is the supreme sight on the black earth.*
> *I say it is*
>
> *the one you love. And easily proved.*
> *Didn't Helen—who far surpassed all*
> *mortals in beauty—desert the best*
> *of men, her king,*
>
> *and sail off to Troy and forget*
> *her daughter and dear kinsmen? Merely*
> *the Kyprian's gaze made her bend and led*
> *her from her path;*
>
> *these things remind me now*
> *of Anaktoria who is far,*
> *and I*
> *for one*
> *would rather see her warm supple step*

and the sparkle of her face—than watch all the
dazzling chariots and armored hoplites of Lydia

Atthis was greatly agitated. "You do not think that Anaktoria for-
gets? No, she could not, she promised, not one second of our time
together. She is true, Lady. And loyal to me, her dearest friend. She
did not want to go to Sardis, it was not her doing. It was her parents.
She obeyed them, what else could she do?"

Sappho thought about this. "Not obey them," she said and rose to
leave.

Atthis ran after her and clutched her arm. "What do you mean,
not obey them? Is there any girl who would not obey her parents?"

Sappho laughed. "It is only my madness. You know those whom
the Muses inhabit are made frenzied and have lawlessness of mind. . . .
If I loved one who dances as Queen Hera walks, with golden sandals
. . . then neither parents nor Erinyes could drag me away."

"But you are Sappho. Another could not be so strong."

"Of that I do not know. As you say, I am Sappho." Then, relenting,
"Shall I stay with you awhile? Perhaps I can bring you comfort. I have
thought of another way to praise Anaktoria. Listen."

> *The charm of Anaktoria's bearing,*
> *her radiant features*
> *would give me more pleasure*
> *to see*
> *than all the chariots of the Lydians*
> *and all their armored infantry*
> *marching to attack*

Atthis responded with apathy.

"I will cheer you with some very old songs."

"Oh, would you? I dared not ask it."

Sappho replied, "First, lie across your bed and I will comb out the
snarls and tangles of your hair. What a state you have allowed yourself
to get into."

"I am so unhappy. So alone."

"You are not alone. I am with you." And seating herself on the bed, she took Atthis's head in her lap and with a comb of jade began to sort out and separate the curls. "I said I would sing to you. Let me begin with this."

> *I saw one day gathering flowers*
> *a very dainty little girl*

"How pretty that is."

"The little girl was you, Atthis."

"Me?"

"Perhaps you were four, I don't know. But you held more jonquils than your small hands could clasp. One dropped and I picked it up and gave it to you. And you were as golden as the flowers you held, and as perfect."

Atthis frowned slightly in concentration. "I think I almost remember, perhaps I do . . . a kind lady . . ."

"There. Now your hair is combed through."

"Don't go, stay with me."

"Shall I bathe you then and put you to bed, like the little girl I sang of long ago?"

"Yes, oh yes. I fear so to be alone."

Sappho took the rings from her toes and ordered the marble pool filled. A pipe coming downstream led through the kitchen, where it was heated by passing above the open hearth. This ingenious method of receiving warm water when one turned the satyr's golden head she had learned in Syracuse and, being much impressed by it, installed the system here in her own villa. When one was finished bathing, other pipes carried the water to the sea.

The pool was filled and tested for warmth by the hand of slaves. When it was pronounced satisfactory, Sappho threw down her chiton and stepped into the polished bath.

Atthis hung back and did not raise her eyes to Sappho or remove her garment.

Sappho laughed at her shyness. "All my girls have seen me naked in my bath. Why not in yours? Come, drop your chiton and enter the water."

Atthis did as Sappho said.

"O mortal-enchanting daughter of Aphrodite!" Sappho exclaimed taking her hand and drawing her down the marble steps. She floated Atthis's body in the perfumed water. "Are you girl or nymph?" she asked bending over her.

Atthis closed her eyes and the water lifted and buoyed her against Sappho, who caressed her, saying, "This is as the gods would have it. Lean against me and pretend I am Anaktoria."

"Anaktoria?"

"Yes, Anaktoria. I will show you the twenty-two places of the skin that are made for love."

"I do not know . . . I do not think . . ." the girl said in perturbation, but her nipples rose against Sappho's touch.

Sappho stroked gently. Love was an art she had studied well. Leaving the bath, she urged the dazed girl to the couch, where she sketched the slender lines of her groin with her finger. "All is rosy and perfect in you." And she ravished her until there was frenzied response in the body she tasted. "You are the sister of my bed," she whispered.

Selene, the Moon goddess, beaming eye of night, looked on their pleasure. Atthis, bewildered yet sated, dropped into sleep, but Sappho roused her to love again, murmuring:

> I loved you, Atthis,
> long ago,
> when my own girlhood was still
> all flowers

For a while Sappho drowsed, too, but she could not miss a second of this night. She spoke to the evening star:

> Fairest of all stars that shine . . .

Atthis tucked her feet under her to listen. It was one of her favorites that Sappho sang to her:

> They said that Leda
> once found hidden
> an egg of hyacinth color

And once more she recalled to her:

> *It was summer when I found you in the meadow*
> *long ago*
> *And the golden vetch was growing by the shore . . .*

Then she prayed aloud, and it almost seemed she prayed to Atthis:

> *May this night last for me as long as two*

With careful strokes she rouged Atthis's nether lips, and the young form undulated with a rhythm Sappho invented for them. Still she must peak once more, and she cried in her throat for release from the frenzy the girl brought her.

But the golden-sandaled one could no longer be held back. The night that Sappho wished doubled, had ended.

Atthis clung to her. "O miraculous Sappho, I see now I never loved, or even knew its meaning, never suspected how it tingles the skin and grips the body in paroxysms that are almost pain. Anaktoria was just my friend, we were two girls. Until this night I did not know how it could be. I am shaken. I fear you will tire of me."

"How could I tire of you, when of all my hetaerae you sing most prettily?" Instead of leaving, in the full light of morning she drew the girl to her. One more time the ache, one more time the rush of fulfillment. "All nights are ours, Atthis."

The days, too, were theirs. Leaving the instruction of her hetaerae to her most accomplished freemen and slaves, she walked in mountain paths with Atthis. Sappho told stories of bearded satyrs with tails and pointed ears, who longed for the flesh of women. These tales made Atthis cling to her more closely. Searching her mind, Sappho found a story or myth for every sacred place they visited. Resting in sweet clover they rolled over on each other.

> *For me*
> *love possesses*
> *the brightness*
> *and the beauty of the sun*

And, squinting, they made rainbow-colored shafts appear.

In gratitude to Kyprian Aphrodite, Sappho and Atthis spent a day in decking and making fair her temple.

Sappho sang:

> *Hither to me from Crete*
> *to this holy temple where you*
> *will find*
> *your lovely grove of apples*
> *And your altars smoked with frankincense*

Many times Sappho settled her head in Atthis's lap and asked the girl to sing to her. The young voice delighted her, and she declared it "more sweet singing than the lyre."

Alone in her chambers Sappho started a new song:

> *Love, fatal creature . . .*

But she was too happy to work and put it by, sending again for Atthis. In a simple cadence she told her:

> *It is time now*
> *for you who are so*
> *pretty and charming*
> *to share in games*
> *that the pink-ankled*
> *Graces play, and Aphrodite*

She teased her, too, with riddles:

> *What is*
> *far sweeter tuned*
> *than a lyre,*
> *colder than gold*
> *softer than velvet,*
> *much whiter*
> *than an egg?*

Sometimes she was conscious that Gongyla watched them. She was sorry the girl insisted on staying on, and sorrier still that she sought for ways to please her. When the hetaerae were set sums to do, it was Gongyla who finished first and looked to her for praise. She could not give even that. The shade of Erinna would not permit it, and she turned away from the hurt in Gongyla's eyes. Why, oh why, could not everyone be happy as she was?

In the midst of their play and their happiness, a missive came from Sardis. Atthis brought it solemnly and gave it to Sappho.

Sappho looked not at it, but at her. "Well? How is it with our sister Anaktoria?"

"It is as you said, O illustrious Sappho. Anaktoria is a fine lady now and much admired. Sometimes her thoughts turn to us."

Sappho said probingly, "We have not thought of her as often as we should."

Atthis tossed her head. "She left, didn't she?" Then creeping close, added, "Her leaving brought me to your side. And in your effort to console me, look what has happened to us."

Sappho appeared to agree, nibbling at the precious body as though it were a fruit. But she was frightened. She knew the gods were jealous, and she sang:

> Afraid of losing you
> I ran fluttering
> like a little girl
> after her mother

Dismissing her fears, she decided it was time for another story. Her store was endless. "In far Samos there was an incisor of gems, who drew dexterously on their surfaces, and with the finest line produced the lineaments of a loved one's features, or a rose, or a verse so small it took another gem to read it. When we love, Atthis, I feel I am inside a gem. I cannot describe to you what your love does to me."

But Atthis was intrigued by another story, one Sappho had told previously. "When the peacock and the woman mated, and she wound her legs around its body and clung with her arms about its neck . . ."

Sappho waited.

"I wonder, was the bird's organ larger than a man's?"

"And longer," Sappho said emphatically.

"Sometimes I wish I were married just to know what it is like."

The words were spoken heedlessly, yet Sappho brooded over them. She ended by sending for her daughter. "Kleis, I do not like being at odds with you, especially now that Gongyla is no longer close to me. If you cannot make up with her, surely that is not my fault." Then taking a different tack, she smiled on her, a warm full smile. "For my part, I have forgiven you. You cannot doubt it, Kleis, because I ask a favor."

Kleis said warily, "What do you wish, Mother?"

"Only this—that you go to the caves of the priestesses and make offering for me of Sardinian coins of much worth, which I will give you. In return, bring back the poppy they grow and a jar of satyrion."

"Yes, Mother." There was heavy judgment in each word.

Sappho endured it. She dared not send a house slave, as she could not bear Niobe's censure, and they all reported to her. A base slave from the fields might be sent, but such a one could be counted on to water the satyrion and reserve a portion of the poppies for herself. And these were the precious ingredients needed to bind Atthis to her.

Kleis was gone a long time. But late afternoon a basket was left outside Sappho's door. Sappho withdrew the ingredients, trembling as she did so. The poppy seeds she ordered baked in little cakes with caraway. These she served Atthis herself. Then, sending away her women, she poured the aphrodisiac, watching with hidden glances as Atthis ate and drank. While she waited she sang new songs hymned to her loveliness:

> I render your beauty the sacrifice of all my thoughts,
> and worship you with all my senses

Atthis began to laugh. It was true that she could not be serious long, but now her laugh was mindless. She tore off her clothes and before Sappho realized what she intended, ran out the door of the chamber and out of the house, where she offered herself to the other hetaerae as they passed singly or in twos and threes.

Sappho did not know whether to run after her or hide in the house.

She watched from behind a wooden lattice. It was Gongyla who finally took Atthis by the hand and led her to her cottage.

The time seemed endless to Sappho, but it was only ten or fifteen minutes before Atthis ran back outside, naked still, screaming wildly, and clutching her mound. To Sappho's horror she ran at and rubbed herself against any protuberance that offered.

Sappho sent a eunuch to lay hands on the girl and bring her inside. Atthis was sobbing hysterically. "Gongyla pretended she would love me," she gasped out, "but when I lay on my back to receive her she poured black pepper into me. My body is on fire. I burn. I burn!"

Together, Sappho and the slave dragged Atthis to the bath and rinsed away the irritant.

Atthis cried all night with humiliation, but Desire had not left her. Only this time none of Sappho's tricks satisfied her; the drug had raised a lust she could not assuage. Where was the delicacy of her golden girl? Where the daintiness, for she masturbated against her Samian shoe, then, grabbing a taper from the wall, plunged it into herself, grinding her body against it. She taunted Sappho, saying, "You, O Sappho, cannot bring me peace. I want a man. I want a man's rod."

Sappho shed tears, but Atthis took pleasure in this, repeating again and again that she could not be eased by Sappho.

At daylight Atthis fell, exhausted, into sleep, but Sappho was turned to stone. She herself, by the power of the priestesses of the snake, had induced this madness. She, teacher of song and all things that were gentle, had thought by gratifying the girl in new ways to tie her more closely. Instead, she had set a fire she could not put out.

And her hetaerae were witness to what had happened. They knew. They laughed. They whispered. Would they leave her? How? In a body, all at once? She was so intent on inflicting these lacerations on herself that only gradually did awareness reach her. She sensed that somewhere there was activity; she caught innuendos uttered with a thickened tongue. Was it the imaginings of an overwrought mind, or was something amiss?

"Apollo," she said, "your throne is truth," and went out of her house. To her surprise she saw that it was morning. Every door stood wide, but no one was about. The hetaerae were gathered in the center of the courtyard, in various stages of dress, and their glance was upward where Gongyla's small feet drooped above their heads, a sandal fallen to the ground.

Nothing stirred but the draperies which the wind moved on the dead girl. Sappho stood stripped of all her powers, even that of speech.

It was Kleis who spoke, her tone ordinary, conversational even. "O immoderate, immoral, this is your doing. Why the gods chose to speak through you to humankind, I do not know. Perhaps it is another joke they play on us." She faced her mother squarely. "With what meter will you fix a broken neck? How rhyme those dangling, slender ankles that one could put one's fingers around? Gongyla could not destroy her love for you, so she destroyed herself. Hail and farewell, Sappho. I go to the caves to live among the snake priestesses. And when you think of it, remember it was you who sent me there."

Sappho had no answer for her daughter. Her gaze reverted to Gongyla. "Cut her down," she said through stiff lips. "Can't someone cut her down?"

Sappho needed forgetfulness and prayed her Way-Muses to intercede with Memory. But Memory would not be trifled with and branded every detail into her. Her hetaerae did not condole with her over Gongyla. Neither did they allude to Kleis, lost to mysticism and drugs, who dwelt in the high mountains from which none dared retrieve her.

Sappho could not be reconciled to the thought of her child unkempt, half naked, with reptiles slithering over her. In her own body she seemed to feel their clammy coldness. What rituals did they practice in their caverns, their eyes blank with prophecy and knowing? She knew that at times lassitude from the poppy spread over them, while at others great strength was in their limbs from the satyrion they drank. To Sappho it seemed her daughter, like the little marble girl at whose feet she once had wept, was lost in time. Once she had a golden-haired child; now, the sisterhood of Dionysos outstretched its hand over her.

Of these things Atthis, too, did not speak. She seemed as innocent and merry as before, laughing, singing, teasing for games and stories, begging to learn the steps of a new dance. There was a child's heart in her breast. And in Sappho's breast there was no heart at all. She felt curiously numb. She saw before her Gongyla, whose draperies fluttered while she herself was still. She remembered Gongyla's caresses before the shade of Erinna intervened between them, watched again her dexterous fingers weave music on the lyre, heard the lilt of her voice.

She should never have allowed her to stay on. She had become a beggar outside the door, waiting for a crumb, feeding on a glance, a random smile. The gods had used them all for sport.

Gongyla was lost to her; but she must retrieve her daughter. Although she knew one did not strive against the priestesses of Dionysos, she knew that she must try.

She trudged alone to the mountain caves in the heat of noon, when mirages played in the dust before her in the guise of deep pools. When she reached them, they were parched and desolate. She stared about, befuddled. Then, gathering her resolution, approached what appeared to be a cave entrance. A voice from the shadows stopped her. "Turn back, Sappho."

"My child," Sappho implored. "I've come for my child."

"You have no child. Kleis is no more."

Sappho staggered. "What evil do I hear?"

"No evil. Kleis that was, has been initiated into our rites. Reborn, she bears a new name secret even from you."

"She cannot be reborn. I bore her, I alone carried her, grew heavy with her, was torn by her, ate afterbirth. Kleis is mine, my flesh."

The voice came sepulchral. "There is no more Kleis."

Sappho fell to her knees and hit her forehead against stones. "Have pity!"

"Did you have pity for Erinna, for Gongyla, for your own daughter?"

"Who are you, that you speak so? I know your voice."

"Long ago, during my novitiate, I came to you, and was afraid to raise my eyes to yours."

"I remember—your name is Doris—you came to order songs for Dionysos. We had wine."

"It was a great house, and you a great lady. But I tell you, Sappho, the wantonness that drives you past yourself will crush you. It is that which will be remembered."

It was true then—the terrible dream—the terrible curse. Her name would be a stench in the nostrils of humankind.

The voice came again. "I pity you, but I cannot help you."

"And Kleis, she that was Kleis?" The question was wrenched from her.

"She is in a world of delusion. When she rouses, she will be well."

"The gods help her and me. Father Zeus, All-Father!" she cried. But what can a man know? "Hera, Mother, it is to you I turn!" She prostrated herself, accepting all.

Her hetaerae did not desert her. They played and sang more beautifully than before. But their eyes rested on her with concern. Sappho emerged from the depths of depression, feverish in her desire for fun and good cheer. She was determined that a carnival atmosphere prevail.

Gongyla was dead. That was sad, but so were her father, mother, and her husband dead, Erinna and little Timas. Her own future was uncertain, and the portents evil. What was to be done? One could not forever bow one's head to the ground. She resolved not to mourn for things lost and people gone from her.

When she woke beside Atthis she looked at the sleeping face as though it were distant from her, the round softness of the cheeks, the lashes that curled against them. Forgetful of what love had done to her, remembering only its sweetness, Sappho murmured, "She loves me well."

And she sang softly that Atthis might be softly wakened:

> I loved you, Atthis
> with all my heart,
> before you yet suspected it

The girl sat up and rubbed her eyes. And into Sappho's mind came another song:

> Like the last red apple
> sweet and high;
> high as the topmost twigs,
> which the apple-pickers missed—
> O no, not missed
> but found beyond their fingertips

"I have never heard that song."

Coldness gripped Sappho's heart; she should have sung something else.

Atthis said shrewdly, "Who did you make it for? The song about apples?"

She had sung it first to Gongyla. But Gongyla was gone. Music couldn't reach her. Without answering, she inclined her head toward Atthis and drank a kiss. "Are your thighs ready to receive me?"

Atthis often acted the child with her. "You were on me all night," she complained.

"Look," Sappho slipped her hand beneath the pillow, "I have a token for you." She pretended to find a chain of silver and lapis lazuli. Atthis exclaimed at the beauty of the workmanship and allowed Sappho what she wished.

When they were replete, each with the other, Sappho sang again:

> *The glad daylight reveals you.*
> *And I know that by your beauty*
> *I may claim you*
> *For eye is the carrier of the disease of love*

"Disease is not a nice comparison," Atthis objected.

"No?" She herself thought it apt. "Well, well."

The hours with Atthis brought the time of payment. They brought Gorgo. The young woman kicked awake the eunuch who guarded the door of the House of the Servants of the Muses and demanded to speak with Sappho of Lesbos.

Sappho, hearing the commotion, came out. Immediately on seeing Gorgo she erased the frown from between her eyes and made all her features smooth. She had not seen her since she retrieved her daughter from Andromeda. However, she sensed a new boldness about her.

"I am here, Lady," Gorgo said, "with condolences for the death of the lovely Gongyla."

The sarcasm, Sappho knew, was a portent of evil.

"I wonder," Gorgo went on in the same insinuating tone, "and I am not alone in wondering, what malady of the soul drives one to such an act?"

"You have a message for me, Gorgo?"

"Do you suppose it could be seeing herself supplanted in the affections of her lover?"

The sparring was over. "Speak," Sappho rapped out, "what you have come to say."

The two women faced each other's anger. "Andromeda, that mistress of spells—"

"Andromeda, that sow—"

"The woman may not possess the rarity of a nature such as yours, O Sappho, who love all things delicate. Permit me to ask, was it delicate to see your hetaera hanging by a twisted neck?"

"That remark is not permitted you, Gorgo. Nothing is permitted you."

"In that you are mistaken. All is permitted me. It is simply a question of what I want."

The nails of Sappho's hands bit flesh. Aloud she said coolly, "You have something to tell me?"

"It is concerning your trip to Samos."

An intimation of what was to come gripped Sappho. "I was in Samos, yes. It was on the occasion of the freeing of Aesop."

Gorgo allowed a small smile to lift her lips. "All that great Sappho does is of interest. Even in the fastness of our hills we heard of your journey, and that you held several conversations regarding marriage with a fellow guest, a young man from Sardis."

Sappho articulated with difficulty. "What do you want, Gorgo? What does Andromeda want?"

Gorgo continued as though Sappho had not spoken. "As a result of these conversations, one of your hetaerae, the lovely Anaktoria of Miletus, was sent as a bride to this same Lydian. And it seems the lady Atthis, whose dearest friend she was, does not even know that you so kindly arranged this."

"What will stop your tongues?" Sappho asked frantically. "Gold, coins, jewels? Name it!"

Gorgo fitted a smile to her lips. "Perhaps we do not wish anything at all, but to see Sappho of Lesbos at our feet."

"Then I prostrate myself." And she fell on her knees before the girl. "I kiss your feet, even hers, if that will satisfy you."

Gorgo withdrew disdainfully.

"Andromeda will let you know what it is she requires. Perhaps it is nothing at all."

"No, please . . . You will have whatever you want. Only . . ."

But Gorgo had left.

From the beginning Sappho had feared this, yet she was stunned. "The gods incline toward *her* sacrifices rather than mine," she cried, tearing her hair. In a frenzy she sent her servants for myrtle branches to drape the walls of her home, for of all trees and flowering things Aphrodite preferred the myrtle. She rededicated herself to the goddess: "In all things I am your servant."

For the precursor of the wile-weaving Kyprus-born . . .

She could not finish her thought, and the next moment was calling on Peitho, goddess of persuasion. Though she promised to burn the fat thighbones of a white she-goat on her altar, she knew she could not be helped. She went inside and shut herself in her room. "We do not know the things we are going to do," she said through clamped teeth as she paced, returning each time to the same spot because it was nowhere.

The day passed and the stars went forward. "Keep watch and be watchful," she told the servants. But she did not know how to guard against her fears. Nymph of the braided tresses, she said silently, they will surely tell you.

What to do?

In the morning she hid her disordered pulse, her mad heart, and went with Atthis to pick yellow gillyflowers by the stream.

"You did not send for me to come to you last night," Atthis said musingly.

"I was working on a song I thought you'd like. Listen."

How especially she loved your singing.
And how among the Lydian women, she shines

"You sing of Anaktoria." Atthis slipped her hand into Sappho's. "I no longer think of Anaktoria. How could I?"

Sappho hardly breathed. Could that be so? She clasped the girl about the knees. "The music of life is brief."

Atthis was surprised at these unexpected words and at the sentiment.

"Swear to me," Sappho said desperately. "Swear by the dread waters of the River Styx . . ."

Atthis laughed. "Why make such a dreadful oath? You know I will do anything you want."

Sappho rushed on without hearing her, ". . . to love me, to hold me dear in the face of . . . no matter. Look, I have brought rings of amber for your toes."

"Put them on."

And Sappho did, while Atthis wriggled her newly adorned feet in delight.

"You swear, then, to love me always?" Sappho asked anxiously.

"I cannot help but love you."

"It must be a great oath, Atthis. I call on Zeus, I call also Earth, Sun, and the Erinyes who dwell below to take vengeance if you swear false."

The dimples left Atthis's face. "Sappho, you have never spoken to me like this."

"Forgive me," she said hastily. "It is the heat of love. It is the goddess born of bleeding Sky, bittersweet, bringing pain. It is your flashing beauty, for as I put the rings on your toes I glimpsed the red pomegranate that tempts me so."

"Is that all?" Atthis leaned back. "My fruit is all for you."

But the precious folds of Atthis's body were almost like passion remembered. While her body quivered with what the girl gave, her mind said good-bye.

Muses, dwellers in the mansions of Olympus, help me, for you are in all places and all hearts. Her prayer was ever the same: Advise me, tell me what to do.

"Come to me tonight," she whispered to Atthis.

When the girl came at the agreed hour, Sappho spoke sharply. "You are long in coming." At once she repented. "If night could be held in the West, on the other side of day, then we could be together longer."

Sappho prolonged the moment of release. She will not leave me, she told herself, even when she learns about Anaktoria. She will not leave me. She will realize how much she needs me, and that no one else can bring her to this madness.

Sappho was frozen and burning, mad and sane, supremely confident and totally distraught. In this state of mind she made a plan. She would take her hetaerae to Lesbian Olympus. They would vacation high in hills of pine and groves of chestnut, where the sea looked small below and the flowers were of blue squill. The idea consumed her:

> I would go anywhere
> to take you in my arms
> again, my darling

The hetaerae were delighted with Sappho's decision, which seemed both novel and exciting. They got their wardrobes together, and Sappho hurried the preparations. She did not want word of their activities to reach Gorgo. At least she would have the summer with no one whispering into Atthis's ear. The girl no longer spoke of Anaktoria and, by the words of her own mouth, no longer thought of her. By the end of summer, it might be true. In three months who knew what the gods would decree. In three months, she told herself, I might be dead.

All the cauldrons of the house were set boiling. Flesh was cooked, freshly prepared dainties readied, bread baked and placed in baskets, fruit picked, pressed wines stored in goatskins, while furs were heaped in piles against the cooler nights. They stowed lutes and lyres, flutes, drums, tambourines, castanets, cymbals, and a kithara of ancient make. The bells of their many sandals tinkled busily, and their carefree voices bubbling with laughter wafted to Heaven. Libation and scented sacrifice were duly made, and the journey promised to be auspicious.

Her hetaerae seated themselves on asses and clambered on carts pulled by mules, all so bedecked by primrose and lily that no vehicle or animal was readily discernible.

Can we climb beyond evil? Sappho wondered. And fear was upon her as she sang with the maidens.

They passed the undying forest where trees had been changed to rock by the will of Zeus, and arrived still in daylight. They paused to admire the view of mainland Aeolis lying at horizon's edge where shading blues of Sea met. Beyond that they had been told was the foreign land of Mysia. They could not be restrained but must dance before the beautiful temple of the Year Maiden. Its columns were of wood, only the tablatures being stone, so deeply carved that the patterns of sunlight fell partly in shade. The motive was floral, and the Argive priestesses made pilgrimages to keep it brightly painted. Recently the temple had been extended with Pentelix marble. The hillside, barren a month ago, blazed with color, for crocus grew everywhere. Persephone, radiant daughter, had passed this way.

The first instrument to sound was the sambyke; then pipes and flutes joined in as they erected woven tents before the temple. Wine from Lemnos was spilled to the gods and long-stemmed goblets passed about. Soon they had a fire going, presided over by a slave who fed it with cedar and sandalwood so that for the whole summer the odor would pervade their camp.

The girls found wild leek, onion, asparagus, and parsley. Atthis discovered a patch of mint. And as night came on, pots of tallow were kindled so that light blossomed everywhere like stars upon the ground.

Sacrifice was made and their first meal eaten. They grouped themselves about Sappho and asked for stories. She told them an Orphic mystery about a priestess who paid a visit to the underworld to recover a stolen soul. Then they would have the tale of the Minotaur, who, forcing intercourse upon a woman, caused her to give birth to the first bull.

Sappho surprised them with a new work. She bent to the lyre:

> *Around the glorious Moon*
> *the bright beauty of the stars*
> *is lost*
> *when her silver radiance at its fullest*
> *lights the world*

Sappho's songs were the pleasantest kind of teaching. The girls took their turns at singing and of them all, Atthis sang best. A musical person is a gift, Sappho thought, as she listened to her uplifted voice. On her part, Atthis, aware that Sappho was moved by her song, had never sung sweeter. When arm in arm they went to their tent, Sappho whispered, telling her again she was

Far more sweet-singing than the lyre

"Know," Sappho said, when they lay upon the couch of skin, "that Love, the limb-loosener, sweeps me away."

There was a subtle difference in their lovemaking. Sappho was not at all times mistress of herself. Often she seemed a suppliant. And when she held the girl to her, she felt again how it was: "Bittersweet and bringing pain." For the sleepless heart in her beat with constant fear.

When would Gorgo discover they had gone? And when discover where they were? If it were only the old sow Andromeda, she could deal with her—coins and jewels would do it. But how buy the silence of one who had in plenty the things she could give? O Muses, dwellers in these mountains, I yearn and I seek to bring about . . .

What?

Only the continuation of that which she had. Only Atthis's head cradled on her arm. But dissonance had entered her life. She could not enjoy what she had for the certainty of losing it.

She knew she held Atthis too closely. If the girl was a moment out of sight, she had to know where she was and with whom. Her thymos drove her; she was chained by her emotions without a will of her own. She took out her stele and polished it with pumice so that when the Muses spoke, she would be ready. But they were curiously quiet. They also waited.

All around her were busy. The girls made cloth from raw wool, carding, weaving, and dyeing it with precious purple from the shellfish of Tyre. Dexterous fingers imitated Milesian cloaks and blanket patterns. And Sappho kept them amused with stories, her own and those of other poets. She related Hesiod's account of Creation: The fair Earth bore Heaven, equal to herself, to cover her on all sides and to be a home forever for the blessed gods. And all the universe became alive with the life men know.

She made lyric dialogue between herself and the chorus, teaching the girls new rhythms and steps which she devised. But at night she cried out, declaring, Desire has no offspring and is void!

Atthis could follow none of this; Sappho's moods and words were contradictory and moved too fast for her. At last, one night she asked gently, "Sappho, is there anything that weighs on you or brings you sad thoughts?"

Sappho smiled at her and replied with the first poem that came to mind:

> *As a whirlwind*
> *swoops on an oak*
> *Love shakes my heart*

Atthis kissed her. "That is lovely. And it means you love me. Yet it is a song I have heard many times, and not recently made. So I know something troubles your heart."

"How you know me. And still are patient with me. Will you always be so? Tell me."

Atthis's protestations did not satisfy her. At the gate of dreams she stood shivering and alone.

As summer inexorably slipped by, the hetaerae became restless. They had enough of the rough outdoor life, and were anxious to return to the opulent existence of the villa.

Sappho, sensing their mood, and indeed being told of it by Atthis and the bolder of the girls, withdrew from them. More and more she brooded in the eyries of wild places or in her tent alone. Images flowed past her; those she had loved seemed present. At times she replaced the name Atthis with that of Gongyla and did not notice. Then she sang directly to her: "Gongyla, come back in your white robe."

> *Death is a misfortune.*
> *Surely the gods think so*
> *for they do not die*

Why must love be destructive, and not as Aphrodite would have one believe? Did all things pass? Even those most intensely felt? And if the gods played such tricks, where was any truth? What about her love for her daughter? Had it changed? And to what? Was Kleis at this moment speaking with gods from a drugged stupor? Then she remembered she was no longer Kleis but someone unknown to her, even her name unknown. What had become of her golden-haired child? In her distress Sappho called to her mother, that other Kleis: "I cannot weave this mesh of mine."

When Atthis came to tell her a happy day shone outside, she replied dully, for she had decided Atthis could no longer love her when she learned what she had done. Little Timas would have loved her, but Timas loved all alike and so her love was nullified. Erinna. Erinna would have understood, if not her love, at least her actions. But Erinna had not resisted Death when it came. Had life become too bitter? Did she feel what Sappho now dreaded to feel?

With love for a slender maiden I am overcome.

Always before it had been she, Sappho, who left lightly without looking back. But retributive Fate had found her in her high Olympic dwelling. Deciduous leaves were underfoot, autumn in the air, and she withdrew still more from her hetaerae. They sent Atthis to speak for them.

She entered the tent that was Sappho's retreat, and said with resolution, "Sappho, you must get up for our sakes. Take off your chain dress and bathe. From your boxes I have chosen a saffron lope and a purple peplos. Praxiona will roast us chestnuts, and you shall be crowned with flowers. For this very day, like a mother with her children, you will take us back to Mitylene."

Sappho got up as Atthis demanded and allowed herself to be dressed for the journey.

"What have you been doing that you stayed so much in the tent alone?" Atthis asked curiously. "Have you made songs for our return?"

"One song only I have, and you shall hear it."

"Now?"

Sappho picked up her lyre which lay ready for packing:

> When I look at you, it seems to me that Hermione was
> never such as you are,
> and that it is right
> to liken you to Helen herself
> than to any mortal girl:
> and I tell you
> I render your beauty

the sacrifice of all my thoughts,
and worship you with all my senses

Atthis fell on her knees. "Such wonders are yours to bestow, great Sappho."

"Only love me, Atthis," Sappho begged, "no matter what you hear of me."

"And what should I hear of you?"

"I do not know. My own brothers are my enemy, and my child. How can I know what is said against me?"

"But your Atthis loves you. Nothing can change that."

"Swear."

The girl laughed. "How many times already have you had me take an oath of love, O Sappho? I give you proof each night and in the days, too."

"Yes, yes. I know I am at fault. And you must forgive me, Atthis. Some god plagues my mind and distorts everything with fancies. But you do promise me?"

This time Atthis only laughed.

The tents were struck amid jubilation, asses and carts laden. There was song on every lip. Sappho did not sing and walked like a shade among her hetaerae. She had gained her summer.

They were still settling in at the House of the Servants of the Muses when Atthis, without making a sound at her inner door, threw it open and confronted her. Her face, contorted with anger, made her a daughter of the Erinyes. "Look at me, Sappho, and tell me it is a lie, if you can."

Sappho found the strength to answer calmly. "What has so disturbed your soul, Atthis? Speak, that I may know."

"They say—"

Sappho stopped her. "No, that will not do. Who says?"

"Gorgo."

Had Earth-Shaker heaved the world?

"Deny it, Sappho. That's all I want. Deny that you arranged for Anaktoria to be married, that during your visit to Samos you met there the young Sardian, and sang the praises of one above all your hetaerae, so that he fixed his heart on her. And this you did to separate us. For you knew I preferred Anaktoria to you, and would never love you if she remained."

Sappho rose slowly and moistened her lips as though to speak, but did not.

"I hear no statement from your mouth. I hear only the silence of guilt. But by the gods, I will force you to say that you did this thing."

"No need, Atthis. I am not ashamed of my love for you. It drives me so that each of my days is arranged around you. It was as Gorgo told you. But think, it was from love, so how can there be evil there? Is not Anaktoria first among the ladies of Lydia? And are you not my treasure, for whom I would plunge my arm into open flame, to the very shoulder? I am swift to satisfy every desire you express, each whim. If it is chestnuts to be roasted, so be it. If it is a lovelier necklace than you now possess, my black ships bring it."

Atthis looked at her, her face no longer reflecting anger. Coldly, she said, "I do not love you anymore, Sappho."

Sappho held herself without movement. "Let me remind you of what you have forgotten, how fond and beautiful was the life we led together."

"You did the worst to me that one person can do to another. You schemed to send away the one I loved."

Sappho began to tremble. A line of sweat broke against her hair and yet she felt cold. The old poem came back to her. With it she begged:

> *I loved you, Atthis,*
> *with all my heart,*
> *before you yet suspected it*

"Or suspected what you would do about it," the girl retorted.

Sappho took a faltering step toward her, but the stiffness with which Atthis drew herself up rebuffed her.

"I do not know what to do. My thoughts are double. You loved me well, Atthis."

"I did not know you, Sappho."

"But it means something! The times I braided your hair with fragrant blossoms, and remember . . . when love has you by the throat, you will do anything. Can you not believe the gods themselves put the plan into my mind?"

> Darling Atthis, can you forget all
> that happened in the
> old days?

Atthis stood her ground. "I despise the person you are, Sappho, under your fine words. I go with Gorgo to Andromeda."

"Not there, Atthis. Do you think to find honesty and gentle dealing there? O Atthis, your words disturb my soul. Yet I see you have decided to leave me."

"Your power over me was built of lies. It is broken."

Sappho's eyes raged with darkened lights, in one of those shifts of emotion she was capable of. "You have trampled on your oath! You swore by the dead waters of the River Styx to love me."

"It was no true oath, since you never showed me your true self."

Sappho did not know how she remained on her feet.

> Daughter of Zeus and weaver of ruses
> Now I address you:
> Queen, do not hurt my heart, do not harry it,
> but come as before when you heard and you hearkened
> a long way away

Atthis was impatient with all this. "Farewell, Sappho."

Sappho looked her in the eyes. "Atthis, I see you hate all thought of me. Well, hate and despise me if you must, but do not go to Andromeda. Go home to your family. I could not rest thinking of you with that foul woman."

"I listened to you once, O Sappho of many tongues. It is Gorgo I trust."

"I am not trying to hold you now. But let me protect you from that woman and from Gorgo. By the gods, by holy Zeus, I ask that you return to your parents."

"I will go with Gorgo."

When she was gone, Sappho stood a moment looking at the place where Atthis had been.

Then she ran after her, out of the compound, into the road. "Atthis!" she called, for the girl's figure was fast receding. "Have pity. I have not the strength to go through moments like this. Atthis!" She still ran but lurched from side to side. There was a tremor in her voice as she pleaded. "Terror hung over me all summer. Do not make me face the truth, which even Apollo cannot cure . . . that you have never loved me.

"Atthis," she called again, for the distance between them was widening. "Will you leave me here on the road?—I had no choice, no choice, Atthis, but to do as I did."

Her eyes glazed. She was beaten. She could not go on. She didn't want to go on. She pulled her cloak about her and laid herself full-length on All-Mother Earth.

When Niobe came upon her she was lying on the road with fever in her cheeks. Niobe ran for a litter and Sappho was carried home. She turned away from food and would have the barest sip of water. Day and night were the same to her, and then from nowhere her daughter appeared, released by the Dionysians to tend her.

It was a reversal of roles: she the daughter, Kleis the mother, who murmured soft words and administered herbal medicine, the knowledge of which had been taught her in the sacred caves. "You must be well, Mother. You still have many songs to sing."

"For Dionysos?"

"Even so."

"And what about you, my daughter?"

"I am no longer your daughter. I belong to the joy-god."

"Can you not love me, Kleis?"

"Not as mortals love. But as a priestess, who loves all."

Sappho turned her face to the wall. She did not want that kind of love. She embraced her illness as she had her poems and her loves; she wanted to be consumed by it.

When she looked up next, Kleis was gone and it was Atthis who tended her. Sappho spoke faintly. "You have done well. I longed for you."

At another time she roused herself and pressed Atthis's hand. "I was longing for you. Bless you."

Sappho fell again into sleep. When she woke Atthis was still there.

"Sweet one," she murmured, "dear Kleis," and for a while she confused them.

"Drink some broth," Atthis urged. Strengthening wine was also brought her.

Atthis sang the old songs. When, after some days, Sappho took up the lyre, Atthis knew that, though pale and weak, she would recover. "Anything must be forgiven love," Atthis said, and kissed her.

Sappho had hungered for this kiss, but when she tasted it, it did not seem the same. "Bring me my mirror, Atthis. No, do not bring it. I will not question my good fortune or look too closely at it. You are here. I am content." Propped against cushions she sang Atthis's praise:

The belovedest offspring of Earth and Heaven . . .

Thinking Sappho was tired, Atthis tried to take the instrument from her, but Sappho would not give it up. "It was ever our way to sing what we could not say."

Nor ever did the gathering sounds
of early spring
fill any wood with the chorus of the nightingale
but you wandered there with me

"How pretty it is."

"Yes, it is pretty. Anything written in pain is pretty, Atthis."

Soon Sappho closed her eyes and seemed to sleep, but when Atthis attempted to steal out, she roused at once. "Do not leave me, Atthis. Sit closer to the window so that the light falls on you more fully."

Atthis rose and positioned herself as Sappho wished.

"Do you forgive me, Atthis? Or are you here in pity?"

"I forgive you."

"You do not mention love. Do you love me?"

"I love you well."

Sappho smiled. "Are you nymph or maiden? You are my nymph of the braided tresses."

Sappho slowly regained her strength and her hetaerae made thankful offerings. Saffron was sprinkled at the entrance to her door. The girls sang her praises in the forest and the courtyard, at work and at leisure. It seemed that the House of the Servants of the Muses was as before.

Sappho made her own gift at her recovery:

> *To thee I will burn*
> *the rich fat of a white goat*

These lines she sent to the priestesses of Dionysos. For she knew her daughter had saved her life, and that she could not have come without permission. Remembering Kleis's hands on her, she was happy. She loves me after all, Sappho thought, and did not feel so alone.

For with Atthis it was not as it had been. The girl found many missions in town. If thread were needed, or stuffs for dyeing, it was Atthis who offered to go.

"Send a servant," Sappho would say, but Atthis preferred to go herself.

She finds it dull here, Sappho thought. And then she thought, Is there perhaps some attraction in the town of Mitylene? The chastising Erinyes put it into her mind to wonder, Is Atthis meeting someone? For certain it is that Aphrodite presides over the whispers, smiles, and deceits which girls employ.

Reinforcing Sappho's suspicion was Atthis's continual reiteration that she did not consider her well enough to indulge in the act of love. This had gone on too long. Atthis would sit by her and sing with her, but startled like a fawn if Sappho's hand so much as rested in her lap. Finally Sappho took up her barhitos lyre of the polished horns which she used at rare but important moments. With her eyes fixed on Atthis she began:

> *I want, darling, to hug you*

Atthis laughed nervously. And Sappho plunged recklessly into what she wanted to ask:

> *Is there any man*
> *anywhere among mankind*
> *you love more than me?*

She fixed a gaze on the girl that seemed to bore through to her soul. "Certain it is that you love another human being more than me."

Atthis denied it and went away crying.

Sappho had her watched, sending a servant to follow her into Mitylene. There it was discovered that she met a young man.

"Describe him," Sappho demanded of her servant in a voice without inflection.

She listened passively and without comment. She knew this young man, she knew his family, one of the first families of Lesbos. His grandfather had been killed in the long-ago war with Athens, and by closing her eyes she brought the face of the young man before her. No feature was awry—a straight nose without bend, fair hair, and eyes like the sea. His mouth? She could not recall his mouth—it must be full and ripe for kisses. His build she did remember—like a gladiator, powerful, with the slenderness of youth. It was reported that Atthis always flew straight to him, and they lost no time but fell at once into attitudes of love.

Now that she knew without doubt, she thought her love must die, but it grew in her. She could think of nothing else. If only she could dig out of herself what she felt, as one digs up vine roots, or even prune it back to something reasonable, something that could be lived with. She could not do it. Instead she sang her hopelessness and her jealousy:

> *He is a god to my eyes—*
> *the man who is allowed*
> *to sit beside you—he*
>
> *who listens intimately*
> *to the sweet murmur of*
> *your voice, the enticing*
>
> *laughter that makes my own*
> *heart beat fast. If I meet*
> *you suddenly, I can't*
>
> *speak—my tongue is broken;*
> *a thin flame runs under*
> *my skin; seeing nothing,*

hearing only my own ears
drumming, I drip with sweat;
trembling shakes my body

and I turn paler than
dry grass. At such times
death isn't far from me

Although some kind of love trance possessed her, she managed to appear calm. She did not show the ode to Atthis or mention the clandestine meetings in Mitylene. She was silent.

She knew she should pray to some god to help her. But how could she do this, when she felt they had stolen her mind? Finally she addressed those she decided must be responsible. "Dread Erinyes, mighty in power, release me! I do not know what to do: I say yes—and then no."

A few days later Atthis went into town to bring back some geometrically adorned vases, the kind Sappho used indiscriminately about the house, in the kitchen and in the garden for woodbines and ivy. She returned without them.

Atthis said all in a rush, "My parents want me to leave you, Sappho. They have betrothed me to a young man. It is against my will, but when does a maid have a say in such matters?"

Sappho gazed not at her but out the window. It seemed she gazed on distant days. At last she said, "I was in love with you once, Atthis, long ago . . ."

Atthis began to cry. She fell to her knees and her tears washed Sappho's feet. Sappho watched this performance with indifference. Atthis no longer loved her. But then, she no longer loved herself. She seemed removed, distant from the weeping girl.

"I swear it is against my own wishes that I leave you."

"So you said."

"It is true. My family . . ."

"Yes, it is your family. Well, you are of an age to marry. But from me, no wedding songs, not one."

"Do not be angry with me, Sappho. It is not through my fault. And we both suffer."

"Where are the vases? Did you leave them outside?"

"What vases?"

"The ones you went to Mitylene for. But I see anguish overcame you and you forgot them."

"Yes."

"O Atthis, say no more. Go the way of your happiness."

"But you must believe that I cannot bear to part from you."

"No games, Atthis. It goes too deep. We have meant too much to each other for that. Go where your path takes you. In this life we shall not see each other again."

Fresh weeping from Atthis. "How can you say that so calmly?"

"Because I cannot change it, and because I know of the young man you have been meeting."

Atthis sprang up. "At least tell me how long you have hated me!"

"I? Hate Atthis? Never. You have brought me more joy than I have ever known. So it is perhaps a balance that the gods hold in their laps, that you bring me also the most pain."

"I could not help it."

"I know. I know." She reached out as though to touch her, but her arms fell to her sides. "Go. There are hard words and soft in me, and I do not wish to use either against you." She closed her eyes and her senses told her when the girl left. "I will never see Atthis again, and indeed I might as well be dead."

Niobe found her sitting quietly in a room where the tapers had not been lit.

"Lady," she remonstrated in great distress.

Sappho waved her away. Once she roused herself and murmured:

> *Whence never again will I come to thee,*
> *never again will I come*

At some hour she got out her stele and on it pressed out the last ode she would write Atthis:

> *With a great many tears she left me saying,*
> *"What a terrible blow—what sadness!*
> *Sappho, I swear I leave you*
> *absolutely against my will."*

And I said in reply:
"Go, be happy, good-bye.
Remember me—for you know how I loved you.

Or if you do not, I'll tell you
so many things you forget
which made our life together a gladness.
All the chaplets of sweet
violets and rosebuds braided
and placed by you on your hair at my side,

all the delicate garlands woven
around your delicate neck
fashioned from a hundred flowers,

all the fragrance of myrrh
fit for a queen and rare
worn on your fresh young skin beside me

While on the softest beds
from the quiet hands of maids
no Ionian was so feted.

There wasn't a single hill,
holy purlieu, rill,
from which we kept ourselves asunder

and never a wood in spring
fretted with the crowded song
of nightingales where you and I
did not wander

She wrapped her lyre and put it by. A rueful smile settled about her lips. This is my doom, she thought, to make songs of my life's end. Atthis had been her last love. Her life as a woman was over. She prayed to altars that had no fire. Weary as she was, a decision must be made, indeed was already made. She would disband the hetaerae, and live retired on her estates with only slaves and servants. She would see her good friend Alkaios, whom she had neglected. And one day Khar would return.

She must rededicate herself, invoke the Muses, listen only to their voices. On the lips of many, she told herself of herself, shall your deeds lie. And to bolster this belief, she sang:

> *While Earth and Sun abide,*
> *who cherish song*
> *shall cherish your renown*

She would be an anchorite:

> *For me*
> *neither the honey*
> *nor the bees*

And with this determination firmly in mind, she ordered an elaborate feast for her hetaerae. They, thinking it was a thanksgiving to the gods for her restored health, were blithe as birds, singing and caroling through all the preparation. Over the courtyard seamen's nets were lifted and heaped with flowers. At the height of the banquet, the attachments to the bower were to be slashed and bouquets drift over the revelers.

As Niobe dressed her hair, Sappho said suddenly, "Good Niobe, for your years of faithful service to me, I am minded to offer you your freedom."

Niobe's eyes brimmed, and her hands in Sappho's hair trembled. "You are my mistress, my pride. To be your chief slave is my life. Do not deprive me of what I love."

"O Niobe, I have not lived five times eight years . . . yet am old."

"It is not so, Lady."

"You, who are my slave, are now my one friend. Sometimes I think the only disgrace is to grow old and be blemished by wrinkles."

"My fingers and the oils I use will fend them off."

"We cannot change the fact that at the beginning of my life Psamethichus was Pharaoh of the Egyptians. Think what that means—

think how many years I have seen close, and heaped my sins upon a scapegoat for purification."

"You are not an ordinary woman. The name Sappho is known throughout the world. Youth is not everything, Lady."

"Is it not? I am surrounded by it. I alone, it seems, do not partake of it."

Niobe worked over her with special care to disprove her words. And when she surveyed herself in the mirror, Sappho was pleased. "You have made me charming, my Niobe. But only the gods can make me young."

She went to her girls and cries went up at once. "O fairest!" "Sweetest player on the lyre!" "Songstress of Lesbos, beautiful Sappho!"

She hailed her girls in turn, but chastised them gently. "Praise to me might be construed an affront to the Muses, who love beautiful things."

"You are beautiful," her girls insisted.

"Not beautiful," Sappho said, "and not 'fairest of women.' My skin is lined, my hair from its blackness turning. But who can cure it? It is not possible. Even as rosy-armed Dawn crosses Earth, Death overtakes. But O Olympian daughters—"

> *Today for you my hetaerae,*
> *these songs right well*
> *will I sing*

They shouted their love as she poured out verse after verse. "Ah girls"—suddenly it was to herself she spoke—"here in the House of the Servants of the Muses, Sappho has grown old."

They would not permit her to continue. They would not hear her, but stamped their feet and tossed their heads, calling out that she was the most illustrious teacher, mentor, a patron to match the goddesses themselves.

Sappho lifted a double-armed goblet to them in a pledge:

> *Toward you, my beautiful ones,*
> *this mind of mine will not change*

For a moment their merriment redoubled, but among the more perceptive an uneasiness grew, until they quieted again. Once more Sappho spoke to them:

> *I reply:*
> *Gentle . . .*
> *you will ever remember*
> *our life together in our youth*
> *For both the pure and the beautiful*
> *we then did. And now that you see . . .*

"No!" came the cry. "No, we will not hear you!"

At this moment the net above their heads was severed and they drowned in blossoms falling from Sky.

Sappho's voice rose above the commotion. "My companions. I have hymned you well, but now our life together is ended, as all things end. My own existence enters a new phase."

> *Of air are the words I begin*

The hetaerae pressed around her and she saw not Praxiona but Erinna, not Margara but Gongyla, not Nariscaa but little Timas.

Her girls importuned her, catching at her hands, her feet, the hem of her chiton. "We do not wish to leave you." "Do not send us away!" "Gentle Sappho, we would stay with you!"

She raised her arms over them in a gesture of benediction, and they were silenced. Thereupon she swore an eternal oath to Memory. Hearing this, they understood they must accept her decision, and they knelt in obedience. Her blessing rang out over their heads: "May you sleep in the bosom of tender companions."

PHAON

*I*N THE YEARS FOLLOWING THE DISPERSAL OF THE BAND of her fair friends, Sappho was sculpted on friezes, her likeness painted on terra-cotta vases; she was even cast in bronze according to a new technique. Sappho, the pride of Eresos, of Mitylene, of Lesbos—even Syracuse claimed her. Solon, great ruler and wise man of Athens, sent gifts. She was called the Tenth Muse, daughter of Aphrodite and Eros, nursling of the Graces, companion of Apollo.

But the world, her world, was changing. Pittakos was waylaid and murdered. Rumor had it that he simply tired of his life and arranged the assassination himself. In the empire of the Persians, Cyrus rose to power. In Egypt, Amasis now ruled. King Alyattes of Lydia died and his son Croesus became monarch there. Sappho felt alien. All she had known was going fast. New names were everywhere and the old lay in the dust.

Aphrodite, that laughter-loving goddess, had withdrawn from Sappho's courtyard and taken with her the dove and the swan, although sometimes a sparrow or two hopped about. It seemed to her the prevailing North Wind was colder than in other years. Eagles and vultures glided over her home. This they had always done, but they swept lower and their wings of ill omen shadowed the ground. The halls of her home held silence and emptiness. It was a place which joy no longer visited.

The three Graces were gone with her hetaerae, especially Euphrosyne, ruler of mirth, and Thalia, goddess of good cheer. Only Aglaia, she of splendor, still presided over the gardens, the groves, and the fields.

Many times, listening to the stillness, Sappho remembered the clash of Armenian cymbals, the quick modulations of lotus flutes, the waving of fennel wands in graceful dance. Though the flutes with their piercing voices were silent, images recurred. Like a column of flame Atthis was leading the chorus, her luxuriant hair braided with ivy.

Now there was neither sistra or sambyke. Torches no longer threw back slender shapes. Nor was there the sound of feet, quick and dainty, flying up the stairs, both inside and out. She did not plait her hair with lavender and roses, nor did waves of joy any longer pour over her.

She lost herself in earlier times. Sappho thought back to the child Sappho:

I want, I want, I want!

And later:

I desire, I desire, I desire!

Had she wanted unreasonably? Desired too much? And her lovers, each so dear to her, but so quickly gone—what had that wild quest meant?

She believed to be bonded with another was the highest good a human can know, and if one encounters the perfect mate, it is the ultimate. Many times with her many lovers she had glimpsed the ultimate. But the Muses alone had lifted her, never wavered or faltered. Only in song was she truly Sappho. To her Muses she had been constant and unflagging—and they to her.

For the first time she stood aloof, judging her work. She was amazed by the raw force she could still employ. Her words she knew were the way in which the world entered her and the way in which she entered the world:

If the battleground were of words,
I could fight gods!

She never ventured timidly but plunged her entire self into work, offering up what she had lived, like a votary, with both hands. Her written books by now reached a total of six.

And I shall leave for thee . . .

As a widow she was free to look in on any event, and her loneliness drove her to occasional parties, galas, festivities, where Sappho listened with pleasure to the sound of a lyre plucked in the Egyptian manner with a quill. It seemed to her that no matter where she went, she met again and again a young man who stationed himself always in her path. If she graced an evening with song, he above all others was entranced. Sappho finally asked his name, and was told Dionesus, who made a good record at the last Olympiad.

One evening he waylaid her, stepping from behind a colonnade where he must have waited hours, and stumbled through an obviously prepared speech, declaring his love.

Sappho looked at the young man more closely. He was twenty years her junior. Had he any idea of this? Or did celebrity erase such differences?

Sappho smiled sadly at him. She even patted his hand as she discouraged his hope.

That night in her chamber she gazed long and thoughtfully into her mirror. The life she had lived, the loves she had loved, the great joys and desires, the losses—all were there to be read.

She saw how a young man might be attracted to her, for the eyes smoldered with words unsung, and her body was as sensual as a young girl's, while the mark of aristocracy was carved into the delicacy of wrists and ankles. But the lines in her face were scars of battles fought and lost. Why had her nine sisters allowed a white swath to steal into her black hair? Who else had they to so skillfully interpret them? "Soon I will be old enough for death. To whom then will you turn, Undying Ones?" She hated being forty-four years old.

Sappho was not to sit out her life in her garden dedicated to the Nine. A messenger with a berried bay leaf in his hair, to indicate he carried good news, knelt at her feet.

"What news," she asked, "do you bring?"

"The fleet of your brother, the Lord Kharaxos, has been sighted. He will this day lie within the twin home harbors of Mitylene."

Blessings were on her lips for the messenger and for the gods. The seven mouths of the fine-sanded Nile had returned him! Forgotten was her brooding fear of age, and the loneliness in which she lived. Like a young girl she ran about the house, ordering a feast as in the old days.

Niobe hummed again at her work. As chief among the slaves she directed their tasks; some she sent into the fields, some to the flower stalls of the city, some to raise the more mature wines from the cistern. A robe was made ready for Khar. "Softer than a light wrap, whiter than milk" were Sappho's instructions. Golden sandals for Khar's feet were purchased, studded with rich gems, a wreath woven for his hair, a garland for his neck. She found time to whisper to the gods in gratitude that she was able to welcome her brother as a prince. Music, feasting, drink—what honor she would show him, the only one of her family left.

She oversaw her dressing with great care and not a little concern. Niobe worked with meticulous attention, drawing the face she wished her brother to see. It did not reflect her recent despondency, nor her solitary life. It showed a fine and handsome woman with great dark eyes that pierced with their own particular seeing.

"All servants, all slaves, and especially those trained in music upon various instruments—in fact, my whole household shall accompany me to the dock, except only the watchers and guards of the house."

Her finest chariots were brought around, decked and ready, even to the polished hooves of the horses and chains of blooms thrown over their proud throats. Sappho, watching, made a note:

More skittish than a mare

The merry troop with flute and tambourine and the beat of drums wended its way through the streets of Mitylene. Alkaios, having received a messenger from Sappho, joined her with a retinue of his own. It saddened Sappho to look on Alkaios these days. The poet had gone to fat and carried a wobbly belly before him, but his height was imposing. His age was ten years greater than hers. Yet if Alkaios was old, Sappho was old. She perceived a man almost as close to sixty as fifty, who was in no way venerable, but constantly laid himself open to jokes and ridicule. In his case, however, they were guarded, for though his wits were usually addled by wine and his eyes rheumy and unfocused, there were occasions when he struck a well-aimed blow with his staff or devastated his opponent with a well-chosen sarcasm. He was wealthy, and so had young boys aplenty, but in all the world there were only two people whom he truly loved, Sappho and Khar. They embodied for him the sweet days of his youth.

Sappho was pleased to see that for her sake he had refrained from drink. His iron-gray hair had been freshly curled and there were glimpses of the Alkaios he might have been. They embraced warmly, with fond greeting, and she read approval of herself in his eyes.

"Enchanting Sappho."

The smile she turned on him was filled with such happiness that he knew she had not heard the rumor. He himself could not speak of it—let someone else, let Khar, if it were true. In the public houses one heard all sorts of things, but this particular bit of gossip was so persistent that he put credence in it and pitied Sappho, for he knew her pride.

At the quay the lead ship was already slipping into quiet waters. Nubians with blue-black bodies jumped from its decks to the mole, securing the dancing bark with strong hawsers. A plank for conveying the goods of the voyage was run to the vessel. Ignoring this, Kharaxos sprang upon the dock. In his manner and grace he was still young, a virile man—and beautiful.

He swept Sappho to his breast, then Alkaios, his old companion, who seemed more like his father.

Kharaxos knelt and blessed the land of Lesbos, giving thanks to the gods for his safe return. Sappho raised her voice with his; by their protection and favor he had once more won through the perilous passage.

When at last they arrived at her house and her guests were seated, with food spread upon the inlaid tables, she asked her brother, "Tell me, dear Khar, why must you spend your days in far lands, even that of Egypt?"

"So I may receive such welcome when I come home," he laughed, and raising his glass to her, "You do not know the admiration in which you are held, Sappho, or what honor it brings me abroad to be your brother."

"Even in Egypt?"

"In Egypt the Aeolic dialect is known. Your songs are as much sung in Naukratis as here."

"If I have brought any good to your life, I am content."

Khar behaved as though he had not lived seven years among Barbarians, as though it were a pleasure cruise to sail the hundreds of stadia that threaded the islands of the Aegean. However, of the open sea between Crete and North Africa, he was silent. But Sappho managed to get him to talk somewhat of his journey.

"More than the pathless sea my sailors dreaded the desert coast by the Canopic mouth of the Nile. Lack of water necessitated forays upon land to sites where wells were marked by other Hellenic merchantmen. Near these cisterns Libyan tribesmen hid to attack and plunder shore parties such as ours. Fortunately my fleet carries many men, and in these battles we got not only water but slaves."

Sappho called on Kalliope, elder sister of the nine Muses, to listen to these tales. But Khar turned the conversation. "And where," he asked, "are all the beautiful maids that surrounded you with music and dance when I was here last?"

"I sent them away years ago."

"But why?"

"I grew weary, that is why. It seemed to me their young voices were out of place here, where Sappho grows old."

"Time dares not touch great Sappho," Alkaios said.

"My slaves were at some pains to make you think so."

Khar put in indignantly, "Old! How can you say that? Why you are but two years older than myself, and I am about to be married."

"Married?"

Alkaios stared attentively at his plate. He had guessed rightly, Sappho had heard no word.

Sappho said, perhaps a shade too lightly, "You could not pine for a girl from Lesbos seven years. It must be someone you met beneath the shade of the palms of Naukratis?"

"Even so, Sister. And I tell you this, the many mouths of the Nile have never washed up at the feet of one so beautiful."

"She would be a Barbarian then? An Egyptian?"

"She is Thracian. You will love her as a sister. Not only is she exceedingly beautiful, but pious as well. She made a pilgrimage to the temple at Delphi, navel of the world, and gave away a tenth of her possessions. The most magnificent gift consisted of quantities of iron spits, such as are used for roasting oxen whole."

"She must be a wealthy woman to have made the trip to the slopes of Parnassus. And the gift of such obeli is indeed magnanimous."

"Yes," Khar said carelessly, "she is used to luxury."

"And the name of this prize among women?"

"She is called Doricha Rhodopis."

For a shocked second the wings of a giant bird beat, replacing the beat of her heart. The pause between brother and sister lengthened.

When Sappho spoke it was slowly and with care. "You disturb my peace, Khar, for there was on the island of Samos a young slave girl belonging to Iadmon, whose invitation to attend the freeing of Aesop was brought by you. It happened that the name of his most accomplished slave was also Doricha. They called her the White Rose."

"It is the same. He sold her for great price to a certain Xanthes, a merchant, who took the girl to Naukratis and set her up as a courtesan."

Sappho looked at him, unbelieving. "Answer and tell me, am I losing my mind? Has Lyssa, goddess of madness, overcome my brain? I thought I heard my brother say he is marrying a slave and a courtesan."

Khar's hand closed over the goblet he was holding and, in anger, broke it. "I did not expect such judgment from you. The girl did not choose the life she led."

"But apparently made a good thing of it. Will her present master, Xanthes, sell her to you?"

"That is why I returned, to raise what I can on my lands, my villa, my cattle. Each night, for many nights, I wrote an offer on the seawall and each morning it was rejected."

"But one morning it was not?"

"Thanks be to the gods."

Sappho smiled her most sweet smile.

"I think I did misunderstand you, Khar. I thought you spoke of marriage. But my mind is much relieved now I see she is to be your concubine, your slave."

"Not slave. I will free her and marry her. I shall return to Lesbos with the White Rose and make her my wife."

There was nothing to indicate that a moment before Sappho had been smiling. "You cannot do this thing, Brother. I know the gods make sensible men to become senseless where a woman is concerned, but there are no slaves in our family. It is a proud lineage. You cannot sully it."

Khar, like his sister, was unused to opposition. "Sappho, the life you've led has not been so conventional that you can tell others how to live."

Control was very near slipping from her. "So, you take the part of Eurygyos and Larichos against me!"

"That you know I have never done. But because you have suffered from gossip, I expect you to be understanding."

"Khar, have the gods blinded you that you do not see? It is her business, her profession, to make men love her. How do you know she is not using you simply to purchase her freedom? Such a woman feigns love easily."

"You do not know her, and you are ready to assume the worst."

"I know her!"

Alkaios looked up sharply, and Sappho continued more cautiously, "That is, I know of women like her."

"None is like her. She is unique, and I am fortunate that she has agreed to have me."

Sappho turned to Alkaios for reinforcement. "Alkaios," she pleaded, "you are a man of the world. Even her gift at Delphi, of unbending rods, is appropriate to her profession. This Doricha has used her ploys on my brother and he is so infatuated that he will ruin himself for her."

Alkaios waved both hands in denying the role she forced on him. "No, no, do not place me in the middle of a family quarrel. I know nothing of the matter. But I think, Sappho, it is possible that you yourself met Doricha when you journeyed to Samos."

"If I did, I do not remember. Why should I remember a slave?"

"When I return to Naukratis, she will be as free as you are." Khar threw his mantle over his shoulder in token that he was leaving.

"Very well, Khar. Buy her. I will even help you. But do not, by those of our family, both on the ground and under it—do not, I pray you, marry such a one."

"And do you not insult my wife-to-be, Sister."

"Khar . . ." Sappho's voice made him pause. "I lied just now because I feared to hurt you. I *did* know of Doricha Rhodopis in Samos. All did. For though almost a child, she was infamous even then."

Khar looked as though he would strike her. "I will hear no more."

"But you will, Khar, and not from me only, if you make this slave your wife."

He strode to the door. "I will return to Egypt without seeing you again."

"And you are right. While you hold to this course there can be no understanding between us."

As her brother left, Alkaios clambered over several cushions with a goblet of wine. "Drink, my comrade. Better to fall on the floor through drink than through sorrow. So, you know the White Rose? I hear she is quite good with peacocks."

"I know nothing of all that." Her tart tone told Alkaios what he wanted to know.

Sappho bowed her head to her hands and said, her voice shaking in disbelief, "I am alienated from my brother."

"He may not go through with the marriage. He may not even buy her. By the time he is returned, the price may have gone up. Or Doricha Rhodopis may have found someone richer."

"But not as gullible as Khar. He is a leader of men, but of women he knows nothing. From the age of ten she was a prostitute. It is horrible to think of the hands she has passed through, the performances she has given. Every officer in the Attic fleet must have rammed coins into her. My poor brother is surely bewitched."

That night she pressed out and sent to Kharaxos these words:

> . . . *with whom in vagrant love you are united*
> *and suppose that to be beautiful*
> *which is public property*

There was no reply.

Kharaxos stayed in Mitylene long enough to sell or mortgage everything he possessed. Sappho heard from time to time how he had disposed of a piece of land, an orchard, even a grove of olives. But when word reached her he intended to sell the home they had grown up in, the villa of their aunt Tyro, she went to him.

Khar had her admitted, but looked at her with a frown. "I thought we had nothing more to say to each other. Except, perhaps, I may look for my sister's blessing?"

"You have my rich blessing, Khar, in all things, but not in the union you contemplate."

"I will marry Doricha."

"And beggar yourself as you are doing? She won't have a poor husband, you know. She is used to the finery of her kind."

"I forbid you to talk about her, especially as I have heard in detail from our brothers about your own parade of girl lovers."

"Khar, I did not come to quarrel. I came as your elder sister to ask you not to sell the home of our youth, the home of our good aunt, who loved us as her own children."

"It must go."

"Why? Is it not grand enough for her?"

"No, it is not."

"How can one man's fortune satisfy her, when she is used to many?"

"I told you not to speak of her. I forbid it."

"I speak as I am minded. But none speak so to Sappho."

"Except she be female, young, and desirable. It is you who have dishonored our house, Sappho."

"Are you leaving on a journey, perhaps of years, with those words for me? Unsay them, Khar."

"Only if you can unsay their truth."

"You know me, Khar. You know Sappho is incapable of ugly acts, for I have all my life loved dainty and delicate things."

"So I thought. But you have no charity for the woman I love because of circumstances forced on her, while you, of your own self, indulged in what Doricha has never heard of."

"Doricha has heard of every practice there is, and engaged in them."

"Enough. I will not listen to more."

"And so we part."

Sappho left the villa she had known so well and the brother she had loved. Her stomach felt as it had when she saw the small feet of Gongyla dangling in the air. Tears are too weak to wash away such moments. There was no help for her, not in prayer or sacrifice, for whatever god ruled this hour had hold of her brother's heart and mind.

Khar sailed without a token. When she heard of his departure,

Sappho locked herself in her room. She hadn't believed it would come to this. Suppose he should die on the sea as Kerkolas had? To banish the ill of such a thought, she spilled the sweet wine of Lesbos, the same Khar carried on his ships, to the god of the blue hair.

Still, to have parted from him so, to have let him go with angry words between them—but what could she have done?

It was ghastly to her that she had held in her own arms the woman her brother was enamored of. What if he found out?

Was an unclean whore who performed obscene tricks and approached her lover on her belly, was this slave to enter into the first house of Lesbos whose proud ancestry stemmed from great Orestes? How they would laugh at a son of noble Skamandronymos! It would not happen, she assured herself.

To ensure that Khar would come to his senses, Sappho assembled a tenth of all on her estate and by oxcart made her way to the mountain fastness of the priestesses of Dionysos, thinking as she went that she might glimpse Kleis.

It took the better part of the day to arrive at the caves, where she saw to the unloading of animals, grain, and wine. All was piled before the entrance. She knelt in the dust and spoke her prayer. "Soften my brother's heart toward me, O god who sports with dolphins. You know I love Khar well. Bring him back in health and strength, that the quarrel may be undone, the words unspoken—and the hold that woman has on him broken."

Dionysos returned no answer, although she stayed on her knees and waited. Yet perhaps in his way he did. For after the visit to the caves there was a change in her. She found it hard to stay as before in the sanctuary of her home and took to roaming as she had when a child.

Her walks led her into the streets of Mitylene. She found she was diverted by the many colors, the movement of people, the sounds of trade and barter. She made an occasional small purchase, something from the stall of the flower merchant, or an opal caught her fancy and she would have it. Shopkeepers bowed, mothers pointed her out to their children, men turned to stare, and girls put their heads together. Later they would say, "I saw Sappho with these eyes."

She sought out the Street of Women and looked curiously at the immodest and ornate costumes. They make of themselves another commodity, she thought. This put her in mind of Doricha, so she left.

Upon her return a runner from Alkaios waited. She was invited to a small dinner party. At first she was inclined to go—there was no one left from her old life except Alkaios—but she knew before the evening was out her friend would be snoring on the floor. She sent the servant away, saying she could not manage it. But the incident evoked a trail of memory. She recalled his first poem to her:

> *Innocent Sappho*
> *of the violet*
> *hair*
> *and sweet*
> *smile*

When Alkaios invited her a second time, she accepted. He had hired a ship for the occasion. Lighted with tapers and festooned with flowers, it glided out of the harbor. The captain, in special greeting and honor, bathed her feet and spread a lotion on them. He was a powerful young man, yet graceful. And as he knelt, she looked down on a crown of chestnut curls. How beautiful the young are, she thought.

The feast was in progress and Alkaios already quite drunk. She didn't mind, but enjoyed the Samian performers who with naked feet trod out the dances of their land. Mostly she enjoyed the fresh breeze stirred by Sea, and the slap of waves as they rocked the craft. It was pleasant upon the water, and the evening passed quickly.

Thereafter she was drawn to the harbor, she supposed because she felt closer to Khar there. One day she recognized the ship Alkaios had hired for their dinner party and looked to see if the captain who had removed her sandals was aboard.

She saw him in the bow speaking with a merchant. Was he arranging to fill his craft with water and wine for another such evening? She continued to enjoy his profile against the sea. It was strong, the forehead sloping to the nose with scarcely an indentation. And the mouth might have been drawn by a master artisan for an Apollo figure. The thickness of his upper arms and shoulders showed the sailor, used to handling rigging and rough work. The litheness about him she supposed was youth. She watched from dockside as he did business with the merchant.

In the days that followed, she went again and again seaward, to the harbor. Usually the ship rode at anchor, but there were times when it had slipped its mooring and was gone. When this happened she spent a restless night and hurried back in the morning to make sure the boat was there. It always was, for its journeys were short. When Sappho realized this she felt light as air.

She conceived a longing, a desire to engage the boat herself. A gala, a party even, was not what she had in mind. Rather it was to lean back against skins and cushions, and floating on dark waters call upon the Muses and make songs, for surely songs sung under such circumstances would be wonderful indeed. Why should she not gratify this wish? It was a simple one, to smell the salt, feel the faint breeze that hovers over water, and hymn her verses old and new.

Sappho sent a runner to make inquiry about the boat and to discover if the young man was indeed the owner. "Find out what you can about him," she instructed, and turned her back, pretending an interest in material for a new shawl.

The slave returned. "His name is Phaon, Lady. He is master of the vessel, and it is for hire for galas, parties, picnics, and the like."

"How does he live when his boat is not hired?" Sappho asked.

"Lady, he is a sponge diver."

"I see." She sent the slave back to Phaon to negotiate a price and designate an evening.

Shortly after this, her servants announced that a messenger approached with bay leaf in his hair. Sappho's heart raced—it is Khar! Khar has sent this man with a token that he loves me as before and will forget the woman.

When the man went on his knees before her, she said, "Speak— who sent you?"

"My master, O great Sappho, is the wise man and ruler of Athens, even noble Solon, whose fame has spread through all the cities of the Hellenes."

Sappho was astounded. Solon was not a lover of women, although on previous occasions he had sent costly oils and more recently a gift of a silver chalice on which the nine sisters were incised. A very handsome present, but a personal message was of another magnitude. "So-lon, ruler in Athens, has business with me?"

"He salutes great Sappho. And on learning that she is making books of her songs, he would obtain them for himself at any cost. He asks if a scribe of highest integrity might be quartered in your home and given access to the material, that it may be copied to bring pleasure to his leisure. For of all pleasures my master knows, listening to the immortal songs of Sappho brings him most joy."

Sappho was much affected by such a message from this mighty ruler, who was one of the seven wise men in the world. In her reply she assured Solon that utmost hospitality would be given his scribe, that he would be lodged with her household until his task was done, adding proudly, "I have six books, which represent the songs I have sung from a girl until now." And she thanked him for the honor he did her.

When a fresh messenger had been sped on his way, Sappho closeted herself in her chamber and took from her woman's chest her most highly polished and true-reflecting mirror. All my fame does not make me a year younger, she thought.

Into her mind came a vision sent by the gods of the beautiful young Phaon, diver after sponges. His was a body powerful as Pittakos's when he returned the hero of Lesbos from the ten-year war with Athens. "How madly my heart once beat for him."

She laughed even now, thinking of the lampoons Alkaios had sung of him. But she recalled well what a hold he had over her, and how he himself had broken the spell, setting her free when he exiled her.

Her ruminations led her to conclude that she was not as averse to the male as she had told her hetaerae. She had grown up at a time when men were absent altogether from Mitylene.

She considered her husband. It had been a long time since she had thought of him wandering in the house of Hades. He had been, she realized now, too indolent for her taste, too foppish with his constant pursuit of new amusements. He had not known how to fan the fires in her. Many were the times he remonstrated with her for her lack of passion, never considering that his own brief thrust was not sufficient to call forth what blazed in Sappho.

If her husband had been inadequate as a lover, it was not neces-sarily an indictment of the entire sex, but one man only. Perhaps her womanhood had been cheated, perhaps her first instinct toward the might of Pittakos had been of the gods. Or it may be the other Sappho, her second self, who now desired.

Sappho put aside her mirror, in fact buried it at the bottom of her chest. But that night she thonged the door to her room and retrieved it. This time it was by the tapers that flared in the night-darkened chamber that she examined herself. It was quite amazing how softened the lines in her brow were and those wrinkles about her eyes that told of too many days of merriment and carefree laughter. As for the streak of white in her hair, it could be dyed with the juice of dark berries and the bark of trees well steeped in boiled water.

The time had definitely come to use the mastics her mother had employed. Such artifices worked very well for a number of hours. And Niobe knew of others: fomentation, sulfur over a low fire mixed with klanet, that rare plant, combined with litharge, a paste which remained on the face and neck three hours. Then the skin was bathed with laten, and the milk of a woman nursing a girl-child was brought to cleanse all. These were followed by oil of almonds, tincture of hydromel, and a decoction of honey and water. Ah, these small alabaster boxes of illusion. What were these cosmetics but fraud and lies? She did not care.

She might be young again, without the reality of youth. In such pretense there was the possibility of a final love. Once more, after these many years, she spilled to Aphrodite and, forgetting her quarrel with the goddess, urgently asked to feel the arms of a lover, to rouse another's body with her own.

The hetaerae had been her delight. But might there not be waiting for her a final untapped joy in the arms of a man who knew how to love? Not a man of her own class with his oboe player and string of boy lovers, but a rough sailor whose forearms were brawny and whose legs were as pillars. Phaon, who stepped with such surety in his rocking craft, whose shoulders were as a wrestler's, but whose waist was slender as a girl's. She smiled to herself, thinking he would have no way of knowing the tricks she was made of, that she was all illusion, even as her songs; a made thing, for the moment only, lasting while song lasted.

All depended on art and torches, for she would never hire his high-curved boat except by night. Light is joy, she thought ruefully, for all but me. Her patroness in this venture would be Selene, the Moon goddess. "And with Heaven's help . . ."

Her slave settled details with the young ship's captain for an eve-ning three nights hence. During the intervening time, a constant train of laden beasts traveled between her villa and his boat, carrying woven rugs and pillows, pelts of tiger and panther. Stringed instruments came next, a harp with a carved Sphinx atop it, a zither, and a lyre. Also taken aboard were alabaster boxes, from which strange and exotic scents emerged.

On the day itself, jars of wine and baskets of delicate foods covered by fine linen with the fragrance of lavender were loaded on deck. Fi-nally flowers arrived, the bark was flanked with them. They were braided to its sides and strung along the mast, they ran along the ropes and trailed the water. As though an afterthought, several torches were secured fore and aft. Slaves also laid at the feet of the speechless captain sandals of gold and a himation of purest cambric, white as Egyptian lyssus.

As night fell, a Nubian slave rowed a cloaked figure to the ship. Phaon leapt to hand in the single form, whose cloak parted, revealing a gossamer wrap. He was unsure whether he touched a statue or a woman of flesh and blood. He dared not raise his eyes to find out, but kept them on the planks of his ship.

"I have inquired and know that your name is Phaon."

The voice held the sounds of lyre and cymbals. He had never heard his name said in that fashion.

"I know further that you are a freeman and have an honest repu-tation. Therefore does Sappho of Lesbos place herself in your steward-ship and depend on your ability to deal with what Poseidon sends."

Phaon bent before her. "Lady, I will do my best to please you."

"I believe it."

"And I thank you for the lending of this beautiful garment and for the sandals of gold."

"They are not lent, but given."

He murmured something, he knew not what. He still dared not look on her, except to observe how tiny her feet were, how perfect her toes, and that on the twinkling sandals were silver bells.

"Lead me, O Phaon, to the place my people have made ready for me that I may compose in the quiet of your ship."

"Yes, Lady." And from the diaphanous tarentine veil, a hand freed itself and clasped his . . . but such a hand. He had never seen a hand like it; his own swallowed it up as a hawk would a small wood dove. The daintiest fingers and smallest wrist he had ever felt lay inside his palm, trusting him as a guide. And when the lady moved at his side, it was the sliding of water, it was the swaying stalk of a narcissus. His own feet, even in sandals of gold, made the deck creak; hers made no sound except for the merry bells. Phaon led her to the piled luxury of skins and rugs and pillows.

"Will I be able to watch you from here as you ply your ship?"

"Assuredly." Then, worried, he added, "Your servants set up this place for you, but if you would be more private . . ."

"No, no, I may need you. You see, I am quite alone." She smiled through the filmy gauze into his face, directly into it. And it was as though great Zeus threw a thunderbolt and struck him full; his wits seemed addled and he himself befuddled as though from drink.

He again lowered his eyes, but Sappho had seen what she needed to know. Her magic was truer far than those love potions once sold by the witch Andromeda.

"The boat is so unsteady," she said, and the next moment she was against him body to body. Instinctively his arms were about her and she felt the hardness she caused in him—he felt her softness, her up-tilted breasts. The next moment he was swallowed by a cloud of aroma and knew a goddess had been in his arms.

"Pardon, Lady." He braced his legs and laid her back against the array of colors and textures skillfully blended. Though the full weight of her hung in his hands for only a second, he saw the aureole of rosy breasts, the fullness of thighs, yet a waist so slender he believed he could span it with his two hands and touch finger to finger. Phaon felt dizzy from the scents she seemed to radiate, but he managed to say, "I pray the Muses bless your efforts, Lady." And he saluted her.

"I pray so too." She picked up her lyre, which Phaon took as a dismissal, for he turned to his duties.

She strummed softly; her eyes, seeming closed, watched all he did.

Nimbly he cast off their mooring stone, made fast the oar thongs, and rowed past anchored craft whose silhouettes showed darkly. Once clear of the harbor he swung his body against the ropes that ran up the sail. The male form exuded an excitement in activity that was comparable to the female in dance. The virility of his person, his co-ordination, lightness, the harmony of movement that characterized his actions, all stirred her, so that her usual plea to the Muses, Add passion to my song, was not needed, although she recited the formula.

The night was warm, unlocking fragrances whose loosened stoppers made the senses reel. There was no longer much for Phaon to do. The wind did his job for him, and he continued to lean against the ropes. Even in a posture of relaxation his body held the hint of dynamic power.

Sappho continued to sing to herself. He strained to hear. She smiled; he also wanted to say, "I heard Sappho sing."

The moon rose, gibbous, as though squeezed from its perfect form by the hand of a child. Night engulfed them. They moved silently, parting black waters. "Phaon," she called.

He was by her in a moment. "Lady?"

"We will return now."

She could feel his disappointment, for he was as transparent as her youngest hetaera.

"It was satisfactory . . . the sailing?"

"It was completely satisfactory, but I have finished my song. However, it is certain the nine Muses travel with me and have enjoyed the outing, even as I. This boat of yours shall be hired again."

"Tomorrow night?"

"I do not know. I will send word."

"You were comfortable, Lady? And you had all you wished?"

"It was very pleasant."

"Then I shall not disturb the rugs and cushions, but leave them as they are."

She nodded; the point was too trivial to discuss. They rethreaded the passage. He furled the sails and lowered the mast beside them, rolling them together into a compact bundle. She knew everything that he did, memorized each motion. When he handed her into the small cockleshell, she thought his fingers lingered over hers.

Sappho sent word by a slave that it was not convenient to come the next day, or even the two days past that. This she did because she was mad to be there. For such desire had leapt upon her as she had not known since the golden days of her hetaerae. She could think of nothing but Phaon, and spent the time until she saw him reconstructing all his movements and everything he had said. Closing her eyes she felt again the lingering fingers that had not wished to leave hers. She began to plan their next encounter.

None knew love's strategy better than Sappho. And what was Aphrodite's strategy? Had the goddess given her a chance to relive her youth? Or was it a cruel taunt?

"I know the path of my wisdom!" she flung at the Kyprian-born, but knew she would not follow it. My brain is blighted, she told herself, because what started in a light, carefree manner had laid hold of her heart. "The chain of Fate binds all." Was Phaon disappointed that she put off the day? Did he think of her as she did of him? Did he think of her at all?

Another question followed closely. "Is it possible," she asked in wonder, "that I love again?"

Once again her slaves made processional and Phaon's craft was filled with fresh incense, even more glorious clusters of flowers, fine soft Amorgos drapery, all magic that presaged her presence.

The small, light vessel danced impatiently, and the same Nubian slave rowed her to it.

As before, Phaon raised her to his ship. He was more beautiful than she remembered, his lashes sweeping his cheek as sweetly as any girl's. He found courage to look directly in her face, but only for a moment. Once again he stared at the planking. "Welcome, O Sappho."

"Peace to you, Phaon."

He did not release her hand but kept it as he led her to the place prepared for her. When she seated herself upon the skins and rich materials, he said haltingly, "Since you so love flowers, Lady . . ." and held out to her a woven garland of violets and crocus.

To accept it she must remove the mantle and coan veil.

Phaon was spellbound, for Sappho's chiton revealed her form— even to the mound of Aphrodite, which her women had plucked clean of hair, rouging and outlining the nether lips.

Sappho lowered her head that he might slip the chain of flowers over her more easily. He knelt to perform this service, and her breasts with their delicately tinted paps swung against him. Phaon jumped back as though he had touched fire.

Coolly, she said, "I give you thanks, Phaon. The flowers were a pretty thought."

She drew the coan wrap about her. It did not obscure, but only lay another fold between them, making her filmy and unreal. Her body seemed shot through with the gold of a constantly disappearing thread. Phaon retreated to his oars and guided the bark from the harbor.

Sappho picked up her lyre and sang as before, very softly to herself. When Phaon secured the sail, she called to him, saying, "O Captain, I would have a companion to share a goblet of white wine with me."

As he came toward her, she was conscious of his male smell even among the perfumes and sweet oils. It disturbed her. It had always disturbed her.

"Will you pour?" she asked, handing him a flagon. It was encrusted with jewels as shells at the sea bottom were encrusted with barnacles. He took the decanter almost reluctantly and spilled to Poseidon.

Sappho frowned slightly. "I see through some oversight my servants put in only one goblet." Her expression changed as though she had at that instant solved some weighty problem. "Therefore you must sit, that we may share it."

"I am not worthy . . ." he protested in real agony.

She smiled sweetly on him. "I make you worthy by my request."

He sat—Sappho desired it, what else could he do? Many scents wafted over him and his head reeled, encompassed as he was by a garden of strange delights.

Sappho sipped from the single goblet, around which ran a frieze of Dionysian dancers. She regarded him over the rim, leisurely.

Aware of her scrutiny, he evaded her glance by lowering his, but that brought his eyes along her body and he quickly raised them again. She passed the cup to him without a word, and without a word he drank. Then exclaimed, "Is this wine?"

She laughed softly in her throat. "Of course not. It is nectar stolen from Clymene, shapely daughter of Ocean, who bedded with Iapetus and gave birth to Prometheus and Atlas and Epimetheus."

Phaon stopped drinking. "Epimetheus," he said, "brings bad luck to those who must toil for their bread."

"Not bad luck, just luck—both good and bad."

"By your hire of my boat I have been granted better luck than I ever knew before."

"Is the pay generous? I did not inquire."

"I did not mean the pay. In your presence, O great Sappho, the world is remade."

She laughed. "By your talk, Captain, I think I was right, and that this simple wine you drink surely is not from grapes trod out by oxen led round the millstone."

"What then?" he asked.

"My ladies may have packed, by mistake, something stronger, a Thessalian brew, perhaps, concocted by Cotytto herself, made of incantations and special potions."

"If witchcraft is your meaning, then is there no need to drink, for I am under Sappho's spell." He seemed to hold his breath as he waited to see what effect the boldness of his words would have.

"Did my music please you then?"

"Yes . . . no . . . you, yourself. I never saw a lady of your rank so . . . close before."

"Oh, if that is all. There are many with more grace than I."

"I believe your veracity, great one, but not your judgment."

Sappho laughed musically, like the cadence of bells. "Tonight I want company, Phaon. Listen and I will sing you a tale." Sappho chose an epic such as would fascinate a man. Her song was about Theseus, who, after slaying the Minotaur, freed from the monster seven boys and seven girls.

Phaon was enraptured. He listened at her feet as she chanted. He is like a child, she thought, a beautiful child. And she wove her stories and songs about him, with each binding him more surely.

She told of King Priam of Ilium when he received the news that his son Hector was returning with a bride, the daughter of the King of Cilian Thebes:

> With power and speed to his legs came the herald,
> Idaeus, announcing this wonderful news . . .

Phaon watched her face and she whispered to him, "These tidings spread all over Asia and turned to legend forever."

> Hector and all his companions are bringing
> from sacred Thebes and the plains of Placia,
> over the salty sea by ship,
> a delicate dark-eyed girl: Andromache.
> Many the golden bracelets

and purple stuffs the winds are bringing
and trinkets bespangled;
numberless, too, the silver cups and ivory chasings.
So uttered the herald, and Hector's dear father
nimbly arose as the news
sped to their friends through the ample city.
Then the people of Ilium
harnessed their mules to the smoothly moving cars;
and all the women in one,
with the prettily ankled girls,
ascended—the daughters of Priam apart.
The men had the horses yoked
to the chariots; every youth
was there; till a mighty people moved
mightily along.
And the charioteers drove
their jingling horses on . . .

She glanced at Phaon. He had not moved. He begged her not to stop, and she told him of the warriors returning after the fall of Troy.

"It is a bedazzlement to hear you," the young sailor said in awe.

Sappho stretched her arms lazily above her head. "I am weary. Take me back."

"Must I?"

She smiled gently at him. "Yes."

"But you will visit my boat another time? Not to hire it, but as an honored guest?"

She studied him a moment, as though making up her mind. "That would be delightful," she said, playing the great lady—when she wanted to press him, mouth him, frenzy him.

He suggested a day. She replied that she would study her commitments and send an answer.

She spent the time at home working out an ode in the epic vein, for this is what fascinated him. She decided to retell in her own way the tale of Prometheus and his theft of fire. When humankind received this godlike gift, Zeus and his race, in vengeance, had no more face-to-face dealings with either man or woman but came thereafter only in dreams and portents.

Sappho was pleased with her story, certain that Phaon would like it. So, she was to be his guest. Guest-lover, she whispered fiercely to herself. For she could not again keep her body from his.

She had conceived a superstition that semen from his young and powerful loins entering her, would act as a potion and keep her young. She needed his youth and beauty, and although he did not know it, he needed her not at all.

She was reminded of a favorite love poem, that of Selene, the Moon, in which it was said that the goddess saw by her pale light a fair young shepherd boy sleeping near the entrance to a cave on Mount Latmos. And she, being enamored of his grace and comeliness, determined to keep him there, just as he was, forever asleep and forever young. She fed her passion for him nightly, rousing him with her kisses, exciting him with her touch, so sensual that in his sleep he moaned and cried out and his erection lasted until she slid from him at morning. The name of the youth was Endymion. And though she possessed him each night and seduced and inflamed him, Selene never let him wake. And he never saw her, who was the mistress of his slumbering body. She allowed him the most erotic dreams of her, and pictured herself to him as she would be: a maiden both wanton and pure, who by accident it seemed, tripped and fell across his prone figure, tearing her chiton so that it did not protect her. She then cajoled the East Wind into stripping Endymion of his clothing. Her lust for him was never ending and never satisfied. And Endymion knew sensations that only gods know when they mate.

"Come to me, Moon goddess, and advise me in my sleep," Sappho murmured. And in the morning, more strongly than ever, she knew she must keep Phaon forever asleep, allow him to see her only by dim torchlight, spin him tales of heroes and bring delight to his body.

She could do this magic because she was Sappho. And magic was the main ingredient of her small self that stretched to encompass what she wished.

So on the night agreed upon, she commanded Niobe to fetch her most skillful women and with consummate art was again prepared. Very lovely she seemed, and enticing. "Yes," she told her women, "I am the Moon."

They looked at one another without comprehension. Niobe alone smiled; her mistress often spoke in such fashion. Riddles, it seemed to the others, but Niobe knew she spoke with gods.

Sappho was driven to her Endymion, who stood in the bow of his long ship straining his eyes toward shore. She was handed down from the chariot and, light-footed, ran to the small boat where the enormous Nubian waited to row her out.

Phaon lifted her to the deck and was instantly wrapped in a cloud of scents, both tranquil and disturbing. "You are like a thistle, Lady. Welcome."

"Thank you. I feel welcome."

He led her to her bower, but this time he had provided the picnic.

"How lovely," she exclaimed at the care with which each item had been arranged. The food was poorer and coarser than she had tasted since high Pyrrha, but it was served with flowers as beautiful as any she had ever gathered.

"It is only Lesbian wine—" he began.

She interrupted. "Than which there is none better. My brothers are both growers and sellers."

"Sit then, Lady, and once the craft is free of the harbor, we will taste of it."

"So grant the gods." And to herself she promised to taste other things as well.

Tonight he did not run up the sail, but let the ship rock gently as he came to her side. They poured to the gods and then he poured for her from the mixing bowl. "May every good attend you, most dazzling of women."

"And to you, good."

They drank, watching each other as they did.

"I have thought these many days on the wonderful stories that you told. It must be like entering another world to be inside your head."

"There are many conflicts there. Sometimes disturbing . . . as you are disturbing to my peace."

"I? How can that be?"

Sappho jumped to her feet. "Stand up. Look me in the face as friend to friend, lover to lover."

Like one in a trance he obeyed. And she managed that when he was on his feet, she was almost in the same place. His eyes traveled the transparency of her peplos, feather-woven by Amathusians, and viewed the marvels of her exquisite body, which seemed to palpate toward him. Sappho met the glance of his deep-fringed eyes. "Touch me—for I am consumed by you."

She whispered the words rapidly at him, but he stood still, uncertain. A lady of high station, the songstress of Lesbos—had he heard correctly?

Was it a lurch of the ship, had either moved? She was in his arms, pressed against him in a way that revealed the differences of their two sexes.

"You are as fire, driven over me by wind," she whispered and did not close her eyes when he kissed her. He closed his. "Ah, Phaon . . ." She undid his garment and her fingers glided his nakedness.

He was rigid and upstanding as a column, and ashamed that it was so. Sappho dropped to her knees to worship.

He groaned aloud with the pleasure of what she made him feel and, with urgency, carried her to the piled cushions, where he crushed her with his weight.

But she would not be still to allow him his way. Her delicately oiled body ever indicated new possibilities of love. Before he could pin her, she evaded, to expose herself in yet another position. She lay upon him head to head, then head to feet. She presented her rounded buttocks and as he reached for her, turned and hovered above him.

Quick as a panther, he had her, nor could she escape to tease in a new way. Now it was she who moaned. A volcano erupted in her, hot lava coursed over her, and she strained for every last sweet drop with which he filled her.

"You are my shepherd boy," she whispered and licked him clean of his own sperm, then massaged gently with unguents which combined the pith of the pomegranate, eggs, honey, the soft part of crabs, the undersides of snails, mussels, and a trace of nettle-seed—all secret restoratives, for she meant to have him again this night. For this reason she wore the right testicle of an ass in a broad silver bracelet on her left wrist. She left nothing undone that would excite his liver again to desire and sexual prowess. Unobtrusively she slipped a piece of southernwood beneath their cushions, for that also strengthened the male for frequent copulations.

"You are not woman," he gasped, when he had his breath, "but goddess."

"It is true, the gods are very close to me in that I am sister to the Muses. But I am mortal woman, and all my nature turns to you."

"I have never felt . . . never known . . ."

"Of course not. I did not say I was an ordinary woman. I am Sappho. And all that I do is with passion."

"I would die for you," he said, and then, "I think I almost did die."

"I also. Your flesh scorches me. Your mouth burns like a wound. Athene must have sent a heron to our right hand."

Phaon laughed. "No heron that, but a seagull."

"Then they are lucky, too."

"It must be so, for you are here—unless I dream."

"I am here." She twined hyacinths in his curls and murmured soft words that did not make sense, or need to.

She told him that the Nine were born in Pieria. He did not know even simple things like that. "Hesiod says they are all of one mind, their hearts set upon song, as mine is set upon love."

"For me?" he asked in wonder.

"For who but you? Am I here or elsewhere? Answer and tell me."

"You . . . are here. Although I cannot believe it. Nor do I understand."

"Seek not to understand. It is a gift the gods have given us." And her insatiable mouth was open to his. He responded lazily, letting her play with him as she would.

Her famished mouth at last moved the sailor to lose himself once more on the tide of passion.

When it was possible to lie quietly, Phaon spoke. "I do not know anymore if I am you or myself," he said hoarsely.

"You are always Phaon, which is why my eyes adore you and my heart is toward you."

"Yet I have heard . . ." He had begun impulsively, unthinkingly, and checked himself.

A chill descended on her. "No, no, you must tell me what you heard. In all things we must be open with each other, nor keep anything back."

"It is because the gods visit you that tongues wag. It is envy. It is nothing."

"I would know this nothing." And she poured down his throat the strong red wine of Lesbos.

"It is of the girls they speak, that for so many years stayed on your estate."

"Yes, my hetaerae, my fair companions. What of them?"

He shook his head. "It is but the talk of taverns and unworthy of being repeated."

She said lightly, "All this is not new to me. I have many enemies. Fame starts tongues clacking. They say I had lovers among them." She laughed. "Which were mentioned by name?"

Phaon hung his head, unwilling to answer. "They did mention an Anaktoria, and beautiful Kydro, and a girl called Atthis."

Sappho enjoyed the inaccuracy. Atthis, of course they had guessed Atthis. She picked up her lyre and, gazing out over the water, sang as though to it:

> *Neither in the girls of Pyrrha or Metyma nor*
> *in any of Lesbos do I take any more delight*

Did he notice the past tense?

She put aside the lyre. "We lived together in innocence, singing lessons from the wonderful Isle of Thought, studying Sky by night. By day we danced ritual steps in the sand, anointing one another with cenanthium from the mountains of Kypros. Many times my Muses would carry me from my friends, and I would sing poems to those fair spirits. It was a small repayment, for happy is she whom the Muses love."

"You are half divine, O matchless Sappho. I cannot believe your love could turn toward a common sailor, a man of no distinction, when all Lesbos, the entire Hellenic world court you."

"There is no reason in love—do not look for reason. It is a holy gift." And she told him the story of Dionysos, who each spring goes crowned with blossoms and ivy to the valleys of Lydia, to the far mountains sacred to him. And of Prometheus she told how he concealed the sacred fire in a hollow reed.

Some of the things Phaon wanted to hear about were very strange. He was interested in the mechanics of her bath. He had never heard of pipes buried in the ground that carried water from the spring to the fire pit in the kitchen, from whence they passed into the satyr's head, which slaves turned to fill her marble bath.

"That is from the gods." He spoke in a reverent voice.

"No god at all," she laughed, "but one of my slaves designed it. In Syracuse all the great houses have such arrangements."

"And the wastes," he asked, "could they not be carried from the house through the same kind of pipe and deposited in a pit some distance from it?"

Sappho laughed with delight that such topics as "waste" intrigued him as he lay upon the couch of love, but decided it was for these mysterious reasons she loved him.

They met every night. They could not be away from each other. She sent him trinkets of gold or hid them on his ship, so he need not risk his life for sponges.

Once, winds swept down from Heaven and waves pounded their boat and broke over the deck. Phaon laughed. But Sappho, terrified that her well-painted face and juiced hair had become blotched, turned from him and asked him to erect a temporary tent.

He thought it was modesty, as her wet chiton clung to her, and was well pleased to do as she wished. Behind the improvised screen she hastily repaired the damage and threw a kerchief over her hair. And so the charade went on.

Phaon was the center of her world. She loved and ravished him and could not have enough of him. But the magic was always spun. There were stories to entertain him and poems sung for his enjoyment.

"Your songs would charm even the wild beasts, could they hear you," he declared.

"If they charm you, lord of my heart, I am content."

One night she came and saw as he lifted her in his arms that his eyes were haunted and sad. When she questioned him, he put his head in her lap and wept. "I have lost a dear friend, Pelagon, son of Meniskos, who, like me, was a fisherman and diver after sponges."

"What happened?"

"So many things can go wrong in the dark of Poseidon's kingdom. One sees a catch a bit farther down, another kick of the feet and you will have it. Instead blood pours from your eyes. This happened to my friend."

Sappho soothed him with kisses, but he lay listless and despondent against her.

After some time Sappho spoke. "Yet your dear companion will not die unnoticed, for listen, Sappho has made an ode to his poor shade." She sang:

> *In memory of Pelagon, a fisherman,*
> *his father Meniskos placed*
> *here a fishbasket and oar:*
> *tokens of an unlucky life*

Phaon kissed her hands. "He will not be forgotten—great Sappho gives him life!" And he remembered his manhood.

Returning late to her home, she found a messenger outside the gate. He dared not enter, for his tidings were ill. There were no leaves of bay in his hair.

Quickly, under her breath she intoned, "Father Zeus, let it not be Khar!" Then to the messenger: "Say what you must."

"In Athens, O incomparable Sappho, the wise and noble Solon lies dying. He wishes not to die until he has heard your last songs."

"Poor man. I have already heard of one death tonight. Like an accursed hound it is ever at our heels. Enter in the gates. I shall not sleep until I've gathered the smell of meadows, the brightness of flowers, the sound of water falling onto stones. I will send all this to Solon and ease his going forth."

She went over her work but could find little that was new. The Muses, jealous of Phaon, stayed away. She didn't care. The passion she brought to her verse, she now brought her lover.

She collected any writings that might have been overlooked at the time Solon's scribe had copied so diligently.

She stopped to read:

> *. . . nor ever did the gathering sounds of*
> *early spring*
> *fill any wood with the chorus of*
> *the nightingale*
> *but you wandered there with me*

"Atthis, Atthis, you held so much of my life. Sometimes I wish for death." She was amazed to hear herself say such a thing. Had she said it? Was it true?

It would be true when the moment came that Phaon looked at her and saw that she was old. For then she would be. And life finished.

Every time those deeply blue eyes of her young sailor looked into hers, she trembled that she would be found out, that the white lead on her face would crack at a wrinkle, or along a laugh line . . . and he would perceive her as old. If that should happen, and it must happen, Sappho was no more.

In the morning she sped the messenger on his way, sending with him a sheaf of poems in one of her slim vessels to Athens.

There was news of Khar in the agora. His fleet had been sighted making for Lesbos. Sappho could not disentangle the emotions this set up in her.

Did he come alone?

With *her?*

As slave or wife?

She was so nervous that she sent word to Phaon she was unwell and could not visit him. Then, changing her mind, went after all, to find him absent from his ship. Where was he? Carousing in some tavern? Perhaps courting a girl his own age, or playing lover-lad to some wealthy judge or prince? She knew nothing of his life. His life was there on the boat with her. That he had any other existence had not concerned her. Suddenly she was mad with jealousy. Where was he this night when he should have been with her?

Was there a girl? How old? Fifteen? Sixteen? O uncaring gods, what tortures you reserve for me! In her room she scrubbed the paint from her face and looked at herself with revulsion, crying at the disfigurement of wrinkles, which only caused new and uglier lines to appear. Her body sagged. The gift of herself that she presented to Phaon was worn, used up. "O Aphrodite, I was wrong. I had forgotten. Cannot these fires in me be quenched? Can you not see how tormented I am? I long and I yearn . . . and it may not be. There is nothing before me but humiliation." She sobbed, as broken in her being as a dropped pot.

She sent servants to the dock to await Khar's arrival and bid him come to her. Bordering on physical collapse, she must still see to everything herself. Each detail of the welcoming of her brother was discussed with Niobe. Leaving nothing to chance, she hurried to the kitchen, selected capons, made changes in the menu. In the garden she directed which buds be tied so they would not open until presented to Khar. She inspected the cleaning and polishing, and hesitated a dozen times over the wardrobe she had selected.

She kept a runner at the twin harbors so when the curved ships were sighted she would have sufficient warning. Khar had gone away angry. But now surely he must realize that his sister's words came from love and concern for him and his welfare.

But she was Sappho, and knew that passion could dissolve the stoutest heart and dissipate the sturdiest resolutions. She must prepare herself for the presence of Doricha Rhodopis. Sappho worried that if Khar kept her as a slave, out of spite the Thracian might reveal she had slept between her legs in an orgy that culminated when the great bird, with outspread dazzling tail and frantically flapping wings, debauched her. Sappho had only to close her eyes to see the creature hopping about, the girl's white body hanging from his feathered one.

What would she do if this were told? Deny? Laugh? What? But Doricha would not speak of Samos. It would destroy Khar's love for her, and perhaps in her pride she still imagined she might marry into the noble house of Skamandronymos—had she told the cooks how to slice the peppers? And had she mentioned the caraway seeds? Khar liked his bread baked with caraway seeds. If only she could rest a moment against her Endymion, against her sleeping lover. If only his eyes would never waken. "O my Muses, where have you led me, on what wild shore have you abandoned me?"

A runner flung himself at her feet. "Lady, the Lord Kharaxos comes. He is even at the gate, led by your servants, whom he detained and made accompany him, that he might surprise you."

Sappho with a glad cry ran down the wide stone stairs to meet her brother at the entry of her home, wash his feet, and bid him welcome.

The double doors were flung wide, slaves knelt and threw confetti, a pathway of embroidered purple cloth was quickly laid and as quickly covered with flowers. Kharaxos handed down from a chariot a woman of blond roselike beauty. One question had been answered.

As Kharaxos came toward her, a kind of presentiment descended on Sappho's mind. She felt the light eyes of the White Rose, and over her brother's shoulder met their calculating gaze. The next instant she was holding him. "Khar? Are you come home?"

"Sister."

"Enter with welcome and blessings."

Doricha Rhodopis was only a step behind with her women. This was the moment. Sappho stepped before her. "You, Thracian, may not enter, though you offered up a hundred iron obeli to your own glory in the temple of Pythian Apollo at Delphi."

The beautiful woman looked her full in the face. Even through time they knew each other. The glance of the White Rose slid to Khar.

"Sappho . . ." Khar's voice, when it controlled violence, was very terrible. "She must enter, and you must bid her welcome. I told you when I left that I would marry her. All my heart is toward her, and you, beloved Sappho, must hymn the wedding songs and rejoice with me."

Sappho was conscious of the White Rose watching with a show of disinterest, as though she knew how it would go.

Disregarding her, Sappho addressed her brother. "It may not be. I know you purchased her at great price . . ."

"And gave her freedom."

She ignored this. "You are, even as I, of the noble house of Skamandronymos. Our line traces unblemished from Orestes and Agamemnon. You may not marry such a one. You have given the woman freedom, Brother, but you cannot change the obsequious nature of a slave, who with every orifice of her body entertained the navy and the army, too."

The White Rose appeared untroubled by these insults; she continued to gaze expectantly at Khar.

"What are you saying?" Khar was beside himself. "You sent your slaves and chariot as welcome, knowing Doricha was with me."

"I did not know."

"I told you."

"I did not believe you would bring her to my very house. I did not believe you had so little thought for our good name."

"What thought have you had of it? Doricha had masters over her, and in spite of it rose to great prominence. The oracle at Delphi purified her, so that she comes to me like a virgin. It is you, daughter of shame, who, hiding behind your great renown, wantonly lured here innocent maids and deflowered them."

"Is it my brother speaking to me?" Sappho gasped. "What lying words have you listened to?" She turned on Doricha, who continued to keep herself removed from the exchange. "I see it is you, bitch," Sappho spat at her, "who has shattered the harmony between a brother and a sister." She approached her menacingly.

A sharp blow across Sappho's chest made her stagger and fall backward. Slaves with drawn swords on the instant surrounded her brother.

"Hold!" she cried. "No hand shall be raised against him in my house."

Khar stood over her. Ares, that terrible god of vengeance, had hold of him. His nostrils extended and deflated in rapid succession, while his face had a look of such fury that only in her own had it been mirrored.

Kharaxos wasn't through. "Eurygyos and Larichos persuaded me to leave a servant to act as my eyes and open them to your indiscretions."

"You spied on me?" she asked with indrawn breath.

"I know of your disgusting affair with a common sailor. I thought, because we are alike in defying society, we would continue the old affection and stand by each other. But it seems you find it easy to moralize, as though you were a paragon of virtue. It is you who are the whore, Sappho, and that's how you will be remembered. And an old whore at that!"

She got to her feet by the help of a portico. "Take that filth from my house"—she choked out the words—"her of the false buttocks. And when she is gone I will burn sulfur and make my home clean."

The White Rose did not flinch—why should she? Khar brushed roughly past Sappho to her side. "Forgive me, Doricha, I brought you to a madwoman."

Doricha smiled at Khar, and spoke to him for Sappho's ears. "It is very sad, Kharaxos, to be met by an Erinye in the form of a sister, whom once you held dear. Is it true that she debases herself with a sponge diver, who in years could be her son?"

Sappho watched them depart. She felt unwholesome, like a leper. The words of such a woman have power to defile. And what of a brother's words, the words of kindred blood?

Khar had struck her. No one had ever struck her. And spied on her! Of everything he had done, that was the worst. Her women brought her inside and put Gilead balm on the bruise that was showing on her breast, but it could not penetrate to where the wrongs lacerated. "Oh, if there could be medicine for grief like mine!"

Only Phaon could comfort her. Why had she stayed away from his ship to be brought to her knees, to be called vile names?

Her hair, which had become disarrayed, was brushed with incense and freshly done with flowers. Spikenard of Tarsos was rubbed into her legs, Egyptian metopion anointed her breasts, marjoram of Kos thickened her lashes. Lastly, a Persian sapphire was lowered into place.

Sappho called for her chariot. Hastening to the wharf, she found Phaon's Nubian slave asleep in his small boat. She woke him and he rowed her toward the ship.

She climbed to the deck as Phaon watched. For the first time he did not leap to help her. Here, too, was change. Things were falling away from her. The young captain who had been her lover, held her with devotion, listened to her songs with awe and wonder, stood and watched her with an expression she could not read. Was it disdain? Mockery? What emotion butchered his face, turning his lips ugly?

"Phaon?" she questioned.

"I was in the tavern just now."

"Are you drunk?"

"No, quite sober. I have *been* drunk, I think, or bewitched. Did you use bought charms on me, or pour something into my drink?"

Discord hung between them as when the strings of her lyre went slack. She said slowly, "I hear your words. I do not understand them."

"I talked to men off your brother's ships, or rather—listened. They did not know I knew you. But it was of you they spoke. They called you old. Are you old? I never thought about it. But I can see now . . ."

"Yes," she challenged him. "What do you see?"

He did not answer directly, but heaped his hurt on her. "They said you were bored with seducing young girls, that you now haunted the piers and low places and bought love from any man who could raise his mast, even though he were scrofulous or a slave."

Sappho's hand went to her heart.

Phaon took a step toward her. "What is it?"

"You have struck me."

"I have not."

"A blow more terrible than Khar's."

"I have not touched you," he reiterated.

"I know," she answered and held out her arms to him.

He did not move.

She stood before him in a welter of tears. "If I have to . . ." And she began tearing off the gold ornaments from her arms, the sapphire from her throat. She threw her jeweled girdle at his feet, pried off her rings of great worth, even the rings of her ears and toes. "Now I order you. Give me the love I have paid for."

Phaon's breath came unevenly, and he stumbled over his words. "I did not say they were true, these things I heard. I only said that I heard them."

"I paid you," she said again through clenched teeth. "By the double portals of Tartarus, you shall love me!"

He came to her and grabbed her about the knees. His head was bowed and his tears fell on the caulked planking. "I love you," he said.

Sappho pulled free. "Crabbed age and youth cannot together . . . live."

"Those things they said, they are not true things."

"Of course they are true things. Zeus's lightning has ripped you from my arms, my body." She climbed back down the ship's ladder. "Row," she commanded the Nubian. And once on land, ordered her own slave to beat the beasts that pulled toward her villa.

"Wait!" she told the driver when they reached her door. "We have a further journey to make." She ran into the house, light-headed as though there was no substance in anything, as though she were a shade. But she knew clearly what she was doing.

She went directly to her treasure room and took fistfuls of jewels, which she rammed into sacks, and as many lion-faced Samian coins as her servants could carry. She had them loaded into the cart. Niobe tried to stop her, but she pushed her aside. "To Eresos!" she told the driver.

All night the road was taken, and the next day and much of the day after that. When they arrived at the town of her birth, she told the driver, "To the Street of Women!"

He demurred. "Lady . . ."

"To the most wretched, the poorest prostitute who plies her trade, a woman who will accept any, a leper even, if he has the price."

The driver, in fear for his life, obeyed her, for surely his mistress had lost her senses. He stopped only to ask the way, then drove into an evil-smelling, decayed part of the village where at the windows female faces peered. He stopped at a wooden door, half off its hinges. "Lady . . ." he pleaded once more.

But Sappho sprang down. "Follow me with this." She waved toward the sacks.

"This? This treasure beyond worth?"

"Pick it up and come."

Sappho pushed open the door, which fell against the wall to reveal a room with dirt floor and filthy straw in a corner. Never had she been in such a room. She heard grunts, and at first thought animals were stabled there. Then, as her eyes became used to the faint light, she saw a deformed beggar and an old crone copulating.

"Whip the man from her!" she ordered.

Her driver laid down the pouches and went back for his whip.

The woman looked up, but the male was half blind and addled in the wits, and continued riding her.

The driver reentered and Sappho, who could scarcely breathe for the stench, simply nodded.

The lash flicked the creature's bared rump, and again. There followed great confusion as the man rolled from the woman, evading the blows by crawling toward the entrance, and the crone huddled, drawing her extremities out of the path of the welt-raising thong.

"Stand at the door!" Sappho commanded her driver. "See that none enter." Then turning to the festering, vile thing crouched in her rags, "Get up. Do as I say. Get to your feet."

"Pity, Great One. Pity me. Let me live."

"You? Such a one as you wishes to live? Tell me your name."

"It is Neara."

"It is Sappho." Sappho spoke with absolute authority.

"The great lady is pleased to speak in riddles."

Sappho kicked one of the pouches toward her. "Open it."

The woman worked at the knot with crooked fingers. When she loosed it and coins and jewels spilled on the dirt floor, she dared not move or even lift her eyes.

"Can you hear me?" Sappho asked.

The woman nodded.

"And understand me?"

She nodded again.

"Here is treasure beyond counting. It is yours if for the rest of your life you say one thing."

"Lady?"

"When any asks who you are, you must reply: 'I am Sappho of Lesbos.' Repeat it."

"I . . . I . . . am . . . Sappho of Lesbos."

"And if you say it not, these riches will be taken from you, and your head lopped off, and boys will use it as a ball to kick to each other in the street. Say then, once more. Woman, who are you?"

The creature trembled as though shaken by wind, but she replied stoutly enough: "I am Sappho of Lesbos."

"Remember the bargain." And Sappho left the place. Expelling the tainted air from her lungs, she breathed deeply. She was contending with gods, and what mortal had ever won at that game?

Yet it was possible. "Aphrodite, it is you I call, be my witness. A fortune in gold, and jewels unnumbered, I have heaped on the scapegoat. *She* is the other Sappho, who has taken on my sins, my iniquities upon herself. It is *she* who is selfish and unthinking, who wants, wants, wants, and is never satisfied. *She* is the one who must have more, more love, more songs, more wealth, more everything. It is *she* who drove her daughter away, her brother, too, and all who loved her, by her uncompromising nature.

"I, on the other hand stand before you, unsullied as you when you stepped from Sea's foam newly made. O Kyprus-born, accept the scapegoat with her great heap of wrongdoings. And let me be pure that the gods may love me and bring back him I hold dearer than the world."

Then more recklessly, "You must accept the scapegoat. I have nothing else to give. Say that it is acceptable, for the tears of mortals are your common drink."

Would Aphrodite hear her, aid her?

The journey back was a blur; she didn't know if she slept, fainted, or lay prostrate. What would happen to her now? What was the penalty for bargaining with a goddess?

She no longer felt the cart beneath her. The jolting caused the many pictures of Phaon to break apart and become jumbled. New images were juxtaposed against a moving network of branches flying overhead and a countryside that flowed as with a strong current.

They told him I was old, his drinking companions in the tavern. They laughed at the fool who was beguiled by an old woman. Against laughter, magic crumbles.

Would the foam-born goddess close Phaon's eyes to her years? For she had not worked all her guile on him, nor told all her stories, nor sung all her songs. She had so much more to pour out to him. Would he forgive her stripping every last trinket of gold from her body and throwing them at him? Would he forgive her arrogance?

He must. For it was no longer she who had done this thing, but the scapegoat. Had she not gone to the town of her birth and bestowed her name—a great and famous name, none more so—on that loathsome creature who sold the hole in her body for a loaf of bread, a crust even?

Sappho laughed wildly. What would the woman do with all her wealth, the flashing gems, the ancient coins of fine workmanship, the many ornaments of precious metals heavily embossed? She would set herself up as chiefest of the prostitutes, a second Doricha. She, too, someday would purchase virtue with iron spits! Her laughter was uncontrollable, like rumbling thunder unloosed.

She wanted to fly to Phaon, go at once to his ship. But how carefully he would scrutinize her now! She must be able to endure his closest inspection. She needed Niobe and her women. She needed a warm bath, oils from many lands, and royal essences, also the whites of eggs and mastic and white lead. She needed all of that to hide behind. And the goddess, Kyprus-born, before whom she made herself as nothing—she needed her intervention most of all.

Aphrodite would make Phaon the sleeping child he had been, loving her, listening to her tales, filled with her enchantments.

When the jolting at last ended and she was at her own door, her eunuch did not recognize the disheveled person as his mistress. He stepped forward to bar her entrance.

She laughed in his face, the wild laugh recently born in her.

Niobe, when she saw her, began murmuring prayers. She led Sappho to her bath.

"O Niobe, good friend . . . do you not know . . . I made a bargain with a goddess."

"Hush," Niobe breathed as though to a young child.

Sappho fell asleep in her marble pool. But on taking a deep breath, she inhaled the good and rare scent with which they were rubbing her palms and the bottom of her feet. Her hair, too, was washed and perfumed. A sponge was plunged into a jar of Athenian oil and passed over her body. A smile appeared on her face, though her eyes were not open. She had never been so weary. They rubbed and massaged her limbs, and she knew no more.

Was this rosy-ankled and golden Dawn, the Dawn that followed the night of her return? She sprang up as one reborn. No sin, no stain was on her. She looked into her heart and found it was the heart of a child. She could forgive Khar anything, even the blow, even the White Rose.

Breakfast was brought, and she called Niobe. "I am feeling well after my good night's sleep; the world is smiling."

But Niobe did not smile, nor did she tell her mistress it had not been an ordinary sleep, but one of two days, during which she lay like one drugged.

Sappho did not notice her silence. "Prepare me, Niobe. I would myself look like a goddess. I am willing to spend the entire day to accomplish this."

Niobe stood unmoving before her.

"There is something you want to say, Niobe? Tell me, but do not let the telling interrupt your hands. I am in a hurry to begin our preparation."

"There is no need to hurry, Mistress. He is gone."

Her heart began to beat crazily against her sides, an uneven pounding. "Who?"

She knew, but she listened while Niobe told her that her brother had entered Phaon's ship. "He did not stay long. Of what he spoke, you know. For after Lord Kharaxos departed, Phaon laid in supplies for a long trip, they say to Ithaca. And two days ago he raised the square sail and was gone from Lesbos."

The world slid away.

"Lady? Lady?"

She fought her way up from the nether world of Tartarus, past the

River Styx. "Niobe, ready me. I will see this brother of mine, this traitor, a final time. Does he forget we are of one house?"

Niobe's hands flew about her; slaves knelt holding precious ointments and jewels from which to choose.

"Good Niobe, you followed me into two exiles. And when I wanted to give you freedom, you would not take it. Niobe, make a last journey with me. Ready the chests for Sea. Take from here all goods that may be carried, and those retainers who are loyal. Provision my fleetest ship. This day we sail after Phaon!"

"Lady!" Niobe's despair shook her voice.

"Do you fear the anger of Lord Kharaxos? Stay then, and learn who is stronger."

"I fear only for you, Lady."

"For me? Surely not for me. I am sister to the Muses. I am Sappho."

"Strange portents scourge the air, Lady. Your brother's wife hates you . . ."

"His wife?"

"They were married, with all your family gathered. It was a lavish wedding, but it lacked greatly, for it lacked the songs of Sappho."

"All my family present? Eurygyos and Larichos can forgive Khar his born slave, his prostitute . . . and they cannot forgive me?"

"That is not the worst, Lady. There are ominous signs. Word comes from Eresos that a woman of the streets, vile past description in her reputation, is telling everyone that she is Sappho of Lesbos. And this creature, who was wretched before, now has riches past counting."

Sappho nodded her head. "What do you make of it, Niobe?"

"I do not know, Lady."

"Know this, then, that we go to Ithaca, to Sicily, to Poseidon's kingdom, to the gates of Hades' domain if necessary. My swifter Syracusan craft will overtake Phaon."

"And then, Lady?"

Sappho struck Niobe full in the face. "Are you saying you cannot make me young again? You cannot make me beautiful? Well, you shall! You hear me, you shall!"

Niobe wept, but not for the blow.

"Do not pity me!" Sappho screamed at her. "I am blest of the Muses. They walk at my side. So, too, does the Kyprus-born. Forces and powers have I more than my brothers. And there is no mortal who can separate me from Phaon. He did not sail away from me, Niobe, but went in fear of the Prince Kharaxos. And he was right to go—he is only a diver after sponges. He cannot stand against the might of my house.

"But I will see this brother I was ready to forgive, who makes a slave a wife and censoriously denounces me and sends off the man I hold dearer than the world. Yes, I shall see this brother. Let him look at me, whom he has so wronged."

"Lady, perhaps if you spoke with Lord Alkaios, he might help or at least prevent . . ."

"Lord Alkaios is drunk in some public house. It is not Alkaios but my brother I will see. And you, meanwhile, make ready for the journey, and never think to see this house, or these fields and orchards again, for you will not. Nor your children either. Now, have you finished? Am I beautiful? Good. Then bring the driver."

The fellow did not come willingly, but was beaten to his post. On Sappho's order they drove off.

Like one of the Erinyes she appeared at her brother's estate, putting his servants into a quandary. "One does not announce a sister," she told them and walked into the main hall, where Doricha and Khar lounged together with a zither player, who sang songs other than hers. They had been laughing, drinking wine, pelting each other with flowers. At sight of her they stopped.

Sappho called on her brother by name. "You shall suffer for what you did to me!"

"Phaon? He was lucky I didn't dispatch him on the spot and leave him to rot on his own mast, run up like a bloodied sail."

"What evil daimone possesses you, that you want to destroy not only yourself, but me? I have only loved you, Khar. Countless are the sacrifices and prayers I sent after you. Costly purple I spread at your feet on your return. What did I ever do to you except warn you against this Medea? Do you know what you have done? Call the Persian mourners, the Cissian wailers, for you have sent your sister out on the wild Sea."

Khar leapt to his feet as though he would seize hold of her and stop her. "Sappho, are you mad to think of chasing after that boy?"

"They are my ships, and you cannot prevent it."

"In what a twisted way you persist in seeing things, Sappho. I am not your enemy. I spared his life, and by sending him on his way, I spared your dignity. If now you will forget him and return to your house, the scandal will be forgotten. But if you go after him, where once you were revered, you shall be laughed at."

Sappho smiled at him the smile he had been afraid of since he was an infant. "I've taken care of my posterity. I promise you when I die, I shall not be forgotten. Six books I leave to Alkaios on which will depend the fame of our age. For this was Sappho's time upon Earth, and I took it all tender and green to my breast. It was my child. I have no other. And if at any moment you are still my brother, bring offerings in my name to the priestesses of Dionysos. I would not want Kleis to go hungry—although I've thought recently that she is dead. . . . You did me much harm, Khar. I never did you any."

"I have saved your reputation, that is what I have done."

"You have driven me from Lesbos. We will not see each other again in life."

As she left, Khar called after her, using her childhood name, "Little Pebble!"

She did not turn.

Niobe and her people were already aboard the ship, and being stowed were what remained of Sappho's worldly possessions. A wool mantle was placed around her shoulders by Niobe's eldest daughter, and for the last time she was rowed from the twin harbors.

In open sea the route to Ithaca was by way of Corinth. They sailed past Chios and Andros, and the desolate island of Leucas, where they had put in on her journey to Syracuse.

At Corinth she inquired everywhere along the harbor for word of Phaon's slower vessel. No one, however, could be sure if he had even passed that way. His small and undistinguished craft was not remembered. Sappho gave the order to reprovision the vessel and make straight for Ithaca. She was prepared to sail until they came to Sea's rim and plunged over it.

The second day a fog descended and all landmarks were obscured. The captain prayed aloud to Poseidon of the blue hair and to Hecate, who gives aid to men who sail dark and treacherous waters.

Sappho did not pray to anyone. She spoke directly to the gods as men used to do. "If wanting to embrace his hands, his calves, feel his firm round arms about me, if this makes me dissolute . . . then the world has changed since Zeus himself loved. My heart is eager. You, Hera, oversaw it. You, Aphrodite, ordained it."

She did not seek the shelter of the tent, but stood alone in a shrouded, unknowable world. It occurred to her that perhaps at moments like this one saw it best, not suborned by its pretty broidery in which the gods dressed it to beguile human senses. This blankness was as true a picture as sunny fields. Was one more true than the other? The world held all indifferently in spite of libations poured and prayers sent up in perfumed smoke.

For this blasphemy, they were driven back upon the route they had traversed. They were pitched northward almost upon the inhospitable bluffs of Leucas. The white fog seemed to harden before her eyes. But it was not fog, it was the rock of desperation, that monstrous white wall of stone rising between Earth and Heaven. For the second time a ship under her steered for the small hidden cove and beached there.

Anything repeated had, for Sappho, great mystery. Why did the lapping waves wash her up here again, all these years later? It was no accident, for calm and storm were under Poseidon's control.

She remembered the shrine to Apollo that she had climbed at the start of her exile to Syracuse. Was it really twenty-five years ago? Had Apollo, who never lied, a message for her? Perhaps Phaon had been blown by a like wind to this very shore. It might be he had left some word at that lonely place of worship, which surmounted the great cliff. She knew this was impossible, and yet it would explain the strange sense of destiny that had taken hold of her.

"I will visit the shrine," she said to Niobe.

"Day will be toward its finish when you reach the god Apollo, Lady," Niobe cautioned.

"I will go."

"Then take a taper for the descent."

"My eyes are cat's eyes; they see well in the dark."

"I do not like this place, Lady. The sailors say that criminals were once thrown from the top to be dashed upon the rocks."

"Yes," Sappho replied, recalling the tale, "with birds tied to their shoulders so that if by some chance innocent . . . they should not die, but be borne gently down."

"You have no birds, Lady."

Sappho smiled. "Nor need of any."

She climbed, remembering the springing steps that once carried her like a young goat up the trail. The way seemed to her now much longer. Her breath was short and seemed to desert her. She took in air by mouth and this made her light-headed. Sweat was crawling on her brow like a fly. She brushed it away. She thought she detected the edge of Gongyla's milk-white dress as she slipped around a bend. But she saw now, it was little Timas, precious giver—and she laughed at the purple kerchief tied about her statue's head.

She stopped to pick flowers, and Atthis bent to pick them with her, as the two of them had done so often. A heavy braid fell over Atthis's shoulder. "Atthis? O Atthis, there is a corner of my heart for you—"

Farther on, she discovered a wild and thorny rose, which she plucked with care and added to the bunch that Apollo might have a token from her. Her heart was pounding. How long it had taken her to understand that love with sorrow is mated. "It's all right," she told Kleis. Kleis had come to take care of her. Tears rolled down her cheeks. Kleis had come. "Thank you, darling."

And she turned to Khar; she could always turn to Khar because they had shared an exile. "Khar, the Moon is white in a sky that still belongs to Day, and neither the dead nor the living can I shake from my head. They climb with me, even Alkaios, a young Alkaios full of pranks." She was young, too. She smiled indulgently at the young Sappho, the young Alkaios.

The last few paces were a scramble. She stood breathless at the summit. Far beneath, breaking white at the base of the cliff, Sea sent up spume.

Sappho knelt at Apollo's shrine, among the broken columns, and laid there the tattered roses that had survived the winds. There were no other offerings. None had recently passed this way.

She addressed the rock-throned god: "You see before you, O healer, a woman. A poet . . . but a woman. Until this moment I thought I came in pursuit of love. But since you are a god and know all, you know it is a vain and foolish quest."

She hummed a moment, a snatch of song, for her Way-Muses were with her. "I had a youth so full by day and night of delicate and dainty things, of dear loves and fair companions. And ever at my side the slender-ankled maidens. O my hetaerae, toward you this heart of mine will never change.

"Why am I here at your feet on this unlikely height?" she asked the god. "Phaon at the last opened his eyes and looked me in the face, and what he saw I do not wish to know. But I am not here because of Phaon. I am here because I cannot go forward and I cannot go back." She smiled at the weathered god as she had smiled at Khar, it was a big sister smile. "We are wrong, I think, to envy the immortals. You must grow very weary."

Slowly she stood and began to sing:

> They say that Leda once
> found hidden an egg
> of hyacinth color
>
> Atthis, I loved you long ago,
> when my own girlhood was still all flowers
>
> Earth of the many chaplets
> puts on her embroidery
>
> Love coming from Heaven
> throws off his purple mantle

She wandered to the very edge of the precipice, drawn there step by step. From this distance, the billows seemed comfortable. The rocks could not be seen:

> I shall put you to rest
> on soft cushions.
> You shall lie
> on cushions new

She raised her arms. There were no birds on her shoulders. But winged words of many loves and many garlands woven held her a moment.

Sappho was surrounded by fair companions. She reached out to the unlimited.

> *Yet I could not expect to touch Heaven*
> *with my two arms*

She took one step more over air, calling to her nine sisters:

> *I long and I yearn*

Rushing through vast air to a new exile, a new freedom, she was Sappho.

> *Someone hereafter, I tell you*
> *will remember—*

Crafts of all sizes, from small fishing boats to Kharaxos's and Sappho's own fleets, dredged as close as they dared to the awesome white Leucadian cliff against which Poseidon spewed his might. Silent slaves, fishermen, and young sponge divers with the grace of an Apollo or a Dionysos sprang again and again into the black waters. They were casting with nets.

On the shore Kharaxos walked with Alkaios. Alkaios was sobbing, Khar's face was ashen as the cliff and looked carved from it. "If you love me, do not speak to me more, for I killed her. I sent her on this mad chase that has ended here. In love myself, I had no pity for her love, that last desperate flaring up. She would have shortly seen . . . but I drove the boy away."

Alkaios sank deeper into misery, nor did he try to comfort his friend. Some ills there are that may not be cured. They walked the small crescent of sand shore in silence and retraced their steps under the high, commanding granite.

A sudden shout went up.

"They've found her!" Khar said.

A light boat was rowed in and beached. A diver, dripping water, lifted the small body ashore. Her brother and Alkaios approached and looked. Every bone was smashed so that the skin was no more than a sack for the pieces. A blanket was placed on the sand and the remains put into it. Khar knelt and tried to make an outline with the semblance of human form, but he could not even set the limbs straight. "Those awful virgins, the Gray Women, know I did not mean this. I swear by all the gods that be, I would give up everything, Doricha, anything at all, to have you breathe your grace upon me." He abandoned his effort to smooth the rubble under the skin and looked distractedly at Alkaios.

His friend's hand fell heavily to his shoulder. "I tell you this: Time will not break the meshes of her greatness."

What seemed to comfort Alkaios, comforted Khar not at all. He turned again to the pitiful heap that, except for the raven hair with its white streak, was unrecognizable. What he saw was another time and another Sappho. With an iron knife he cut a lock of hair as dark as hers and commingled them. "Voyage with a fair breeze, Little Pebble."

Alkaios continued staring at what had been Sappho of the violet tresses. "Not all the streams of all the rivers that flow below and on Earth can wash away this life." He cut a lock of his own gray curls, as Khar had done, and laid it upon her.

A bowed form of an old woman wrapped in a mantle the color of the sand shore, moved. It was almost as though one of the rocks on the beach moved. Niobe walked to the blanket and stood looking down at her mistress. "You told me, Lady, to accompany you in this exile." And before any knew what she would do, thrust a knife deep in her bowels.

Her corpse was laid respectfully at the feet of the poet.

Alkaios began a dirge, his voice stumbling so that only some of the words were heard, although the cadence was felt. Rough sailors who had lent their help in recovering the body of Sappho of Lesbos stood and wept and tried to hear Alkaios's ode:

> . . . *Misfortune* . . .
> *a sharer in sorrows* . . .

Khar's tears fell on the misshapen bundle at his feet, and he tore his clothes. Alkaios went on:

> . . . *for the incurable decline of life is at hand but*
> *panic springs up in the terror-stricken breast of the*

*hart . . . maidens . . . ruin . . . the coldness of sea
waves . . .*

The funeral chant ceased, but no one moved. They remained frozen in attitudes of grief and desolation as though they had been mourning figures captured on a temple frieze or on a black vase.

At last from the crowd a gnarled, weathered fisherman stepped forward. He had foraged a little way up the trail that led to Apollo's shrine and found wild roses growing in a declivity between sand and stone. With coarse, reddened hands he laid them on Sappho's distorted form, and in the soft Lesbian accent said simply:

> *Though few
> they are roses*